CHICAGO QUARTERLY REVIEW

Volume 40
Fall 2024

Senior Editors
S. Afzal Haider, Elizabeth McKenzie

Managing Editors
Sean Chen-Haider, Gary Houston

Fiction Editor
John Blades

Poetry Editor
Jake Young

Associate Editor
Mona Moraru

Contributing Editors
Christina Drill, Jennifer Signe Ratcliff, Umberto Tosi

Editorial Staff
Chuck Kramer, Stuart Woodhams

Graphic Design
David Ladwig

Board of Directors
Lois Barliant, Peter Ferry, S. Afzal Haider,
Anna Mueller Hozian, Richard Huffman,
Elizabeth McKenzie, Kathryn Vanden Berk

Cover art "Thirty" by David Ladwig

The Chicago Quarterly Review is published by The Chicago Quarterly Review 501(c)3 in Evanston, Illinois. Unsolicited submissions are welcome through our submissions manager at Submittable. To find out more about us, please visit www.chicagoquarterlyreview.com.

Proud Member

[clmp]
COMMUNITY OF LITERARY MAGAZINES & PRESSES
W W W . C L M P . O R G

TABLE OF CONTENTS

NONFICTION

POETRY

ART/GRAPHIC NARRATIVE

EDITORS' NOTE

If you believe you're seeing your first issue of the *Chicago Quarterly Review* but have the feeling you've picked up a copy before, it may not be déjà vu all over again. We have been publishing this magazine for thirty years.

Back in the Spring of 1994, the *CQR* was born out of conversations among a group of Chicago writers who also happened to be friends. We shared a belief that the work of many good and talented writers was not reaching a readership through conventional venues. So in the early days of the *CQR*, in need of submissions, we published the work of writers and editors of our acquaintance whose work in some way matched our vision and personal biases. When we celebrated our 25th anniversary in 2019, we invited our staff to contribute in the tradition of the olden days, and here on our 30th we have done so again.

Our true joy, the labor of love or love of labor comes when we can showcase the writing of young and new as well as seasoned and established writers.

We now have many hundreds of submissions to choose from. We are small but with time we have carved a niche in the independent literary world. We have been honored to appear in *Best American Short Stories, Best American Essays, The Pushcart Prize Anthology,* and *The O. Henry Prize Stories.* Our special issues have been reviewed and used in university courses, including our Chicago Issue, Italian Literature issue, South Asian American issue, Australian issue, and our Anthology of Black American Literature. A special issue on Native American writing, guest edited by Brandon Hobson, is now in the works. The heart and soul of *CQR* is our all-volunteer staff, and we are still blessed with a growing group of friends who grant us their time, energy and enthusiasm. ∎

POLICARPO
Patricia Engel

Gabriel never had trouble meeting women when he wasn't supposed to be meeting women. Now that he was divorced and it was finally appropriate, it was as if he'd paled into wall plaster or dissolved into the grass like fertilizer. Women walked right past him even as he tried to demand a meeting of the eyes. In his younger days, he would have thought internet dating beneath him. He used to scan newspaper classifieds and think the people placing those ads insane, casting anonymous lines. His daughter was the one who convinced him a dating app was different. More customized. "Everybody does it," she said. "What? Are you supposed to approach a rando in a bar like some kind of psycho?"

He didn't always understand her slang but he got the point. Courtship was now a defensive art. He was sensitive. Evolved. Unlike other men he knew, he'd never cheated on his ex-wife until he had no other choice. Cassandra would say there was *always* another choice. He did not confess his infidelity until long after their divorce but that was strictly to hurt her when she found a boyfriend. Until then he'd been discreet. The confession had been one of their last conversations, a means of seeking absolution. Since their daughter was nearly thirty, college debt paid, there was no more reason for them to speak.

October rain pebbled the window. A morning resembling night, too cold to leave bed before a few alarm snoozes. Gabriel fondled his phone, which rested beside his pillow each night. When he woke to piss, three or four times before dawn due to his weakened prostate, he'd tap the screen, hoping some special message from the past or future had found its way to him, but it was usually just spam.

The woman he'd been chatting with through an app's private-messaging option only sent her three-sentence contributions at respectable hours and waited at least another four before responding to anything he said. He had managed to schedule dinner with her for Friday. They would try the new ceviche place on Grand. She'd asked if it was the cuisine of his people. "Not really," he said. He was from Bogotá. The mountains. "We're beef eaters." She told him she'd watched the first season of some drug-smuggling TV drama. "No wonder you left!" she wrote. He didn't know what to type after that.

She owned one of those suburban shops where you get drunk on California wine while painting a still life or a Van Gogh replica with your friends. He would never go to one of those places. Not if you paid him in actual Van Goghs. But in some of her profile photos she was pretty in the way that his wife used to be. Slenderish and sharp featured. Brown hair that curled at her chin. His wife also used to play the guitar and sing folk ballads and listen to him go on about whatever for hours. Nobody listened to him now.

Gabriel opened the app. Nothing. He'd once offered the woman his phone number so they could switch to voice-to-voice communication but she said it was too soon and instead asked for his email, which he'd supplied, though she never wrote him there.

He checked his main email account just in case, the one listed on the website he'd made when he retired early from the bank and started "consulting." Then the email address he used for internet purchases and news subscriptions, and finally the one tied to a fake name that he used when signing up for things he really shouldn't be signing up for. An online psychic membership. A conspiracy theorist newsletter. The matchmaking service for men wanting to connect with women not interested in love, just money. Not prostitutes exactly. He never met any of them. He just liked to snoop their pages, study their faces and taglines about wanting to be spoiled and have someone pay their rent or tuition, then wonder about women he saw moving about their day in real life.

He was back on his main email account when a new message slid to the top of the list. The subject in bold: "Your father." His first thought was religious propaganda meant for the junk folder. For a while he'd signed up for one of those prayer-a-day lists until he got bored of it. He opened the email anyway.

"Our mother died last month. We are sending your father back to you. He'll land today at Newark at 3:40 p.m. His mind isn't very good so don't be surprised if he doesn't remember who you are."

* * *

His apartment was a newer condominium in a box building with a gym, a screening room and other amenities that were supposed to convince people they should want to live off a highway between a gas station and a Panera Bread. His daughter shared a place with two girlfriends in Hoboken. His ex-wife was the only one who could afford Manhattan, with her career as an author and public speaker. It still cracked him up when he wasn't depressed about it. How, when he met Cassandra, her only ambition was to marry. She was ten years younger than he was, had never held a job and her degree in Communications was mostly ornamental, a time-filler till the wedding. They'd planned on having several children but when Lily was born, Cassandra said, *No more.* She was an adequate mother. He could never say otherwise. But there was a stiffness that came over her every time their daughter rushed to hug her mother's legs or looped her short arms around her neck. Cassandra developed a pinched nerve from carrying the child, so the baby was sentenced to stroller distance and even then, Cassandra usually left her strapped and parked while she sat on a bench and stared at strangers' children at play.

The accident was the best thing that happened to her. He said this once during a fight. She should thank him for not slamming the breaks quick enough when the pickup truck ahead of their sedan came to a sudden halt. She woke in the hospital a week later without any memory of the last decade, including most of their marriage. She remembered having a baby then a kindergartener, but this fourteen-year-old in front of her was somebody else's daughter. He held Lily on the sofa as she wept. He knew then it was a kind of death for them all. There would be years of family and individual therapy draining their savings. Cassandra's superficial memory returned for the most part, recognition for the order of her life and routines. But she was a different woman at her core. She settled into her former craft room with a laptop and began to write. Next thing they knew, she was giving lectures at women's clubs, hospitals and nursing homes about resilience and reclaiming her identity. Deciding to start a YouTube channel was where it really turned. Gabriel couldn't recall if it was the week before or after that she told him she didn't love him and maybe never had. She likened their marriage to a hostage situation. In her lectures she said that it was through amnesia that she came to discover her true self beyond captivity. He still didn't understand what she meant by that.

He'd believed he was a good husband because his father had been a bad one. He kept most of the books and framed photos from their family days because Cassandra became a minimalist in her new life. They lined the edges of his three bookcases. A scene of the young parents kneeling on the beach around their fat little girl, as if venerating a saint. A stranger took the shot with a camera he'd bought for the vacation to Curaçao. It was on that trip that he realized how easy it would be to be sleep with another woman. He'd always imagined it a complicated endeavor. The lying and logistics of duality. A bartender at the resort told him he could dip into her cabana in the staff's quarters in the morning. Tell his wife he was going out for a walk. They'd just had a conversation about how they would each spend their final hours if it were the end of the world. He'd surprised himself by saying he'd like to swim naked in the sea as far as his stroke would take him and then let himself drown. His wife did not mind when he went to drink at the bar alone. In fact, she encouraged it. Perpetually annoyed, she would shoo him away with a magazine as she sunbathed and the baby slept in the umbrella shade. "Go *do* something," she'd say, as if Gabriel stood around doing nothing all day, as if he did not deserve this vacation that he'd paid for by working very hard sitting before a computer screen at the bank while she refused to breastfeed because it would ruin her tits.

He took his computer to Panera because they were nice there and the food wasn't bad and it was full of housewives in gym clothes and young professionals without facial piercings and neck tattoos for the most part. Being there didn't make him feel so old or so unemployed even if he was technically forcefully retired. He scanned the airline flight status page. His father was due for an on-time arrival. Fifty-five years since they'd seen each other. His father always ran around with other women. Secretaries, receptionists, the ladies who worked at his accounting office. A stocky man with glasses and little hair, one would never guess he could be so oversexed. Gabriel's mother forgave and forgave. He and his sister, Luisa, discussed a few times in adulthood the mystery of her grace. How she never threw him out, even when he reappeared after sleeping away for days, then weeks. One morning their father announced his departure. He'd met a woman in his dentist's waiting room, an expatriated Colombian named Raquel, and would be going home with her to California. They never saw or heard from him again.

There must have been a goodbye of sorts but Gabriel can't recall one now. A moment when his father looked upon his children and wife one last time before leaving. He remembers in her first year post-amnesia, when Cassandra worked with a doctor to conjure the images of the accident with no success, that the doctor concluded that the mind is often wiser than we are in hiding what is most painful in self-protection. "Some memories should not be uncovered," he'd said. Cassandra was troubled by this surrender. When she left Gabriel a few years later, she told him she could not invoke any memory of ever having been happy in their marriage and now she didn't even want to try to remember because they would feel manufactured, planted. It surprised him how her saying so made him doubt the authenticity of his own memories of their life together too.

When Gabriel and Luisa buried their mother, they acknowledged, both divorced, that they were each other's only family now. He called her in Bogotá earlier to tell her about the email from Edgardo and how he'd emailed him right back since he didn't have his number asking what the fuck he was talking about and was he sure he had the right guy?

"Policarpo Fuentes was married to my mother, Raquel, for fifty-three years. We loved him like family but our mother is gone now and he's not our father. He's yours."

Ninety years old and they just put him on a plane? Gabriel wondered what Edgardo had told Policarpo. Did he know he was on his way to his son? Did he even remember having children? And how would they identify each other at the airport? He thought about this as he drove into the parkway's smog-blurred horizon. At the turn on Lyons Avenue, right near the burned-out apartment building he always speculated about—who'd lived there, if anyone had been home, the cause of the fire and why it had remained like this for years already, not a soul moved to repair the meteoric holes in its walls and collapsed roof—he wondered if he would recognize his own reflection at that age.

He stood in the arrivals area until an airport employee rolled out a small dark man rumpled into a navy suit in a wheelchair, a cane across his knees and a small suitcase at his feet.

"Is this Policarpo?"

The airport worker nodded and together they helped the old man stand.

"Papá," he said, and the word felt old and new. A word he hadn't uttered in decades, only heard spoken by his daughter before, despite his best efforts, she started to lose her childhood Spanish and switched over to *Dad*.

Policarpo stared.

"I am your son," Gabriel said.

"I am your son," Policarpo repeated.

"No. You are Policarpo. My father."

"You are Policarpo."

* * *

Lily called to say Cassandra would be on *Good Morning, America* tomorrow to promote her new book. Somehow, she'd used her career as an amnesiac to ricochet into another career as a relationship expert; this new book was about rebuilding your life after a bad marriage, preaching a doctrine of taking younger lovers in lieu of domestic partnership.

"I'm so glad I could contribute to your mother's success," Gabriel grumbled.

"Don't take it personally, Dad. Women really connect with Mom's story."

A therapist told him it wasn't unusual for a child to make excuses for the parent that leaves. This was the same therapist who wanted to put him on antidepressants but he'd resisted. He wanted solidarity from his daughter, similar to how he'd aligned himself with her when she was a child and Cassandra had deemed her an intruder. They were somewhat close in that they both enjoyed skiing and being offended by the other's political views, but he knew she often slept at her mother's place and went with her on work trips as a loosely paid assistant. Sometimes he imagined telling Lily that when she was an infant, Cassandra hated the awkwardness of holding her, her baby smell, complained of her burping and crying and told her husband that if she'd had a son, she would have loved him more. This tiny bitch, she'd once screamed in tearful fury, had been born to ruin her life.

Of course, he would never tell Lily this. Or that he had not exactly been faithful to Cassandra. Not just once but several times with five different women over fifteen years. But they were not affairs, which require effort. His escapades didn't add up to much if you thought about it, considering he maintained an active sex life with Cassandra the whole time, meaning whenever she was in the mood, which was not that often, and she never found out, and these relationships were not romantic, just incidental, spored from encounters in hotel bars while on business trips, with the exception of one woman, who shampooed his hair at the barber shop, and he didn't think of these dalliances at all anymore, except on nights when he felt especially alone, so they might as well have never happened. He was sure Cassandra had told Lily he was a cheater but if confronted, he was prepared to deny it. He preferred to have his daughter think him ever loyal. Even if now, single in his late sixties, he could tell she more often thought of him as pathetic.

"Your grandfather is here," he told Lily when she finished bragging that her mother's new book was on track to be another bestseller. "Don't you want to meet him?"

Policarpo was sitting in the armchair across the sofa from him, watching the highway lights through the picture window. Maybe it looked something like Fresno or even Bogotá to him.

"Are you for real? I thought he died."

"It was *like* he died," he said, then felt bad about his words. His father was very much not dead, even if his skin puckered across his wide skull, pocked, liver spotted and whiskered. He could not get over the permanent look of terror in his father's eyes. He almost pitied him.

"He's going to stay with me for a bit until we figure things out."

He meant that he still had to convince his sister to take him in. She was the one with the big house in Rosales. The maids and drivers and the money and the time.

He watched his father and was flooded with the vision of them remaining roommates forever, two old bachelors far beyond their prime. "Where are the women?" they would ask each other. "Where have our wives and families gone?"

"I don't know, Dad. You're putting a lot of pressure on me. I'll think about it."

When he and Lily said goodbye, Gabriel checked his email. Finally a message from the woman on the app. A real first and last name attached to her address, not just the profile avatar he'd come to know her by. He whispered it a few times, trying it out in sentences like, "This is my girlfriend, Maddie Rogers." "Let me introduce you to my wife, Maddie." He'd been divorced long enough to be intrigued by the idea of marrying again. With Cassandra, he'd dreamed so often of solitude and space, freedom from the daily wash of apathy he'd misread as mystique during their early years together. They met on the subway when she was studying to become a florist, which he interpreted as a passion, though she quit the program within months to study acting but that didn't lead anywhere either. Sometimes he watched those nightly news programs about husbands who hire someone to murder their wives and thought, *I get it*. But now, in the vast wildlands of the Third Age, what he wanted more than a life partner was a witness to his dying.

Maddie said she was looking forward to their date on Friday. She added three smiling faces and one blowing-a-heart kiss. It seemed excessive. His daughter sent him those at the end of texts sometimes but he understood it could also mean flirting. Friday was still four days away. If Policarpo was still here, Gabriel would have to leave him alone for a few hours. He would be okay. He didn't know where he was mentally but he certainly wasn't a danger to himself. Gabriel had put his father to sleep in his bed. It pleased him that he was much larger than the old man shrinking and fetal under the blanket like a toddler. "I could strangle you with one hand," he whispered before leaving him to take the sofa.

He pulled out a box of photos Luisa had sent years ago, black and white, frayed at the edges. He paused to examine one in particular. Two children standing along a wall next to their grandmother in a wheelchair. A dog curled at the boy's feet. He could not remember the dog's or even his grandmother's name now. Forgetting names was the first sign of dementia, he'd read somewhere, but in his case, it was intentional. When he met Cassandra, they'd described their childhoods to one another but he'd been purposefully vague. In her latest book, she said her unnamed ex-husband had been raised fatherless, in a matriarchal household, but it was not enough to undo his masculine damage and shame.

* * *

Luisa called the next morning. He was on his second coffee, having set an alarm to watch Cassandra on television talking about her new book, long haired and breast-implanted. He knew Lily was offstage somewhere soaking in secondhand talk show glory.

"How's it going over there?"

"He doesn't know who I am. I say my name over and over and it's like I'm making animal noises. He can eat and piss on his own but his mind is shit."

"We can put him in a rest home. A nice one. We'll both chip in."

"Why should we? He never did anything for us."

"Because we are better than he was and we have our consciences to think of."

She'd already been calling around, getting the rates at different facilities in Colombia since they were less expensive than in the U.S. Somewhere small, like the family-run homes with space for just a few seniors. Other places were like resorts, extravagant decor with all sorts of services, in-house doctors and spa-like therapies.

He heard a shuffle and turned to see Policarpo entering the living room, leaning on his cane as if it were another appendage.

"Policarpo, do you want to speak to Luisa? Your daughter?"

He said this as a way to taunt them both. He knew his sister would sit on the line through their father's silence until her brother said, "You see? Nothing. He's a ghost."

When they were children, Luisa had been the last to understand that their father would never return. She insisted on setting a place for him at the table for every meal until her mother started punishing her for humiliating them. Gabriel and Luisa did not share a bedroom but he heard her cry at night. When children in the neighborhood asked where their father had gone, Luisa made up stories that he was a soldier fighting for the Americans in Vietnam while Gabriel would simply reply that he was dead.

When Gabriel announced that he was leaving to study in the United States, she was convinced he had a secret arrangement with their disappeared father, whom he'd live with, that together they'd conspired to abandon the other half of their family.

He took Policarpo to Panera Bread because soup seemed like a good meal choice for a man of his condition and he didn't have a problem managing utensils. They sat at a table along the wall with a view to the parking lot. Policarpo looked around and set his eyes set on a girl a few tables away. "Maria," he said several times, though only loud enough for his son to hear. There were no Marias in their family. He'd heard from a family friend his father had bothered keeping in touch with that Raquel had three sons, Edgardo being the oldest. No Marias in their family either.

"Why did you leave us?" Gabriel asked.

He knew Policarpo would not have an answer. When he became a citizen, Gabriel had used the opportunity to have his father's name legally excised from his identity. He'd been baptized Policarpo Gabriel Fuentes Lara but now he was just Gabriel Fuentes with a blue passport and not even a middle initial *P* left on its pages in remembrance.

"You were a real piece of shit. A puto. You ruined our lives. You annihilated our mother with sadness. You left us orphaned. I am a mediocre man because of you. I would have turned out better if you'd been better but you decided to follow your cock to California."

He said all this in Spanish but noticed his words caught the ear of the couple at the table next to them. Their eyes flashed over him then they glanced away and went back to their conversation.

"I should drop you in the Hudson River. Leave you in the woods on some mountain so the bears can tear you to scraps. Nobody knows who you are or where you are. If they find you alive, they will lock you up and nobody will ever look for you, just like you never looked for us."

Policarpo watched him. Gabriel was sure he understood. The old man was just pretending to be a stranger to his own son, coward that he was. He knew his children were arranging to set him up in a cushy nursing home back in Colombia. He'd be set. It was all a scam. Gabriel could feel it. But then his father started coughing and it was clear he was choking on a bean from his soup. A woman came out from behind the register and performed the Heimlich maneuver. With a squeeze, a cough and some spit, he was saved.

* * *

In the evening, Luisa called with more news. With their mother's pension, his father would be a beneficiary of government funding that would provide for his nursing home care. Yes, he'd left the country over fifty years ago. And he'd been married to another woman for most of them. But he'd never divorced their mother because it wasn't yet legal in Colombia and by the time it was, she had already died. All they needed, his sister said, was to prove Policarpo had been by their mother's side till the end of her life with a photo. And since there were none of those, his sister said, maybe they could ask Edgardo for one of him with Raquel.

"It's the right thing," Luisa said. "Our mother would have wanted us to do whatever we have to do to take care of him. It's an act of charity."

Gabriel had never seen this woman his father left their mother for. He imagined her sensual and beatific, like Sophia Loren in *Two Women*. She would have to have been to justify his abandonment. He emailed Edgardo explaining their end of the situation.

"Let me get this straight," Edgardo replied. "You want to pass our mother off as your own?"

He then emailed Maddie. They'd been discussing the weather. "All this rain makes me nostalgic for Paris," she wrote. She'd gone there twice with her ex-husband. Not her first ex, who was a firefighter, she clarified. Her second, the veterinarian, who'd died of heart failure. She hoped to return one day, preferably in autumn, her favorite season.

They'd already established that they both enjoyed traveling but Gabriel wrote back that he actually hated Paris and much preferred Rome, which still presented a degree of unclichéd charm.

She responded that she couldn't understand how any sane person with any sense of culture could hate Paris. "You'd have to have something seriously wrong with you."

He returned to the profile he'd first swiped on when they met, if you could call it meeting when you haven't seen the person in the flesh or heard their voice. In her photos she was always smiling as if she had perfect teeth, which she did not. She would have benefitted from a nose job, but he supposed she was past the age where a woman cares about altering her face. He was sure Cassandra had already had a facelift. On his high-definition television her skin looked flattened and taut, like wrapping paper. He had loved her once. He wondered about that love. Had it left with her, relocated into her new apartment in the city, been lost in the move or fallen dormant, maybe even self-cannibalized? He thought there should be a warehouse for all the unused love in the world. He would rent out a storage unit and put his love for his father and his wife there in a weatherproof container, so he would know where to find it if he ever needed it again.

Maddie had no children. "By choice," she'd said in one of their chats. But in a later conversation she let it slip that her first husband had left because of her infertility. Her weight fluctuated in different photos. Maddie doing yoga poses was thinner than Maddie in Bermuda shorts standing on the side of a boat with a view of a harbor behind her.

"Do you have an accent when you talk?" she'd written in an early exchange.

He said he was sure he did but doesn't everyone?

She said she didn't mind accents. She loved Antonio Banderas.

He closed his eyes and tried to imagine fucking her to determine if all this conversation was a worthy investment of his time. The last woman he'd slept with since divorcing was a former colleague from the bank. One of those women who know every sex position and basically do all the work for you. Maybe it wasn't fair but he got the impression that Maddie would be lazy in bed. And that she'd talk a lot and if you didn't agree with her opinions she would mope around the house in silence and maybe even cry.

* * *

The photo from Edgardo arrived. Policarpo with Raquel, a woman whose head barely reached his shoulder. Her features a disorganized mess, certainly not more attractive than his mother, not by any interpretation. A woman who, even with decades removed, could never have been considered point-blank beautiful. But there was a comfort between them, the way they rested on each other, an ease he never saw between his own parents. His father looked like someone else, peaceful, not the chaotic, sabotaging man he'd been in Bogotá. With Raquel, he'd lived a half century undisturbed.

In Policarpo's suitcase, Gabriel found a brown suit, two shirts, another pair of trousers, three undershirts, three boxers and three pairs of socks. One belt. The only shoes were those on his feet. Tucked into a paper envelope was one thousand dollars in cash. He called his sister and told her about the money. She'd sent in the photo right away and by the next day had his home funding approved. It wouldn't cost them a peso.

They agreed that he'd use the money to buy Policarpo's fare back to Colombia and buy him some new clothes before dispatching him once again. He would spend a few days with his daughter at her home before she delivered him to the elder care facility she'd chosen for him near the coast, where it was warm and arid like California.

The earliest ticket Gabriel could get was for early Saturday morning. Over breakfast while his father ate raspberry yogurt, Gabriel said, "I'm sending you back to your country. You'll see your daughter again. Somehow she doesn't hate you like I do."

Yogurt slipped from Policarpo's lip onto his chin. Gabriel could not help wiping it for him with a napkin. He then checked his phone. Maddie had emailed to confirm their date that evening. "I know we don't agree about Paris but I think we'll still have fun," she said. She ended her statement with many exclamation points. *Unnecessary*, he thought. Such punctuation should only be used in an emergency. Otherwise it just conveyed panic.

He started to type back that he was tied up with an unexpected family situation and would need to reschedule but realized it would sound like a lie even if it was true. He wanted to ask Lily for advice but she hadn't communicated since he'd last prodded her, "Don't you want to meet your abuelo before he leaves for good?"

"Yuck," she wrote, followed by a vomiting emoji. "Abuelo? Don't call him that."

* * *

Gabriel arrived at the restaurant ten minutes early. He often did this before a date to make sure he secured the best available table, established a rapport with the server and could glance over the menu so as not to be surprised by the prices later. When she appeared, he stood up to meet her with a handshake and a light kiss on the cheek. This was the real Maddie: thick like the sailboat photo but much more attractive, and her nose didn't seem as lumpy or her teeth as jagged; pink lipped and warm to the touch.

He wondered how she would describe him to others. Thin legged and wide waisted? They might be the same pant size. She might say you could tell he once had a good head of hair despite his scalp now shining through the graying remainders.

By the end of the dinner their hands were resting comfortably one atop the other. They'd refrained from ordering a whole bottle but had had three glasses of wine each. She owned her house in a nearby town and had two German shepherds. Gabriel shared that he sometimes contemplated adopting a dog but thought them as almost as much work, money and worry as a human child. They talked about stupid movies, favorite novels and their mutual hatred of divorce lawyers. About how neither was religious but had both come to wonder more about God in recent years. Gabriel detected a melancholy in Maddie that somehow charmed him, made him want to draw her into his chest and hold her there tenderly.

He asked when he could see her again. She suggested they take her dogs for a hike in the Palisades on Sunday where the views, she said, were amazing. They could make a picnic if it didn't rain. She would make sandwiches and he would bring the merlot. It flattered him that she did not question whether he could keep up with such strenuous physical activity. A date like that, Gabriel concluded, did not sound terrible.

When he returned to his apartment, he checked on Policarpo, who slept with hands folded over his sternum, so cadaveresque that Gabriel had to make sure the old man was still breathing. He held his palm above his lips until he felt warm breath graze his fingers. *What will it take to kill this guy?* he thought, though he would admittedly be relieved to send his father back to the motherland intact and congratulate himself for the bastard's safekeeping.

He was interrupted by a memory of his father sleeping beside him in his childhood room in Bogotá, having drifted off in the middle of telling his son a story. He recalled the whistle of his father's snore against the shuffle of traffic. An accordion rested against the wall. Policarpo often promised to teach him to play though he never did.

His father would die alone. Even if in the care of nurses or doctors or underpaid attendants; even if one was holding his hand at the moment of transition, he would be adrift in the realm of strangers and strangeness, far from anyone he'd ever loved or who'd ever loved him. A just fate if there ever was one, Gabriel decided.

Gabriel thought of calling his daughter or at least texting her. She was always slow to respond. He was sure she never kept Cassandra waiting the way she did him. And then the sudden intrusive thought of calling Cassandra, telling her that he was grateful for their years together even if neither of them turned out to be who the other had really wanted or hoped for, even if they were better apart than together. *I loved you then*, he could say and mean it. And then maybe he would press her to try to remember one last time if she had ever loved him in even a small way, before marriage, before the baby, when they had shared promises and dreams, when they had vowed each was the exact person the other had been waiting to meet since birth and it felt as true on their lips as death.

She never answered his calls though. Maybe an email would get through.

Instead, he drafted a note to Maddie, who still hadn't given him her phone number. She wanted to take things slow, she'd said at dinner, and he was fine with that. He would tell her he had a really nice time tonight. Use that ultrasafe American phrasing he'd learned from his daughter that was meant to be sweet without seeming pushy.

He wanted to write more. "I think we could be something. I hope this is what I want it to be." He never felt more foreign than when he tried to assemble language for intimacy. He stopped himself, deciding to try again in the morning when the wine wore off, and instead went back to the bedroom to watch his father sleep. ■

IN SEARCH OF *HERZOG'S* CHICAGO

Charles Kenney

On the elongated block of West Augusta Boulevard that spans the distance between North Rockwell and Washtenaw Streets, in a neighborhood referred to as Humboldt Park, Ukrainian Village, or West Town depending on how dated or specific the map you are referencing is, heavy traffic whirs past dilapidated greystones; the door of a Puerto Rican liquor store chimes irregularly as it is opened and closed. The residential streets that branch out from this thoroughfare are dwarfed by stately catalpas, whose branches hang over the pavement like the limbs of old women reaching down for coins. Bomb Pop flags flutter on the porches of prewar two-flats. Quick Spanish mixes with the accentless contralto of suburban transplants. And, as is often the case in Chicago, a green street sign with the avenue's legal name hangs above its honorary counterpart: a diminutive brown rectangle listing to whom the street is dedicated.

In most of the city, such names are long and polysyllabic, often Polish or Lithuanian, Mexican or Greek. The font is routinely shrunken to accommodate first, middle, and last names. On this street, however, empty space abounds. Ten capital letters written in bold Highway Gothic stand out in a dark sea of beige: Saul Bellow.

To the curious passerby on a midnight waltz from the Empty Bottle to the bars of Western Avenue, the name might seem like a verse stolen from the New Testament. *Saul bellowed as he was cast from his horse on the road to Damascus.* It is not a surname that rings with familiarity in the ears of Chicagoans as Daley or Pritzker might, not even one that lines high school reading lists alongside Cisneros and Sinclair. It is as Jewish as it is American. It is as much of Chicago as it is of Montreal or Saint Petersburg. It is a name trapped under dust on the early shelves of public libraries, whispered across the iced-over alleyways of Hyde Park, and spoken on pairs of wrinkled chili pepper lips that dwindle in number with each turn of the Sharpie-smudged calendar.

When Saul Bellow published his sixth novel, *Herzog*, in 1964 and was subsequently vaulted from limited literary acclaim to national relevance, a Chicago as unaware of him as today's is did not exist.

He held a professorship on the University of Chicago's Committee on Social Thought. He had already won the National Book Award for *The Adventures of Augie March*, a novel set almost entirely in the city, and would repeat his success within the year. A Nobel Prize would follow in just over a decade. He was not the most famous man in Chicago (and honorary street signs did not yet exist to enshrine such fame), but he was a man "about town," as he might say. His was a name that, though not every face walking down Michigan Avenue in a frenetic, rush hour mob would know, a decent, readerly few might. The success and scandal of *Herzog* was, in many ways, the beginning of this more serious notoriety.

Split between New York City, the Massachusetts Berkshires, and Chicago's Hyde Park, *Herzog* is by no means Bellow's homeliest novel. The opening line of *Augie March*: "I am an American, Chicago born," is traded for its neurotic, self-inspecting alternative, tied to no mass of land but the barren plain of the unconscious: "If I am out of my mind, it's all right with me." It is a novel nearly epistolary in style, its pages ripe with circuitous, nonsensical correspondence to old lovers and dead politicians, to his lawyer, Sandor Himmelstein, and his president, Dwight D. Eisenhower. "Dear Mr. President," he writes. "Internal Revenue regulations will turn us into a nation of bookkeepers." "Dear Mama," he pens. "As to why I haven't visited your grave in so long …"

Descriptions of bathrooms in cramped West Village apartments and the sodden elevator shafts of the Upper West Side are as common as those of Clark Street thruways and the convex ceilings of State Street theaters. *Herzog* is not a Chicago novel in its ethos, nor does it intend to be. Bellow had recently published several of those and self-evidently did not wish to write another. But it *is* a novel intensely concerned with memory, and when its protagonist, Moses Herzog, allows his thoughts to wander back to his childhood home on Chicago's Jewish West Side (or when he must physically return there to sort out the divorce he has left festering), the ensuing descriptions of the lakeside city, while not as plentiful or varied as in his earlier work, carry a resonance far shapelier—one reserved for the nostalgic and which can only arise when distance is placed between a boy and his home. It is not the perfect memory of yesterday, but the muddled, forgotten reminiscence of yesteryear, dirtied and aged like wine, making its taste all the sweeter.

When I began rereading *Herzog* this past April, I did not do so with any intention of finding the metropolis Bellow memorializes within its pages. I live in Chicago's Lincoln Park neighborhood. If I ever need to be reminded of the city's beauty, I can step out my door and see rows of Victorian apartment buildings that stretch from the forest preserves to the lake. There is nothing hidden here. No brilliance that Bellow describes that I cannot go out and find myself. When I finished the novel on a Saturday morning and stormed out of my apartment into the cold of an early spring, I was not looking for the place I lived. I was instead searching, desperately, for Bellow. And, since I could no longer find the man, I went in search of his city. To see whether the Chicago Bellow writes of so lovingly still existed, to see whether Hyde and Humboldt Parks and the dainty clubs of Division Street and the dilapidated Goose Island flophouses still stood, and, if so, whether they carried a trace of the magic his words seem to inoculate them with.

The day had a Bellovian quality to it, by which I mean its beauty was so apparent that the world lent itself to being described in exhaustive, unexacting detail. The sky was not merely blue, but a spectrum of many hundred blues—beginning at the horizon, a deep vein of ultramarine lined the lake bed and bled upward into navy and turquoise before finally lightening to that delicate shade named after the sky itself. The El slunk underground with regret and the Metra knew no better, sparks flying from its wheels as if its tracks were the strike paper of an endless matchbook. I boarded one of its half-empty cars and headed south, to that university where Bellow's later novels seem as much a part of the neighborhood as any gargoyle on Rosenwald Hall or the shallow parabola of Promontory Point.

If there is an emotional center in *Herzog*'s Chicago, then it is undoubtedly Hyde Park. That narrow rectangle of city encased by Washington Park and the western shore of Lake Michigan is the only place where its narrator ever nears the present tense. It is the neighborhood in which Herzog's divorce from Madeleine Pontritter is chronicled at the novel's beginning; where the two begin renting a house several months before adultery splits them apart; and where the story concludes when Herzog approaches the old three-flat with his father's nickel-plated gun in tow to watch his ex-wife's lover, Valentine Gersbach, lovingly bathe his daughter, Junie, from the gangway window. Herzog visits other neighborhoods in Chicago when the novel takes him back to its streets, whether traveling by car or memory, but they are always on the way out of or back to his storm windows and bursting tomato plants on Harper Avenue.

I entered Hyde Park from the south, via the Midway—a sunken

stretch of lawn situated between East Fifty-Ninth and Sixtieth Streets that was built to accommodate sideshows during the World's Columbian Exposition. It forms the southern border of the University of Chicago, and, depending on who you ask, the neighborhood itself. I trod carefully across its grass, using the sidewalks but not caring if I happened to veer off them. I carried myself much as Herzog did on an anonymous June day in the early 1960s when he is described as "wheeling the child's stroller on the Midway, saluting students and faculty with a touch to the brim of his green velour hat, a mossier green than the slopes and hollow lawns."

The grass I walked upon had not changed from Herzog's time as far as I was concerned. It was April so each blade was perhaps less verdant than he had seen them on that high summer afternoon when "the warm lake wind drove" him westward, "past the gray gothic buildings," but it was no different in substance. An avenue of life, the Midway still bore students and trees and shouts from one end to the next. It was still an interruption of asphalt with traffic of a different, more human sort. The contrast lay in what surrounded it, in what Bellow did not mention because there was nothing to mention. While the ivy-choked Rockefeller Chapel still hulked over its northern face and copses of gothic classrooms waited patiently nearby, on the south side of the Midway, tall glass buildings now glimmered with sunlight and the distant rooftops of high-rise apartment complexes hung behind them. To the east, in the direction of the lake, where white plumes rose from the smokestacks of Gary, the yellow necks of cranes arched around the concrete skeleton of what will eventually become the Barack Obama Presidential Library. And in the center of the grassy knoll, the ruins of a melted ice hockey rink backlit an intramural soccer game. The park itself was the same, but its surroundings had been thrust into the new century.

As I stood on that slope of green and gazed out at realities that both confirmed and questioned my belief in whether Bellow's Chicago remained, the obvious became more dumbly obvious. Of course the places he wrote about still existed. There they were to my left and right, stone-hewn and filled with students. The city's limits had not shifted east or west, the lake had not been dredged back any further. No fire had raged with enough power to render the urban landscape unrecognizable since the 1870s. Chicago was still largely as it had been—at least in these old neighborhoods near downtown. The question was not whether I would find brick streets and trolley lines if I dug through the shining black pavement. It was whether the comedies of Bellow's characters were still capable of being lived in this neighborhood or any other.

I walked across Fifty-Ninth Street onto the University of Chicago's campus. Open doorways led me into abandoned hallways; echoing footsteps led me onto the quadrangle. It had been an unseasonably cold week. Though it was early April and the winter had been mild, snow had fallen the Thursday preceding and the frigid weather one might have expected from March was persisting into spring. The buds of trees were pink with life, but not quite blooming in the way one might expect, as if they were waiting for a more permanent parting of the clouds. The day was similar to one when Herzog trudged across campus to consult his friend, Lucas Asphalter, after an argument with Madeleine:

> This was two days after the March blizzard. You wouldn't have known it had been raging winter that same week. The casement window was open on the Quadrangle. All the grimy cottonwoods had sprung to life, released red catkins from their sheaths. These dangled everywhere, perfuming the gray courtyard with its shut-in light.

The windows were closed in my Chicago, but I could see through their glass—that same brittle glass Bellow might have sat behind—that each was hinged and crank-handled like in the old days. In the middle of the quadrangle, surrounded by subtle anachronism like that, you could almost trick yourself into thinking *Herzog*'s decade was at hand. Ivy-clad buildings with jutting dormer windows and red-tiled roofs obscured any trace of modernity. Students certainly lounged in contemporary dress—loose fitting, sheer, more often made of polyester. There were posters for club meetings on the trees and Wi-Fi routers buzzing in the windows. Time gave itself away just as easily as it hid. But the places and individuals that most caught my eye were of that different, more temporally ambiguous era, bespectacled, bearded, and in the tweed or tartan I could envision Bellow wearing. It was in that recessed area of campus, away from the brutalist structures of the library and metal spires lurching over the Midway, where I could imagine a scene from the novel unfolding.

Still, though, somehow it wasn't Bellow's Chicago. It was too perfect. The lawn was manicured. The trees were pruned. The granite and limestone were polished or else covered in veins of ivy that webbed out with such precision each one must have been trimmed daily. While there were moments when the quadrangle veered towards Bellow's ideal—half glances when I saw students sitting around chalk-dusted sidewalks discussing Marx or the Middle East—it was never, as Bellow so often describes Chicago, "clumsy." It was not the city Moses Herzog details when driving from O'Hare to his father's house in a "hard-top, teal blue" convertible "under the greenish glare of the lamps and dusty sunlight amid unfamiliar signs."

> He did not know these new sections of Chicago. Clumsy, stinking, tender Chicago, dumped on its ancient lake bottom; and this murky orange west, and the hoarseness of factories and trains, spilling gases and soot on the newborn summer.

And so I walked from campus to Fifty-Seventh Street, where the university bleeds into neighborhood, in search of that more authentic city. Tourists queued outside the Robie House for a scheduled showing. An alfresco café attached to the Seminary Bookstore drummed with conversation and the clinking of ceramic coffee mugs. I was walking with a friend. I had convinced them to come with me because it seems every northsider wants to travel down to Hyde Park but can never find an excuse, and we stopped to buy sandwiches at Medici's bakery before continuing north to Hyde Park's commercial district.

On those liminal streets we soon reached, between bookcases and restaurant tables, I found what I was looking for. The neighborhood was well kept, as most of Hyde Park is, but there was a humanity to it that the campus and its adjacent streets seemed to lack. Single-family homes with white clapboard siding and trees blooming in the front yard stood next to Edwardian apartment buildings with idle air-conditioning units dangling from half-opened windows. Tumbleweed alleyways, the pavement of which had been peeled back to reveal cobblestone, were pockmarked with black-and-blue recycling bins and bits of broken glass. Old women sat on porches with books in their laps. Rickety cars drove by playing their music too loud, but if heads turned it was only out of coincidence.

There was deficiency here. The sidewalks were chipped. The paint was peeling. If Saul Bellow's novels are about anything (and *Herzog* is no exception) then they are about failure, at its grandest and most ridiculous scale. Moses Herzog is not merely divorced. He is twice divorced, thrown from his home, cuckolded by his closest friend, forced into spending his life's savings on worthless property in the western reaches of Massachusetts, and separated from his children by orders both formal and impromptu. The environments Bellow's characters inhabit mimic their mental states. A novel like *Herzog* could only have taken place in a town like Chicago— in clumsy, stinking Chicago. And when his characters do find themselves in the more polished cities of this world, there is either a significant degree of discomfort (Herzog flees Martha's Vineyard less than an hour after arriving) or it is in those districts that would perhaps feel more at home along the rocky coast of Lake Michigan. When Herzog is in New York City it is not to see Broadway shows, but a "great metal ball swung at the walls" of an apartment building so that "everything it touched wavered and burst, spilled down" until "a white tranquil cloud of plaster dust" rose into the sky. Bellow's characters search for the degraded and find ways to turn it sublime. Construction workers throw "strips of molding like javelins." Paint and varnish smoke "like incense."

As I walked through that more vulnerable stretch of Hyde Park, I was reminded of the wonderful clumsiness. I was reminded of a journey Herzog made on a street that could not have been much different from the one I found myself on.

> He drove directly to Woodlawn Avenue—a dreary part of Hyde Park, but characteristic, his Chicago: massive, clumsy, amorphous, smelling of mud and decay, dog turds; sooty façades, slabs of structural nothing, senselessly ornamented triple porches with huge cement urns for flowers that contained only rotting cigarette butts and other stained filth; sun parlors under tiled gables, rank areaways, gray backstairs, seamed and ruptured concrete from which sprang grass; ponderous four-by-four fences that sheltered growing weeds.

I let my eyes saunter down the alleyways between those houses. For if there is ever a place in Chicago that *is* unchanging it is those narrows. They have often been left unpaved. Metal dumpsters house colonies of rats. Sagging power lines form a canopy when trees cannot. It is where Chicago hides its dead and where the dead would rather be.

> Grit spilled on the concrete; broken glass and gravelly ashes made his steps loud. He went carefully. The back fences were old here. Garden soil spilled under the slats, and shrubs and vines came over their tops. Once more he

saw open honeysuckle. Even rambler roses, dark red in the dusk. He had to cover his face when he passed the garage because of the loops of briar that swung over the path from the sloping roof. When he stole into the yard he stood still until he could see his way. He must not stumble over a toy, or a tool.

* * *

On a street corner in downtown Hyde Park, we waited between a Whole Foods and Capital One Café for an Uber to drive us to Saul Bellow Way. The morning had passed, and Humboldt Park was the second neighborhood I had become convinced might carry some trace of *Herzog*.

Moses Herzog is itinerant when visiting Chicago, flying with a bottle of whiskey to the forest preserves, stopping for lunch at downtown sandwich counters. He traverses the city by foot and vehicle, seeking out the individuals who people his comic world. But, despite his travels, the vast majority of the novel's Chicago moments unfold, not coincidentally, in the neighborhoods he lived and grew up in: Hyde and Humboldt Parks. The former is where his adult life plays out, those events that precipitate the book's conjugal impetus. The latter is where his childhood is remembered and where he, briefly, returns to relive it. Since I had been to one, I continued on to the next.

If Hyde Park has been something of a time capsule for the past half century—remaining largely the same academic enclave as the rest of the South Side has shifted in demographics and investment— then Humboldt Park has been its opposite. Unanchored by a university or waterfront property, its fortunes have wavered by the decade, dependent on much more whimsical purveyors of fortune: industry and immigration. A poor and Jewish neighborhood when Bellow was raised there, it soon became the center of Chicago's similarly impoverished Puerto Rican community. And, since the 1990s, when significant investment began to creep into the city's northwest, it has become increasingly gentrified. Two- and three-flats have been razed for sleek apartments with cantilevered balconies. Restaurants with tasting menus have opened beside seedy neighborhood bars. The 606—an abandoned railway line repurposed into a walking trail à la New York City's High Line—cuts through the neighborhood like a malignant vein of gold might slice through a mountain, infecting every street beside it with investment, interest, and determinant movement.

The most striking thing one notices when exiting a car that has driven from Hyde Park to Humboldt Park, however, is the noise. Hyde Park, particularly on the streets surrounding the university, is a quiet neighborhood, far away from freeways, more accustomed to foot traffic than its vehicular alternative. It has no peers to Humboldt Park's Western, Division, and Augusta Streets, no arteries to shepherd people through it other than those who intend to be there. Cars, businesses, hospitals, schools, bus stops, and curbside crowds—anything that produces noise—are more plentiful in Humboldt Park. It is a neighborhood that is alive in a much more serious sense than a college campus. It is a working part of town where money is the currency, and money talks, often loudly.

As I walked through the neighborhood and saw what was causing the noise—the mufflers of chrome-plated Honda CRVs, the far-off wailing of ambulance sirens, music being piped into convenience store lobbies—I realized it was of a different sort than in *Herzog*'s Chicago. "Clumsy lumber porches" no longer creaked underfoot in each backyard. The shovels of men with "gritty beards" no longer chimed as they scooped "soft coal" into "furnace rooms" under kitchens. Fathers like Mr. Shapiro no longer shouted newsboy chants as they peddled "rotten apples from South Water Street in a wagon." The clamor of today was more metallic, less human. But the environment *Herzog* paints was still largely as I found it. When strutting down those streets lined with bungalows and horseshoe apartment buildings, one can almost picture what the neighborhood might have sounded like when Yiddish was being spoken instead of Spanish and the sky was blacked out by the soot of nearby factories. *Herzog*'s narrator describes such a street, not dissimilar from the one I found myself on, and I could envision the life he must have heard around him:

> Leaving the Expressway at Montrose, he turned east and drove to his late father's house, a small two-story brick building, one of a row built from a single blueprint—the pitched roof, the cement staircase inset on the right side, the window boxes the length of the front-room windows, the lawn a fat mound of grass between the sidewalk and the foundation; along the curb, elms and those shabby cottonwoods with blackened, dusty, wrinkled bark, and leaves that turned very tough by midsummer. There were also certain flowers, peculiar to Chicago, crude, waxy

things like red and purple crayon bits, in a special class of false-looking natural objects. These foolish plants touched Herzog because they were so graceless, so corny.

The neighborhood was as it had been. I might not have been in front of the house Herzog describes, but I found myself beside one nearly identical to it. And the street was as I imagined it would be: busy with people, cars, and conversation, imperfect in precisely the way Bellow's worlds must be.

There are no longer flophouses on Cherry Street or honky-tonks on State Street. I am no longer able to buy "books of all sorts out of the thirty-nine-cent barrel at Walgreens." When I attend Blackhawks games at the United Center, "tobacco smoke" no longer lies "like a cloud of flash powder" over the ice rink. That cheap, dirtied Chicago is in the grave with its author. But I *am* able to find the places where those feelings that his city stirred up still arise. It is not everywhere in Chicago. Bellow, after all, did not live in the gilded towers of Gold Coast. His Chicago is in the dive bars of Ashland Avenue, the classrooms of public high schools, and the synagogues of Kenwood. It is in the living rooms of Humboldt Park bungalows and in the words spoken across their mothballed, body-worn couches. Bellow's Chicago is no longer a place so much as it is a people who carry it wherever they go.

I rode the Division Street bus back to my apartment on Fullerton Avenue. A cold spring rain had begun falling—dense, pelting liquid caught somewhere between snow and sink water. The bus shuddered as it sprung over potholes and paused for cane-wielding old men. A young mother across the aisle from me scrolled through her phone while her backpacked son gazed out the window. Two men in construction neons leaned against their seats, speaking Spanish on phones to women across the city. Just before we crossed the river onto Goose Island, the buildings began to thin as the highway took shape. A Polish church with two onion-domed steeples stood beside the exit ramp as if it had been built to be a drive-in movie theater.

Chicago, like any great city, is in a state of perpetual rebirth. Highways are built and neighborhoods razed. Fires burn and ashes are scooped up. Thousands emigrate from them and millions more immigrate in. What Bellow captures of Chicago in *Herzog* (and what any author tied to a city must) is that interminable, immovable part of the city that will remain no matter how its façade is distorted. The soul of a city lives not in its bricks or fiberglass, but in the people who pass between the walls they comprise. Does Paris look as it did when

Hugo walked its streets? Do the shops of Joyce's Dublin still welcome *Ulysses*'s customers? I would assume not. But their characters are still walking those same avenues, perhaps with different names, perhaps with jobs in insurance rather than factories.

Bellow's Chicago is not in any high-rise along the lakefront nor in the organization of a collegiate quadrangle. It is alive in the people who sleep in such structures and trod across the grass surrounding them. When sixty more years have passed and *Herzog* celebrates its 120th anniversary, Bellow's name will be as anonymous as those who lived sixty years before him. (Do many remember Verner von Heidenstam, who won the Nobel Prize in 1916?) Chicago's monuments will have been toppled and rebuilt. Perhaps every place I visited on this cool Saturday in April will have been replaced by structures of sleek glass and steel. But Chicago—in whatever form it assumes to accommodate a scarcer, hungrier planet—will still be inhabited by a people who *can* know the feelings Bellow's characters know. Because they will breathe in the same warm wind that blows off the lake on cold autumn nights; because they will commute to that same river-bound downtown; because they will watch baseballs crack against wood on the North and South Sides; because they will be a part of and animating the city that Bellow and his characters helped shape. ■

ODE TO THE SHOULDER
Dorianne Laux

The splinter in your eye is the best magnifying glass available.
—Theodore Adorno

I loved you before I was born, forming
inside my mother's fist-sized sea, her inner
ocean, her little whale. But before you
shattered I hardly knew you were there,
allowing me, with the greatest generosity,
to bend down and tie my shoe, to swing a bat,
watch the ball tumble like a sewn up planet
through the air. When I tugged at a flower
and pulled it out of the earth, roots frayed,
you helped me hold that beauty close
to my breast bone and breathe. Thank you
for turning the jump rope, lifting the cup, digging
in the garden, holding onto the broom handle
and sweeping up the leaves, plumping
the goose down pillow then slipping my arms
beneath it to feel the coolness between
the sham and the sheet. When I climbed
the ladder, you climbed with me, when I fit
a coin into the slot and pulled the handle
my palms filled with tokens and I felt like a queen.
For a moment I thought That's enough.
And the next moment I wanted more.
Tonight I enter my body and see your bald head,
old friend, white as a skull snug in its socket,
the machine oiled and perfect, working
it's lifetime of magic, lifting my arms
to the gift of sunrise, a ball of light
rolling skyward up the side of a hill.

REVENGE OF THE LIMBO BABIES
Claire Oshetsky

Aunt Betty was a bitter divorcée with a serious drug problem and a restraining order that prevented her from wandering within a hundred-foot perimeter of her own children, and that is why she decided to tell her nieces about their terrifying brush with death. It happened before they were even born.

"In the beginning there were four little babies asleep in your mother's womb," Aunt Betty said. "Then a big needle came and sucked two of you away. You two were the dumb-lucky ones. You were spared the needle."

The twins waited for the rest of the story but their aunt was done. She was looking up at the ceiling. Their aunt was thinking about something else, maybe. The twins were growing accustomed to their aunt's way of trailing off in the middle of things but they wanted to hear more about the four little babies, and about wombs, and so they interrupted her ruminations.

"Spared the needle?" the tall twin said impatiently. The tall one's name was Mathilda.

Her aunt jumped as if she had been poked, and then she looked at her nieces and remembered how she'd been telling them a story, and went on.

"That's right," she said. "Your mother called it *selective reduction*. I call it *cold-blooded murder*. I pleaded with your mother! I said to her, 'Sandra, please, please, *please* don't kill your children! It's a sin! It's a terrible sin! I will raise those two extra babies myself!' But did your mother listen? No! She did not!"

Their aunt rolled her head around in an elliptical way for several seconds. She may have wept.

"What were those other two babies' names?" Harriet said. Harriet was the sensitive one.

"Those babies never had names," her aunt said. "And now those poor nameless babies are in limbo. They will never see God."

Their aunt sniffed at the tips of her fingers, and then she rubbed her fingers across the front of her shirt as if to wipe away something that displeased her, and then she lit a cigarette, even though she wasn't supposed to smoke in the house, and then she tapped the ashes into a dirty old coffee mug left over on the table from the morning.

Harriet and Mathilda knew some interesting facts about their aunt. They knew she had lived outdoors for a time. Now she lived with them. Whenever their mother wasn't home, their aunt took care of them. She prayed over them. She sprinkled water on their heads.

"What's a womb?" Mathilda said.

"Don't you girls know about a womb? The womb is a beautiful room inside your mommy's tummy. It's where babies live, until they are born."

"What kind of room is it?" Harriet said. She was thinking maybe a womb looked like her upstairs bedroom, only small enough to fit inside her mommy's tummy. Her sister Mathilda, on the other hand, was thinking maybe a womb looked like the pink plastic playroom in her Barbie Dreamhouse. Aunt Betty was staring at the wall. The twins could tell something unexpected was about to happen. Sensing danger to themselves, their hands curled into fists. Their nostrils flared. Mathilda got ready to run. Harriet got ready to cry.

"Gimme some cuddles!" their aunt said suddenly, and she made a grab for them both. Mathilda dodged away. Aunt Betty needed to make do with Harriet alone. "I got you, you little nub-bub-bins!" her aunt said, and blew her fat lips into Harriet's neck. Her aunt's lips made an uncouth sound. Harriet pushed her aunt's moist face away. Her aunt let go of her just enough to let Harriet wiggle herself out of her aunt's lap and escape, and now she stood apart, ready to jump if her aunt made another grab for her.

Her aunt's arms hung limply, as if she'd given up on life itself.

"That's right, run away!" she said. "You girls are the same as the rest."

Harriet and Mathilda did as they were told. They ran away, upstairs to their bedroom, to get away from their aunt, and to bounce on their beds.

"Room, womb, womb, room," Harriet said, bouncing.

"Boom! Boom!" Mathilda said, and made up a new game on the spot.

She told her sister Harriet all about the game. Her sister agreed it was a wonderful game and they should play it right away. But they couldn't agree on what to call their new game. Mathilda wanted to call the new game Limbo Babies, and Harriet wanted to call it Big Needle, and before the girls could agree, the game began without them, when a big needle came thwopping straight through their bedroom window—thwop, thwop!—stabbing at the air and searching for them blindly, because this needle had no eye.

Mathilda ran to the farthest corner and crouched. Harriet collapsed to the floor right where she was and whimpered. The needle swayed and deliberated between the two of them and then it swerved in Harriet's direction. Seeing that her own dear sister was in danger of getting thwopped away through the window, Mathilda grabbed her American Girl doll up from the floor and screamed: "Take this doll instead! Take this doll instead!"—and the needle sucked that doll straight out the window and disappeared.

"I don't like this game," Harriet said.

The girls heard the front door open and close.

They heard their mother coming upstairs.

"How are my precious girls?" their mother said.

She kissed them smackingly on their flushed cheeks.

Aunt Betty had followed their mother upstairs. Now she was leaning in the doorway and scowling.

"I think your girls might be a little under the weather, Sandra," she said. "Your girls have been strangely sullen all afternoon. Harriet feels warm to me."

"Oh, they're all right," their mother said.

* * *

Dinner that night was macaroni and cheese because it was Tuesday. Aunt Betty looked meaningfully at her nieces from across the table. Her look spoke to them telepathically. Her look said: "Those limbo babies never had a chance to taste macaroni and cheese." Harriet looked away. Mathilda began to arrange her elbow noodles artfully into a long snaky line on her plate.

"Harriet and I made up a new game," Mathilda said. "It's called Big Needle!"

"Big Needle is a very strange name for a game," their mother said.

Their mother was the elegant one in the family. She was a natural beauty and lived her life doing good works for others. Just then their mother was distracted by a thought that had something to do with needles, and then she remembered that her girls were past due for their vaccinations. Then she grew absorbed with the pattern that her daughter Mathilda was making on her plate, with the elbow noodles—what a creative child!—and after that thought she heard, with sudden clarity, as clear as a church bell on a bright winter day with yesterday's clean snow all around, the sound of her own mother's voice, inside her head, and remembered the way her mother's voice had sounded, ever so many years ago, when her mother said: "Sandra, don't play with your food!" And she was happy to realize once again that she was a very different and much better sort of mother than her mother had ever been.

"Mathilda, don't play with your food!" her sister Betty said.

It was not so surprising that her sister said those words because the two of them had grown up with exactly the same mother. Sandra smiled nostalgically. She thought Betty was looking much better these days. She secretly congratulated herself for giving Betty another chance when everyone had been ready to give up on her. Now look at her sister! So happy and healthy, and drug-free, too! She reached over and squeezed her sister's hand. Tears came to both sisters' eyes, because Sandra had given Betty another chance when no one else would.

"I love you, sister," Sandra said.

"I love you, little boop," Betty said.

"Pooka, pooka, pooka," Mathilda said.

"Scribble, scrap," Harriet said.

* * *

When dinner was over it was Aunt Betty who tucked the girls sweetly into bed for the night. Outside the wind was blowing in mysterious ways and making the curtains swing and sway even though the window was shut.

"I think I can hear those limbo babies in the wind," Aunt Betty said. "I think those limbo babies are trying to get in!"

Harriet put her head under the pillow.

"I can hear those babies, for sure," Aunt Betty said. "Those babies are saying: 'Whoo, shoo, it should have been you.'"

Aunt Betty closed the door on the way out even though Harriet liked it open a crack to let the hall light in. Mathilda went straight to sleep but Harriet couldn't sleep. She kept listening for the limbo babies. She kept waiting for the needle to come. When she heard her sister's sleep-breathing she climbed into bed alongside of her—mostly because Mathilda's bed was farthest from the window—and she put her arms around Mathilda's middle and felt better.

And then it was morning.

* * *

Three mornings a week the twins went to a school where the

children learned to count on rosewood abacuses and this was one of those mornings. A picture window stretched end to end along the south wall of their classroom. From the window you could see the playground and the sky beyond. The sky that morning looked vast and unsettling.

"Reading time!" Teacher called.

It was the kind of school where teachers sat on chairs and the children sat on the floor in a circle. The children gathered. Teacher began to read a story called *Llama Llama Red Pajama*.

"Don't look, Harriet, but those two limbo babies are outside the window, looking in," Mathilda whispered straight into Harriet's ear.

Harriet didn't look.

"I can hear those babies calling," Mathilda whispered.

Sometimes Mathilda was the mean one. She couldn't help herself. She was seven minutes older than Harriet and she was the natural leader. Sometimes the power went to her head.

"Those babies are saying maybe you fooled the big needle last night, but it's coming back for you, Harriet. It is going to suck you straight to limbo. You will never see God."

"Twins, stop that whispering," Teacher said. "You are not respecting your peers."

Harriet looked down at the patterned carpet. Try as she might she couldn't help but hear those crinkly sad voices of the two little limbo babies. She couldn't make out the words. But Mathilda could.

"Those limbo babies are telling me their secret names," Mathilda whispered.

"What are their secret names?" Harriet asked her sister.

"Twins!" Teacher said. "What is the matter with you? Harriet, take your hands off your ears at once!"

"My neck hurts," Harriet said.

"My sister and I had bad dreams last night and we are very tired," Mathilda said.

"You both look flushed!" Teacher cried, and she ordered them to the nurse's office, where Nurse took Mathilda's temperature and declared it to be one-oh-one. She didn't check Harriet's temperature because the word "twins" was like a compound noun to her.

"Twins, I'll need to call your mother," Nurse said. "Lie down on these identical little cots until your mother comes. You will need to stay home until you are well again."

"You scamps don't look so sick to me," their mother said when she got there.

* * *

The next morning Harriet's temperature was ninety-eight-point-one and Mathilda's temperature was ninety-eight-point-three and their mother took them back to school, naturally. They were happy to go. Mathilda's fever had broken. Harriet had nearly forgotten about the limbo babies. Their little friends all gathered around and gave them shy hugs and pats. All was well until the door of their classroom opened at an unfamiliar time of day and the air in the room changed to one of sharp anticipation. In walked the principal, with two little girls.

"Boys and girls, I have an announcement to make," the principal said. "Two new students are joining your class. Their names are Mona and Nona. How lucky we are to have two sets of twins in our class! Please make them welcome, dears."

"IT'S THEM," Mathilda whispered in her sister's ear.

Harriet fainted, just like that. Teacher called for Nurse. The mother could not be reached at her work number, but the girls' aunt picked up the phone at the home. The aunt said she would come right away. By this time Harriet had recovered, a little, but she insisted on running out of the class. Now she was sitting on a playground swing. Nurse sat on the swing next to her. She spoke to Harriet in consoling languages. Mathilda stood close by. The children in the classroom looked out at the tragic tableau. They pressed their little noses against the glass. Even Mona and Nona.

"Not to worry, not to worry!" said Aunt Betty, when she came at last.

"That's right, you'll be all right," Nurse said.

The child stood up, relieved to see her aunt had come. She wiped her tears away. She told Nurse she was better now. Nurse kissed the pale child on the top of her head. She watched as the aunt bundled those twins into the car. She waved as the aunt and the girls drove off together and she kept on waving until the car was gone from sight. Later Harriet and Mathilda's mother would say over and over again to the authorities: "How could the school hand my children over like that? How could they?"—but the school's official position was that it was completely unreasonable of this mother to blame them, because the sister was on the "good person" list that authorized her to pick the children up from school. The mother had signed the paper herself. The mother would claim the paper was forged but she couldn't prove it.

In the meantime Mathilda and Harriet sat in the back seat and listened to their Aunt Betty hum an unfamiliar song.

"Those two limbo babies came to our school!" Harriet said, through hiccups.

"You don't need to worry about those limbo babies ever again," their aunt said.

Her hair was a different color. Her clothes were strange.

"You girls are going to be my very own little limbo babies from now on," she said. "And I will be your very own limbo mother, forever and ever, and I will love you and look after you until the very end of our lives." ■

JUNE WEDDINGS
Joseph Millar

Suppose the virus was spreading out
over the heaving lungs of the South
and suppose the store
where they sell wedding gowns
stayed open during the quarantine,
its arched backdoor agape like a mouth
that's not afraid to be infected,
the gowns floating like solitary clouds
behind the shimmering glass
and the planet holding so still right now
I would hate to leave it,
never having seen you in such a dress
though married these many years ...

I watch you lean over the flower bed
listening to something in the afternoon wind
under the big eucalyptus
and leaving the rest of the world behind—
wherever you are, in whatever time—
for beauty will never apologize
for the trouble it's caused in everyone's lives—
whatever it owes to the roses and moon,
or the volcanoes under the sea
the sound of bells or an old country tune
before the season is done.

THE VAULT
Lisa Allen Ortiz

S ome people have a sixth sense, but that's not what Charlene had. Charlene had the fifth sense twice. She could smell twice as strong, twice as far.

"It's those cavernous nostrils in that patrician nose," Victor said. He loved Charlene. He loved her nose.

Charlene could smell the ocean from Entrada Road. She could smell if milk was sour without opening the carton. She could smell swimming holes from the highway. She could smell lightning before it struck. Shampoo your hair and Charlene could name the brand you used. Skip washing it and she could tell you how many days it'd been. She could smell salt. She could smell water. She could smell ants in the wall.

"I could take you on the road," Victor said. "I could get you on *America's Got Talent.*"

But Victor wouldn't. And Charlene didn't want to. They'd been married thirty-two years. They raised three children, two sons one daughter—all good, all grown. With a life like that, you don't need the road. With a life like that, you don't need to show America your talent. With a life like that, you can keep your talent in your own house and feel seen enough, known enough. With a life like that and any sense at all, you can smell something coming, not far off, something acid and ashy.

Charlene was an RN. Victor ran a machine shop. Charlene worked swing shifts at the ER. She liked swing shifts. She liked double shifts. She liked nights in the nurses' station, smell of latex and peracetic acid, smell of swollen appendix and swollen pancreas, smell of cast plaster and plastic mattress covers.

On her days off Charlene quilted. "I'm practiced with needles," she told her patients. She patted their arms. They watched her expert fingers put IV needles in the tops of their hands. "I'm a quilter, not a quitter," she said. In her sons' old room she stretched fabric on a frame. She ironed cotton scraps and pinned them to patterns: God's eye, nine patch, basket, anvil.

Yet the acid-ashy smell grew closer. It intensified. Charlene opened the window and sniffed the yard. She got down on her knees and sniffed under the stove. She sniffed the dog food dish and the compost bucket. But the smell was not in the world. The smell was on her. She showered, and the smell remained. She bought new soap, and the smell soaked through. Pungent, carbolic, the smell emanated from her own skin. It originated from the philtrum below her nose.

"Will you smell my arm?" she asked Victor and lifted her arm to his nose. He inhaled. He spasmed his nose like a rabbit and then he licked her arm. Gently, he bit it, holding her skin between his teeth.

"Smells like heaven," he said. "Smells like blue sky. Smells like the path to some place I'd like to visit later."

"How about my hair?" Charlene asked. "Does my hair smell bad? Does my head smell like there's something wrong with it?"

Victor sniffed dramatically and then put his whole face in her hair, tussling it by flapping his cheeks.

"Polka Dot," Charlene said. She lowered her head to the dog's nose. She put her wrist at his muzzle. Polka Dot slow-blinked his pearling eyes. He sat.

"Some dogs can smell cancer," Charlene said, and Polka Dot wagged his tail. "Some dogs can smell unexploded bombs." Polka Dot offered his paw for a shake. They'd had Polka Dot since their youngest was seven.

Anyway Charlene didn't need Victor or a disease-smelling dog to identify the smell her skin exuded. She recognized the smell. It was the smell of impending death. She had a hunch the death would be hers.

"You're a good dog, Polka Dot," she said all the same.

"You're a good man, Victor," she said.

It was raining and they made a fire in the woodstove and drank red wine—smell of cedar, smell of dirt, a little fruit—blackened glass, smell of smoke, smell of sticks, damp dog, flames, the couch. Charlene stretched her arm away from her nose. She tried not to smell her own upper lip. She stretched her body out on Victor's lap and smelled him. He smelled like Christmas cake. She thought about kaleidoscope quilts. She smelled the rain and rain-wet dust on the windowpanes.

The next morning because it had rained the night before and Charlene and Polka Dot liked the smell of rain the night before, they set out for Long Trail. Because it was Charlene's swing shift day, they had time. Because Charlene and Victor had been working the same jobs from the same house for thirty years, they had a system. Victor made coffee while Charlene showered. Charlene walked Polka Dot while Victor showered. Victor made toast for when Charlene came back. Charlene liked her toast cold, no butter, plenty of jam. Victor liked fixing Charlene's toast. That morning he chose strawberry jam. He left the jar of it out with the round-headed spoon, two slices of toast foot-to-foot on a plate.

The rain stopped, and the sky cleared enough so the sun could enliven the air. Steam twisted up from the soaked branches and ground. A van was parked in the turnout by the gate to Long Trail, a white van with a red stripe. Its windows were steamed. It smelled of gasoline. It smelled of vinegar and human breath. Smelled like dogs. Smelled like bad luck. Charlene worked in the ER so she knew the smell of bad luck.

"Good dog," Charlene said, and she and Polka Dot walked past the van and into the woods. Smell of redwood bark, smell of acorn shells.

Charlene thought about luck. She thought about coin flips. She thought about calling heads or tails and then watching the round shape a flat coin can make in the air. Charlene thought about toast and jam. She thought about time and how long luck might outpace time. She smelled the wet green of the redwood needles and the flat-wet trillium leaves. She thought about glaciers calving. She thought about birth and babies and grown-adult children. She thought about Victor. She thought about liquid nitrogen and severed limbs and how long a limb can survive without its body. Charlene thought about generations. She thought about generators. She thought about rain. She thought about tree roots. She thought about tree limbs and tree roots and the imperfect mirrors they make of each other. She thought about Victor. She thought about quilts. She thought about pinwheel patterns and churn-dash patterns.

Because she was thinking these things and because of the smell of last night's rain, and the smell of her own skin, Charlene didn't smell the dogs. Because they didn't bark, she didn't hear them. Because they came from behind, she didn't see them. Polka Dot turned. Charlene's gaze followed Polka Dot's. Two dogs were running full out, one brindle, one blue, their eyes fisted.

Charlene shouted at the dogs. She shouted for help. She shouted for Polka Dot to run. Go home, Polka Dot! Go home! But the wet sponge of the forest absorbed all her shouts. Polka Dot stayed and nobody came and the two dogs sprinted down the time-slushed trail, their eyes fixed on Polka Dot and Charlene.

The brindle dog sunk its teeth into Charlene's thigh, and the blue dog opened his mandibles against her abdomen. Polka Dot caught the brindle dog's foreleg, so the brindle dog unclamped from Charlene and grabbed Polka Dot's spine. The blue dog yanked Charlene's trapezius muscle, and Charlene heard her own clavicle snap. She smelled her own marrow. From Polka Dot's throat came a foundering sound. Then the brindle dog lunged into Charlene's face, so her nose entered the cavern of the dog's mouth, and in the clamp of her pain, Charlene smelled—ammonia, butane, solvent, substance, torment.

The dogs shook themselves, scattering from their fur: bone fragments and droplets of saliva and blood. They trotted away, back the direction they came. The smell of trees. The smell of branches, mushrooms, leaves, hemorrhage. Smell without limit. Smell of all. Smell of redwood duff and the provenance of each damp needle of duff. Redwood sorrel, each heart-shaped calyx, each stringy shoot.

Polka Dot exhaled. In the leaking space of her chest, Charlene's heart spasmed and stilled.

As an RN Charlene knew that when a body died, what was living in that body lingered for a fixed amount of time. Six minutes was what the hospital gave a dead person to resuscitate. If six minutes passed and the living part did not return to the body, the body was declared officially dead. Charlene tried to count. She couldn't count well because she was floating. This floating sensation had been described to Charlene as a symptom of dying, so the floating was not a surprise. What was revelation was the clarity of sensation the floating allowed.

Floating Charlene smelled more than twice as far. She smelled without limit. She heard and saw details and totality combined. She saw her own face at a magnified distance, every pore, both old scars, each new puncture, gash and laceration. Her floating zoomed out, and she saw the entirety of her skull and her hair. Her shoulders and torso were explicit under an elaboration of ferns. Floating Charlene smelled the complexity and origin of dirt. She smelled Polka Dot's fur, how each hair had a smell of its own. She smelled the particles of his breath, his still-functioning heart and lungs. Polka Dot whale-eyed in the direction of floating Charlene.

One. The idea of one. Singularity. Two. The smell of two. The way two numbers sounded one against the other making of themselves a third that melded into five, the child number, then its sibling six. The ferns. The roots. Accounting. Equations. Floating Charlene rose up. The countable parts of herself fell behind.

Charlene floated back down Long Trail the way she and Polka Dot came. She caught up with the two dogs and floated above them. They trotted shoulder to shoulder. Charlene heard each of their paws hitting the gravelly mud of the trail. Charlene saw-smelled their fur. She saw-heard their kinship, their feeling of rightness. They were satisfied dogs. They felt better. Their ears had been cut years ago and the cut parts ached in the rain, and in heavy rain the ache entered their heads, the cutting revived, the pain and the flickering light, the tool that was used, the cries of the woman, the shouts of the man. Now that hurt eased. The effort and focus of the attack warmed and dried their cut ears and so their skulls warmed and dried too. The distress in their skulls settled. Because they had attacked, their insides were now quiet and calm. They arrived at the van with the red stripe on the side and whined and writhed outside the side door.

Ian, half-asleep, slid it open.

"What did you two fuckers get into?" he asked.

Floating Charlene smelled tan oak leaves, buckeye, the rust of the van. She smelled Ian's skin, his fingernails, the wet at the back of his neck. She smelled the blood-ink of his tattoos, the seminal fluid dried on his abdomen and hip. She smelled stainless steel and glass.

The dogs jumped in the van.

Josie opened her eyes.

"The dogs were outside," Ian said.

Josie looked at the ceiling of the van.

She said: "Smells like calico. Smells like hospital. Smells like toast."

"You're still high," Ian said.

"I'm not high," Josie said. "I'm just right."

She stared up, at the movement of the scarves she had tied in a pattern across the metal ceiling of the van.

"I love waking up in this van," Josie said.

"Did you hear me?" Ian asked. "The dogs were outside."

"Baby, you let them out. Remember?"

She said the remember part gently. Ian had a habit of sometimes forgetting, and the habit of it was a hurt.

"You slid open the door," Josie whispered. "Sometime this morning."

They'd parked outside La Honda next to a trail that went into the woods. It rained all night while they slept. Now it was sunny and the windows were thickened with steam, a bright-white eclipse on which sunlight billowed like curtains. Josie felt nice. She felt nice because she felt free, and that's what Josie liked most, feeling free. That's why they lived in the van. It was her dream to live in a van because a van doesn't need to stay in one place. You park somewhere new all the time.

But it wasn't Ian's dream to live in a van. What Ian wanted was to feel safe. Because Ian wanted to feel safe and Josie wanted to feel free, they got the dogs, but getting the dogs has been a whole thing, and conversation about the dogs had been tense, the meaning of the dogs, the intention and implication of having the dogs. Something about it didn't seem right to Josie, the getting and having of dogs. Also Josie didn't like what Ian did to their tails and ears.

They had to be cut, Ian said. If they weren't cut they'd get infected. They'd be torn off in a fight. Cutting their tails and ears had to be done. Ian got drunk at the Two Palms Motel and cut the ears and the tails with bolt cutters. That's how his foster dad did it, he said. It had to be done, he kept shouting. So much shouting then howling and the vodka poured to sterilize the cutters and ears, and the too-bright buzz of the bathroom light at Two Palms Motel, then the too-thin towels they used to soak up the too-muchness of blood— it was Josie who sopped it all up. It was Josie who bandaged the stumps of the dogs' tails and ears.

"Something's not right," Ian said. "I heard something."

"What did you hear?" Josie asked. She was enjoying the light on the scarves, the shadows of watery leaves on the van's steamy windows.

Ian pulled himself into the driver's seat.

"I heard a woman walk by. I heard a dog," Ian said. He used his hoodie to clear a circle in the windshield steam. Josie stretched her arms up.

"Ian," Josie said, "have you ever heard about those rich people who freeze themselves when they die?"

"Why are you asking?"

"I don't want to live in a vat."

"Get dressed," Ian said.

"We shouldn't have clipped their ears," Josie said.

"It's not about that, Josie. Don't make this about that."

Josie put one foot at a time through her jeans and lifted her hips to button the waist.

"These rich people pay to put their bodies in vats. Their bodies are floating in there. They float in a liquid that freezes but never grows hard. It's dark and without sound or smell. They're all waiting. The idea is they'll wake up and be saved. The idea is that one day we'll know how to keep a body from dying. They're waiting for that. Even if I had all the money in the world, Ian, I'd never do that. There must be some kind of reason we die, don't you think? I don't know.

I don't think anyone knows though they pretend that they do. Just accept it is what I want to do."

Josie buttoned up her flowery shirt.

Ian dipped his head to look through the circle he'd cleared in the steam. He turned the wheel, so the van moved away from the yellow gate and the trail, down the rutted road toward the town and the highway. Around the van, the wet trees wedged tight until the margin of the little road widened and the trees gave way to small houses, parked cars and overgrown yards.

Josie clambered up to the passenger seat.

"I guess people don't believe in heaven much anymore," she said. "But, Ian, I sort of do. I mean I believe in God in a way, some kind of entity, a collective deity-thing-place that's helpless but kind. Because look at us!"

She rolled down the window and stretched her arm out into the cold.

"Look at us! We could do anything we want! We could go anywhere!"

"It's cold," Ian said.

She rolled up the window halfway.

"We could go anywhere, Ian. But not forever. We'll get old or we'll die young. Then we'll be helpless and gone."

There was the sound of the dogs licking their fur. The sun was bright through the steam on the windows.

"I'd freeze you if I could," Ian said, and he put his hand on Josie's knee.

Josie sighed. She covered his hand with hers. Loving someone meant you let yourself sometimes be misunderstood. Josie let her thoughts be alone in her head. (But her thoughts weren't alone. Floating Charlene was in there, in Josie's thoughts, in the electrified barrier between Josie's brain and her skull, in the complex cavities of her nose, in the waxy nests of her ears.)

Between the two front seats of the van, the dogs licked their legs and their paws. They licked the fur of the other, tasting particles of Charlene's flesh, droplets of Polka Dot's blood.

Josie, through the vignette of steam on the passenger window, watched little houses pass by. She saw a guy on his porch, holding his coffee and putting on boots.

"People get trapped in their lives," Josie said. "They live trapped the same as those dead bodies in vats."

The guy sat on his porch with his coffee and boots, truck down on the street. He sat in front of his house with its walls and its door, and Ian looked out the van window at the guy.

"Do you hear a wailing sound?" Ian asked.

Josie heard the van engine, the steam condensing on the windows. She heard the contented licking and sighing of the dogs.

"I can't live like this, Josie. I have no place to be," Ian said.

"Ian, the dogs are all wet. They're all sticky."

"If we had a regular house, we wouldn't have to drive off all the time."

"Luck," Josie said. "Where our bodies land, that's what we get."

"People make choices, Josie," Ian said, shaking his head. "We made choices. But we can make other ones. We can fix things. We can makes some of it right."

Josie pulled a towel up from under to the seat. She wiped the dogs' faces. She cleaned the corners of their eyes, the tops of their heads, between the roots of their triangle ears. She wiped down their necks and their chests. She rubbed down their legs and swiped out the mud from between the pads of their feet. She rubbed the towel along their spines to the docks of their tails.

Above Josie's hand and the towel, floating Charlene swirled. She lingered a second above the dogs, then floated out through the van's half-rolled-down passenger window.

Time, floating Charlene tried to reason.

Luck, she attempted.

Go home, Polka Dot. Go home.

Sometimes you let dogs run wild in the forest, and sometimes dogs come down the trail at you. Beside Charlene's body on the edge of Long Trail, Polka Dot stood up. He trembled and whined. He slow-blinked his cataract eyes and sniffed the neck of Charlene's body. He licked the contortion of her wrist—Charlene's body, glassy-eyed, mud-packed, gutted, its skin abrasions already jeweled with fern spores and wasps' eggs.

Come home, Polka Dot! Come home!

Victor sat on the bench by the door with his coffee. So much is conjecture or dogma or remnants of faith. A living body can't imagine or work out the logic of its own appearance nor grasp the implications of its impermanence and fatality. We are that inside ourselves. We are so beyond ourselves. Star-bound. Star-made. Nebulae, asteroids, star-caves— the world soaks itself up. Charlene's floating was soaking. As dirt soaks up rain. As rain and sun alchemize to green leaves, all around Victor, floating Charlene became what she once sensed.

Polka Dot!

Past the yellow gate and the turnout where the van had been parked, Polka Dot stopped to cock his head. Sounds of the forest and road fell into the portal of his teeth-torn ear. Through his milky eyes, the redwoods blurred into the sun. He lifted his abraded nose and molecules of scent fell into the vault of his skull—particles of tree bark and dog skin, molecules of house, molecules of Victor, of floor, door, of toast and strawberry jam, of wine, of quilts and embers, of Charlene.

On the bench, Victor sat in his socks. He pulled on his boots and arranged the tongues of the boots over the tops of his feet, pulling the laces even and tight. Three, two, one. Later, Victor would feel that Charlene stayed as long as she could. Later, he'd feel a sense of her remained, swirling in an updraft of breeze. But first Victor would see Polka Dot limping up the road. Polka Dot walking alone. Victor looked up from where he sat— bent over his knees, tying the bows of his boots into knots. ■

A STORY FROM THE LAST BOOK
Charles Holdefer

"Von! Von!"

He was counting money on his bed and he stopped. He looked over his shoulder but he didn't answer. He turned back to the bed and resumed counting.

"Come down! I know you're not asleep."

For the last six months he'd rented an upstairs room from Mrs. Swanson, who was also the owner of the Blue Star Diner, where Von worked as a cook. Her white house with an ornamental turret was the largest in Lamoni. She was a widow fifteen years Von's senior and was usually drunk by noon (or 4:00 p.m., at the latest). She leased more than a thousand acres of inherited farmland and lived off yearly reckonings on crop shares. Bonnie Swanson believed that she was being cheated but it had become more important to her to stay drunk than to do something about it.

She rarely left the house anymore. Her habits had started to take a toll on her appearance. A palsy sometimes passed through Bonnie's left side like a slow-motion bolt of lightning. She'd also become afraid to drive a car. She'd had a number of scrapes and the last one, a collision that put a young mother in the hospital for a week, had profoundly shaken her. It could've been much, much worse! She had to get drunk just to stop thinking about it. Now, if she needed to go somewhere, she let Von do the driving.

"The car is yours!" She bobbed back and forth in the passenger seat. "You can have it. I'll sign it over to you. I don't know what I'd do without you, Von."

He gripped the wheel and stared straight ahead. "It's okay, Bonnie."

Von brought home coleslaw and pork tenderloins from the Blue Star, and sometimes he had to beg her to eat. This was his first job since leaving the Navy and he didn't want to lose it because jobs were hard to find and he was saving up for his special plan. But the situation was getting tricky. On occasion Bonnie threw her arms around him and sobbed, "Oh, Von, you're so good to me, you really are!" On other occasions, when she was really low, she swore vilely and told Von that he was nothing more than a parasite who paid only thirty dollars a month rent and ate his fill at the Blue Star and fucked every little waitress and skinny-assed girl who came in through the door.

"That's not true, Bonnie, and you know it."

Now she called, "I know you can hear me!"

Von sighed and gathered his money into a pile and slipped it behind the headboard. He lifted his eyes and said, "What should I do?"

Above his bed, its nose thrust forward, was a moose head. He'd found it at a pawn shop in Kansas City. It was splendid, almost five feet across if you counted the antlers.

"You want me come up there?" she called.

He hurried out to the hall. At the bottom of the stairs stood Bonnie, gripping the railing. The belt of her robe lay on the carpet behind her, and her robe hung open.

* * *

When Von was two years old, his father had accidentally crushed a coworker under a lime spreader, and instead of admitting his error, he'd tried to hide the body in a field of sorghum. He'd received a life sentence. Von had no recollections of the man. His earliest memory was from a later period, when he and his mother had come north and she was living with a fellow called Dan who worked in the coal mines. There had been a picnic, maybe it was the Fourth of July. Von had wanted to carry a watermelon. "No, it's too big for him, he'll drop it," she'd said, but Dan disagreed.

"No, he'll be okay."

Dan was kind! Von hugged the watermelon to his chest. It was tiger-striped, big and green and sweating.

When it slipped from his clutch and split open at his feet, the vision of red flesh stabbed his eyes. The glistening black seeds. Shocking!

Now his mother was scolding, Von began to sob, and it seemed as if the melon was his own head. Dan tried to comfort him, but Von knew—oh, terrible!—that it couldn't be undone.

* * *

Later there was Uncle Gerrit's farm. He wasn't really an uncle but a brown-toothed, tobacco-spitting older man that his mother had married after Dan went away. Look: the cat in the barn had a litter of kittens, sucking at her side, and Uncle Gerrit tossed the kittens into a gunnysack, end over end, mewing, and then plunged the sack into a five-gallon bucket. Bubbles broke the water's surface with a silence worse than cries. Von ran away and crawled in the bushes and wept until everything went black.

He hated the farm. By the time Von started school, Uncle Gerrit expected him to help with the chores every morning. At school the kids knew that Uncle Gerrit wasn't his real father and word had got out that his real father was in prison so they taunted him, expected him to fight and live up to his reputation as a convict's son. Von was taller than most boys his age but he was thin, almost translucent behind his spray of freckles. When he swung his fists he lacked force, he was awkward and easy to dodge. This only increased their mocking. One day, his teacher pulled him aside and told him that he should ignore the taunts and work harder and make the most of things, because the world was his oyster.

Von listened and nodded but he didn't understand this speech. He didn't know what an oyster was.

It was a tremendous relief when school let out for summer. But lonely, too, on the farm where, now that he no longer had to catch the school bus, it was assumed that he was available to work all day. And at night there was a ritual after supper when Uncle Gerrit yawned and put down his paper and went up the stairs and slung his bib overalls over the banister, and not long afterward Von's mother finished her dishes and slumped her shoulders and trudged up the stairs after him, and not long after that, Von heard the bed's headboard banging the wall as his mother and Uncle Gerrit did what they always did. Von blinked and chewed on a finger or vigorously began to pick his nose.

In the morning, Uncle Gerrit was the first one to rise. He climbed back into his overalls and tromped downstairs on his way to the outhouse for his other evacuations.

"Time to get goin'!" he called.

Go where? Von thought. *All there is, is here here here!* On several occasions he inquired about his real father, but these questions made his mother angry. "He's not here for you, is he? You'll never see him. Get him out of your mind."

Once or twice a summer, usually around the Fourth of July, Von was treated to a trip to a public swimming pool in a town called Oskaloosa. They picnicked at the city park, and then his mother and Uncle Gerrit left him at the pool for the afternoon while they went to visit the farm implement show. The pool was a pleasure, but it was also a trial, to fit in with the town kids. Von worried about his appearance, his cut-off shorts ballooning around his chicken-white legs. He didn't know how to swim, either, and by mistake he discovered that he couldn't float. At first he'd been content to stay in the shallow end, where he adopted a strategy of walking on the bottom of the pool and moving his arms as if he were swimming, hoping that anyone watching him wouldn't be able to see a difference. But one Fourth of July he was too tall for this ruse, he stood high out of the water, while the kids his own age were in the deep end, splashing and paddling and jumping off the diving boards. All the fun was over there.

So Von climbed out of the pool and walked briskly to the deep end. He approached the edge and looked down at the chlorine-blue water. Really, how hard could it be? He took a deep breath—and let himself fall in.

Instantly he sank, a roaring filled his ears, and though he moved his arms and kicked his legs, he continued downward, till his big toe cracked against the concrete bottom. *Ow!* He tried to stretch out his body and float upward, because he'd heard that a person's body naturally floated. But when he attempted this, he drifted sideways. It wasn't working.

Now it occurred to him that he could drown.

In his mind, he saw an image of his body at the bottom of the pool turning slowly like a piece of spat-out chewing gum.

What now? His chest felt tight, he couldn't hold his breath much longer. Von regained his footing and tilted his head upwards, where legs scissored and colored swimsuits moved like kites in a liquid sky. He felt cheated. *Why not me?*

Above, the bodies waved, out of reach. Glumly, Von set his jaw and began to trudge up the slope toward the shallow end of the pool. He'd have to figure out a solution.

* * *

"Close your robe, Bonnie, will ya? We can't do this."

He regretted what was developing between them but he wasn't surprised. A few days earlier, she'd fiddled him in the salon. It was the second time. It began when she ran a hand across his torso. "Look at you. You're so beautiful, Vonny, and you hardly know it."

He felt what was happening to him and he didn't want it but he couldn't stop it. His body did not obey.

"Lordy, look at that," she said. "Vonny likes me. He goes straight up, doesn't he?"

The first time she touched the front of his trousers, they'd ended up in Bonnie's room with its big lumpy bed and wallpaper of splotchy flowers. The second time they didn't even get as far as her room. It went fast, the sound of her breathing, the clicks of her throat, the snap of elastic. Her skin smelled of olives—womanly—pleasantly stronger with a little sweat. The floor of the salon hurt Von's knees but soon they reached the verge and she shuddered and a moment later he spilled, groaning, and she shuddered some more, gripping his shoulders very hard.

Afterward, he helped Bonnie sit up, and then without a word went upstairs to his room and closed the door.

* * *

Back at the farm, Von could not put the injustice out of his mind. But then it occurred to him that maybe he was like everybody else, only he needed more time to figure it out. He resolved not to give up. *Maybe*, he reasoned, *if I could hold my breath longer, I'd have time to figure out how to float.*

He found an old tin bucket, wiped out the cobwebs, and brought it to the hand pump, where he filled it, and then carried the bucket to the orchard, because this was a private matter and he didn't want anyone to see him. He stopped at a grassy spot behind a plum tree. He set the bucket down, the reflection of leaves and blue sky shimmering on the surface.

He knelt and, taking a deep breath, he plunged his head into the water. The shock of cold made his temples pound, but he counted to thirty before straightening up again, panting, wiping his eyes. There. That wasn't so hard. He could learn how to be at home in the water.

The grass around the bucket was wet from overflow. Von caught his breath and tried again. He counted to fifty. He stretched it to sixty. Could he last longer? It hurt but he concentrated till his ears began to pop and ring and he believed he could hear the trapped echoes of mewing kittens. *Ninety-eight, ninety-nine, one hundred!* He pulled out his head, gasping and triumphant, water streaming down his face.

"Shit's sake!" Uncle Gerrit stood by the fence, watching. He shook his head and spat. "I always knew there was something wrong with you."

* * *

Did Uncle Gerrit go out of his way to hurt him? That same summer, Von's mother announced that she was pregnant. Von shouldn't have been surprised, given what he knew of life on the farm. Still, he felt betrayed. His mother grew very large and suffered in the heat. Several times in Von's presence, Uncle Gerrit said, "Now I'll have a real son."

In the winter his mother gave birth, but little Jerry lived only six weeks—there was something wrong with his heart and lungs; his face would go from rosy to purple as his tiny hand curled around Von's finger, and Von looked down, reluctant to pull away. The morning of the funeral, Uncle Gerrit wept at the kitchen table. For the first time Von felt sorry for the man and even, in some unspeakable way, responsible for the grief, because something lacking in him had set in motion these events. He felt as if he had dropped the watermelon again. But he'd wanted poor Jerry to live, too! Really!

"Uncle Gerrit?"

"I can't talk right now, boy. Give me some peace."

Von went out to the machine shed and unscrewed the gas cap on Uncle Gerrit's Allis-Chalmers tractor and inhaled deeply from the tank. He'd done this before. The first gust was nothing, the second gust would give him giggles, and the third gust—which he knew he shouldn't do because of the aftereffect, but once he started giggling he no longer cared—*whooo!* He sat back on the oily dirt and laughed and laughed, and for a whole minute he couldn't screw the cap back on, because the Allis-Chalmers tractor kept swimming in front of his eyes. By the time it stopped swimming, and he could replace the cap, his head would begin to hurt. It hurt terribly.

* * *

School was the same but more so. Von could repeat things that a teacher said, but reading was difficult for him. The letters danced before his eyes; he lost track from one line to the next, and soon he lost interest. One day his tenth-grade English teacher asked him to read aloud a story assignment he'd written, but Von stumbled so many times that the teacher, Mr. Willard, snatched his paper from him and had another student read it:

Every day Experience
Bowser, my old faithful hound, which had seen his best day for lack of teeth,
hearding and seeing he was worthless, so I decide to get rid of him did not want
to take him to the dog pond. I thought I would take him out to the timber fastened

a box of dynamit on his back and attached a fuse to it. after doing this I tied Bowser to a tree. after exchange of last words and greetings, I lit the fuse and started away. The old dog happend to get scent of danger, broke lose and run until he caught up with me. I was almost frighten to death started to run for the dynamit on Bowser back might explode at any time. The dog beeing a hound could keep up with me. Through the tree I spied a lake and, although I couldn't swim jumped in. Going down for the last time, my old faithful dog jump in, the water putting the fuse out. He caught me by the collar and pulled me to shore, getting up took the dynamit from Bowser back, we both went home, reaching home rather late I put Bowser in the barn and I return next day found Bowser my dog dead. With careful exam I found he had died with heart trouble.

"So that's an everyday experience?" Mr. Willard said, and the entire class laughed.

Later that day, during a lonely hour of study hall in the library, Von took down a dictionary and tried to look up the word *oyster*. He had a vague idea but he wanted to know. He found the *O* section of the dictionary; but the fine print began to swim under his eyes. *OYSTER… OYSTER…*

Suddenly he was so frustrated that he was tempted to get up and start walking and never come back. Leave the library—leave school. Outside was the street, and freedom. Von had already skipped classes in the past. But this time he would leave *forever*. Leave this town. Leave his mother and Uncle Gerrit.

But would they care? Would anybody care? It was very important that his departure be noticed. If he wasn't missed, Von reasoned, then he might actually be doing everybody a favor by disappearing. Like his real father—invisible in prison, as far as the world was concerned. If Von left town and wasn't missed … why, *the whole world was a prison.*

He slammed the dictionary shut and rubbed his eyes. He couldn't cry here, in the library. *I need to get outside first*, he thought. When he stopped rubbing his eyes, though, he noticed that Kitty Galeazzi was watching him from a nearby table. She tucked a book under her arm and came over to him.

"You okay?" she whispered.

Kitty Galeazzi was a quiet, dreamy girl whose father worked in the coal mines. She wasn't popular, she was no bouncing cheerleader, she was scarecrow skinny and had a huge nose; she wore the same belted red dress every day and her socks tended to droop around her ankles. She couldn't make them stay up.

Von blinked at her, wordless.

"You okay?" she repeated.

Von sniffed. "Sure. Just reading."

"The dictionary? Gee, you *are* literary. I didn't know till the other day. I liked your story. I thought it was very original. Mr. Willard is a stinker and he doesn't appreciate that. What are you reading in the dictionary?"

"Uh, looking at *O*." Von changed the subject. "What are you reading?"

"*Castle of Tomorrow*. It's wonderful," she said, and then proceeded to tell him all about it, how Manfred Muller was her favorite writer, and when she finished it she would start it all over again. She'd skipped her homework because she couldn't put it down, she said. Did Von like Manfred Muller's *The Secret Chamber*?

Von admitted that he hadn't read it, and then added, "I've been sticking to the dictionary. Almost got as far as *oyster*."

He wanted her to like him, but she struck him as intensely strange. It wasn't just that this was the first time he'd seen her big nose so up close. (He knew that some kids called her Beak, and she had a habit of lifting her hand to touch it—sometimes it seemed she was trying to cover her nose, other times that she was pulling on it, trying to make it even larger.) Von had never read a book for pleasure and it had never occurred to him that someone might choose to *reread* a book. What was the point? But there must be something to it. Just talking about *Castle of Tomorrow* made Kitty's dark eyes snap, and her little mouth grew animated. She looked so ... happy. And certainly Von wanted some of that.

"Want to see a poem I wrote?" she asked.

"Sure," he said.

Again, she might as well have levitated, as far as Von was concerned. But he was fascinated. She reached her skinny arm into a ring folder and pulled out a sheet and handed it to him. There was nothing on one side, so he turned it over. This side was almost empty, too, but for several precisely printed lines in the middle. Von read:

> *BLANK PAGE*
> *What was here*
> *Before I danced*
> *With inky feet.*

"Wow."

Then he noticed other details about her. The way she held her shoulders very straight, and the way her teeth suddenly emerged like an avalanche when she smiled, pleased that he was impressed by her poem. Now Von grasped that, amazingly, he was on the verge of acquiring a girlfriend.

"Do you know 'The little man who wasn't there'?" she asked.

Von blinked.

She began:

> *The little man who wasn't there*
> *I saw him standing on the stair*
> *He wasn't there again today*
> *Oh, how I wish he'd go away!*

"My grandma sings that sometimes," she continued. "From the first time I heard it, I couldn't get it out of my head. Those words—I mean, they're just like the little man! The words! And now they're in my head! But I like it, too. Now you won't be able to get it out of your head, either."

Von nodded, swallowing deeply.

School was almost finished for the year, but he and Kitty found time for other conversations and, in a rash moment, Von promised that he would read *Castle of Tomorrow* over the summer. "You need to come out of your shell," she told him, and though he wasn't sure what she meant, he was ready to believe her. Von was growing, his chest was getting broad, and already the previous summer his trip to the Oskaloosa swimming pool had taken on another dimension. He'd practiced holding his breath and was very good at it; and though he confirmed, unfortunately, that he still couldn't float, he managed to enjoy himself by taking long strolls at the bottom of the deep end, looking up at the kicking legs of girls, a grin breaking across his face and bubbles escaping from the corners of his mouth. A large bulge distended the front of his shorts. Something he'd brought from the farm.

But this summer was an agony. Because once again he was trapped in the country and this time, he was in love. Nothing meant the same anymore. Uncle Gerrit wanted him to pull cockleburs in the cow pasture but now Von was openly defiant, and he idled. "What's the matter with you?" his mother asked him. "A roof over your head, all you can eat, and you think you can just sit around? That's not the way life works." Upstairs in his room, Von tried to read *Castle of Tomorrow*, but it was tough. The words started swimming away from him. He couldn't rise to their level and this made him miserable. What would Kitty think? Would she give up on him? Oh, this was heart trouble, worse than Bowser's.

Alone in his room, he spent long hours trying to write Kitty Galeazzi a letter, but it didn't sound right; it didn't add up to all he had to say, everything he felt. Eventually he settled for writing a poem on the last page of *Castle of Tomorrow*:

It's true

I love you.

It was short, but to the point. She would find it the next time she reread the book, and she would know the author. She would understand how he felt.

The next day at lunch his mother put a platter of steaming sweet corn on the table. It was a hot day and the corn would make everyone hotter, but that was all right, because it was such good corn in this young season. Now it was the best.

"I don't think Von will be having any," said Uncle Gerrit.

Von's mother stood up quickly and went back to the stove and pretended to be busy.

"What do you mean?" said Von.

At first he didn't believe that Uncle Gerrit was serious. Von was hungry and ready to eat three ears, maybe four. Sometimes he tweaked Uncle Gerrit about eating corn because Uncle Gerrit had strong opinions on the right way to do it. Uncle Gerrit ate his ears horizontally, going down one set of rows and then back up the next, like his tractor in a field. Von's mother, in contrast, ate her corn circularly, turning the ear and going round. Uncle Gerrit told her that this was a peculiar method and she listened to him and nodded but persisted in this manner all the same. That was her personal style. Von, for his part, took random bites. He attacked the ear *here*, and then turned it round and chomped it *there*, and now maybe a nibble *over there*, on the far end. He had no reason for doing so other than provoking Uncle Gerrit, who he knew observed him and found his method positively maddening. That was why, now, he thought that Uncle Gerrit was tweaking him, too. He couldn't mean it.

But, in fact, he was serious.

Uncle Gerrit pulled the platter away from the center of the table, out of Von's reach. He selected an ear and buttered it. Next, the salt. He took his time. Now, the first bite. And a second bite.

"I planted this corn," he finally said, a dab of grease on his chin. "I picked it this morning. Who shucked it? I did. While you were moping around up in your room. No corn for you, kid."

"I weeded it!" Von shouted. He brought his fist down on the

table, plates rattled. "Every day!"

"There's enough for everybody," Von's mother called from the stove, but she didn't come forward.

"No, it's the principle," Uncle Gerrit insisted. "He needs to learn."

From there, the argument degenerated. There were violent reproaches, embittered demands. Soon Von could stand it no more and he kicked back his chair with a crash and on his way out of the kitchen grabbed an ear from the platter, which he took outside and ate with no salt or butter under a box elder tree, looking out at the rolling fields, in a frenzy so ferocious that long after the kernels were stripped, he found himself chewing and gnashing on the bare ear, he was so damn mad.

Eventually, instead of going back in the house, he threw the ear in the ditch and started walking the six miles of gravel road into town. He knew what he was going to do. He had a plan. There was a recruitment center in Oskaloosa. He was going to join the Army.

* * *

The plan didn't work overnight, as he'd hoped, but it still went quickly. The Army refused him but then he approached the Navy and lied about his age, said he was seventeen instead of sixteen, and in barely three weeks after the big argument with Uncle Gerrit, Von found himself in a recruit training barracks in Mississippi.

Boot camp was hot and humid, and the drills weren't easy, but on the whole it wasn't so bad, compared to the farm. The only thing that went seriously wrong was when he discovered that the Navy required a swimming test. The thought tormented Von for several days till he went to his recruit division commander, a stubby man named Travis. "You see," he confessed, "my problem is I don't float, sir. I'd do *anything* to get out of the swimming test. If I get kicked out of the Navy, I'll have to go back to the farm." Von's voice cracked. "I can't sleep when I think about it, it gives me heart pumpitations. But I *can* hold my breath. I'm really good at that, sir. You just try me."

Travis stared at him for several long seconds. "You just passed, Einstein." He walked away, shaking his head and muttering.

* * *

Von spent four years in the Navy, circling the globe in the guts of a destroyer. He learned about life from other sailors, some of whom had seen action on the USS *Collett* in the Battle of Inchon. These were hardened men who were not easily impressed but, because they reserved their scorn for higher targets, they were fairly indulgent of Von, though they didn't always understand him and sometimes couldn't resist amusing themselves at his expense. In Gulfport they got Von so drunk, so violently ill, that he vomited blood. That same weekend they'd hooted in laughter at the way Von averted his eyes when a fat prostitute with a wobbling midriff descended a hotel lobby staircase, *click-clack, click-clack*. The lobby carpet smelled like a rotten pear and was pocked with cigarette burns. Von followed the prostitute through a beaded curtain, where, before he was allowed to proceed into the next room, a little old woman sitting on a stool with a crocheted shawl over her shoulders ordered him to take out his penis. Von teetered on his feet, he felt he was drowning. He didn't want to show his penis to *her*. But the old woman insisted, and Von complied, whereupon she gave him a quick inspection, concluded by a pinch of her bony fingers, to test for gonorrheal drip. "Ayye," Von yipped. The old woman removed her hand and readjusted the shawl on her shoulders. "All right," she said. "You can go in."

And that was just the beginning of his education. Von learned how to pour oil from a twelve-gallon barrel without spilling a drop, how to sleep standing up, and how to perform a slick piece of sleight of hand to vanish a still-lit cigarette. He saw lucent glaciers in Greenland. He discovered an aptitude for cooking, the pleasure of chopping and the smell of raw food on his fingers. He fell in love with a busty young woman on a bicycle in Copenhagen. He didn't speak to her; he simply saw her on her bicycle, as she stopped at an intersection and put one foot down on the wet black paving stones; she looked over at him, standing on the corner, and she smiled. She was unbearably beautiful. Then she gave her bike a push and pedalled away into the March mist. Von never saw her again, but at that moment the entire world became unbearably beautiful, because it contained this woman on her bicycle. An indescribable gladness filled Von's heart.

Of course the other men spoke often of girlfriends and whores and wives. One night, when they were at sea again, Von announced that he had a sweetheart back home. Her name was Kitty.

"Whoa—listen up, everybody! Von's missin' pussy!"

Thereafter they sometimes teased him: "What's yer girlfriend's name again? *Pussy?*"

"No, it's Kitty," he answered, every time.

In his bunk, as the ship's engines chugged and reverberated through his body, he pulled the blanket to his chin and wondered about Kitty Galeazzi. What was she doing now? Had she forgotten him? Sure, he'd fallen in love with the woman on the bicycle but he knew that it was not fated for him to start a new life with a beauty in Copenhagen. Whereas he'd started to nurse a fantasy—a special plan—of returning home in triumph, and settling down with Kitty Galeazzi.

She'd liked him, he was certain. And he began to see a way to make things work. He knew that he was steadily maturing and becoming more accomplished—these were solid facts—so now he was more confident. Although he would never be bookish like Kitty, or impress her in that way, when she saw him next, he would have other things to offer. He savored an image of their life as a couple.

The image largely derived from a movie he'd seen before his first Atlantic crossing, as a freshly minted seaman third class, at a theater in Norfolk, Virginia. It told the story of rabbit farm that had gotten out of hand so that there were rabbits everywhere—it was a comedy, and that was the joke, which grew in scale over the course of the movie, more and more rabbits!—but the story didn't matter, that wasn't what interested Von. Rather, he was struck by the characters of the next-door neighbors to the rabbit farm, a businessman and his artistic wife who called each other "darling." It wasn't clear what business the man was in—mainly he was a collector who smoked a pipe and wore a silk robe with a fancy knot and lived in a house with books and paintings and an enormous moose head above a settee where his wife lounged in a flowing gown and read a book.

This household fascinated Von. These people stuck in his mind. How would it be, to live like that? In this kind of gentle harmony? He knew the décor was fake and its world was being made fun of, but he didn't approve, because this image seemed to gesture toward something larger, finer, soulful. There was too much mockery in the world already. He was tired of mockery, and he ached for something different.

The rest of the movie was annoying, with all the rabbits and the problems when they invaded the house, hopped on shelves or tumbled out of drawers. Von didn't think it was funny or laugh along with the audience. Rather, new possibilities nourished a private fantasy he could share with no one.

"Kitty, my darling."

She removed her nose from her book. "Yes, Von, my darling?"

"Are you feeling delighted?"

"Oh yes. Thanks to you!"

He extracted a pipe from the pocket of his silk robe. A match flared, he grinned, and twin toots of smoke escaped the corners of his mouth.

* * *

"Von! Von!"

He'd taken the job at the Blue Star and moved in with Bonnie because Lamoni was less than an hour's drive from the farm fields of his youth. It was close to Kitty. He was saving up money. By his calculation, one thousand dollars wasn't enough. The next time Kitty saw him, he should have at least two thousand dollars in his pocket! That could launch them. He would take her by the hand. Look into her dark eyes. *"What did you think of what I wrote in the book?"*

"You want me to come up?" Bonnie called.

"No! Don't come up."

"You're being naughty, Von. I won't bite. Am I going to have to teach you a lesson?"

"No."

"Here I come-come!"

"No!"

Von descended the staircase, step by squeaking step. This wasn't part of the special plan, no, definitely not. But what could he do?

Suddenly he recalled his mother on the farm, climbing up the staircase to be with Uncle Gerrit. He slowed down and reached for the railing. Then, unbidden, Kitty Galeazzi's favorite poem came to his mind. It had stayed in his head, just as she'd said it would.

> *The little man who wasn't there*
> *I saw him standing on the stair*

That's me, he thought sadly. The poem is about me!

"Von, what is it? Come on, sweetie."

He blinked. Bonnie smiled up at him. He resolved: *This will be the last time.*

* * *

Daybreak.

He slipped quietly out of Bonnie's bed.

He went upstairs and put on a clean shirt and removed the $1,306 that he'd hidden behind the headboard. It wasn't the full $2,000, but it would have to do. He stuffed clothes in his Navy seabag and then crept downstairs and put it in the back of the car. He came back inside and tiptoed to his room, where he whispered, "Here we go." He removed the moose head from the wall.

Step—step—step—when he was one from the bottom, he heard a flush and rush of water. He froze. The bathroom door rattled and Bonnie came out. He stood so still that she almost didn't notice him, but then, with a startled cry, she brought her hand to her throat.

"What the—? *No!*"

Von took the last step and moved toward the door, but Bonnie got there first and blocked the way. "You'd walk out like this? How could you?"

"Get out of the way, Bonnie. My rent is paid."

She began to wrestle with him, gripping an antler and pulling, but he was stronger and he pushed her back once, twice, and the third time, when she clung, he used extra force. She fell to the floor. She looked up at him, weeping, and beat her fist on the floor. "No! This is so cruel!"

Von made it through the door and went to the car, where, with some difficulty, he fit the moose head into the passenger seat. Then he went around to the other side, got in, and drove off.

* * *

Soon he was approaching his old territory, breathless that things were moving so fast. He'd assumed that he would have more time to work out details, but plans would have to be adjusted. Besides, he took comfort in a story he'd told himself about the poem he'd written in Kitty Galeazzi's favorite book. Surely she had found it and realized it had come from *him*. As a consequence, she would expect his return.

That was the wonderful, sustaining part. However much time passed or wherever he wandered in the world, his part of the book was still intact, burning quietly like a little flame. *He* was there in those words. Von thought of this book as the Last Book, because no matter how many other books existed or how many smart people read them, the collection would always be incomplete and people would always be ignorant if they did not make room for *him*. In the Last Book, he was worthy.

But now that his story was unfolding before his eyes, it made him nervous. He arrived in town and started inquiring about Kitty Galeazzi. "Who?" asked a red-cheeked woman at the bakery. She didn't know who Kitty was. But at the feed store, another fellow understood immediately. "Oh yes—I remember Kitty Galeazzi. Now she's Katherine Flynn. Lives on the old ice house road." The fellow peered at Von. "Do I know you?" Von turned away.

Minutes later, he parked the car and walked the length of the street, unsure which door to knock on. He saw no one. Next, he followed an alley behind the houses.

Then he saw her. She stood in a tiny backyard where a big-haunched man was pounding garden stakes. Kitty, even skinnier than before, listlessly stood by a toddler who crawled on yellow grass and tried to eat a cricket. She looked up, startled at the sight of Von lurking by the fence. She squinted, as if trying to recall who he was. Then came a moment when it seemed that she knew. Kitty drew up her shoulders straighter. The sound of the hammer. The child crawled. He realized that she wanted him to go away. Von's mouth fell open and he walked on.

* * *

"Maybe I should've said something," he told the moose. "But she didn't even come over. She just stood there like she wanted me to disappear." The moose's nose pointed straight ahead, and the car seemed to drive itself. They were on the old school bus route. Soon he was heading up the lane to Uncle Gerrit's farm. The familiar landscape, the gnarled trees of the orchard, appeared dreamlike on the other side of the windshield.

He got out of the car and walked up to the back door. "Mom!" he called through the screen.

No one answered.

"Mom!"

Then came a shout behind him. He saw Uncle Gerrit picking raspberries beside the machine shed. He went over to the man and learned that his mother had abandoned Uncle Gerrit, and Uncle Gerrit didn't know her new address. "She stayed with me for your sake, you know. She always wanted you to have a dad. But when you left, she moved on, too." He looked at Von with watery blue eyes. "How are you, boy?"

Von could not pursue this conversation. He turned his back on Uncle Gerrit and returned to the car.

* * *

"I got $1,306. That's something, isn't it? I don't owe nobody!"

Now he stood in the cemetery in Oskaloosa. It had taken him

twenty minutes to find the plot he was looking for, but eventually he came upon the spot, the patch of green under the broad sky.

The name on the stone: Jerry Zinnegar.

"Brother," he said, "what now?"

He stood up straighter, balling his fists as he'd learned to do in the Navy. He looked at the tombstone and he wanted to cry, to cry very hard, but it was tough to get started, to pry himself open. What should he cry about first? Where to begin? He was actually a little envious of Jerry.

"You don't know what you missed," he said. "You *can't* know."

Then he began to cry. He was riven, and he believed that he would never stop. ■

Gary Young

Small birds hover outside my window, their wings beating wildly to hold themselves aloft until I rise and fill their feeder. Perhaps I ask too little of them. At the foot of Mt. Inari, among the treats offered to pilgrims going up or coming down the mountain, there are grilled sparrows splayed on bamboo spikes like tiny crucifixions. People eat them whole: bones, feathers, the tiniest bit of flesh.

THE GREAT MIRROR
Karen Joy Fowler

Somewhere in the dustier part of the archives, I have a memory from my childhood of something once seen on television: A man is creeping furtively through a room. A glimpse of sudden movement makes him gasp. But it is only a mirror, only his own reflection. He laughs with relief, salutes himself. He bows to the mirror; he capers. Maybe he is a musketeer—I think I remember merry thrusts and parries, perhaps a plumed hat. Then finally comes a gesture unrequited. There is no mirror. The man is facing a twin brother (identically dressed, what luck!) he never knew he had.

Recognizing oneself in the mirror can be a tricky business. I haven't done so since I turned fifty.

In 1970, the psychologist Gordon Gallup Jr. developed the mirror test as a way of determining self-awareness. To date, those species that recognize their reflection as their reflection include all the great apes, bottlenose dolphins, orcas, elephants, and European magpies. Further research suggests that some of these same species understand themselves as distinct beings in time; they remember their past, they anticipate their future. The political philosopher John Locke proposed such psychological continuity as the very definition of a human being.

But neither political philosophy nor science is the law. Several years back, the Nonhuman Rights Project brought three cases in New York State, each seeking recognition of limited legal rights for some captive chimpanzees in dire circumstances. Expert witnesses attested to the psychological continuity of the chimp plaintiffs, to their understanding of their own suffering as something long-standing and ongoing. That this testimony did not carry the day does not mean that the scientific evidence in support of it is not detailed, extensive, and irrefutable. But judges have been deaf to such evidence since at least 1977, when, in Hawaii v. LeVasseur, the argument that dolphins were humans in dolphin suits was first tried and first failed.

No doubt the judges in New York were equally unconvinced by the chimps-are-persons arguments. No doubt they were constrained by precedent. At least one said that he was reluctant to be the one to take the large leap a finding in favor of the plaintiffs would require. But this also is true. In making their decision, the judges were thinking like chimpanzees.

Here is the flip side, the B track, of our recognition of the rich capabilities of our chimp relatives. If they are more like us than formerly understood, it must also follow that we are more like them. This mirror goes both ways. And actions based on a firm distinction between us and them are prevalent among chimps, up to and including territorial warfare.

Based on my readings of the work of Jane Goodall and Richard Wrangham, of Frans de Waal and Richard Conniff, and many others (and with apologies for anything I have misunderstood), here are a few other things we seem to share with chimps:

1. We both seem to have an innate sense of fairness. This is most often expressed as a feeling that one has not gotten one's due and less often as a feeling that one has taken too much and should put some back.

2. We are both sensitive to hierarchy (as every high school student knows). Individuals are often more concerned with what those beneath them are getting away with than with those above. Meanwhile, those at the top are highly affronted if deference is not shown. How many political careers have been fueled by this? How many family dinners ruined?

3. Alpha males are admired for their aggressive display behaviors and display behaviors are common. Take another quick look at our elected officials. So very common. (Both definitions of the word *common* applicable here.)

4. Coalitions are built through conscious strategies of reward and punishment. They are also deliberately and strategically broken up with the same. These efforts are often motivated by jealousies, ambitions, hurts and solace, friendships and lust.

5. We both soothe ourselves with junk food.

And finally:

6. Both chimps and humans show an obsessive interest in the sex lives of others. Both show a particularly obsessive need to control female sexuality. Our myths, our faiths, our laws, our history, and our lives are strewn with such attempts. You can hardly make a move without tripping over one.

* * *

I am the daughter of a behavioral psychologist. I was once asked in an interview if my father truly believed that humans had no inner lives. He would never have said that. He was also a poet, an unpublished novelist, and a great reader of novels. But he did think that humans were far less thoughtful than we credited ourselves with being. Clear away the brush of reason and rationality and you expose the real us. Current psychological studies suggest that character plays a surprisingly small role in human behavior. Instead, we are highly responsive to trivial changes in circumstance. We are like horses in that, only not so gifted.

Now that we understand emotions as material things—chemical, physiological, and mappable—I have no doubt that my father would have agreed with David Hume that we act from feeling first. Logic always lags, rationality is always playing catch-up, and it is always possible to find some reasonable-sounding reason for doing what you were going to do anyway. Language has been proposed as a critical difference between humans and chimps, but it often appears that the primary use we make of language is to obscure or ornament our essential primate selves. The correct response to most reasons given is suspicion.

Our essential primate selves are not necessarily bad people. Combine our primate sense of fairness with our primate capacity for empathy, and you have us at our very best. But good or bad, the inclinations listed above are surely pervasive. They buttress our laws, our religions, our stories and arts, our marriages and wars.

More than a decade ago, novelist Colin McAdam and I both wrote books with chimpanzees in the cast. When we met at a conference in Texas, we agreed that once you start looking at human behavior through the lens of primate studies, it is very hard to stop. More than ten years have passed, but this is the enlightening filter through which I now find myself viewing such things as 9/11, 1/6, 10/7, Donald Trump and Vladimir Putin, Congress and the Supreme Court, government shutdowns, Citizens United, the Dobbs decision, the hush-money case, Marjorie Taylor Greene and Matt Gaetz, the zombie life of Comstock, Stand Your Ground, anti-woke book banning, immigrant bashing, slut-shaming, and Fox No-News. Ignore the verbal incantations of the Sunday talk shows. Scratch and sniff. If it smells like an ape, it might be an ape.

This is the particular mirror in which I currently view myself. Just another of the great apes, though considerably short on greatness.

* * *

Charles Darwin, one of our greatest great apes, was among the first to use the mirror test. The ape in the mirror was a captive orangutan at the London Zoo named Jenny. Darwin visited with

Jenny, recording his impressions in his notebook and in a letter to his sister. Jenny had already been shoved into a dress and taught to eat with a spoon. Darwin watched her dealing with her handler, making tools out of bits of straw, and looking with what appeared to be comprehension at her reflection. He saw his own kinship to her.

So did Queen Victoria, who observed Jenny making and drinking a cup of tea. She was "too wonderful," the Queen wrote later. And also "frightful and painfully and disagreeably human."

We are left to imagine what Jenny's impressions of Queen Victoria might have been; words failed her. ■

BAT FAT
Lou Mathews

"I got a guy," Jaime Rubin says, "who was present at the creation. Graduate student. Albany. Winter of 2006. Second one into the cave."

We are parked outside Bowdler's, three faded screenwriters on a bus bench in the winter sun, waiting for noon opening, and Jaime is sketching out our latest investment opportunity. Entrepreneurs and screenwriters have similar skills: we do our research, develop a story, and sell it. Since Jaime can no longer sell his ideas in Hollywood, he tries them out on us.

Jaime is riffing on an *LA Times* story he emailed us last night. It's Jaime's favorite writer, Thomas Maugh, who specializes in science and anthropology and generates more screen treatments than any writer in town.

Maugh's latest was about a bat colony in New York that starved to death, attacked by this white fungus that made them burn calories even while hibernating. Jaime also really liked the common name given to the affliction, white-nose syndrome. Reminded him of his glory days as a staff writer on *Gimme a Break!*

Oscar Grunfeld purses his lips and pulls down on his pursed lower lip with a thumb and forefinger, which is how you know Oscar is seriously thinking. "I read that article. This sounds very much like bee colony collapse syndrome."

Jaime is incensed. "Not even close. Insects versus mammals. Eyes on the prize, Oscar. Bee colony collapse? Tragedy, yes. Dividends, no."

"Tragedy," Oscar says, and then he goes walkabout. It is his only concession to age, which we think is early eighties; a word sometimes provokes a reverie.

"One Armenian dies, a tragedy," Oscar says. "A hundred thousand Armenians die, that's a statistic. Your Joseph Stalin said that." Oscar was, when he could still afford it, a Trotskyite/anarcho-syndicalist. Now he owns apartment buildings. The landed man among us. He still has hopes for humankind. For tenants, not so much.

"Eyes on the prize, Oscar. Key phrases," Jaime says. "Sedentary mammals lose weight."

"Big deal," Oscar says. "When did anyone ever see a fat bat?"

"So what's the pitch?" I ask.

"Davis, Davis, Davis," Jaime says, "this one is *so* obvious, I thought even you would get it. What is the number-one, surefire money-making program in this country?"

"Probably *American Idol* or some other halfeness"—Oscar means half-ass, but he sometimes converts to Yiddish—"reality show." He sounds bitter.

"Wrongo-bongo," Jaime says. "Number one, all-time, anytime, guaranteed is a weight-loss program."

"This is true," I say. "I've been doing the South Park Diet, on and off, for two years."

"Don't you mean, South Beach Diet?" Oscar asks.

"Naw, I modified that one. I do South Park."

And Jaime says, "Wait for it, wait for it ..."

"South Park is a low-carb, low-brow diet. You cut out bread and cuss a lot."

"Badda-boom," Jaime says and does his crashing cymbal noise. "Okay, Spielbergs"—Jaime's term for Einsteins—"and among weight-loss programs, what is the crème de la crème, the Holy Donut Grail?"

Oscar and I are not at this moment Spielbergs or even Katzenbergs. We shrug.

"A passive weight-loss program," Jaime crows. "We're Americans! If you give us a choice, take a pill, enjoy an orgasm versus have sex, have an orgasm, we'll take the pill every time. The whole point with this fungus is that the fungus does the heavy lifting."

"Let me see if I've got this straight," I say. "You got a guy, a grad student, who can get you this fungus?"

"Unlimited supplies. These fungi are known as *GEOMYCES*"—we can actually hear and almost see the capital letters in Jaime's voice—"and all they require is cold, ideally a forty-two-to-fifty-five-degree climate, and a warm mammalian body to feed on. My guy's got a pair of yaks, cause they like the cold. He keeps them in a refrigerated shipping container and twice a day he combs the fungus off them. He gets nearly eight pounds of Grade-A *GEOMYCES* a day. Starter kit for the average dieter is half an ounce. Do the math. The only drawback is that *GEOMYCES* have to be refrigerated, which makes shipping more expensive. If the temperature gets over sixty degrees, *GEOMYCES* die."

"That does seem a disadvantage," Oscar says, not even bothering to pull on his lip because this is so obvious.

Jaime stands up from the bus bench. "Wrongo-bongo, déjà voom! Again, Oscar." Jaime looks like he's about to float. "That's the genius part. That means the suckers have to come to us. Or buy their own refrigerated room."

I'm catching on. "So you're going to rent a meat locker and fill it full of fat naked people and cover them with a white fungus that sucks calories out of them?"

"This reminds me," Oscar says, "of Terry Southern's novel *Flash and Filigree.*"

"Fat, naked, *sedated* people, Davis, and they are going to be sedated with the finest combination of recreational and twilight drugs available, but it ain't going to be no meat locker. We're gonna run this joint like a Malibu Detox Mansion. Strictly high-end.

"I mean eventually, sure, we might fill up a frozen food plant in Vernon with the HMO and Medicare crowd, but to start with, it has to be definitely high-end. Caché equals cash. We start with a few celebrity clients, the word gets around, we'll have to hire screeners to keep out the riffraff." Jaime is in the middle of the street by now, jabbing, then pointing, then punctuating with his famous floating-hand diorama. In the seventies he wrote a documentary about a renowned Chinese dance troupe. The dance master taught Jaime this move, "the rolling wave," a series of languid watery gestures that give the impression that Jaime's hand disconnects and floats away from his wrist.

"I mean, suppose Elizabeth Taylor is up for a Lifetime Achievement Oscar. You give La Liz this choice: one, spend one week in a medically supervised happy coma, and you are back to your *National Velvet* weight, or two, a month and a half at the No-Fun, No-Drinkies Fat Farm with the hourly enema plan. Which do you think she is going to choose?

"And of course, then you get into the ancillary income. Try to imagine what *National Enquirer* would pay for photos of the naked Cleopatra? I can see the headline now: *Melons covered with mold in the cold!* I'm just so sorry that Marlon didn't wait until I could provide him with the weight-loss program he deserved. Or Orson. God I could have helped him.

"And that's just the *deserving* high-end. You think I couldn't convince Paris Hilton, and that other one, the other stick figure, her friend for half-life?"

"Nicole Richie," Oscar says.

"How do you *know* that?" I ask.

"A successful writer needs to stay current."

"Yeah that's the one. You think I couldn't convince them two geniuses that they need to lose a few ounces?"

Oscar sticks out a lip, does his Edward G. Robinson thrust-head-bob. "How you going to hang them?"

This interrupts Jaime's flow and happy surveyal of all he sees and shocks him into full rant. "Hang 'em?" Jaime says. "We don't hang 'em! Whattya talking? We got four showrooms at the Malibu Fat-Free Mansion. Different rates. We show them the four levels, outline the options, they sign the contract. We give them a comp massage, put 'em under, and roll 'em out. Once they're in Comaland, who knows whether the daily floral bouquet, tantric massage, pagan prayer cycle, aromatherapy, Chumash sage ceremony, or Kosher acupuncture is actually delivered. We stack 'em up like cordwood in the cold room. Why would we hang them?"

"Because, flat," Oscar says, "flat is not good. You have to turn them. There is the bed sore problem, but also, if they're flat, the fungi only have access to one side of the body. This means it takes longer for the fungi to do their job. You lose money. The *GEOMYCES* need a full-time, all-access pass to all parts of the body, don't you agree?"

Jaime looks a little stunned, but then you can see him working it. "But not upside down," Jaime says. "They're not bats. They're fat people, who usually come accompanied by high blood pressure. Upside down would kill them."

"Who said upside down?" Oscar says. "What?"

But Jaime has done what he always does, reclaimed his turf, one of his small victories, the kind that got him banned from every studio in town. "Actually," Jaime says, "I think we need to sell it as an upgrade. *The Upright Suspension in the velvet-trimmed Big Baby Bouncer™.* Yeah, this will work."

The door to Bowdler's swings open and Kenny Ishikawa, the day bartender, blocks it open with a trash can and starts pulling chairs down from tables.

"Ahh," Oscar says, "time for a libation."

Jaime takes a stand, "Are you guys with me on this? The last surefire, ground-floor opportunity of your lifetime?"

"No cash," I say.

"No enthusiasm," Oscar says. "Come, Hymie"—Jaime's preferred pronunciation—"let me invest in a libation for you."

But Jaime has talked himself up, the way he used to, when he was known as one of the best pitchers in town. He is high on himself and needs no alcohol to sustain that high.

"Drawing the line here," Jaime says. "I'm going to go home. I'm going to work on my prospectus. And then I'll head for Musso's, where some real investors may still be found."

Kenny comes out to retrieve the trash can, and as he lifts it, Jaime calls to him, "Yo, Kelsoe. Buy these losers a drink. Put it on my tab." Kenny switches hands and waves vaguely at Jaime. "Lack of commitment," Jaime says. "You see how uncommitted that was? That slack, loosey-goosey pretend wave. The problem with this country, *hahh*"—it sounds like a hair ball coming up—"*hagggh*, is that lack of commitment."

"Onward," Oscar says. "Onward!" Oscar salutes, emphatically, then walks into and is absorbed by the dark recesses of Bowdler's. I follow him.

* * *

We don't see Jaime for a few weeks, and when he rejoins us at Bowdler's, it is hard to gauge his attitude. He doesn't seem chastened, but he is not the inflated Jaime we saw last. The balloon didn't get popped, but maybe it lost a little volume. Jaime walks through the door, nods to Kenny, and sits at our table. He flattens his hands on the table and spreads his fingers. "Gentlemen," Jaime says, "I'll accept that libation now."

Oscar decides to torment Jaime by buying him that promised drink and not asking what happened.

Oscar, as though he is continuing an interrupted conversation, says: "Did either of you know Terry Southern? No? No? Before your time." Jaime's vodka martini with fresh-ground pepper, two olives, and an onion arrives. "A wonderful train wreck waiting to happen. Incredible talent, incredibly abused." Jaime lifts and sips, and Oscar catches him midsip. "In case you should ever feel sorry for yourself, think of Terry Southern.

"He rewrote *The Killing* for Kubrick, no credit, almost no money, then wrote *Dr. Strangelove*, and Kubrick screwed him again, both credits and money. Southern wises up, swears off Kubrick, and then gets totally screwed on *Easy Rider*, and that vas worse because now he vas being screwed by amateurs. I mean, Kubrick is Kubrick. A worthy adversary. But when your throwaway genius is credited to a Dennis Grasshopper? It killed him."

"That's sad," Jaime interrupts. "Let me tell you another sad story ..."

But Oscar rolls on. "When he died, they went to that Grasshopper and asked for help, to keep him from a pauper's grave, and you know what that insect said? He said he didn't want to set a precedent. He said that if he had to buy funerals for all the writers he had screwed, he'd be bankrupt in a month. Fehh. It's the business we are in."

Jaime can stand it no longer. "Do you remember the last time we talked?"

Oscar tosses off his crème de menthe and slams the cordial glass down. "How can you not know Terry Southern?"

Jaime glares.

"So, Ja," Oscar says. "Tell us about the bat fat."

"It worked," Jaime says. "It actually worked. So close, but there was just this little problem with the delivery system. The *Geomyces*"— Oscar and I both note that they are no longer capitalized—"were really good at sucking calories, but they couldn't hang on."

"Hang on?" I say.

"They slid off."

"Slid off."

"Skin. They didn't much like smooth skin."

"Skin," Oscar says.

"The thing about bats," Jaime says, "is that they are furry little fuckers. Completely covered with hair. Which was good for the *Geomyces*. So they could hold on. Humans are relatively hairless. Orderly opens door, one puff of air, valuable *Geomyces* are floating up around the vents."

Jaime arrays his onion and olives on a napkin, downs the martini, and holds up the empty glass. "Yo, Kelsoe," he says. Kenny, who is charitable today, hands over a ready-made exchange martini. Oscar and I turn and stare. Kenny settles back next to the cash register and picks up his book. Today he is reading a favorite, Jean Rhys's *Wide Sargasso Sea*. Beside him are two more ready-made martinis. Kenny senses our stares and looks up. "What? At least he's trying to do something." Oscar and I are staggered. It never occurred to us that Kenny might listen to anything one of us had to say.

Jaime pops an olive. "What we figured out was it would have to be a two-step process. First step, you would have to grow hair all over your body so the *Geomyces* would have something to cling to. That would be a deal-breaker for most women, and the depilatory factor only screwed it further. Once they'd lost the weight, full-body waxing. Then laser. Maybe some radiation …"

"Ouch," Oscar says.

"Not cost-effective." Jaime pops an olive, then closes with an onion and downs his second martini with a swirling flourish. Kenny again makes a gracious exchange.

"You don't seem that daunted," I say.

Jaime sips. "It set me back for a day or two, particularly because I'd found some *serious* investors, but I think it's going to work out. I sold off a half interest to a guy who thinks he can find enough fat hairy guys to make a profit."

"No shortage there," I say. "Start with the Weinsteins, work your way up to Rudin."

"You should have started with Coppola," Oscar tells me. "The obvious choice if you weren't such an anti-Semite."

Jaime waits for us to settle down, like that genius fifth-grade teacher you had who knew exactly how to read a class. We settle.

"I think I'll be okay," Jaime says. "Once you immerse yourself in the world of weight loss, you learn there are myriad ways to skin that particular cat." A gleam ignites in the depths of Jaime's eye. "How much do you know about tapeworms?"

Oscar and I glance at each other. "Obviously not enough," I say.

Jaime expands, once again, to full entrepreneurial size. "In many ways, tapeworms are the ideal diet aid. No restriction on caloric intake, no need for unwanted exercise. Their only drawback is that when tapeworms reach maximum size, thirty meters, they become injurious to their hosts, and if they should reproduce, the fuckers can kill you.

"But I think there is a workable solution. All we need is tapeworms with a shelf-life." We wait for it. "I gotta guy," Jaime says, "a Doctor Musharaff, Mushariff, one of those, who can deliver to me irradiated tapeworms of any size, in any quantity. These are prime Pakistani tapeworms, not those feeble two-inchers the Indonesians are flooding the market with.

"Great appetites. Because they are irradiated, they are sterile and will die peacefully within six months, once they have achieved our goals. We can predict a thirty-pound weight loss in that period, but of course you can always upgrade, buy more than one if you want to lose more or lose it faster. And of course, the vacuum enemas would be complimentary."

"Irradiated tapeworms," Oscar says slowly. "I must say, Jaime Rubin, you are a man with courage and vision."

"I know it," Jaime says grandly. His famous floating hand gesture encompasses us, the room, and Kenny, who rises involuntarily, reaching for that third martini. "I wouldn't be where I am today without that vision."

It is the wisdom of the room, one I have learned to trust. We reverse here the process that the chambered nautilus uses to create its world. The nautilus begins with a microscopic chamber and builds spiraling outward, larger and larger, sealed and airtight rooms. We three, and our tender, Kenny, have retreated, year after year, from a lifetime of education, work, struggle, humiliation, and employment to this small place where we are secure and well entertained, and Jaime trusts that he edifies and amuses. It is a style and a comfort. A small chamber with music we agree on. ■

BARBACK
Dan Millar

It's a strange angle, viewing this
from a crouched position
where sideways movement
across the rubber mats
causes tire marks on your knees.
On your knees
but you are not praying.
You feel like the least
spectacular organism
in this Manhattan
shit holy fiasco:
oafish, skinny, sucked-in,
clumsy, bull brained,
but natured mildly,
just a little off socially,
lacking confidence,
and never feeling
mediocre enough.
The bartender, seen
from below with his
collared white shirt
and black slacks,
knows what he's talking about always:
sports, fashion, backpacking
through Europe,
skating, samurai swords,
and kite surfing.
He's full of red roses,
butterflies, and sarcasm,
his chiseled face
like that of a superhero
smiles easier than
anyone you've ever known.
Your head on the other hand
is a pin-ball machine,
colorful lights blink, red, blue,

green, silver
metal balls rolling and
bouncing sporadically.
Sick to your stomach
from nicotine gum
and drinking gallons of cherry coke.
You, my friend, are a bar-back.
Lugging two cases of beer,
on your shoulder in a black t-shirt,
yelling at the dishwasher
to hurry up in Spanish.
If you could, you would
tell the bartender
to change the keg himself,
to get his own glasses and silverware.
Sometimes you think about going home,
leaving work and flying
back to San Francisco.
You think of leaving
the girlfriend that sometimes
smells like other men,
the damp booze-soaked
wad of ones from
an overly touristy night.
You think about China Town,
Golden Gate Park, sourdough bread,
24th street, Bernal Heights
and the Lower Haight.
The glasses finally finish,
the dishwasher
passes you the rack,
you bump your way backwards
out of the dish room,
and stack them gently
under the counter.

THE BOOKMAN VANISHES
Priscilla Turner

We drove overland like travelers in the Old West, across Texas in the oven-baked landscape of June. My husband and I could have flown, but Larry McMurtry had drawn us, like other "citified Northerners," into what he called the heart of the heat. A decade ago, we journeyed through the Great Plains' southern fringe to a forlorn, forgotten place, McMurtry's hometown, Archer City. In 1987 he had bought four old buildings to house secondhand books for sale, which he numbered at four hundred thousand volumes. Over hundreds of miles, through terrain McMurtry described as "space, a huge sky, and a sense of distance," we metaphorically entered his early childhood's "bookless" years. On our pilgrimage from Seattle to Oklahoma City, McMurtry's bookstore lay square in our path.

Like secondhand bookstores, much of what we saw in Texas seemed on the edge of extinction. At a stop in Lubbock, we came across what appeared to my Northwest sensibilities like a pretty gussied-up backhoe operator. He was a trim older man wearing a neatly pressed Western shirt with a bolo tie, unfaded jeans, cowboy hat, and boots, tearing into a plot of earth on a street of new big-box stores, sending up clouds of ruddy dust into the drought-stricken expanse. Lubbock sits atop the world's largest aquifer, which environmentalists, to local dispute, say is being drained by big agriculture at a dangerous rate. We sped through Dickens, "The Unofficial Wild Boar Capital of Texas," desolate, half-boarded up, and not named after *David Copperfield's* author.

We finally arrived in Archer City to find the town little changed—to our eyes anyway—from its bleak appearance as Anarene in Peter Bogdanovich's 1971 black-and-white film adaptation of McMurtry's novel *The Last Picture Show*, set in the early 1950s. McMurtry and Bogdanovich cowrote the screenplay, which closely follows the novel. Just outside town, someone had planted another of the weary, sun-beaten "Pray for Rain" signs we'd seen all across Texas. Booked Up, McMurtry's bookstore, was located in a former Ford dealership, the kind that once were small-town business anchors, in the decades when people shopped downtown for everything from canning supplies to sedans. Of course, one old car dealership was not large enough to contain all the books, which spilled over into three warehouse-style buildings across the street.

Beyond them, Archer City's Center and Main Streets featured mostly plain single-story brick-faced structures with a couple of taller, early twentieth-century fronts to punctuate the flat roofs, along with the restored Royal Theater, where *The Last Picture Show* was screened the night before the auction McMurtry and his partners staged in August 2012. At seventy-six, McMurtry had decided to relieve his son and grandson of the responsibility, reducing his stock by two-thirds and drawing book buyers from major secondhand bookstores across the country. He could have made more money selling online, but he took special pleasure in bringing throngs of those citified northerners from major independent bookstores, like Powell's Books in Portland, to Archer City. The temperature hit a hellish 116 degrees. McMurtry billed it as the Last Book Sale.

Once in town, we noticed that we'd have no trouble banking, buying insurance, consulting a lawyer, or praising the Lord. McMurtry had hoped to create a version of the Welsh book town Hay-on-Wye, and for a while, book tourism was a viable draw for his and other local businesses. Susan Sontag called Archer City his theme park when he showed her around town. But by the time we arrived, the boom had faded. If we wanted to buy much more than a convenience store bag of chips, a pair of cowboy boots, or a sack of feed, we'd have to keep driving. Except we were longing for books. There were still a lot left.

McMurtry first started in retail secondhand bookselling in 1971 with the Booked Up legacy store in Georgetown, in Washington, DC, where after more than thirty years he and partner Marcia Carter were chased out by rising rents and the poshing-up of the neighborhood. In the decades between founding the original store and moving to Archer City, McMurtry and Carter branched out with bookstores in other cities, notably Dallas and Houston, but eventually consolidated as the fate of secondhand bookselling fell, buying up the stock of other sellers as they folded.

In his 2009 memoir *Books*, McMurtry wrote that after his writing career got underway, "the hunt for books was what absorbed me most." He asserted that "writing was my vocation ... no longer exactly a passion," but that from the mid-1970s on, he considered himself primarily a bookman. At first, he said, bookselling was a way to subsidize his reading. It was a watershed moment when he could no longer read every book he stocked. But reading *Books*, it easy to see that as much as McMurtry wanted to carry on the trade, he also believed in his singular role to memorialize it. *Books* reads in places like a slightly comic collective tribute to legendary, now-defunct secondhand bookstores and long-dead book scouts all over the country, like the denizens of Book Row, a six-block stretch of Manhattan dominated by secondhand bookstores for seven decades, until the 1960s. McMurtry remembers the Dallas bookstore where he bought his first secondhand book after a high school track meet. The owner, he said, used to hide particularly valuable books in paper bags under tables in dark corners. McMurtry was fascinated, he said, by dying breeds, himself included. He reflected on the "matter of reading. What if it does stop? … In commerce extinctions happen often. It didn't take electricity long to kill off the kerosene lantern."

Since McMurtry died in March 2021 at age eighty-four, I've often thought of how neglected his role in book trading has been, how his titanic passion for finding, owning, reading, collecting, and selling rare and secondhand books should be celebrated as the monumental achievement it was. By the time he died, already half-forgotten, he was known for a handful of books that had been made into high-grossing, award-winning films or TV miniseries, for his screenwriting, but not his bookselling or collecting, not for amassing what had been called the largest book collection in Texas outside of a library. He claimed he didn't like calling books "rare" but allowed that "antiquarian" was okay, "if you want to fancy it up." He showed up occasionally in Archer City, sorting, pricing, and shelving books, famously grumpy when asked for an autograph, yet still intent to keep his hands on the goods, because as the grandchild of West Texas ranching pioneers with a ferocious physical work ethic, sitting at a "strange machine" and typing all day did not qualify as work. Bookselling at least involved hefting boxes.

* * *

The physical aspect of being surrounded by books, perhaps even buried under them, spines and covers and pages that aren't disposable with a click, speaks not just to the art of collecting, but also to seeking and learning and obsessively reading. Nicole Krauss defended the merits of retail print-and-paper bookstores more than a decade ago in the *New Republic*, in the years when rising rents and Amazon's shooting star were shuttering them all over the country: "If we wish to be changed, to be challenged and undone, then we need a means of placing ourselves in the path of an accident."

Many secondhand book buyers, even if they are not collectors, regularly wander the accidental path. McMurtry reported that a young woman came into his Georgetown store, with no apparent intent, and left with a carful of books. One of my most memorable accidental finds involves Katherine Anne Porter, a Texas native whom McMurtry, with the exception of a few stories, unrepentantly dismissed from the ranks of true Texas writers, an opinion for which he took a lot of heat. But after dodging her for years, I finally came to reckon with her in a place where McMurtry, wearing his duct-taped cowboy boots, would have felt himself at home.

My husband and I had gotten stuck overnight in a small western town known for its rodeo. We ate a late lunch at a place called the Starlight Lounge, sitting near a guy, with the requisite boots and hat, who'd just come from his court appearance for a DUI. He pounded doubles, reviled the judge, and then got up, announcing to his buddy that he was driving home. An hour later, fortified by two gin and tonics, I bought a beat-up copy of the 1962 O. Henry Prize collection in a small, dusty storefront a few doors down from the bar. That's where I discovered Porter's short story "Holiday." It's set on a prosperous Texas farm in the early twentieth century and centers around a German patriarch who reads *Das Kapital* every night, while presiding over a large household that cruelly subjugates his disfigured daughter to a state of virtual slavery.

The first paragraph of "Holiday" hooked me, striking me as something akin to Tolstoy's dictum about unhappy families, a frame through which to look at the world. Porter's "great truth" is "that we do not run from the troubles and dangers that are truly ours, and it is better to learn what they are earlier than later, and if we don't run from the others [the lesser, distracting troubles], we are fools."

McMurtry, who was a Stegner Fellow with Ken Kesey, believed himself to be an indifferent teacher and ran away from the foolish trouble of making a stable living from teaching as soon as he could. "What does PhD stand for?" one of McMurtry's uncles wrote him. "To me it's posthole digger." If you had asked McMurtry what his great trouble was, the one he could not run from, I'm guessing his only answer would have been a scowl or a wry West Texas put-down. But I'm probably not alone in thinking it was his strict allegiance to the written word, exactly as he first encountered it when an older cousin, headed for World War II, dropped a box of boys' adventure books at his grandparents' "bookless" ranch house, where McMurtry spent his earliest years.

* * *

Of course, McMurtry had showier, more lucrative credentials than bookselling, about which he made little fuss, at least in his interviews or memoirs. His work received mixed reviews. He allowed that he'd written only two "really, really, really good books" in his long career. Popularity, he said, did not confer greatness. But McMurtry was a workhorse at the chore he said he didn't hate. He authored fourteen nonfiction books and thirty-six novels, whose screen adaptations brought him fame that the books alone could not. Among them were *Hud* (adapted from his very first novel, *Horseman, Pass By*), *The Last Picture Show, Terms of Endearment*, and the TV miniseries *Lonesome Dove*. Starting in 1970s, he also wrote screenplays and teleplays, collaborating as time went on with his writing partner Diana Ossana. McMurtry's work, as adapted for film, garnered thirty-four Oscar nominations, with thirteen wins, many for major Hollywood stars, while his TV adaptations scored huge audiences, celebrated actors, and many Emmys and made his books bestsellers. McMurtry and Ossana's last screenplay to make it to film production, *Joe Bell*, was released four months after McMurtry's death.

Other awards and high honors also piled up behind him. He won the 1986 Pulitzer for *Lonesome Dove* and a 2014 National Humanities Medal for his lifetime contributions to American arts and letters. During the first years of the tragic fatwa against Salman Rushdie, he served as copresident of PEN America with Sontag. All the while, McMurtry traveled the world collecting books, everything from "an account in French of a very early trans-Sahara auto rally" to his beloved Virginia Woolf diaries. When Sontag spent a night in his Archer City home, he reported that she insisted on rearranging part of his twenty-eight thousand volume personal library, which he called an "accumulation." It included everything from novels written by poets, an impressive collection of H. G. Wells, a multitude of reference works on the American West, a first edition of *The Great Gatsby*, and two thousand volumes of travel narratives by women, at least one dating from the late eighteenth century. McMurtry said those women were often running away.

It's a scene for a novel. Sontag was known as restless, often traveling, though she could never visit McMurtry at his primary home in Tucson, because she so loathed her memories of living in that desert town as a child. McMurtry may have indulged in caviar with Sontag in Manhattan but his boots were planted in West Texas. He bought Archer City's country club, which had belonged to the richest man in town when he was a kid, to make it a second home.

* * *

As if to ward off the scourges of fame or any note of the contemporary bright, loud retail environment, Booked Up was kept like a testament to McMurtry's sensibilities. We ran through the front door into the former Ford showroom, chased by the heat, met by the hush of hundreds of sound-absorbing volumes. A sun-faded movie poster for *The Last Picture Show*, signed by the film's stars, hung high above a round table and chairs that suggested a living room, circa 1953, faced in knotty pine, but generously serviced, of course, with bookshelves. As teenagers, Jeff Bridges and Cybill Shepherd found their first film roles in *The Last Picture Show*. The ghosts of their youth seemed to circulate here too, with some rare, large-format volumes lying open on tables in the small space. McMurtry's co-owner, Khristal Collins, was minding both the store and her daughter, who sat with a toy in her hand in a playpen by the cash register.

We made our way from the showroom into the adjoining vault-like former garage, where the shelves stretched toward the high ceiling and the cooler couldn't keep up with the heat. The pheromone of aged paper and print hung in the air, that unmistakable dusty, barky, leathery smell. In a 2020 scholarly paper titled "The Multisensory Experience of Handling and Reading Books," Charles Spence, an Oxford professor, headlines one section "Best Smellers." He cites a well-known quote widely attributed to Ray Bradbury, one that's often dredged up whenever print-and-paper book lovers mourn their form's loss, much in the same way a traditionalist Roman Catholic laments the extermination of the Latin Mass: "If a book is new, it smells great. If a book is old, it smells even better. It smells like ancient Egypt." Spence cites an anonymous source, saying that reading an e-book is like using an ATM. His article features a photo of a researcher extracting an eighteenth-century Bible's scent for an "odour-wheel." The room's smell made me feel I'd entered a place that, in spite of its owner's atheism, contained its own kind of holy.

The section in the bookstore where I stood housed hundreds of volumes on the nineteenth- and early-twentieth-century history of the American West. McMurtry rode this theme to fame in the *Lonesome Dove* series, but he also came to be "thoroughly sick" of it, according to a *Texas Monthly* interview. It was McMurtry's fate to become synonymous with his most famous novel. He said he intended "to subvert the Western myth with irony and parody." But he believed the book ended up being misread by millions as the *Gone with the Wind* of the West. Yet, the appetite for the mythic cowboy was so great,

McMurtry knew he'd never get out from under it. Reporting on the 1993 Branch Davidian massacre for the *New Republic* in an article, "A Return to Waco," he tried to talk some officers into letting him through a roadblock outside Waco. "Curious to see what it would get me," he wrote, "I played my ace, *Lonesome Dove*. It promptly got my picture taken with the two highway patrolmen."

In the bookstore, I pulled down a rare, oversized scholarly book on the Plains Indians, beautifully illustrated with vintage plates, at a price equaling what I might have paid for twenty-five secondhand books. The volume reminded me that while I was never a great reader of McMurtry's fiction, I loved his reviews and essays, mostly on the history of the American West, in the *New York Review of Books* and other publications. His writing is learned and plainspoken, flecked with words like "tetchy." Even as McMurtry's reviews light on such brutal, corrective facts as the "black book" of Native American genocide, "a catalog of horrors, butcheries, exterminations," his voice is alive with a sense of wonder. In a 2004 review, he freely admitted being challenged and undone—for most of his reading life, he had conceived of the West before Lewis and Clark as "having been more or less empty," when in fact it "teemed." Among many other things, he noted a scholar's assertion that the five-story ruin at Pueblo Bonito in Chaco Canyon was "the only apartment building of comparable size in America or the Old World until the Spanish Flats were erected at Fifty-Ninth Street and Seventh Avenue in 1882." He didn't know whether that was true, but he said it was "a notion to chew on."

Why I chewed on that notion just at that moment, I've never been sure. Possibly it had to do with the sense of where McMurtry's own massive city of books might be headed. Above me hung a sign that said, "When will Mr. McMurtry be here? At his whim." So much for whim. McMurtry's intellect, personality, and taste, as forceful as his voice in those long-ago reviews, were everywhere.

We crossed the street to one of the warehouses, knowing that we would soon reach the books in our price range and help depopulate the stock. Though he'd done well at the auction, McMurtry was irritated that he still had thirty thousand novels to get rid of. Fiction had ceased to interest him in the mid-1980s, as his fascinations migrated to the great wars of twentieth-century Europe, to figures like Bismarck, Churchill, and Stalin, to the extinction of the Hapsburgs, Romanovs, and Ottomans (those dying breeds), to the twentieth century's two world wars. In the warehouse, the leftover novels were merely cheap, five dollars each, just about as relevant to twenty-first-century life as the narrow, fluted, short-handled shovel my grandmother used to stoke her coal burner.

The books had been auctioned in lots, shelved on high, wide cases and marked by chalked numbers on the cement floor. The effect was off-kilter, with some lots already gone, their white shelves emptied, while others were picked over, with gaps where volumes had been plucked out. Those shelves came to mind later in the trip, when we drove through neighborhoods in Moore, Oklahoma, leveled by a tornado only a month before. On one street, houses were untouched. On the next, the back walls had been ripped off, and on the next, there was nothing but flattened debris.

Virginia Woolf wrote, "Second-hand books are wild books, homeless books." McMurtry marked the books in his personal collection with custom plates carrying his family's ranch brand. The concept of books on the run, as rambling strays (or in McMurtry's case, loose livestock), is hard to give up. In the half-empty warehouse, we were joined by a handful of middle-aged white women who'd driven up in old Subarus and Toyotas with out-of-state plates and political stickers favoring liberal causes. We warily edged around each other in the sweltering heat, discreetly scanning each other's hauls.

Next to a copy of *Animal Farm*, I found the single published novel of a gentle, solitary man I'd met in a writing group, a book likely read by a relative handful of people. My husband picked up a first edition of a William Saroyan play, clearly misplaced, priced at $150. When he turned it in for reshelving at the cash register, Collins's gratitude made me think of the stories in McMurtry's memoirs, of catching the rogue volume on the sly and of the inevitable runaways in such an enormous corral of books.

Our journey to McMurtryville officially ended at a steakhouse in Wichita Falls, the big city in *The Last Picture Show*'s tiny universe, some twenty-six miles from Archer City. We struck up a conversation with a tall elderly man—wearing the standard hat, boots, and bolo tie—about our visit to Booked Up. He established himself as a reliable narrator by saying he'd line-danced with someone close to McMurtry and spun a tale about McMurtry's purchase of a small-town Texas bookstore's entire stock, owned by a "stove-up" old man, whose retirement McMurtry was funding for what seemed like a fantastic sum. Our narrator had helped the old man load books from a library sale into a beat-up station wagon to beef up his stock for McMurtry. It seemed like a fitting endpiece to our time in Texas. In this telling, McMurtry was no more than the famous local eccentric searching for gold in dusty boxes of abandoned library books.

* * *

If an image of McMurtry lives in my mind, it's the one of him at the 2006 Academy Awards ceremony, wearing a tux jacket over faded blue jeans and cowboy boots, hair rumpled, tie askew. He and Ossana had won the Oscar for the screen adaptation of Annie Proulx's "Brokeback Mountain." McMurtry reminded the audience that the screenplay had come from a book and said, "From the humblest paperback exchange to the masters of the great bookshops of the world, all are contributors to the survival of the culture of the book, a wonderful culture, which we mustn't lose."

Though McMurtry's Oscar plea made me tear up, he brought to mind the Christian evangelist who hijacks any opportunity to bring people to Jesus. But even so, he must have been aware of the irony of how his success as a screenwriter bankrolled his bookselling. After all, Hollywood mammon had made him one of the masters of the great bookshops of the world. McMurtry reported in *Books* that the money he earned from writing scripts mostly paid for the Archer City enterprise, allowing him to buy up the stock of secondhand bookstores closing around the country.

An even greater irony is that McMurtry's lifelong knack for attracting Hollywood's attention coincided with the technological advances in both publishing and TV production that diminished the appetite for printed books. His *Publisher's Weekly* obituary cited his influence not only on the shape of the modern Western, Texas literary history, and bookselling, but also on "Hollywood's page-to-screen industrial complex." In other words, he prequeled streaming media.

One way to track McMurtry's fate is to follow *Lonesome Dove*'s progression through the media loop. The story started as a screenplay, which McMurtry sold but bought back years later for $30,000 out of frustration because John Wayne could not be talked into taking one of three leading roles, though the story goes that Jimmy Stewart and Henry Fonda were persuadable for the other two. Then McMurtry wrote the novel, which was adapted into one of its era's most popular miniseries, with Hollywood A-list film actors and a host of Emmy awards. Then came the prequel and sequel novels, with their award-winning TV adaptations, also featuring prominent film stars. And, of course, the books sold famously after making it to TV.

I read something about McMurtry on an antiquarian book site

that amused me. He wasn't billed as an Oscar-winning screenwriter, a prolific and popular telescreen writer, and a bestselling author, who also happened to sell books. He was noted as the only antiquarian bookseller ever to win an Oscar.

* * *

The secondhand bookstore nearest our current home is housed in a spacious two-story, light-filled Northwest-modern building that overlooks a bay and wooded islands. Denny, the proprietor, wears a tattered hand-knit beanie over a wispy white ponytail and plays eclectic tracks on a nightclub-quality sound system. ("Yes," he told me when I commented on an acoustic Hendrix recording, "Jimi was here just this morning.") He offers credit or "cabbage" for my books.

McMurtry thought Chekhov was the writer most suited to depicting the book trade because he "had a natural sympathy for fringe cultures." Since the pandemic, knee-high book pillars have arisen in Denny's shop like obstacle-course stations, too neatly placed to be described as a hoarder's stash but numerous enough to raise the question about whether a pathology might be at work. Denny told me that the day that McMurtry's death was announced, a couple came in looking for *Lonesome Dove*. Fortunately, he had a hardcover copy in excellent shape, but he was disappointed that that's all they wanted. McMurtry's many works line several long shelves, where I found a ragged copy of his 1968 essay collection *In a Narrow Grave*, which, in addition to smelling like the books in my childhood public library, contains a chapter in which McMurtry recounts a rapid stem-to-stern Texas road trip, a personal cross-country race. He passes near his grandparents' homestead just before dawn, topping a ridge to see the lights of Archer City. In his early thirties at the time, he observes that this view no longer gives him the sense of rootedness it did returning home from college. He writes, "I had begun to suspect that home was less a place than an empty page."

And now, someone else is filling it. It shocked me almost to tears to learn that while staying open for a year or so after McMurtry died in 2021, Booked Up closed. The store and stock were sold to an investment firm owned by Chip Gaines, who with his wife, Joanna, boosted HDTV into shiplap orbit with their show *Fixer Upper* and launched their own lifestyle home-renovation empire in Waco, Texas. The Gaineses' sensibilities, shaped by a nostalgic pseudo-agrarian aesthetic and an ever-upbeat outlook closely tied to their evangelical beliefs, couldn't be more opposed to McMurtry's. But Chip Gaines's parents also grew up in Archer City, and he spent fondly remembered summers at his grandfather's ranch.

I, alone, it seems, did not know that under the signature name Magnolia, the Gaineses had eclipsed HDTV with a host of enterprises that included a TV network, a home siding line, a home décor line sold at Target, a HarperCollins imprint, and the Magnolia Market, a two-block open-air retail complex in downtown Waco. After they bought Booked Up, Chip Gaines released a statement saying he'd always loved McMurtry's work and was "honored and excited to preserve this incredible book collection with the respect it deserves."

In November, 2023, the couple opened an elegantly renovated boutique hotel in Waco, named Hotel 1928 for the year it was built, notably one year shy of the Great Depression. The website's home page is a shot of the library, featuring a Persian carpet; deep, tufted antiphonal leather sofas; a commanding fireplace; a marble-topped coffee table; and an ebony-shelved backdrop of vintage hardback books, artfully placed for color and size, a small portion of Booked Up's stock. The books, published in the early twentieth century, were chosen to enhance a Roaring Twenties design scheme. Their prices, still penciled in, are said to range from ten dollars to thousands. A plaque honors McMurtry.

Two months after the hotel opened, I asked a staffer by phone whether she'd seen people reading the books in the library. Playing board games, yes, but reading, no. When I asked whether volumes were ever stolen, imagining guerilla book liberators or unscrupulous collectors, she stammered. Their guests would probably never do something like that. Later, I read Texas native Colin Ainsworth's essay on his visit to the library in the *Paris Review*. He had the fleeting thought that he could easily steal a book—he was holding *Moby-Dick*—all the more valuable because McMurtry had possibly held it too. He put the book back. In the gift shop, Booked Up volumes also are shelved behind the counter, within spitting distance of the Hotel 1928 scented candles and signature coffee mugs. A staffer told me recently about a common confusion. Guests ask about buying the books, but they are "strictly for décor."

As I write this, the Gaineses' plan for the Booked Up buildings and probable thousands of remaining books are unknown. Like many small towns, Archer City could use an economic driver, and some there would be happy to see the Gaineses command it. If McMurtry once returned to Waco, it's possible that Waco's power brokers could contemplate returning the favor. In that case, Archer City will become a decidedly different kind of theme park than the one Sontag christened.

McMurtry no doubt would have had an acerbic comment not so much on the Gaineses themselves but on the megacommerce impetus that has rocketed them to a $50 million net worth, and on the disparities between appearance and reality that allow for such things as umbrella branding and social-media influencing, especially as they might relate to Archer City. In *The Last Picture Show*, McMurtry's characters are consumed by the mechanisms of desire and then chronicle its disappointments in ways that exceed his hometown's narrow frame, in ways that cannot be scrubbed clean— think adults sleeping with high school seniors, nude teenage pool parties, prostitution, adultery, brutal mockery of old-time religion, even bestiality. It's impossible to see how McMurtry's true stature in writing and bookselling could flow into another wholesome Magnolia revenue stream.

McMurtry's driving ethic was authenticity. He noticed needling cracks, seismic faults, and cheery hypocrisies. In his novels, vanities are laid bare, and beauty and notions of honor are often matched with random, unpredictable violence or tragedy. In his bookselling and collecting, he curated across broad intellectual, artistic, and literary interests. He also clearly enjoyed his eccentricities. He took literary celebrities to stock car races, liked his Hershey bars half-melted, claimed he could read and drive at the same time. Whether or not the Gaineses choose to trade on McMurtry's legacy in Archer City, there can be no mistake. The bookman has vanished. ∎

SIX DRUNK BOYS IN A DODGE CORONET

Miles Harvey

Decades later, they can't agree on how it happened or who was behind the wheel or what stretch of Roosevelt Road they were on when it took place, but they all remember the moment itself with a kind of uncanny clarity, as if they were still in that car when it went into the spin, six drunk boys sitting there with monk-like calm and attentiveness while everything whirled around them, the slashing streetlights, the blurring snow, the airborne bottle of Jim Beam, the pungent mist of whiskey, their own screams, the screech of another vehicle's brakes, the headlights coming at them from all directions at once, now in front, now in back, now in front again, brighter and brighter and brighter and brighter until each of them knew with absolute certainty that they were about to die together, a strangely tranquil feeling. And then the world went silent and they found themselves stumbling out of the car in the wrong lane of the road, the snow falling slowly, a pair of crimson taillights fading into the night. And then they began to laugh.

They're in late middle age now, except for the one who just passed away from colon cancer, and when they run into each other at his funeral, the first time they've all been together in who knows how long, they laugh about that incident again, each of them suddenly remembering how close they once were, how they'd drive around the western suburbs of Chicago for hours, howling at inside jokes that only they found funny and listening to cassette tapes of Crack the Sky, a band nobody else in their hometown knew about and nobody else in the world could ever possibly love the way they did as a group, a shared intimacy they've never quite felt since. And maybe hoping to recapture that feeling, they go to a bar after the wake and raise a glass to their friend, who had been, they all agree, the brightest one, the one all the girls liked, but who wound up stuck in an unhappy marriage and staying put in Downers Grove, where he punched the clock for years as a landscape supervisor for the park district, things not quite working out the way any of them had expected. And after a couple of hours, having run out of things to say to each other except *remember when,* they call it a night, all of them promising to meet like this more often, all of them sure it will never happen, luck and time no longer being on their side. And so, with quick handshakes, tentative hugs and tender glances, they say goodbye for the last time—no more running jokes, no more stories, no more sharing whatever it was they shared, though tonight they'll all go back to their homes or hotels and dream the same dream, the world spinning, the headlights growing brighter and brighter, the end zooming in on those drunk boys in the car. ■

IN BONNY DOON
Christopher Buckley

for Gary Young

2 slim apple trees flourished
outside your studio, a dozen
redwoods and Sierra Red Firs
edging a circle of salt grass
and ferns where sun fingered
the small, yellow, apples …
honey-rich—3 or 4 bites was all,
and they were gone.
                I'd fill
a grocery bag to take back
with me each year, once we had
survived our 20s and calmed
a little … and I remember
the deer arriving after first light,
content to crunch the windfall,
leaving us to reach up the best
we could for what remained …

Now, not even twigs are left,
just over-grown winter grass.
And if you were not as far away
as age and time have put us,
I'd drive up as I did those summers
we built retaining walls to hold
your house in place, singing out
with Ernesto and Jon as we hoisted
and pitched rocks up from the creek
below.
          Were we all still present
in the world, we could sit on the deck
of Hitchcock's old house and not think
of the future anymore, think nothing
of looking down at the water rushing
away to be lost in the sea, and recall
those troubled/untroubled times, the fruit

and easy sweetness of those days, and thus
be satisfied for a while yet, and let
the sky try to find us, hidden among
the lengthening shadows of the trees.

The Devil's Oatmeal

by Kathleen Founds

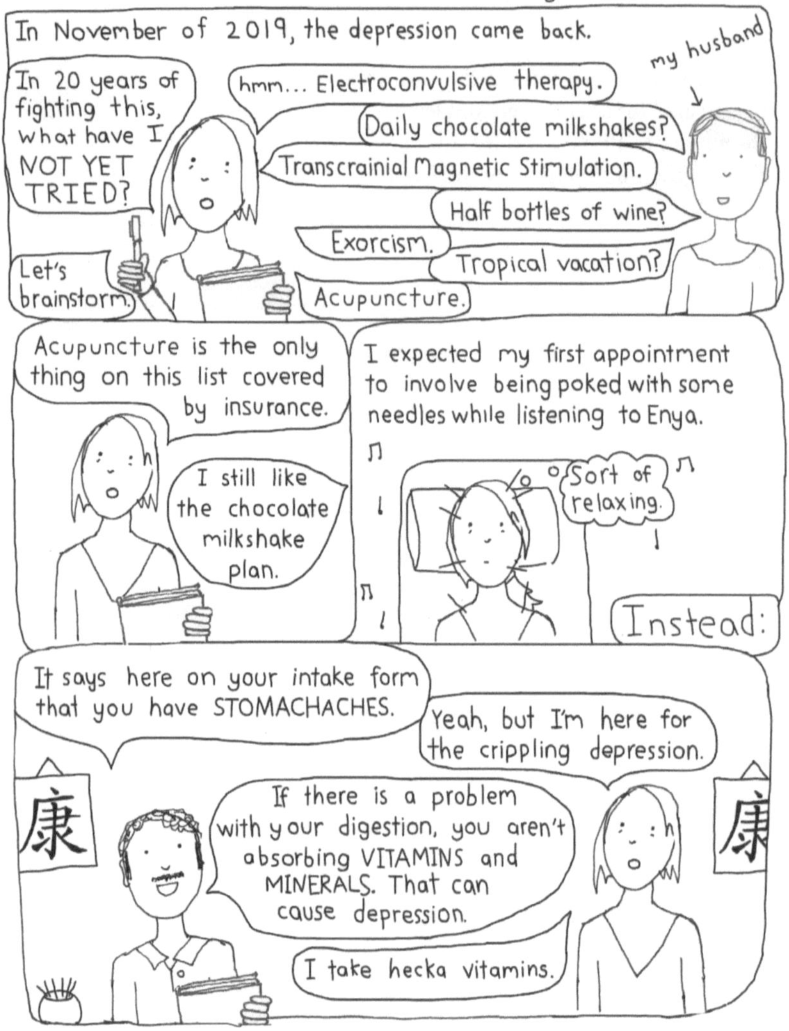

At the next appointment, the acupuncturist checked in.

BLOOD
Roy Parvin

Only Marco's heart raced most days. By now, four-plus years removed from his double victories in the 1998 Giro and Tour de France, it was an open secret that the great climber was in steep decline. He'd had various run-ins with the sport's governing body, Union Cycliste Internationale, and there were rumors about drugs. Yet the press along with rank-and-file *tifosi* continued to adore Pantani like a character from a Puccini opera—heroic, but deeply flawed.

To disguise himself, Marco wore a Kangol hat to cover the famous bald egg of his head. He and fellow cyclist Mario Cipollini needed to ensure that nobody, including their respective team managers, caught wind of this meeting. The two riders were convening at a hotel in Prato, midway between Cipo's home on the Mediterranean Rivera and Marco's on the Adriatic.

As per plan, Marco had taken the elevator up to the thirteenth floor, exited, walked down the hallway to the stairwell, then descended one flight to the deserted landing below. Nobody would ever know.

Except it appeared that Cipo was a no-show. Marco couldn't pull in a signal on his mobile in the shaft of the stairwell to see whether he'd gotten cold feet, annoying to have to wait, but at this point what choice did Marco have.

As it turned out, Cipo was only running late. He didn't bother to come in camouflage. The two couldn't be more different. A sprinter, a climber. Big and small; handsome and not. Despite his lion's mane, Cipo was older. Marco had begun losing his hair as a teenager. With his splayed ears, he resembled a small woodland vole.

"*Ciao*, Marco," Cipo said in greeting, patting Pantani on the back. He smiled broadly, still preening from his fall victory in the World Championships. Cipo was always smiling. He had a beautiful life.

For a few minutes they exchanged small talk. Marco merely shrugged when asked about Christine. The last he'd heard she was in Spain. Cipo of course was married, although in the name of publicity, he enjoyed floating rumors about other women. Perhaps he believed it drew attention away from the fact he was a one-dimensional rider, a sprinter, nothing more. Cipo had never finished a single Tour de

France. In the book of Italian greats, beginning with Alfredo Binda, he'd earned an asterisk.

"*Certo*," Marco answered when Cipo finally got around to asking whether he'd been training. It was true, more or less. Marco was good for a few weeks of roadwork, before falling off the wagon and losing himself in Rimini's nightlife. Even with his career in limbo, he managed to make headlines.

Cipo had given him the once-over, the way they did in a race, one rider determining how much was left in the other's tank. Perhaps he was also checking for drugs, not the ones to ride faster, the other kind. Forming a joint team had been Cipo's idea. He'd already dangled the plan to the press, the first Marco heard of it. Cipo had played to the cheap seats, claiming he was only extending a helping hand.

The sports columnists dined on the news, fervent offseason speculation of whose team it would be, a sprinter's or a climber's. Then right before January, Marco found an envelope that someone had slid under his door. No stamp, just his first name. Perhaps his coke dealer or one of his nightclubbing friends. All the note contained was the address of a hotel in Prato in the historic district, along with a time and instructions about the elevator and stairwell. The handwriting looked like a six-year-old's. Cipo. Marco hadn't told anyone at Mercatone Uno or even his parents. He hired a car because his license had been revoked. Along with being desperate, he was curious.

* * *

Eventually Cipo got around to the idea of a mutual team. "Can you imagine?" he said, leering, his big rubbery wolf face. "You and me together. Unbeatable."

Marco leaned over the stair railing. It was difficult to stand for too long. His lower back bunched up. He considered taking off his ridiculous hat but left it on. With his arms on the railing, he looked as if he were bent over the drop bars of a bike. "But how would it work exactly?" he said.

"You take the mountains. I win the valleys." Cipo shook his head. Wasn't this obvious? Perhaps the rumors he'd heard were true. Marco's brain had gone soft from all the drugs.

"Not the mountains and valleys," Marco allowed. He meant practicalities. Cipo needed a sprint train of support riders to deliver him to victory while Marco required a smaller number of *domestiques* in his service in the mountains. There wouldn't be enough teammates for both. Perhaps more important, who'd be the team sponsor, and what would come of their respective teams? At the least, the prospect portended a divided squad from the start.

Cipo frowned at Marco now for not playing along. Their voices echoed in the vacant air shaft, the hotel largely vacant after the holiday bustle. Marco had been clean every day since the New Year, a tiny gift he privately carried around. He'd begun smoking crack by then, much earlier than reports later had it. Alone in a hotel room in his underwear, Marco hit the pipe every fifteen minutes as he obsessively stripped the componentry off his bike frame and rebuilt it again. Crack for him wasn't like coke. It made Marco mindful of conspiracies, paranoid someone was shadowing him—his team, UCI, a bar owner wanting to settle an unpaid tab. In any case, he changed hotels on the Adriatic often.

Cipo waved a hand at Marco's question about their respective teams. "Details."

Marco stared over the railing into the narrow column of open air. "There won't be room for everyone."

"No," Cipo agreed. "But things always work out in the end." He meant a team factotum would dispatch the dirty work. "Anyway, Marco, you miss the point. You forget it's a new year, and France has a big party planned this summer." Cipo leaned his arms on the railing, smelling of hair product and cologne. Marco finally understood. Cipo was referring to the hundredth anniversary of the Tour de France. The truth was never simple in professional cycling. It was more like a compound molecule with various trace elements. Nothing was ever what it seemed. Helping Marco, it was becoming clear, wasn't the primary objective. Rather, Cipo was intent on forming an Italian super team to crap all over France's centennial moment. He'd been banned from the event the past two years, not for drugs, but for being an incomparable *stronzo*, the race-day histrionics, his early exits.

"I have no war with the French," Marco said. Unlike Cipo, he'd won the Tour.

Cipo stared out over the railing. He was like a dog that required constant petting. The end was in sight for him. Cipo no doubt felt it in his bones. He wasn't as relevant as he'd been. "At least think about it," he suggested.

Marco promised he would. It still rankled him that Cipo hadn't called about the idea of a team first. He'd been in too big a rush to prove he owned a heart.

"This isn't only about racing," he assured Marco. "We must defend our blood."

Marco thought Cipo was referring to the fuzzy science of testing. No drugs had ever been found in his system, only hematocrit values deemed "anomalous." UCI was apparently in the business of chasing ghosts. But as it turned out, Cipo hadn't intended his comment that way. He meant it in the way of countrymen, that they were both from the north, *polentone*.

"I will," Marco promised about weighing Cipo's scheme. It was only the beginning of January, the rest of the year unwritten. Loyalty was a short-blooming flower in pro cycling. Who could say?

* * *

The meeting gave Marco one more secret to carry into the New Year. Despite his myriad doubts, he was intrigued by Cipo's proposition. A bit of intrasquad competition might be the thing to finally wake him up. Immediately after returning to Rimini, Marco made an appointment with a doctor to fix his nose, along with pinning back his ears. The nose was from a crash several years back, the ears, vanity, the prospect of having to stand next to Cipo in team photos.

Shortly afterward, Marco flew to the Balearic Islands for Mercatone Uno's first offseason training camp of the year, only for trouble to find him again after returning home to the Adriatic, a relapse before the next camp in the Canary Islands. Despite all of this, Mercatone Uno couldn't afford to get rid of him. Marco's image rights were worth a fortune. At least it was coke rather than crack, which meant nightclubs, fender benders, paparazzi, a scene in a hotel hallway with a partially clad stripper named Barbara. Meanwhile the sport burbled with rumors and conjecture about the two stars joining forces. Marco was unable to reach Cipo on the phone.

Yet all was good as long as Marco was on a bike. He displayed tantalizing flashes of his old self at Coppi e Bartali in March. Afterward Mercatone Uno whisked him off to Spain to put some distance between Marco and bad influences back home. For over a month he managed to stay clean, the longest time in years. One night there, his mobile rang. Cipo apologized for being out of touch. "Children and in-laws," he groaned before congratulating Marco for his showing at Coppi e Bartali. Marco could hear music in the background, laughter, some sort of get-together.

"I'm in Spain," he said. "Training."

Cipo laughed. "*Chi non lavora, non fa l'amore.*" No work, no love.

On his side of the line, Marco laughed also. He felt like a cyclist again. "I'm glad you called," he said. Marco had begun to worry about the fate of their prospective team, but perhaps after Coppi e Bartali his stock was rising.

"I have a favor to ask," Cipo said before mentioning Luca, Marco's masseur. *Finally*, Marco thought. It was getting rather late in the day to put a team together for the Tour. At least Cipo had begun to take the prospect seriously. Marco had a number of thoughts about squad composition as well as team support.

As it turned out, it wasn't quite that. Cipo hemmed and hawed. It sounded like a parlor game was going on, people barking out words. Cipo said he was wondering about Luca's work status.

"Don't worry," Marco promised. "As teammates, you'd enjoy the same access to him that I do."

"Of course," Cipo said, although what he meant was borrowing Luca now, while Marco was training, before any contracts got signed. "Just a local exhibition."

Marco didn't know what to say. This felt like gamesmanship, Cipo probing how much he could get away with. Everybody in the peloton had an angle. It was only a team sport until a breakaway. Perhaps all this talk of a team was only about poaching Luca. Marco didn't really need Cipo toying with him. It had begun to feel like he'd caught the first bit of momentum in years.

But then Cipo backed down from the request. "Yes, probably wiser to wait for the lawyers," he agreed, laughing.

So, it was only that. Marco had recently read in one of the gossip columns about Cipo and a movie starlet. Always something. He'd have to get used to that. Cipo was a showboat. He once again asked after Christine. "We still talk," Marco allowed. "But my focus for now is training."

"Ah, love," Cipo said. "Only our sport is more strange."

* * *

Then the wheels began to fall off any hopes of mounting a squad in time for the Tour. It didn't matter anyway. Neither Cipo or Marco were invited to compete, only to the centennial festivities out of a perverse sense of French courtesy.

But even meeting up with Cipo in Paris proved unworkable, some dodgy business with his current team. First the manager insisted on talking with Marco, which smelled fishy. Then eventually when Cipo did call, he set up a rendezvous with Marco only to postpone later on.

Things weren't quite over. Into the offseason this odd dance of advance and retreat continued. Rumors. Questions of Marco's fitness or the financial health of Cipo's team, whose owner was said to be in grievous debt. All this time the press was clamoring for a meeting between the two stars. It would be appropriately theatrical in the Italian way, highly choreographed and photographed. Nothing would really be accomplished. The picture of the two together would be the point, a moment for all of Italy in addition to the miracle of opposites attracting.

That never happened. Marco had too much pride to make the necessary overtures or accept a smaller contract. The entire gambit proved to be little more than a contrivance, a good old-fashioned publicity stunt with the bounty of Marco's image rights at the center.

So, he flew back to the Adriatic. Cipo would still sometimes call, always late at night, his goofy voice from the opposite coast of Italy. Promises of procuring one of those new Carrera frames for Marco, endorsement possibilities, invitations to dine with soap opera actresses. Marco would let the calls go to voicemail.

* * *

He hadn't always wished to be a cyclist. For a little while, in his late teens, when it seemed things could go either way, Marco considered radio repair as a vocation. This was before there was an under-twenty-three category and helmets weren't compulsory, a nearly bald boy competing against grown men.

Marco had climbed every incline in all of Romagna by then. He just hadn't put all the pieces together. Already he had that strange posture in the saddle, like a hen over a sharp egg. The older riders taunted him, got in his head. Mostly he hadn't learned how to marshal his anger.

Radio repair, by comparison, seemed a more stable enterprise. Marco didn't have many other chances. But he liked hanging around the workroom after hours. Radio circuitry was like an orderly road map. What Marco prized most of all was sticking his head in the old tube amp jobs, the howl of static at both ends of the dial, an unearthly peal in which he believed that if he turned the dial just the right way, it was possible to pull in the old broadcasts of the Italian greats. Nencini descending a mountain with the finesse of an alpine skier. Gimondi. Bartali.

Marco could never find quite the precise frequency, only snatches of conversation he couldn't decipher. This was before everything.

Before turning pro or placing second in the amateur Giro. Before he became fastidious about his training and gained a reputation for being difficult to control. Even then, Marco had ulcers from worry. In repair school everything had its place. He'd already decided he'd tell people that since he wasn't good enough to be on the radio, he'd gone into the business of fixing them. A joke. Also he could wear a workman's cap to cover his bald head.

* * *

Sometimes now in Rimini Marco still biked. Not for gain or glory. He was back to being a night creature and could always commandeer a village bicycle after the discos closed, a machine too decrepit to miss or bother locking, gearing shot, rims out of true, leaning against a lamppost or wall, there for the taking.

The streets would be empty, houses dark. Marco could pedal in circles right down the middle of the street, nobody awake, nothing to hurt him. It was impossible of course to roll very far in that part of Italy without encountering some kind of rise, often short but steep coastal stinger hills. The bike would wheeze, Marco along with it, the climb briefly evoking La Plagne, Col de la Croix, the heights he'd reached. Sometimes he had to get off and walk, nearly two stone over his competing weight, bloated, in no kind of shape for it. He never thought about the steep descent on the other side. Marco believed there was still time for a comeback. He only wanted to get to the top. ∎

SPORTSMANSHIP
Richard M. Lange

At nine o'clock, Carla decided that she was too hungry to care how one angle within a triangle could be deduced from the other two and closed her textbook. She crossed the living room to her father's office, where he sat smoking his pipe and staring at the rainbow of graphs and statistics that filled his computer screen.

"Should I call her again?" Carla asked.

Carla's father, Clark, was twenty years older than her mother. He'd been in his fifties when Carla was born. Hair Q-tip white, flesh loose under his chin, he was regularly mistaken for her grandfather. He didn't answer.

"Dad, there's a man at the door with a gun."

"That's fine," Clark said, before turning suddenly. "What?!" When he saw that Carla was smirking, he shook his head. He was not a fan of teenage antics. "Okay. You have my undivided attention."

"I'm starving. Should I call her again?"

"Yes. This is ridiculous."

Carla's mother, Susan, had gone out for drinks with her friend Jackie and some of the other women from work and was now two hours late. She'd been spending more and more time out with "the girls." In addition to weeknight cocktails, they took a two-hour walk along the ocean on West Cliff Drive every Sunday morning. In March, they'd gone on a spa weekend to Palm Springs. In a few weeks they were going camping in Big Sur.

When Carla was younger, her mother was always around. She'd be in the kitchen, cooking lasagna or roasting a chicken or making a cherry pie from scratch. She hand sewed curtains to replace the upstairs wooden blinds. At Carla's soccer games, she sat in a folding beach chair on the sidelines, slightly away from the other parents so she could skip the chitchat and concentrate on the action, on Carla. When Clark's brother and sister-in-law visited from New York, she cleaned the house upstairs and down, covered the dining table with a cloth and put out small crystal bowls of olives and nuts.

But after Carla finished elementary school, Susan got a part-time job in the city's General Services Department. She bought new clothes, started wearing lipstick. At home, she shared stories of her coworkers with Clark, who listened patiently but didn't seem too interested. She got a promotion and stepped up to full-time. She decided the house was too big to take care of on her own and hired a service, Merry Maids, to come twice a week. Instead of cooking every night, she brought home takeout. She was more energized but that energy could be frenzied and chaotic. When she broke a wine glass, or accidentally washed something silk on hot, or got home from the store to realize that she forgot the milk, she cried. If Clark told her to stop being so dramatic, she yelled at him until he locked himself in his office.

Carla knew she was supposed to be proud of her mother. She was out in the world getting stuff done, building a career. But there was a lot about the old version of her that Carla missed. They used to pick tomatoes together in the garden and lie on the daybed in the den watching *Parks and Recreation* on DVD. If Carla was at the table doing homework, Susan would be ten feet away on the sofa, reading one of her relationship books, ready to help. Carla hoped that, when the excitement of the promotion and the new friends at work wore off, Susan would calm down a little and get back to being the quiet, attentive person Carla remembered.

Carla's call, like the earlier ones, went to voicemail. When she reported this to Clark, he grumbled. "If you're hungry, I'd advise seeing what you can find in the kitchen."

Carla was at the toaster, slicing a raisin bagel, when Susan's RAV4 swung into the driveway. Keys jangling, she entered with a tight smile and dropped her purse on the counter. Instead of asking about Carla's day, or apologizing about dinner, she kissed Carla on the cheek and hugged her dramatically, as though one of them had just been rescued. She smelled of cigarettes and wine. After cupping her hands over her nose and taking a deep breath, she headed for Clark's office.

Carla stepped closer to the opening between the kitchen and living room to eavesdrop but Susan had closed the door. Carla drifted back to her bagel.

Minutes later, Susan emerged. Her eyeliner had run but she was no longer crying. "Carla, sweetie, I need to tell you something." She looked frightened and pleading. "My feelings for your father have changed. So I'm going to be moving out of the house."

Carla's tears came immediately. "What?"

"I know, baby. I know. But it'll be okay. It's for the best." Susan sat down and put a hand flat on the table and took a big breath—apparently, there was more. "I'm going to move in with Jackie."

Carla didn't like Jackie. She was stern-faced and bossy, forever disappointed. Once, when Carla was brought along on one of the girls' dinners out, Jackie asked her what she'd been up to and Carla mentioned "The Grape Lady," a funny YouTube video she liked. Jackie snorted. "You kids and your stupid internet." Another time, commenting on Carla's height, Jackie said, "If you were prettier you could be a model." After the model comment, Carla mentioned to Susan that she thought Jackie was kind of mean. "She can be brusque," Susan allowed. She explained that, the year before, Jackie's husband had left her for a twenty-three-year-old woman he'd met online. "So we need to be compassionate toward her while she works through that."

Jackie's daughter, Stephanie, was equally unlikeable. She was one of the smartest kids in school and believed herself an authority on every topic under the sun. She particularly disapproved of "attention whores"—girls who had too many piercings or wore too much makeup or dyed their hair dramatic colors. If you disagreed with her, you were the most pitiful creature on earth. It was bad enough that Carla had to share classes with Stephanie, but this year Stephanie had joined the volleyball team, where she was a waste of space. Uncoordinated, with no vertical, she never gave more than minimal effort. She was already a homeroom leader and a member of Model United Nations, so playing volleyball was just a way to pad her college applications.

"Am I going to stay here?" Carla asked.

"That will be your choice. But I'm really hoping that you'll eventually come live with me and Jackie. At least most of the time."

"How long will we stay?"

"Sweetheart, don't you understand what I'm telling you?"

"I guess not."

A moment before Susan responded, Carla understood. "Wait. You mean that you and ..." Carla's mind flooded with images: Susan and Jackie nursing fruity drinks and gazing into each other's eyes. The two of them holding hands on their Sunday walks. Writhing naked in a Palm Springs hot tub. "So you're telling me you're gay?"

"That's not how I'm thinking of it. Let's just say I have strong feelings for Jackie. But I need you to keep that part to yourself for right now. This is going to be hard for Stephanie. Jackie wants to wait until she gets used to having me around the house before we tell her the whole story."

"But I get all of it in one blast?"

"You're very mature and I knew you could handle it."

"Great. Terrific." Carla took a calming breath. "For the record, I have no problem with you being gay. If you're gay, that's totally fine. But why does it have to be Jackie?"

Susan begged with her eyes for understanding.

* * *

When Carla awoke the next morning there was a brief painless moment before the previous night's news came flooding back in. The images she had of her future, of birthday parties and Christmases and graduations, now included Jackie and her loud gravelly voice, her underhanded insults. Stephanie would be there too, looking bored and acting superior. Carla realized she might be stuck with Jackie and Stephanie *forever.*

Her parents were normally up and about at this hour, Susan running the hair dryer in her bathroom, Clark downstairs making coffee and watching the stock market on CNBC. But today the house was silent. The night before, following her big announcement, Susan had packed a few things and left for Jackie's. When Carla went upstairs to bed, Clark was still in his office with the door shut. Though it was possible he was still sleeping, it was more likely he'd gotten up early and gone to work. He was the head of finance for a real estate investment hedge fund in Scotts Valley. Whenever he and Susan weren't getting along, he spent as much time as possible out of the house.

Carla showered and dressed. For breakfast, she dug a nearly forgotten Luna bar from her backpack. As she walked the cold blocks toward school, the streets seemed empty, the houses shut against her.

In the hall on her way to first period, she ran into Yvette, her best friend.

"What's wrong?"

"Whole bunch of stuff." Carla realized she might cry. "My parents are getting a divorce. My mom is in love with Jackie."

Yvette was on the volleyball team with Carla and felt the same way about Jackie and Stephanie that Carla did. The look on her face was that of someone hearing about a gruesome killing.

"Yeah. Bit of a surprise. I'm not supposed to be telling anyone because they haven't told Stephanie yet. So you can't tell anybody."

"Okay. Wow. That means that you and Stephanie are going to be ..."

"Don't say it. Don't *ever* say it."

"Sorry. I know. It's gross." Yvette wrapped Carla in a hug.

That afternoon, as Carla and Yvette changed for volleyball practice, Stephanie was two spots over, speaking in her domineering voice. For the past three practices, Coach P had been making the team do down-and-ups—a squat, a push-up and a jumping jack in quick succession—and Stephanie was complaining about it. "Is she, like, trying to *kill* us?!" At some point in her monologue, Stephanie threw Carla a sneering look and turned away.

Carla ignored her and finished changing. When Carla stood up after tying her shoes, Stephanie shot her another look.

"Can I help you?"

The other girls stopped their conversations.

Stephanie wore a smug little smile. "It's just weird that your mother is staying at my house because she's divorcing your father and doesn't have anywhere else to go and you're not saying anything about it."

Yvette started to speak but Carla put a hand up to stop her. Carla wanted very much to tell Stephanie the truth here and now, to obliterate her in front of the whole team, but she saw it was better to keep her in the dark and give her the chance to say even more things that, one day very soon, would prove quite idiotic. "I guess I was trying to keep my personal business private. But too late for that, apparently. Hopefully, she won't be staying long."

Stephanie struggled for a comeback. "Yes, hopefully."

The rest of the team looked at Carla with pity.

Out on the floor, the girls started with stretches and laps around the court, and then paired up for passing drills. Carla traded volleys with Yvette, while Stephanie and another girl volleyed next to them. When Carla was younger, at every one of her soccer games, her mother stressed the importance of good sportsmanship. Even if the other team threw elbows or talked trash, or even cheated, her mother insisted that she shake hands and offer congratulations. But after last night's conversation, her mother's thoughts on sportsmanship—or any topic—didn't seem so important. Carla gave Yvette a look and inched sideways toward Stephanie.

Thinking the game was to hit Stephanie with the ball, Yvette sent a high arcing pass in Stephanie's direction.

Carla took two rapid steps and threw a shoulder into Stephanie that knocked her down.

Across the gym, balls hit the floor and conversations went quiet.

Dazed, ponytail across her eyes, Stephanie looked up.

"Sorry," Carla said. "I didn't see you."

Stephanie was holding the elbow that had broken her fall and—unfortunately, in Carla's view—kept her face from hitting the hardwood. She winced pathetically. "That really hurt. Why don't you watch what you're doing?"

"It was just an accident. I already said I was sorry."

* * *

After school, Carla was in her room when her mother pulled up, apparently having left work early. Carla watched from the window as Susan made several trips in and out of the house, loading the RAV4 with suitcases, boxes and clothing on hangers. The sight was disorienting. The woman down there was not just a mother. She was an adult person with thoughts and dreams and desires that had nothing to do with motherhood. She had made a decision and was taking her life in a new direction.

Before the incident at practice, Carla had been trying to reconcile herself to the idea of moving with Susan over to Jackie and Stephanie's. But it was like trying to imagine living in Brazil or Botswana. Moreover, this big Victorian, with its wooden floors, claw-foot bathtub and dormer windows, its previously normal-ish parents, was the only home she'd ever known. The huge backyard, partly shaded in summer by the giant sycamore but sunny in winter after the leaves dropped, where birds flitted in the concrete fountain, was Carla's favorite place in the whole world. Now that she'd made it clear to Stephanie that she hated her guts, the idea of living with her seemed even more remote.

When the RAV4 was full, Susan came upstairs and knocked on Carla's door. "Sweetie, are you in there?"

Carla didn't answer.

Susan opened the door and stepped hesitantly into the room. For a moment she seemed unsure of where to stand or sit. Smelling of perspiration and lilac perfume, she sat next to Carla on the bed and put her hand on Carla's shoulder.

Carla shrugged the hand away.

"I'm sorry. I know you're upset."

"Stephanie made a nice little scene today. Now everybody on the team knows you and dad are getting a divorce."

Susan closed her eyes in irritation. "I apologize. She was asked to keep what Jackie told her confidential. Did you tell her what I told you? About Jackie and me?"

"I'm not doing your dirty work."

Susan exhaled relief. "Thank you. She'll get the whole story soon enough. I know she can be a pill." Susan's tone suggested there was more to this, that there had been negotiations between her and Jackie that hadn't gone smoothly. Susan forced a smile, trying to regroup. She took Carla's hand and held it firmly. "It's all going to work out in the end. I promise."

Carla glared at her.

"I wanted to check in about your game on Saturday."

"Don't worry about it. Yvette's mom is driving us."

"Okay. Well, I guess I'll see you there then."

"You don't *have* to come."

"I know. But I'm coming anyway."

On Saturday, when Carla entered the Soquel gym and started warming up with Yvette, she avoided looking into the bleachers. She wasn't sure if Susan had come or not until, a moment before the umpire's whistle to start the match, she heard a loud and unmistakable, "Let's go, Carla!" Stephanie wasn't here today—she rarely played so it wasn't unusual for her to blow off volleyball for one of her many other activities. This should have meant that Jackie wasn't here either but, again without looking, Carla wondered if Jackie had come in order to spend time with Susan.

Carla recorded twelve kills in the first set. Once Santa Cruz went up 10-1 in the second, Soquel's blockers poked at Carla's kills one-handed—played what Coach P derisively called *toreador defense*. Santa Cruz won 21-7, 21-5. Carla walked the line to high-five her glum-faced opponents and then, eyes down, loaded her gear into her backpack. When she finally looked up, Susan was standing near the open double doors, talking quietly with Yvette's mom. Jackie was nowhere in sight.

"Nice game, girls."

"If you can call it that," Yvette said. "I thought they were supposed to be good this year."

"They did their best," Susan said. "They'll get better."

Normally a group of parents and daughters went out for lunch after Saturday games, but there was no mention of that today. "We'll see you guys soon," Yvette's mom said. "Ready, Yvette?"

"Aren't we going to eat?"

Yvette's mom spoke patiently. "Carla and her mother need some time alone together."

"Oh," Yvette said. "Right." She touched Carla's arm. "Call me tonight."

In the car, Susan tuned the radio to K-WAVE—*light rock, less talk*—and hummed along with Kelly Clarkson. "So what are we in the mood for?"

"I'm not hungry."

"After *that* game? Nonsense. You need to eat."

"Then wherever. I don't care."

"How about Surfrider? We haven't been there in a while."

Carla shrugged.

All the way to the restaurant, Susan filled the car with her usual post-game praise: "Your hands were two feet over the net. And some of those kills ... My goodness ... They looked fired from a cannon."

This act Susan was putting on—pretending everything was okay so she wouldn't have to feel bad—was only making Carla angrier.

At the restaurant, the hostess waved toward the mostly empty tables. "Wherever you like." Carla made a beeline for a high-backed booth in the corner.

As they perused menus, Susan reached across the table and patted Carla's hand. "I'm proud of you."

"I heard Dad crying in his office." This was true. Clark had the door closed and was muffling the sound with a shirt or a pillow but it was plain enough to hear. Carla thought about knocking but she didn't know what she might say. She had never in her life needed to comfort Clark.

"I'm sorry to hear that. I'm actually surprised he has any feelings about this at all." Susan paused and started again more thoughtfully. "I understand it's a shock. But I can't tell you how right all this feels. After I told Clark about my feelings for Jackie, I cried too, but with *relief*. I'd been dragging something for miles, hundreds of miles, and suddenly the rope snapped."

"I had sex."

Susan twitched as though something had been thrown at her face. "With whom?"

"Some guy. We did it in his car." All of this was a lie. Carla had been French-kissed by a boy on the last day of school the previous year, a boy who never called or texted afterward, but she'd never seriously made out with anyone.

"What guy?"

"Just some guy from school."

Susan's eyes filled with tears. "Carla, why are you speaking to me like this?"

"You're being very honest with me so I'm being honest with you."

"You're doing this to hurt me."

"How am I hurting you? I'm just telling you about my love life."

Susan opened her mouth but didn't speak. "That's fine. You had sex. I hope you used protection."

"It hurt, actually. I bled. The guy has a pretty big cock."

"Carla!" Susan looked around and leaned closer. "I'm sorry. Do you understand that? I'm truly, truly sorry. Do you think when I was a little girl that my dream was to be married to someone I didn't love? To suddenly, at the age of forty-three, fall in love with a woman? I can assure you it was not. It just happened. Sometimes you get visited by the unexpected."

"Tell me about it."

* * *

Two weeks after Susan moved out, Carla and Yvette heard that Natalie Degarmo, a senior, was throwing a party. Natalie's parents were out of town and her older brother was buying a keg. Carla and Yvette had never attended an unsupervised party. To date, their partying life was sneaking sips of wine during sleepovers. But Carla had never felt such a strong need to be part of the crowd.

Both Carla and Yvette had curfews—nine and nine thirty, respectively—so they got permission for Yvette to spend the night and then, after Clark went to bed, tiptoed out the front door. The walk to the party led them up the long hill of Bay Street, almost to the university, then left on one of the semirural roads off Western Drive, where the lots included detached barns and horse corrals. The address they had was on the mailbox in front of a very large and brightly lit two-story house with an enormous lawn.

Natalie answered, looking surprised to the point of confusion. "Volleyball girls. What do you know?" She hesitated a moment and then stepped aside. "*Entrez*."

Carla and Yvette entered a hardwood expanse the size of a classroom. Straight ahead, people were on leather couches and cushioned chairs or just standing, watching two boys play video games on a massive flat-screen. The boys called each other *faggot* and *cocksucker* as they frantically worked their controllers. To the right, in a granite and stainless-steel kitchen, a keg sat in a tub of ice next to a massive table covered in pizza boxes and plastic cups. To the left, under a polished wooden staircase that climbed to a landing, a sound system with a pulsing readout played Bruno Mars. The ceiling was thirty feet up. "You want a beer?" Natalie asked.

Carla and Yvette traded glances. "Sure. Okay."

Two hours later, Carla and Yvette were on the balcony, where they'd sat down to let their legs dangle through the wooden railing. The whole downstairs was shoulder to shoulder. A second keg had replaced the first and people were milling through the kitchen like cattle, refilling cups. In a cleared area next to the dining room table, some boys were doing spins on a hoverboard, falling off and laughing themselves sick. The roar from below was a tornado of sound throwing off specific, disjointed phrases—"I got *sooo* scorched," "Where's my *phone?!*," "Hey, Jeff! *Jeff!!*" Working on the end of her second beer, Carla's brain felt warm, afloat, like it did after a hard workout.

"I have to pee," Yvette said.

There was a bathroom just behind them but some surfer girls in hoodies and UGG boots were in there sharing around a lighter and a small metal pipe. The smoke drifting out stung Carla's throat. "There's another one downstairs behind the kitchen."

"Come with me."

Apparently as some side effect of the floaty sensation, Carla was feeling melancholic. "Just go. I'll wait."

While Yvette was gone, Carla took another sip of her beer and decided it was warm and disgusting and that she'd had enough. To make it look like someone else's, she reached as far as she could and set it down.

Some boys climbed the stairs and turned down the hallway to Carla's right. They were giddy, whispering about something and moving quickly.

A minute later, two more boys followed and did the same. Carla stood and went to investigate.

Down the hall, she found a sign handwritten in thick Sharpie taped to a door—"Do Not Enter!!" The door was open an inch or two and she pushed it wider. The room was dimly lit and warmer, almost humid. It was a master bedroom—presumably Natalie's parents' room. The walls were bookcases of different-sized wooden shelves and cubbies. Weights and exercise equipment were strewn around. A crowd of boys was watching something. When Carla stepped forward, she saw, on the edge of the bed, two boys sitting on either side of a girl. The girl and the boy on her right were making out. The girl's face was obscured by the boy's head and her own long hair but Carla could see that the girl was topless. As he kissed her, the boy moved his hand from boob to boob. The second boy was rubbing the girl's shoulder. Carla recognized him from school but didn't know his name. A junior, maybe a senior, he was short and thick, hair forever a shaggy mess. He seemed to be waiting his turn. The first boy paused his kissing and the girl's head drooped forward. She was plainly drunk. When she managed to raise her head again, her long curtain of hair parted and revealed her face. Stephanie.

"Whoa," Carla said, involuntarily. She put a hand over her mouth.

The sight was such an inversion of everything Stephanie claimed and seemed to be, Carla's first instinct was to laugh. As she stared, transfixed, Stephanie kissed the first boy again and turned and kissed the other boy. Carla realized she was acting out. She must have finally been told the truth about their mothers.

Good, Carla thought. *About time.* The boys Stephanie was kissing were skater dudes, remedials. The crew watching looked about the same. The stories were going to fly around school and Stephanie's reputation was going to *die*. She would, at long last, be forced to shut up. Carla hoped Susan and Jackie heard the stories too. They might realize just how much pain they were causing and think twice about things. In fact, the worse the stories, the more obvious it would be that they were creating a problem.

Carla turned and left the room.

When she reached the balcony, the stoner girls were in the spot where she and Yvette had been sitting and the bathroom door was closed. Carla leaned against a wall to wait. Down below, the people in the big central room were packed even more tightly together, their noise an even louder tornado.

As Carla watched the chaos, a voice in her head told her she was doing the wrong thing. Stephanie was a brat and a pain. As Jackie liked to say about certain people that she and Susan worked with, "She needs to be brought down a peg." But Carla could still feel the energy in the bedroom. She remembered the way Stephanie's head fell forward. Maybe Stephanie had been drugged.

Carla went back down the hall but now the bedroom door was closed and locked. She knocked but no one answered. She knocked harder and yelled to be let in. A voice from the other side said, "Go away!"

Carla returned down the hall and approached one of the stoner girls and tapped her shoulder. The girl wore a colorful hoodie and had long tangles of sandy-blond hair. She turned, her eyes half closed.

"Can you help me, please?" Carla asked.

The girl chuckled. "What?"

"My friend needs help."

The girls addressed each other. "What's she saying?" One of them pointed to the closed bathroom door and told Carla, loudly, "You need to wait."

Carla spoke louder. "I don't need the bathroom! I need you to come with me!"

The girls shook their heads. "We're good."

Giving up on these idiots, Carla turned to head down the stairs. A group of boys, having been pushed from the clot of bodies, had taken seats on the bottom six or seven stairs. When Carla reached them, she tapped the closest one on the back. "Can you help me?"

The boy turned and leered. "Sure, baby. I'll help you." The other boys laughed.

Carla wanted to push through the boys, or leap over them, but she feared getting trapped on the other side of them. She could feel herself running out of time and reclimbed the stairs. Tears in her eyes, she went back down the hallway and slapped the door twice with her palm. It pressed toward her slightly. Someone on the other side was leaning against it.

She ran back to the stoner girls. They were laughing stupidly at something, most likely at Carla and her panic. She was really crying now. She had a childish urge to call out for her mother. For perhaps the first time since watching Susan back her RAV4 down the driveway, Carla felt the full force of her mother's departure.

She drew in a big quivering breath and unleashed a scream.

The scream made the stoner girls go quiet and caused people at the bottom of the stairs to turn their heads. Two older boys worked through the group of laughing boys and started climbing. Looking unsure if this was serious or joke, they hesitated. Carla took a few steps down the hall, trying to indicate the way, and screamed again. The bedroom door flew open and boys began hustling out and moving past her. Carla entered the bedroom and found Stephanie alone on the bed, flat on her back, arms out to her sides. The last two boys were standing near her. Carla screamed again, driving the boys out. Two of the stoner girls and some new faces gathered in the doorway. Yvette was there too, looking fearful. Stephanie, who had initially looked unconscious, was moving now. "Are we trouble?" she slurred. Her jeans were still buttoned.

Carla had another scream at the ready. She wanted to unleash it at Stephanie herself. She really did hate her—for who she'd always been and for getting drunk and putting herself in danger and needing to be saved. For making Carla look like a crazy person. But, instead of screaming, Carla found Stephanie's shirt on the bedspread and, pulling first one arm and then the other, helped her sit up. ■

SELF-PORTRAIT WITH MAGPIE
Matthew Wimberley

—after Phil Levine

1.

Already having stolen
the eye, the quick burst
from the juniper, I listen
as you call out
against the empty sky.
Conventicle of thieves—
sometimes I say
a line of poetry to myself
I know I've heard before
& make it mine. At least
at twenty-three that
was the game—living
on kindness and dust
and an income like wind,
which came and went
as I'd walk the way
from West Fourth
up through Washington
Square, past hustlers
touching the black manes
of knights, and I'd sit
just beyond the edge
of the sycamores'
shadows, and watch even
my life go by. *Go*
West, Whitman wrote,
& out near Taos, a year ago,
I saw my first magpie
who also saw his or her
first me. It was
Levine who said someone
told him magpies could talk—
that they'd steal
a ring left out

on a Formica table.
By then, my father's rings
were gas money
and it would be years
before I was married
and rose in the early light
for the first time
as a father, and so
there was nothing more
the bird could take—
though I must
have offered ash,
the glint of a corkscrew,
sweat on a flat palm.

2.

I breathe in the thick perfume
of pinyon this morning
until the last of winter
burns on my tongue,
looking for
a white and blue
flash of wings,
and hear you
cry over the wind,
the light
scintillating through the reeds
on the lake's surface.
Southern Colorado
4/23/24
the palindrome days
and the road to Cortez.
Unlike before, my offerings
are lined up
on the table before me—
this pen and all the ink
darkening time
so I might write
my daughter's name
and get down the boat

she drew last week,
the smudge of blue
for waves it cut through,
a white surf,
and the wave like
the curve of Sally's
stomach, growing
towards late summer
and the sound
unlike any voice
before, a heartbeat
like a deep space
object but also the dark
of space, the sky last night—
if you could see it
like I did—dust
rising against
the moon
one way
and the red
glow of Betelgeuse
the other, over the mesa's
silhouette, and the man
who pointed
his headlights right at me,
asked me to leave—
& I've taken the snap
of it and the idle
of his black Ford,
the crunch
of gravel
on the unlit road
which could take me
anywhere and make me
whole or ragged—like you
or like sorrow or laughter
waiting when I turn
over the cracked earth
where I've gone ahead
without anyone's permission
& done what I had to do—

somewhere barbed wire
rattling on a worn fence
in a field I wanted
to walk through, something
you'd admire and want
all for yourself. Juniper
rustling when I look
the other way.

THE BEAR
Joy Lanzendorfer

Mallory had walked a half mile down the trail before she started worrying about bears. It occurred to her that they must live in this forest. There were thousands of trees in the North Carolina mountains, so many that they blocked the sky. Naturally they would house wild animals, some of which were bound to be large and ferocious.

Helplessness seemed to radiate from Mallory's body like a pheromone and she picked up a stick and clutched it to her chest. It was as thick as a cucumber and about as long, and she knew it wouldn't protect her from a bear. One swipe of a claw and that'd be it. Still, she held the stick with both hands as she continued down the path, scanning the leaves for movement. She should have left a note in her cabin explaining that she'd gone on a hike. It would be just her luck to be attacked by a bear and die out here alone in these woods. No one would know what had become of her.

Then Mallory stopped and told herself to calm down and name the emotion she was feeling: anxiety. She could hear her life coach, Trudy, telling her, "Trust yourself." She, Mallory, a forty-eight-year-old adult, could take a hike in a strange forest and be fine. She wasn't going to be attacked by a bear, or get lost. She would follow the trail to the highway and then walk back to her cabin at the residency. Nothing bad was going to happen. As Trudy said, "You have more power than you think you do."

Resolved, Mallory resumed her hike. It would be a shame to spend a month at this writing residency and not at least go for a walk. After all, she'd earned it. She'd written ten pages of her new play so far, a dialogue between Sylvia Plath and Marilyn Monroe that takes place in a dream. She might even finish the draft if she concentrated the remaining days. So here Mallory was, trying to get some goddamned nature. The Blue Ridge Mountains. A beautiful place, even if her husband, Gentry, wasn't impressed by her getting into the residency. "Why go to the middle of nowhere?" he'd said when she told him about it. No words of congratulations. No discussion of how the scenery might inspire her work. "Do you even know how to build a fire in a fireplace?" he'd added. Gentry only liked LA and New York. The fact that she was staying in a cabin in the woods made him nervous.

Good, Mallory thought. *Be nervous about me. For once.*

To the left, the ground dropped off into a ravine so that Mallory was looking down at more trees. The sheer number made her dizzy. She'd grown up in the city. Even one tree was a lot.

A sign was attached to the closest trunk. It had been there for so long that the bark had formed a burl over one corner. It said:

Boundary National Forest Behind This Sign
No Hunting Past This Point

Mallory stopped, anxiety zinging through her again. The only thing worse than running into a bear would be running into some redneck hunter.

As she was thinking this, a cloud of mosquitoes came up from somewhere and swarmed her face. Mallory swiped at them, but they only flew back and tried to land on her eyelids. Apparently, she'd sweated off the bug repellent she'd found in her cabin. It hadn't occurred to her to bring it along, even though her legs were covered in bug bites. It took her a week to understand that the harmless-looking gnats in her cabin were biting her. Midges, they were called. She'd looked them up on the residency computer.

Jogging down the path, Mallory tried to distract herself from the mosquitoes humming in her wake. The point of this walk, aside from seeing nature—which was being a pain in the ass—was to think through the ending of her play. But her mind kept straying to her last conversation with Gentry, from when she first got here. She was sitting on the floor of the cabin holding the rattling landline to her ear because there was no cell coverage at the residency. Gentry was distracted, and she could hear Becca in the background chattering with her friends. Mallory imagined Becca—the girlfriend; her so-called sister wife—in a bikini, her breasts bouncing in a nylon sling. During the conversation, Becca had called for Gentry to "come play with us" and he'd said, "I gotta go, Chops," and hung up.

He'd called Mallory Chops since college, from Pork Chops, a nickname about her pink thighs. Although Mallory had always been thin, suddenly, sitting alone in her cabin, she felt bloated with fat. She imagined Porky Pig's stout legs, the flabby thighs trailing down to hooves. Not like Becca's long brown limbs twining luxuriously around Gentry in bed.

For twenty-five years, Mallory's life with Gentry, a Hollywood film editor, had been filled with parties, movie premieres, and play openings. Along the way, she'd carved out a respectable career for herself as a playwright, although the awards and occasional newspaper write-ups didn't ever seem to equal much money. Then one day, Gentry announced he wanted to have an open relationship with Becca, a pert twenty-two-year-old with a stomach so flat it was concave. Mallory had gone along with it at first, because this was how people were now. They had open relationships and complicated genders, and as an artist, she should experience such things, break her boundaries, explore, change. But then Gentry said he wanted to bring Becca into the marriage as a second wife, like he was starting a harem, and what had seemed cutting-edge had turned into something so ancient and sexist that she had felt tricked. For who was benefiting from this open relationship? Gentry, of course, who now had two women taking care of him, cooking for him, sleeping with him, waiting on him. It was amazing, Mallory thought, how creative men could be in arranging such things for themselves. And the worst part was when she tried to explain the sexism to Becca, the girl told Mallory, in a condescending tone, that she should share Gentry. "I know you've been hurt a lot in life," Becca said, nodding in agreement with herself. "I know that's why you're having trouble letting Gentry be free." She leaned forward, her Disney-princess eyes widening. "But, Mallory, we have to let go of our insecurities in life so that we can truly love." And Mallory had wanted to pour her turmeric latte over the girl's head.

So here they were, at an impasse. The residency was a distraction, but soon she would have to decide what to do about her marriage. The truth was, whenever she thought about leaving Gentry, Mallory felt exhausted. There were so many things she'd never done on her own without Gentry, like rent a house or pay taxes. Even if they split their finances, she'd have to get a job. Playwriting paid almost nothing. And Mallory hadn't had a job—a real one, with a boss—for decades.

Ahead, bushes hung over the path like an arbor, forcing her to duck underneath the branches. She realized she'd forgotten to worry about bears, which felt like a small triumph over her anxiety. On the ground was a rock about the size of Mallory's fist, and she picked it up. It sparkled in her palm, and she thought, *Fool's gold*, before putting it in her pocket.

The first thing Mallory saw when she came out the other side of the branches was a man with a gun.

She stopped abruptly. The sound of her feet stopped with her.

"Afternoon," the man said.

Mallory eyed the gun. "Hello."

He was wearing hunting clothes—camouflage pants and a T-shirt. A pale-blond beard spotted his chin, and his skin was so white, it was almost bluish. His eyes went down her body and back up again. Mallory crossed her arms over her chest.

"You out here by yourself?" the man said.

Mallory considered saying that a husband or a boyfriend was behind her on the trail, but then rankled at the thought. She shouldn't have to lie.

"I'm just getting some fresh air," she said.

The blond threads that passed for eyebrows went up. "Excuse me, ma'am, but there are copperheads in these woods."

She frowned. It figured she'd be worried about the wrong animal.

"Thanks for the warning," she said, edging around him and hurrying on while simultaneously fighting the paranoia that he would aim his rifle and shoot her in the back. Most likely he wasn't a murderer, but if he was, what would stop him from taking her out? No one knew she was here. They were alone in the middle of thousands of trees. She should have left a note in the cabin.

The man jogged toward her, pebbles crunching under his boots. Before she knew it, he was beside her on the path, gun swinging on his shoulder. When she sped up, so did he.

Oh God, Mallory thought. *I am going to get shot. Or assaulted, and then shot.*

"Are you from that art thing they have on the hill?" the man said. "What's it called?"

She didn't like that this man had guessed where she was staying. For a moment, she considered lying and saying that she was visiting friends, but she doubted he would believe that she knew anyone up here.

"Brecknell Art Center," she said.

"That's the name. Are you an artist?"

"More or less."

She glanced sideways at his gut, which pressed against the enormous bedsheet of his shirt. The gun flapped against his side like a child's crutch.

"That's real interesting," he said. "I always wonder what you artists do up there. My name's Lester, by the way."

He held out his sweaty palm. Mallory heard the whine of a mosquito in her ear as she looked at the wet hand. Why, at her age, couldn't she think of a way out of shaking it? Reluctantly, she gave the man her hand and he caught it in both paws and pumped her arm.

"And you are?" he said.

"Madison," Mallory lied.

Something rustled in the bushes, and she jerked toward it, thinking, almost automatically, of bears. Then it occurred to her that this man could have a buddy somewhere, some equally pasty guy hiding in the foliage, pointing a gun at her.

She started on again, and again, the man matched her pace. For a spell, there was nothing by the sound of their steps in tandem on the trail. It felt like Mallory was floating above herself, watching her body walk beside Lester, a monster who had materialized out of a 1950s horror movie.

"Where you from?" the man said. "Let me guess. You got a New York way about you."

He wasn't wrong. She was from New York originally but hadn't lived there since she'd moved to LA with Gentry.

"California," she said.

"Well, how about that? I'd like to go there some time. I'm a little wary of planes, though. I don't mind telling you that." He adjusted the gun as he spoke.

"Are you hunting out here by yourself?" she said.

"I was, but I didn't have no luck. I was looking for bucks. You ever had venison?"

"I'm a vegetarian."

He glanced at her with his mouth open. "I have to say, I feel sorry for you on that account. Are you that other kind too, what's it called? Vegan?"

She wasn't, although Gentry was. Mallory had tried to go vegan, but it had been too hard. "No. Listen, Lester, I'm trying to take a hike here."

"I see that, ma'am. I see that. And how do you like our beautiful country?"

Anger began to overtake Mallory's fear. She'd almost directly asked this man to leave her alone, but did he take the hint? No, he just went on walking beside her, his stupid feet smashing the leaves on the trail.

"It's nice," she said, deadpan, looking at Lester.

"It is that. I wouldn't swap places with nobody. You go to cities and people don't care about each other. You don't know nobody and nobody knows you. It's a bit different up here."

His cheeks had gotten red, and she thought he might be getting angry about the brutality of cities. Or maybe it was just the exertion. In her pocket, she tightened her fist around the rock.

"You married?" Lester said.

"What?" Mallory said and didn't know how to answer that. She truly didn't.

"I'd guess not," Lester said with a smirk. "If I was to guess, I'd guess not."

Fury flared inside Mallory again, making her feel stronger in the shadow of this man's overwhelming presence. "Yes, I'm married."

"Well, you don't say. I figured your man wouldn't like it, your being out here alone in the woods."

Ahead, the trail narrowed between dark, reaching branches. The only way to proceed was single file, which seemed like a bad idea. Already the bushes had pushed her closer to this man so that she could feel the heat coming off his body.

Lester swept off his hat, revealing blond thready hair, and scratched his head. "After you."

"That's okay," Mallory said. "You go first."

Reaching up, he pulled the strap of his gun more squarely on his shoulder. "I'm going to have to insist, ma'am."

A shiver ran down Mallory's back as she went ahead of him on the path. Somehow Lester kept getting his way, bullying her into walking how he wanted her to walk. It was just like Gentry. She always ended up doing what he wanted.

With each step, Lester's boots crunched behind her. The branches closed above her head like claws. *Bear claws*, she thought. Mallory recalled a TV show that warned women never to go to a second location with a kidnapper. That wasn't exactly what was happening, she knew. This man wasn't going to hurt her— probably?—but if he wanted to, she wouldn't be able to stop him.

Then she heard the whoosh of passing cars, indicating they were nearing the road that led to the residency. Once she reached it, it was a straight shot to the safety of the cabin. This hike from hell was almost over.

She was almost running by the time they exited the thicket. But then Lester's fingers curled around her bicep and she shrieked, fumbling for the rock.

"Shush," he said. "Ma'am, look."

Ahead, a snake was curled like a tangled hose in the path. Mallory jerked her arm from Lester's grip.

"It's all right," he said, peering at the snake. "It's a kingsnake, not a coral snake. See that? The red and black stripes are touching. Red touches black, won't attack, red touches yeller, bite a feller."

Although Mallory didn't want a science lesson just then, she found herself staring at the snake. Its red bands were against the black bands, which in turn were encased in stripes of bright yellow. She gathered from his comments that there was another kind that looked similar but was poisonous. Lester moved forward, kicking his feet at the snake. It slid off the road lazily as if infected with the southern charm she'd heard so much about.

Finally, Mallory walked onto the grassy bank beside the highway. Lester came out behind her, grinning.

"I'm happy you made it out without getting snake bit," he said. "My truck's over there. Do you want a ride?"

He indicated a pickup truck parked in a turnout. Mallory put a hand on her hip. So this had all been a drawn-out act of chivalry to protect her from snakes.

"No, I'm fine," she said, swallowing back the impulse to thank him. "I want to walk by myself."

He tipped his hat. "Nice meeting you, Madison."

A minute later, Lester drove out onto the road. His hand came out the window, waving as he disappeared around the bend.

* * *

Mallory decided she was proud that she'd said no to the man, even if it was late in their interaction. As Trudy said, she should take every victory, no matter how small, as a sign of growth. Encouraged, she resolved not to tell Gentry about the incident. Instead, she dug into the play and in a burst of clarity, finished the draft with a poignant image of Marilyn brushing Sylvia Plath's hair, woman comforting woman. Finishing her work filled Mallory with elation and the sense that she could get along without Gentry just fine. Maybe, she thought, she really could start over on her own.

On the last night of the residency, she treated herself to a trip to Asheville, an hour's drive over the Blue Ridge Parkway. Halfway there, she stopped at a rest area to look down at the sea of treetops covering the mountains. The trees looked much better from above. It was October, and blotches of lemon and cinnamon stood out like flowers in the blue.

In town, she ate grilled eggplant at a bar while drinking sangria. When she came out, she decided to sober up before driving back to the residency. Again she resisted calling Gentry and instead dialed a friend from LA who worked in theater. The friend mentioned seeing Becca and Gentry at a café, arguing. "Becca was crying," the friend said. "She was wearing sunglasses. I wonder if they're breaking up."

Hearing this made Mallory realize that even if Becca left Gentry, she didn't want him back. Her emotions toward him felt cold, dead. Abruptly she made a decision: She would leave Gentry after the residency. It was time to step into her power, as Trudy always said. She would move out, get the new play staged, and apply for work teaching creative writing. She had the credentials, and besides, how many plays had she put on in her life? At least a dozen. The path before her seemed paved and clear, and for once, Mallory wasn't afraid to walk it. She couldn't wait for her next session with Trudy to tell her about it.

It was evening by the time Mallory felt sober enough to leave Asheville. Her phone map suggested an alternate route around the mountain instead of over it, but she trusted the way she'd come. It was better to rely on her own experience instead of listening to a cell phone, she concluded in her newfound confidence.

A third of a way over the mountain, Mallory realized her mistake. There were no streetlights on the Blue Ridge Parkway. It was black and moonless, and the only lights were her headlights. On either side of the road were steep drops, and it wouldn't take much for her to veer off and plunge to her death.

To take her mind off it, Mallory turned on the radio and bluegrass filled the car. "My girl is red-hot," a man crooned. "Your girl ain't doodly squat," the chorus replied. *Gentry would hate this music*, Mallory thought, turning it up, trying to resume the goodwill from earlier. She wouldn't think about tumbling over the ravine. She wouldn't feel guilty about being tipsy and driving the rental car. Even though it felt like she was isolated on a remote planet, if she looked at the headlights and kept the car in the lane, she would reach the turnoff for the residency eventually. Tomorrow she would tell Gentry she was leaving him and start her new life. Her second half, better than the first. Maybe she would move back to the East Coast. She could get a farmhouse in Vermont, or some such place, and write by a fire while snow drifted onto a woodpile.

As Mallory was thinking this, a bear walked into the road. It was strolling across the street from trees that had appeared on the right and didn't seem to notice the car barreling straight toward it.

It took Mallory a second to register that an animal was crossing in front of her. Her next thought was how small the bear seemed, not much bigger than a dog. She slammed her brakes and the car swerved toward the ravine. Yanking the wheel, Mallory managed to pull the nose back to the road where the bear was still advancing. There was a jolt and a sickening crunch as the rear wheel of the car went over some part of the animal. It rose high enough that Mallory fell toward the door.

Then all four wheels were back on the road. The car righted itself and Mallory drove on. The bluegrass music continued to play. The headlights lit the empty road. It seemed to Mallory that she could just go back to California and shrug the incident off like a bad dream. The bear, and its injuries, would stay on this mountaintop. It would be like it had never happened.

But the coldness of this thought, and the sense that it was something Gentry might do, made Mallory open her mouth and scream.

Now she had to know how badly the bear was hurt. Desperately, she looked for a rest area so she could turn the car around, but there was nothing but trees on either side of the road. To go back meant a three-point turn in the middle of a black street, and she was too upset for that, so she had no choice but to drive deeper into the woods. The music had lost its comforting humanity and was a clock ticking away time. She flipped off the radio.

When a turnout at last appeared, Mallory spun the car around and went back up the mountain to see if she could help the bear. At the top of the hill, she knew she'd passed the place where she'd hit it. There were no lumps on the road, no furry body off to the side. At a rest area, she turned around again and went down more slowly, but the road was clear. The bear had vanished. Even in darkness, she would see an animal that big in her headlights.

By now, Mallory was hyperventilating. How she wished for some way to see beyond the headlights, but there was nothing but this hostile forest and unrelenting darkness. More than anything, she wanted to see people. Not just people—cities. Garish streetlights and gas stations and strip malls. Even a traffic jam would be welcomed just then.

Finally she turned at the gap that led to the residency and entered a small town with a Walmart. In the parking lot, she got out to check on the rental car. The streetlights made everything yellow and dim, like looking through night-vision goggles. She'd imagined blood on the door and organs caught in the undercarriage, but the only thing she could make out were small spots on the headlight, which could be bugs, or mud, or anything, really.

There was nothing to do but drive back to the cabin, wheeling slowly through the black streets. When she pulled up at last, the katydids in the forest sounded like thousands of clacking castanets. She hurried inside, head down, thinking that she was sick of that noise. Sick, sick, sick.

She grabbed the landline and dialed Gentry's number, fingers flying over the key pattern. It showed her age, she supposed, that she still memorized phone numbers.

"Hello?" Gentry said, his voice faint against the buzzing line. How familiar it was, like something from a childhood memory.

"Gentry," she said.

"Is that you, Mallory? I've been trying to reach you all week."

"It's me."

"What's wrong?"

Mallory sunk down on the cabin floor. She didn't feel hysterical anymore, just unsettled, like she wanted to cry but couldn't.

"I hit a bear," she said.

"What?"

"A bear. With my car."

She put her face in her hands.

"Are you all right?"

In the background, Becca's voice. "What's wrong? Is it Mallory?"

So Becca and Gentry hadn't broken up. Becca was still there, sitting in Mallory's chairs, sleeping in her bed, putting her things in the closet. Slowly taking over, like crabgrass.

Then Gentry's voice, muffled, talking to Becca. "She hit a bear, I think. I don't know. Are you all right, Mallory?"

"I'm fine."

"How did you hit a bear?"

Again, Becca's voice. "Is the bear okay? Is Mallory okay?"

The situation was taking on the surreal timbre of a nightmare. Maybe, she thought, it was all a misunderstanding somehow. For there was no way she could have hurt something as powerful as a bear. Maybe she'd imagined hitting it, but that would mean she was having a psychotic break of some kind.

The bear had seemed so small.

"I was driving and it walked into the road," she said. "If I hadn't hit it, I would have gone into the ravine. I didn't mean to do it."

"Of course not," Gentry said. "It's that place you're in, that's all. But you're okay, right?"

"Yeah, I told you, I'm fine."

"Good. And how's the play going?"

There was a pause while she tried to remember the play, and then tried to figure out why Gentry was asking about it. "I finished the draft."

"That's great. Listen, I've been trying to reach you. I met a theater coordinator from San Diego while playing bocce ball at a winery. I told her you were writing about Marilyn Monroe and she's into it. She might want to put on the play. Is it okay if I send it over to her?"

Despite being upset, Mallory was flattered. Gentry was on her side as usual, talking her up to people, getting her work.

"It's not ready for anyone to see it," she said.

"Well, get it ready. This woman, Amber, saw your last play, *The Receptionist*, and loves your work. And she knows an actor who can do a good Marilyn. So polish it up and I'll send it to her next week. Okay, Chops?"

And all Mallory's plans about teaching jobs and the East Coast seemed so difficult compared to this easy opportunity. It would be foolish to throw it away, and for what?

"Okay," she said.

Again, Becca in the background. "But what happened to the bear?"

Mallory stood up and walked to the phone base. "Tell Becca the bear wasn't lying in the road when I turned around, which is a good sign, right? Maybe it's okay."

"Yeah, that is a good sign. Animals that are seriously injured don't just walk away."

"Right," Mallory said, nodding. "Right."

"Listen, Chops, we miss you. This month made us realize how much you keep things together around here. We can't find anything and Becca isn't such a good cook, it turns out."

"It's true," Becca said in the background.

Mallory noticed the midges floating in the corner. It would be the last night with them too.

"See you tomorrow," she said.

They hung up and she went to her suitcase, pulling out her pajamas. Then she rubbed lotion on her hands without looking at her skin. She didn't like how old they seemed now, the knobbiness of her knuckles and protruding veins. Becca's hands were plump and soft, like a toddler's.

Mallory got in bed and wrapped herself in the comforter so that the midges couldn't get in. Then she lay there, listening to the katydids outside. With the blankets over her ears, they sounded like a roaring sea.

It was almost worse that the bear hadn't been killed. Instead, it had limped—dragged—itself into the woods to die. For it must die, she thought. No animal could survive something that huge hitting it unexpectedly while it was walking by itself, utterly alone.

And in that unceasing storm of sound, Mallory knew that tomorrow she would go home to Gentry. She would take the crumbs he gave her, until he stopped.

* * *

The next morning, the car seemed fine. There was no blood, although the spots on the headlights were suspiciously thick and reddish in color. In the morning light, Mallory thought the bear might have survived after all. As Gentry said, injured animals didn't simply walk away. There was no gore on the wheels and the road had been clear when she turned around. Maybe the accident wasn't as severe as it had seemed.

She was halfway to Charlotte before she stopped at a Starbucks and ordered a latte. Coming outside after standing in line, looking up from her phone, she finally saw it: The rear passenger door of the car didn't have blood on it, but it did have a dent. Half the door was caved in.

Mallory crouched in the parking lot, gripping the coffee cup in her hand. How had she missed this before? The smashed space that the bear had created with its body took up the entire lower half of the door. She'd been so busy looking for blood, she hadn't expected this different kind of damage.

Slowly, she touched the crumpled metal with her fingertips. It seemed impossible, but there it was: Evidence of her guilt, proof of what she'd done. Mallory had hit the bear. ∎

HAZY
Paul Skenazy

Where do I start? I'd ask why, but I know why. I write. Writing got me through adolescence and coming out. It gave me a byline, paid me to watch baseball all my life and introduced me to Kurt—gave me an excuse to introduce myself, to check in with him over the years while he played, coached and lived in his closet.

These days my head is radio static when I'm quiet, chalk grating on a blackboard most of the time. Grief leads to memory, memory to confusion, confusion to more grief. I wander around the house touching things that were his. I water the cactuses—we called them ours but they were always his—too much, walk out to the balcony and stand staring at them too often. Too often for what? What is it that I *should* be doing instead? There's no one to take care of but me. There's Kurt's brother, Paulie, absorbed by dementia, settled in the Memory unit at Sunset House. What is Kurt to him these days: a name? whiffs of some scene that floats through his gray cells and then disappears? I have no idea. These days I envy him the blank spaces where his mother and father, sister and brother once lived. I water the plants, visit Paulie, make myself food, walk, look at the time, come back to this chair and write some more. I've got a wooden box sitting on the desk next to me that contains Kurt's ashes. Why do we use the possessive talking about ashes, like the person, soul and body, is inscribed in them? And if it's not, why do I feel like I'm talking to them?

* * *

Sunray, Texas, where Kurt grew up, didn't have much of a high school baseball team, but they were better than most of the schools in the county. Paulie and Kurt stood out, along with a quiet, tall pitcher called Hazy. Irving was his real name, the one on the scorecard: Thaddeus Irving. They called him Hazy for the soft look in his eyes. Kurt said he never looked directly at you. He didn't hang with the rest of the team—just walked off after practice, slapping his glove along one leg, then switching to the other. Kurt didn't talk about him often: I got some memories as pillow talk our first nights together and rare moments when Kurt got sentimental; and there were a few oblique asides in the notebooks Kurt kept all his life when a pitcher gripped his curve the way Hazy did or landed on the left side of the mound the way Hazy did with his follow-through. I've pieced the story together, made it up I guess. I don't know if I'm describing what happened or what I imagine happened. Either way, this is the version I live with.

* * *

Hazy and I did nothing more than warm the bench through the first four games. Prozowski, this awkward Polack, was behind the plate and pitchers from last year's team went to the mound. We lost three of those four games. I guess Gus, our manager, who taught gym three periods and civics the other three, figured he had nothing to lose by putting the two of us in the lineup. Before I went out to the bullpen to warm Hazy up, Gus came over and put his hand on my shoulder the way he did when he went out to the mound to change pitchers.

"I don't know about Irving," he started. "He's got some skills but I don't think his mind's on the game the way it needs to be. See what you can do about that."

I nodded as if I had a plan of attack. I saw what Gus meant when Hazy threw all seven balls we had in the bullpen so wide they bounced against the left field wall. I ran out to collect them, ran back and handed the lot to Hazy. He stood there looking around at something, I couldn't make out what.

"That's enough for me," he said. "I'm ready." Then he turned toward the dugout.

"You haven't thrown a strike yet," I yelled after him.

He didn't turn around.

"Generally don't till I do," he said, slapping his glove against his leg.

I got my gear together and followed him but when I got to the dugout he was nowhere to be seen. I found him in the locker room tossing a rubber ball against the wall, catching it on a bounce, then throwing it back. He didn't seem to notice me so I turned around and went back to the tunnel heading into the dugout.

"We'll beat 'em, Buster," I heard him say behind me.

I looked back. He was talking to the wall, or the rubber ball, or something.

* * *

We were the home team so we headed out to the field to listen to the national anthem. He threw four warm-up pitches. The first had the ump ducking, the second went into the metal batting cage behind the plate but the other two were close. Close enough that I thought maybe Irving knew something I didn't.

But it was distracting to give signals to a pitcher who didn't even seem to be looking at me. He looked in my direction, maybe, but not focused. He didn't bend down and stare like most pitchers do, focusing on my fingers in the crouch. Instead he just stood there, tall, Abe Lincoln-like but without the beard. Thin like Abe too. Nothing on his face, but nothing. His eyes stretched out along the horizon like a wide-angle lens.

I walked to the mound after three straight balls. I came up to his shoulders, Laurel to his Hardy. He was staring along the first base line. *Staring* is the wrong word: he just looked off somewhere, not so much in a direction or at any object, just off in the distance. I slapped him on one cheek, and that brought his attention down to me. But I still wasn't sure he was looking at me, the way you know a dog does if you're offering him food. His eyes seemed clouded over, like wisps of some gossamer cloth were settled there. Like calm weather, waiting for a wind to blow through.

"You okay with what I'm calling?" I asked.

He nodded, but it looked like his attention had moved elsewhere.

"Want to try a changeup? Curve? Stick with the fastball?"

"Whatever," he drawled. "Hang in there. I'll find your glove."

I went back behind the plate. He walked that man, walked the next on four pitches, then the strikes started coming. And never stopped for the five innings he was out there. By then we were ahead, 6–2, he'd struck out seven, hit one guy and thrown one so far over my head it might have gone into the second deck if we'd had one. He had a sinking slow curve and, once he found it, the best control I've ever seen in a high schooler. Not a lot of speed by major league standards — mid-to-high eighties depending on the day. But I got used to his MO: after a few throws that looked like he shouldn't be on the mound, he'd find his range, hit the corners, and carry the team on his shoulders. He only lost twice in the regular season, a 1–0 game the day after homecoming, when none of us except Hazy could stand straight let alone swing, and a 7–3 licking when the coach pulled him in the first inning after he gave up seven walks in a row. The way he wouldn't look at you drove Prozowski, the other catcher we had on the team, crazy. The one time Gus tried him out catching Hazy,

Prozowski didn't last six pitches—"I won't catch him," he screamed, tearing off his chest protector and mask while he walked to the dugout.

"Kurt! Get out there," Gus growled while I quickly put on my gear.

Hazy and me, then Hazy and Paulie and me once he made the team—we were the team. It doesn't take much in high school: a few good players can make up for a lot of middling ones. We won county three years in a row, though we never got past the second round of the state tournament. Hazy stayed the same all three years he played: quiet, kept to himself, looked like he wasn't even interested in baseball every time he pitched. When he wasn't on the mound, he sometimes didn't even sit on the bench, just stayed in the locker room throwing that ball against the wall.

* * *

It was the middle of junior year, just after we got back to school from Christmas break, that Hazy and I made love. It was the first time he looked at me, or at least that's how I remember it. He came down the hall with his trademark blank look, then stopped at my locker. I was dropping off my history books, getting the anthology for English next period.

"What's up, Hazy?" I asked. I didn't expect an answer; it was just what I said to him whenever I saw him.

"Meet me at the backstop, Buster," he said. An order, I guess, but in that low, slow monotone of his that made it sound more like a PA announcement.

I didn't know what to say. He'd never talked to me beyond a nod unless he was on the mound.

"Meet me at the backstop," he repeated.

"Sure," I mumbled.

He nodded and turned away.

"When?" I asked his back.

"Last period. Skip gym. Bring your mitt."

* * *

So I did. He had his glove with him. I got down in my crouch, not expecting any balls I could catch. But he stared at me, looked directly at me, even bent down as if looking for a sign though I didn't make one. And he threw a strike. Heart-of-the-plate strike. I threw it back to him, crouched again, and another strike.

It went on like that for ten minutes. Then he walked off the mound and headed to the equipment shed, this small building behind home. It was supposed to be locked, but it never was. No one stole anything and the guys could use the stuff if they wanted to with their families, on trips and the like.

When I walked in, Hazy already had his shirt off. I stood there, the late-afternoon light at my back. It was a shock and yet it wasn't. It was something I'd wondered about for more than a year. I walked over to him, hugged him, and he hugged back. He looked down at me, then off. Off in his usual way, while he undressed me and we spread a mat out on the floor.

* * *

We didn't meet often, but often enough that I felt we were a couple. I never knew what Hazy felt, or who he was, really. He didn't say much, I didn't either. It was hard to deal with, being gay in Texas in the 1960s. There was one guy our year, Ronnie, who stuck out, dyed his hair bright yellow, wore a gold earring, dressed in shiny shirts and flashy pants. He had a thin, high voice, seemed to relish playing the pansy. At least until one April day he showed up to class in blue jeans and a Western shirt, his face a mess, his voice an octave lower. He made it through to the end of that semester, then disappeared. Mostly it was jokes and innuendo, towel slaps on the ass. And in the locker room, during the season, you knew not to make waves. Like the army: no harm no foul.

It went on like that, Hazy and me, catch and fuck, catch and fuck. In and out of baseball season. Once a month, every other week. He called, I came. I asked him the usual questions—when did you know? He didn't have an answer: I've been this way forever. It's why I don't like looking at people, why I stay away from the rest of the team. Easier. I try not to shower after a game, go home in my uniform. How did you know about me? Because you stopped trying to make me look at you. No one does that. Except my mom, who's always suspected and never asked. I think she's into ladies, but I don't ask either. He never asked me when I knew. I probably would have given him the same answer he gave me: forever. Long before Dad stopped beating Mom, before he stopped using his belt on Paulie and me; before he left us. Long before high school, though I went to dances and made out with girls because I thought I needed to. I didn't mind that, liked it in fact, more or less.

Hazy disappeared from my life after we lost to Dallas in the state tourney. He pitched a good game but we couldn't hit and made three errors. When he got off the team bus, he walked away same as always, banging his mitt along his left leg, then his right. I looked for him in the halls the last weeks of school but he couldn't be found. I asked a few people who had classes with him and they either couldn't remember if he was there or thought he wasn't. I went by his civics class and asked Gus, our manager, about him.

"Hazy's outta here far as I know. Said he didn't want to bother coming to class and I didn't see any reason he should. He turned in all the assignments, A work. Good enough for me. He even looked me in the eye when I shook his hand goodbye. Funny guy. Great curve."

He didn't attend graduation.

There were a few scouts at our last games. They came to see Hazy and me and one or two guys on some of the other teams. I'd talk to them on the sidelines after a game or watch as they moved over to Gus, checking out what he thought of us. Hazy avoided them. He never stayed around after a game, just sidled off the mound and was gone before I had my mask off. Once a scout ran to the pitcher's mound right after the last pitch and grabbed Hazy's arm. Hazy turned, looked over the guy's head at me and shook the scout off. Gus told me Hazy still got an offer from the Royals for their summer league but he told them no. By the end of the summer I'd heard he'd moved. He and his mom. To Houston, New Orleans, one of those towns. While I signed with the Cubs and headed to Lodi to play for the Crushers. His last surprise for me was two weeks before graduation, when Paulie came by after his shift at Kroger with a cactus.

"Hazy came in, bought this, and gave it to me to give to you. Said to tell you it doesn't need much in the way of care, why he chose it. Said to say you'd understand." ■

BROKEN
Alicia DeRollo

My mother is dying.
Her death is haunting,
a slow torture.
Although she feels it, each time,
she forgets.
For her, there is no
getting used to dying.

She lies in bed most days,
a glaze of sedation blurs
her once vivid eyes
staring now into fog,
split seconds of clarity
and confusion, always, of
who she is and how she got here …

My dad stands outside
covered in dirt,
surrounded by charred trees,
oaks and madrones that need
to be felled before they
can no longer stand
on dead roots,
shells of what was once alive.

He spends his days pouring concrete
into deeply excavated holes,
foundations created where
homes once stood
before the mountain was aflame,
now with ocean views
after everything has burned.
The absence of life looks beautiful
today, as the sun sets,
silhouette of a dream
that offers him a reprieve

from the memories of what was.

There are hundreds of seedlings
newly planted in his yard.
I caught myself staring at the
tedious task, my daughter
cross-legged,
pushing seeds into starter soil
one inch down,
covering them with dirt,
placing them in sections. 160 olive trees,
the orchard dad talked about
in younger ambition
after a pilgrimage to Greece
two decades ago.

He's rebuilding, or mending.
Solar panels will supply
energy for an irrigation system
and if all goes as planned,
next spring,
rows of cucumbers, red-leaf lettuce,
squash and more
will replenish the desolation
in this isolated fortress.

Mother lies still, and
I come to her side.
Her lucidity is a shock to me.
I feel tears streaming down my face
as sounds from her mouth
take shape.
I haven't heard her speak
in years.
She's squeezing my hand
and I wonder
how much she remembers
as she says, "I'm sorry,
I didn't know."

She lies back down and her

eyes close. I'm hoping she
has her memories in her dreams.

I join my father outside.
He's made coffee.
Our silence is a heartache
even the new life around us
cannot mask.

My mother will die
before the cucumbers form
and I will think of her
as I walk through this garden

where my children will run with
excitement, picking vegetables,
learning about olives
and the grandmother
whose soul surrounds them.

COMPOSING THE END NOTE
Kat Meads

For a little while (in the big scheme of things), I composed obituaries—or, rather, recast obituaries, condensing first-run obituaries to an accepted word count, supplying even more truncated wrap-ups of long or abruptly shortened lives, summarizing the origin, associations and achievements of the deceased, a practitioner of necessary elision.

No one offered instruction on how best to get the job done. Writing the obituary column was an offshoot part of a part-time position. And yet the survivors of alumni at a certain Bay Area university relied on a part-timer with other ambitions to extrapolate and judge the highlights of the existence of a person they loved, perhaps even cherished, her three-to-five-sentence paragraph the means by which to announce to other alumni that they had lost one of their own.

The In Memoriam column originally appeared on the back pages of the university magazine, a fiftyish-page quarterly publication. Regardless of positioning, in the university's semiannual marketing surveys, readers reported that they first turned to the Class Notes section, then to In Memoriam, a reading order seemingly unaffected by sharper typefaces, splashier covers or more topical feature stories. In essence, readers first checked out the brags of the competition, then checked which alumni they no longer competed against. As the university grew, so grew the number of its dead alumni. A point of reckoning was upon us. At one of our weekly staff meetings, the newly hired editor declared that obituaries were taking up too much valuable space in the publication; that the dead, to put it bluntly, were not—or were no longer—university donors. His immediate boss, also at the meeting, also a new hire, agreed. I remember voicing feeble protest along the lines of "but ... second-most-read section." I like to think, at this remove, that the dissent was not entirely motivated by a fear of my part-time hours becoming even more part-time, but certainly fear was in the mix. In any case, a compromise was reached. The In Memoriam column would thereafter appear only online, readers directed to that online location by a boxed notice included on the last page, bottom right corner, of the print publication. At the time of the switch, I was still writing obituaries that mentioned service in World War II and Korea. At the time, it didn't seem unreasonable to doubt that all surviving spouses of World War II veterans owned a computer with a reliable internet connection.

My mother, who was of an age to be a World War II widow and who never once touched a computer, subscribed to the daily newspaper published in the nearest town. It arrived in the afternoon, usually after my mother had finished her pressing work of the day, and with her afternoon cup of coffee she settled into a favorite chair, which offered a view of the front yard and woods, unrolled the *Daily Advance*, paged through to the obituary listings and started her reading there. I say read, but perhaps the more accurate word is study. If the death notice pertained to someone in her immediate community, as likely as not she was already aware of the demise and knew the deceased as well as the survivors. Nonetheless, there were other details to parse: confirmation of the funeral home handling the arrangements, the date and time and location of the funeral itself, whether or not a graveside service would follow the church service, which minister would be officiating. In my mother's community, whether or not the dead had "stepped foot in a church" anytime in collective memory, the ritual of a church funeral service was mandatory. Bible verses had to be read, hymns had to be sung, the family seated on the front pews had to be assured by the minister and by implication all in attendance that the soul of the corpse fitted into the casket before them had long since departed for a better locale. Whether or not every person among the bereaved believed in the sequence, whether or not all in the church believed it, was of no consequence. During a funeral service, one comported oneself as if one believed.

When my mother died, two employees of the nearest town's funeral home, the same funeral home that had overseen my grandmother's funeral, my father's funeral and the funeral of virtually everyone who had died in the community in which my brother and I were born and raised, arrived late afternoon and sat in chairs at the kitchen table while my brother and I sat side by side on a bench across from them. I remember thinking that, while I had somewhat mastered the job of excerpting and condensing the obituaries of alumni of a university three thousand miles away, I would never have been able to master the logistics of the job being then performed: consulting with the relatives of the recent dead. What if those relatives were speechless with grief? What if they nonsensically raved? What if they could not bring themselves to fix on even the smallest detail of the many that must be decided? Because my mother's death was not the shock my father's had been, my brother and I were able to convey our mother's wishes with minimal back-and-forth. My mother wanted to be, and was, cremated because my father, breaking community protocols, had chosen to be cremated and she followed her husband's lead. When we reached the point in the conversation when one of the two funeral home employees in our mother's kitchen gently asked what we would like her "obituary to say," I remember noticing he held a notebook but not a tape recorder. And because I am familiar with notebooks and taking notes, I wondered how accurate a transcriber he would have been had we needed that particular Twiford Funeral Home service and whether the published version would have resembled what I would have remembered my brother and I sharing about our mother's life. It was then I pulled from my pocket our mother's handwritten obituary, composed many years before, and handed it to the funeral home employee who had come prepared to take notes. He scanned the page, then asked, again gently, if we wanted to "add anything," and we said no, that the obituary she had written was the obituary she wanted published. I remember feeling relief when the point was settled because if the public obituary was a replica of the one our mother had written, we, her children, could not be accused of tampering with her version of her life or rewriting its content to suit our tastes. This happened not to be an outlandish worry. Both my brother and I had been privy to caviling family discussions about death notices, complaints lodged about what was and was not mentioned in what order and with what emphasis. Complaints, in other words, about the obituary's composition.

I am now of an age when most in my circle have dealt with the death of parents and are now dealing with the deaths of partners, spouses, friends, colleagues and, in two harrowing, unthinkable instances, children. I have, in the last month, made more in-honor-of donations to chosen causes and charities than I have during the whole of my life. I have written more letters of sympathy, struggling to convey a concern and sorrow that avoids the standard clichés, even as I remember in my fresh grief being comforted by clichés and amplified condolences. A slight acquaintance had said: "My heart breaks for you." A cousin had said: "It doesn't seem like it now, but it will get better." On the steps of my parents' house, the house too full of people to enter, the father of a family known forever had said:

"Your daddy was the best friend I ever had."

I have, either in due course or in a course accelerated by the pandemic, taken up my mother's habit of obituary study. Unlike my mother but like most who currently read obituaries, I read them online. Primarily I read the obituary listings posted on the Facebook page of the funeral home that buried my parents. As expected, I scan first for names I recognize. Thereafter I read the obituaries of strangers, freer to focus on narrative choices. I am—again, unsurprisingly—most struck by write-ups that dispense with the usual measured, neutral tone and opt for some flash and over-the-top superlatives: "Jackie's personality was both charming and captivating. She was a pure joy to be around. She was beautiful with a flawless complexion." Or trade in anger: "The Bible says that all Christians suffer. Jesus suffered and was hated and misunderstood during His earthly years, and arguably still. In the end, even his friends turned their backs on him. His servant Claire Alice Stevens Moore had a hard life but never dwelled on it." I also read the comments that follow the official obituary. "Poor Hazel. I really liked her. She was such a kind person. She did not deserve what was done to her." The next commentator asks: "What happened to her?" An intriguing question that goes unanswered.

It has lately occurred to me that the fiction I have written, taken altogether, is low on body count. I'm not convinced that statistic is a result, as many an instructor had advised, of steering clear of deathbed scenes, but I don't have an alternative theory. In my deserter novel, a character dies because it made sense that a character already ill and exposed to the elements would die on a mountaintop in winter. In my mystery novel, a character dies because someone has to die in a mystery although mine dies accidentally in the third to last chapter. I did once write a novel narrated by a ghost, but that setup is the very definition of an offstage death. And then, as if I'd been working very hard in my tallying not to remember, I remembered my novel about a young woman who takes her own life, a character whose trajectory toward death and the development of death as solution in her mind so permeated the book that it proved a very difficult one for me to finish. And only then did I realize that I have not written what I classify as a novel since.

Another something I have not written, or pre-written, is my obituary. Unlike my mother, I can't fathom taking on such a project. Which "facts" to foreground? Which to soft-pedal? Which to skip altogether? If I wrote my obituary, I would have to edit my obituary.

I would have to be ultra aware, supremely conscious, of how the finished product would be received. I would be shaping a narrative for an audience. And hasn't there been enough of that already? Isn't that what I've been doing here? ∎

ODDBALLS
Peter Ferry

Even before she stepped off the plane from Dallas–Fort Worth, Ethel Long had made the decision to abandon all formality, to leave behind a lifetime of self-consciousness and race awareness and to assume the prerogative of the elderly, the foreign and the innocent; she would speak her mind at all times. The result was that she became an object of amusement to the Dutch townspeople. She spoke no Dutch, not even *goededag* or *tot ziens*, and her English was both loud and heavily accented in East Texas twang. "Ya'll know what I mean" was her characteristic retort to anything, and it was generally true. "Give me about a pound of that potato salad, will ya, darlin'?" She left it to the shopkeepers to do the conversion, which most did without complaint. When she walked down the little shopping street in the village, people looked up and smiled.

Pieter seemed to have taken his cues from his grandmother. Not at first, of course. In his earliest memories, he was a tiny boy sitting in the middle of the floor playing with blocks and listening to his mother and grandmother talking, and thinking three things. The first of these was that he understood what they were saying. The second was that they didn't know he understood what they were saying. The third was that he should never forget that he understood things he was not intended to. *When I'm a dad*, he would think, *I won't forget that my kids aren't dumb, that they know a lot more than grown-ups think they do.*

One of the first things that he "knew" was that while the palms of his hands and the soles of his feet looked much like those of Dutch children, the rest of his skin did not. It was a different color. It was brown. He remembered feeling sorry for Dutch children because they were so pale. He thought that they had been bleached because he had watched his mother use bleach on a stained tablecloth. His hair was different, too, and sometimes other tiny children would reach out and touch it. The two mothers would be talking somewhere over there, and the little girl he was playing with would toddle across and reach up and touch his hair. He was what his mother called "special" and his grandmother called "one of a kind," so from the beginning he knew that he wasn't like the other kids, at least some of them. In fact, when another Black boy appeared in his kindergarten, he was taken aback. He was no longer quite so special.

Of course, it didn't help that the teachers put the two Black boys together for no apparent reason other than that they were both Black. And although he couldn't have been older than five and was probably four, Pieter made that assumption and was offended. Offended enough to think of it years later as the first time he had been socially conscious of his race. That day he played with girls although he was to remember one of them looking at him as if he had broken a rule. Maybe he had. He was also to remember the other Black boy crying. Was it because of him? It must have been; why else would he remember it? Funny how so many of his associations of that year were concentrated in that one morning. Otherwise, all he could remember of kindergarten was a boy he liked who had a pronounced cowlick, a large-bosomed teacher who had body odor and a gentle voice, and a day his grandmother was late in picking him up. He had been frightened. He had sat alone waiting for her in an office empty except for one teacher marking papers, a very small boy in a very large chair.

Later Pieter went through a period when the fact that he was different caused him a good bit of grief and got him into a number of fist fights, especially when other kids teased him by calling him Zwarte Piet. Like most little kids, all he wanted to do was to be the same as everyone else. Then one day, his mother, with a sad little smile and a shake of her head, said, "My, you are an oddball, aren't you?" and he took it as a compliment. It became his mantra, his MO, and as often the only Black kid in the village, it was not a difficult role to fulfill. There were other Black kids in the school on the army base where his mother taught, but none lived in the town, none had a Dutch stepfather, and none spoke Dutch as Pieter did.

In large part, this was his stepfather's doing. It was Alfons who had insisted that Pieter go to the local kindergarten and always spoke to him in Dutch. The result was interesting. In fairly short order, especially when he started first grade, Pieter went from feeling that he belonged in neither the town nor on the base to feeling that he belonged in either and just maybe both. For one thing, he was one of the few kids in the base school whose parents were not being regularly redeployed. This meant that he and his mother quickly became senior members of the school community. At an early age he found himself interpreting for his school friends and sometimes their parents, often standing beside them at store counters, desks or service windows explaining something in English or saying it in Dutch. He also found himself explaining school procedure, history, custom and tradition to his teachers and even to the school administrators, who understood things in a military culture but not always in a Dutch one. "At the end of the term," he would say, "kids hang their satchels and backpacks out their bedroom windows. It's just what they do here. It means that they have passed."

Understanding his relationship with Alfons van Hest was more difficult. In the beginning, Alfons called Pieter "my boy," which, of course, he was not, and Pieter called Alfons "Opa," which sounded ridiculous and actually means "Grandpa." So for a couple years while they were figuring out who they were and what they were and what they were going to be, they weren't much of anything to each other. And as is often the case, it took a fight to make things right.

Alfons had been in the habit of greeting the customers in his butcher shop at Christmastime as Saint Nicholas, or Sinterklaas as he was known in the Netherlands. In the Dutch version of the story, Saint Nick has a long white beard but dresses in ecclesiastical robes, arrives each November on a boat from Africa, is celebrated on December fifth, which is Saint Nicholas Day, and is dignified rather than jolly. That job is left to an elfin blackface boy named Zwarte Piet, who is a playful prankster and Sinterklaas's foil. Alfons thought it might be fun if Pieter played that role. After all, everyone in Holland loved Zwarte Piet. Everyone except Pieter Long and his mother. Pieter's grandmother Ethel rolled her eyes, shook her head, and stayed out of it, but so embarrassed were Eleanor and Pieter that for a while they had trouble overcoming it. They talked to each other in English over, around and through Alfons, as if he weren't there. He sulked and pouted. He bought Eleanor elaborate pastries and Pieter the strong licorice candies called drop that Dutch people like. They deigned to accept these. Eleanor was biding her time trying to figure out a way out of this mess. Pieter, on the other hand, was building up a head of steam. He finally blew when Alfons innocently introduced him to a neighbor as "my son."

"I am not your son!" he screamed in English. "And you are not my father!" This took place in Alfons's shop, which was full of customers, all of whom fell silent, turned and looked. What they saw was the big Dutch man go down on his knees and clasp the Black boy to his body. "Let me go! Let me go! Leave me alone!" screamed Pieter. "I hate drrrop!" he said, even pronouncing the rolled *r*.

Alfons hung on and sobbed instead. He smothered the little boy in his stomach and Pieter found himself hanging on, too, maybe to keep from being swallowed by the big man's body. He was almost hugging Alfons, if in self-defense. Maybe he *was* hugging him. No one knew what the butcher was blubbering about, but they didn't need to. Then Pieter's mother was there. And it wasn't at all certain what she was doing or who she was doing it for or to, and that wasn't necessary either, because whatever the three of them were doing, they were doing it together. Eleanor and Pieter were shocked by and then sobered by and finally moved by the big man's display of emotion. It is possible that they didn't know until then how much they meant to him. At any rate, Pieter never dressed up as Zwarte Piet, and Alfons never again played the role of Sinterklaas.

* * *

When Pieter Long was eleven, his mother and grandmother took him to Texas for summer vacation. Eleanor waited that long because she wanted the boy to have some sense of where he came from, but not too much of one. And she wanted to feel like a stranger. She wanted people to have almost forgotten her. She wanted them to remark on her clothes, to dredge up old memories, to say, "Well, I'll be darned." She wanted people to say, "She went off to teach in Europe and never came back. Uh-huh. Got her mother over there too."

And it was all true. Eleanor had started her own small tutoring service specializing in businesspeople. She taught Dutch people English and sometimes Americans Dutch. In order to do so, she'd had to master Dutch. Eventually she stopped teaching at the Department of Defense school altogether. In the meantime, her mother, Ethel, became a local character, playing the role of the "sweet old American" as opposed to the ugly one. She rode a three-wheeled bicycle and Wednesday afternoons she played mahjong on the army base. She and Eleanor were point and counterpoint. While Eleanor virtually became Dutch, her mother gleefully did not. She spoke only English, and she refused to eat raw herring even when it was served on a bun with onions. "Uh-uh. No thank you."

Alfons didn't go with Eleanor, Ethel and Pieter to Texas. He wasn't invited. Later Pieter would wonder why. Were they embarrassed by him? By his Saint Bernard demeanor, his banana fingers, his oversized everything, explosive laughter and relentless eagerness? Were they afraid of some kind of racial incident because he was white and they were not? Or was it a class thing? Was it about the education that both of them had and he didn't? Were they afraid that he'd spit out American beer and laugh at yellow mustard?

Perhaps they thought that people would take to him too readily. Maybe it was really about them. Pieter certainly noticed that his mother and grandmother were different people in America. They were more proper. Put more accurately, they practiced a certain propriety that they did not in Holland. They walked slower, stood straighter, spoke more carefully, dressed every day as if they were going to church and held their heads a little higher. Pieter watched their reflections in the train window out of Memphis and across Arkansas and Louisiana and down into Texas. Who were these people?

And he watched himself. Who was he? He saw other Black kids looking at him. He didn't think he looked different than them, but apparently he did. A kid in the train station asked him, "Where'd you get them shoes?" In Texas he caught other people being curious about him. At the church they went to, people crowded around them. He was introduced formally: "Pieter Long, Malcolm T. Long's grandson."

"Oh." People shook his hand. A little boy called him "sir." He heard another say, "He talks like one of those English boys you see on channel thirteen."

"Say this," they would ask him, and then laugh when he did. "What do you call that?" they would ask, and then laugh again, but not unkindly. Rather it was as if he was a fascination, an African or a talking dog. They asked him if they had movies over there. Television? What kind of car did his family drive? Did he know who Michael Jackson was? P. Diddy? Did Dutch people really wear wooden shoes?

"Well, when they work in the garden." That one got a big laugh.

Did he live in a windmill? Finally he realized some of them were making fun of him. Only then was he proud to be Dutch; he'd never before that moment even thought of himself as Dutch. Only then did he look at the American kids as provincial. "Have you ever been to Paris?" he would ask them. "How about Amsterdam?" He taught them to say swear words in Dutch, and they would run around laughing and shouting, "*Kut, klote, tering! Godverdomme!*"

He had one tiny six-year-old cousin everyone called Otto, who watched him carefully and constantly. He stood very close to Pieter, often touching his sleeve or pantleg. Pieter found him annoying. Finally, he said, "What can I do for you, Otto?"

"My name's not Otto. It's Harold."

"Otto ain't who he is," said another cousin, who was eleven, like

Pieter. "It's what he is. He's autoistic."

"What's that?" asked Pieter.

"Kinda like being a retard," said the other cousin.

"No it's not," said Harold. "Besides the word is 'autistic.' And Mom says I'm very smart."

"Sure you are," said the other cousin.

The next day the little guy was there again standing too close. "Hiya, Harold. What do you want today?"

"Got any candy?"

"Candy? Got some Dutch candy." Alfons had sneaked a bag of very strong, ammonia-smelling drop into Pieter's suitcase as a kind of joke exactly because he knew Pieter didn't like it, and now Pieter saw a way of getting rid of Harold and the licorice at the same time. To his surprise, Harold loved the stuff. Then Pieter knew quite suddenly that Harold would love anything Pieter gave him. He looked at the kid again. He had never been anyone's hero before.

"Delicious!" said the little boy. "Scrumptious! What's it called?"

"Drrrop," said Pieter, exaggerating the roll of the *r*.

"Drrrop," said Harold.

"Hey that was good."

"Drrrop," said Harold again, grinning.

Pieter began to look forward to Harold coming around. Maybe it was because the kid didn't treat him as if he were an alien. Nor did he insist on talking. Harold was quite comfortable being quiet, and Pieter realized that speaking only English all day long was tiring. He began to speak to Harold in Dutch. Strangely the kid seemed to understand. "*Ja*," he would say and nod. "*Ik snap het*," which was a phrase he picked up from Pieter meaning, "I get it."

I'll be darned. He really is smart, thought Pieter. He began to teach Harold Dutch words. Harold repeated them. His pronunciation was flawless; he was a perfect mimic.

One day Harold said to Pieter, "You and I are alike."

"What do you mean?"

"We're not like them." He nodded toward the other kids.

"Hmmm. I guess we're not," said Pieter with a little regret because he had been trying to be "like them," but also with a little strange pride and a little appreciation for Harold's perceptiveness. "You and me," he told Harold, "we're oddballs."

They began to call each other that. "Hey, Oddball."

"How you doin', Oddball?"

Coming out of church that Sunday, Harold took Pieter's hand, almost as if Pieter were his mother. Pieter extricated himself as gracefully as he could, at the same time sending a little message. Harold didn't get it. He smiled up at Pieter and took his hand again.

When Pieter, Eleanor and Ethel left for the airport to go home, Harold's mother drove them to the train station and Harold rode along. As the train pulled out, he stood on the platform waving. Pieter waved back.

At Christmastime back in Holland, Pieter sent Harold an assortment of Dutch licorice. The postage alone cost more than he spent on his mother's present and Alfons's combined. The postmaster looked over his glasses. "You sure about this?"

"Yes, sir."

"Who is this Harold?"

"He's my little cousin."

"Well, he must be a pretty special young one."

"Yes, sir, he is."

Sometime later Pieter got a Polaroid in the mail from Harold's mother of his cousin with a grinning mouthful of licorice so big it blacked out his teeth. Peter smiled. "Oddball," he said. ∎

ODE TO OIL
Pablo Neruda

—Translation by Wally Swist

Nearby the noisy
grain, from the waves
of the wind in the oats,

the olive tree,

silver volume,
stern in its lineage,
in its crooked
terrestrial heart:
the graceful
olives
polished
by fingers
that made
the dove
and the sea snail:
green,
innumerable,
most pure
pieces of nature,
and there
in
the dry
olive groves,
where
just
blue sky with cicadas
and hard ground
exist,
there
the prodigy,
the perfect
capsule
of the olive

fill the foliage with constellations:
later
the vessels,
the miracle,
the oil.

I love
the homelands of oil,
the olive groves
of Chacabuco, in Chile,
in the morning
the platinum feathers
of the forest
against the wrinkled
mountain ranges,
in Anacapri, above
over the Tyrrhenian light,
the desperation of the olives,
and on the map of Europe,
Spain,
a black basket of olives
sprinkled with orange blossoms
as if by gusts from the sea.

Oil,
hidden and supreme,
determining the stew,
base for the partridges,
celestial key of mayonnaise,
soft and tasty
on lettuce,
and supernatural in the hell
of the archiepiscopal mackerel.
Oil, with our voice,
our choir,
with intimate
powerful softness
you sing:
you are the Castilian
vernacular:
there are syllables of oil,

there are words
useful and accented
like your fragrant matter.
Not only the wine sings,
but also the oil;
it lives in us with its mature light,
and among the goods of the earth
apart,
oil,
your inexhaustible peace, your green essence,
your brimming treasure that descends
from the springs of the olive tree.

ODA AL ACEITE
Pablo Neruda

Cerca del rumoroso
cereal, de las olas
del viento en las avenas,

el olivio

de volume plateado,
severo en su linaje,
en su torcido
corazon terrestre:
las gracilles
olivas
par los dedos
que hicieron
la paloma
y el caracel
marino:
verdes,
immumerables,

puisimos
pezones
de la naturaleza,
y alli
en
los secos
olivares,
donde
tan solo
cielo azul con cigarras,
y tierra dura
existen,
alli
el prodigio,
la capsula
perfecta de la oliva
llenado con sus constelaciones el follaje:
mas tarde
las vasijas,
el milagro,
el aceite.

Yo amo
las patrias del aceite,
las olivares
de Chacabuco, en Chile,
en la manana
las plumas de platino
forestales
contra las arrugadas
cordilleras,
en Anacapri, arriba,
sobre la luz tirrena,
la desesperacion de los olivos,
y en el mapa de Europa,
Espana,
cesta negra de aceitunes
espolvoreada por los azahares
como por una rafaga marina.

Aceite,
recondita y suprema
condicion de la olla,
pedestal de perdices,
llave celeste de la mayonesa,
suave y sabrosa
sobre las lechugas
y sobrenatural en el infierno
de los arzobispales pejerreyes.
Aceite, en nuestra a voz, en
nuestro coro,
con
intima
suavidad poderosa
cantas:
eres idioma
castellano:
hay silabas de aceite,
hay palabras
como tu fragante materia.
No solo canta el vino,
tambien en nosotros con su luz madura
y entre las bienes de la tierra
aparto,
aceite
tu inagotable paz, tu esencia verde,
tu colmado tesoro que desiende
desde las manantiales del olivo.

OTHER PEOPLE
Emily Coletta

Hilleborg suggested we lie down in the field and wait for the harvester to run us over. The harvester driver was a man named Lars Larsen, who wore overalls without shirts and in whom Hilleborg, two years my senior, was abundantly interested. Lars had a flat head and puffy arms and looked dumb, to me. I cannot confirm if he was free of sock in his wellies, but it wouldn't have surprised me. Ever present he was, clopping around. Hilleborg pinched her nipples before talking to him.

"Girls," Lars Larsen said.

"Nice day for a harvest," I said.

"Don't talk," Hilleborg told me.

She wedged a hay bale into her crotch and looked at Lars, who had pearled himself into the harvester's clamshell. I threatened my canker sores. Lars fiddled with the controls.

"Come on," she said. "Let's lie down in the field."

The harvester devoured the field in a still far-off fashion. My little brother, a few months old, had been wailing through the night. Sleeplessness sandbagged my limbs. The sun broiled my scalp.

"He's going to be sorry," Hilleborg said.

She hiked up her shirt. Chaff stuck in her belly creases, something I could have extracted with my fingernail, had we been in different circumstances. Grasshoppers landed on us, fleeing Lars and his harvester.

"Gross," she said.

I wanted a glass of water. We could go to the demonstration farm, where the German volunteers swung scythes and convinced Clydesdales to pull a plow as was done in the old days. We could drink water from the hand pump and pilfer carrots. There was little that satisfied me more than a cold carrot, eased from the ground.

All my ideas were about things we had done before, not these things of Hilleborg, which we had not yet done.

"They're not gross. Their homes are being destroyed," I said. Beyond my lack of imagination, I was recently vegetarian and responsible for the animal kingdom.

"Why don't you take your shirt off?" she said.

"I want a drink of water!"

"Your bra too!"

Now we were shouting.

She waited until Lars was about twenty meters away, then she sprang up and pulled me alongside her. She pressed her mouth against mine. All through the harvester's quieting, she groaned and raked my back. That's when I figured, incorrectly, that my life would end—frozen, clumsy, my chest a ribbed baking sheet against the new breasts of Hilleborg.

* * *

I wouldn't necessarily have remembered this, in such acute detail, had I not run into Hilleborg at the grocery store.

Hilleborg, in the intervening decades, had become torpedo shaped and powerful. She reminded me of that Russian spy whale on the news, the grinning one, who required social interaction and settled for stealing and retrieving electronics from kayakers. There wasn't anything in her personality to suggest this. The resemblance stemmed from the clamp of her mouth, the powder on her face, and my feeling that she knew more than I did. Veins ran their blue circuitry through her temples. She was back for a funeral and, having left the country shortly after the harvester incident, she spoke with the accent of an old Danish hick.

"He worked in the post office. You'd know him if you saw him," Hilleborg said of a deceased uncle. I thought of the anonymous old men in the post office, of whom I saw so little, having a mailbox of my own. I stood there, receiving the information, and nodded with consolation. A mature woman, a grocery shopper, a catcher-upper.

"Where are you staying?" I asked.

"Klørup."

I had been to Klørup for a golf brunch with Matias. Matias didn't golf, but it was early in his time with his company, and he was still making an effort to appear game and sporting. Historically, his efforts were adequate to make my life enjoyable.

"My aunt lives out there. She's been there since we were kids," she said. "Do you have kids?" she continued, looking around, shaking her pasta as if to lure them.

"No. And you?"

"Mine are four and seven," she said. "You're married."

She pointed at my wedding band. I could spin it, which surely portended something. "I was married too. Now divorced."

Hilleborg then returned the pasta to the shelf and bid me

farewell. She'd be here for another week, in the first house as you turn towards Klørup. She gave me directions that were too detailed for my interest in visiting her. Told me she was a massage therapist.

On my way home from the grocery store, I began to think that Hilleborg was lying to me. That she didn't have children or a dead uncle. She hadn't even bought the pasta. She was back to punish me for having tattled on her. I knew this was ridiculous, but it didn't stop me from imagining Hilleborg in the basement of her Connecticut home, standing at a large board, circling my face with chalk and reaffixing thumbtacks, yarn, and painter's tape gone less sticky over her twenty-year investigation.

At home, Matias's car was in his spot. I had the groceries. It was Tuesday. I had gotten careless with my life. I could have ceased living as easily as I removed my clogs in the entry.

* * *

After dinner, as was his custom, Matias read. His neck bent in an unhealthy way. His mouth hung open. This man was supposed to give me long-fingered, intelligent children and calendar years of both bliss and wooden structure. I sat near him as his attention flowered elsewhere. For a half an hour after his reading, he remained unresponsive. Perhaps, during this time, he affixed information to parties who would appreciate it. I thought to ask him this, pleased with my hypothesis, of which I was convinced before asking him.

"Matias—"

"Yes?"

"What are you reading?"

"A book about Swedish conservatism."

"When you read, about something like conservatism, are you remembering bits and pieces for someone who might be interested in it?"

"Not really."

"Really?"

"Do you do that?"

"No, not really I guess," I said.

I did the washing up. *Now he is going to shower*, I thought to myself, and was pleased when I heard the water run.

My discomfort about Matias's sexual requests presented itself as feeling hungover, in the mornings, or sick to my stomach, in the evenings. It exacerbated my hay fever and sciatica, as if, in weakening me, I would have to turn to him, as he turned to me, with weakness. I could forget about it, but my body could not.

I searched for Hilleborg on the internet. There she was, ten years younger, with a closed-lip smile. She had linked to her profile massage videos in which people shook and groaned. I could have read instead. I could have deleted emails. Matias was already asleep, his brain pulsing with learning, eyes covered with a mask.

On the cluttered island of pre-sleep, I recalled how Lars Larsen had chased us, shirtless, through the fields. He pushed Hilleborg and told her to never do something like that ever again. He said that she had endangered our lives. Hilleborg cried all the way back to my house, where my mother was asleep on the living room couch.

"You need to be quiet," I told her.

I pulled over her head one of my training bras and a shirt she had borrowed before. She was incapable of providing preference, snotty in the face.

In the kitchen, I assembled a tray with cheese, buns, two glasses, a tall, unopened bottle of hyldeblomst saft, and, graciously, a package of ham for Hilleborg, who had remained omnivorous. I drank straight out of the tap, great gulps of water, one eye on my sleeping family, the other closed to keep the water from splashing into it.

"I'm going to cut off my hair," Hilleborg said, collapsed against my dresser.

"I can't get the little scissors, they're in the coffee table," I said. "Besides, you have really nice hair."

"I'm going to cut off my hair."

I tried to get her to eat, built for her a ham-and-cheese bun, brought it up to her face, where she fanned it away, barely able to lift her arm.

"Honestly, I couldn't at a time like this," she said. "He is a disgusting man."

When she finally took a bite, she spit the meat and bread back onto the tray, where it sat, a wet, chewed bolus, until I pinched it with a sock and, suppressing a gag, buried it in the bathroom trash.

"He is a disgusting man," she repeated.

* * *

On Wednesday, Matias rose, breakfasted, packed his lunch, and got dressed. I had gotten into the habit of staying in bed as long as possible, remembering my dreams, which cast me in situations more meaningful than those in my waking life. Only once Matias left, leaving the imprints of his morning routines—counter wet with his wiping, toothbrush in its hole, pointed always away from the toilet—did I check my assignments for the rest of the week.

I was to go to Klørup. A sure coincidence, but I couldn't help but to think of Hilleborg, scheming in her basement.

Her aunt's house hunched behind a thicket of hedges at the edge of town. A sign on crimped metal legs read "Massage" and listed a telephone number, the last few digits squished to fit. I continued on to the house where the state had directed me, via a third-party contractor, to clean house.

My client—elderly and slow-moving—showed me the cleaning supplies, the cupboard where the cat food was kept, and her greenhouse, inviting me to take whatever I wanted. The greenhouse was empty save one vigorous oregano. Perhaps I was to take something nonmaterial, some understanding, or moment, yet to be revealed. I could see into the neighboring yard, a replica of this one, with a small lawn, wide back door, neat hedges.

A teenager entered without knocking.

"This is Sofia."

The girl's hair was lime green, cropped to a radioactive fuzz. Her eyebrows were done in the same green and terminated at the pupil. She shimmered with youth, or else had applied a new generation of makeup capable of making women micaceous and unencumbered. She wore a corset as a shirt. I clenched my toes.

"I met a neighbor. Outside the cul-de-sac. Young guy. We got caught up in backgammon," she said, verily skipping to the fridge. No amount of backgammon could generate that spring. *Is this the message?* I wondered, firm-lipped and trousered, but wanting, very much, the understanding my client seemed to have promised me. My client put two, shaking, thumbs up.

"I'm glad you met someone," she said to the girl.

* * *

Hilleborg spent the night, the day of the harvester incident. In the gathering dark, she used a net to raise my guppy out of the tank. I only employed this net when I changed the tank's water, airlifting the fish for some short, terrifying moments before depositing him in a pint glass and dutifully bucket washing his gravel. Hilleborg barked with laughter. She poked him on the soft side of his body. It felt like she was poking me.

"I think he's been out enough," I said.

"How do you know he is a boy?"

"I don't know."

"He should be punished. Let's see who can leave him out longest."

She put the fish on the carpet. I scooped him up after a moment's flopping and put him back in the tank. It was the first time I had touched him. We left the top off the tank. I left the top off the tank.

"You're a coward," she told me and went to sleep.

In the morning, my fish was dead on a napkin. Hilleborg lay in a muddle of blankets on the floor.

"You killed my fish," I shouted, pounced on her.

"You're crazy. He jumped out of his own accord. The top was off," Hilleborg shouted back.

She then bit me, hard enough to leave marks, and ran away, still in my striped shirt. I hid my fish in the top drawer of my dresser, ashamed of it, and sat with a blaring blankness before descending to the kitchen. My mother held up the home phone.

"Has Lars ever made you uncomfortable? Lars, the field hand?"

"Uncomfortable?"

"Has he ever said or done anything that made you uncomfortable? Maybe something of a sexual nature?"

"No," I managed.

"Hilleborg's mother called and said that something happened yesterday that has really upset Hilleborg and that it has to do with Lars."

I then bared everything, greedily. That Hilleborg had insisted we lie out in the field and take our clothes off. I left out the part about how he chased us. That seemed to be an appropriate punishment.

I saw child Hilleborg just once more, a flash of her, running out of sight from behind her front window. A For Rent sign went up at their house and the spigot got a new, coiled hose. Cushions appeared on the porch swing. I never returned to play in the fields. I made another friend, closer to my age and tediously interested in Iron Age history, before my family moved south.

* * *

Matias cooked again. Reasonable, he was, latticing lasagna. Heavy, he made it, this reasonable husbandness, rendering his deviance light in the balance. At the dinner table, the clock ticked loud enough to hurt my jaw. The bricks of the house were six thick and deafened the sounds outside in favor of the chewing and ticking and throat clearing inside. In this inside, Matias announced he was going fishing with

Klaus on the weekend.

My sciatica flared.

"Where is the bait?"

"At Klaus's," he said.

"His wife would not abide the bait," I said. I did not recognize myself anymore. These days sprouted strangeness. Everything was fine when I had to go to work. But he would be leaving on the weekend.

"What do you mean?" he said.

Saturday arrived and I indeed had nothing to do. I watched Klaus and Matias outside, with their sensible hats and vests. Klaus drank coffee out of a travel mug, wore boots up to his knees. A nice man. My life would surely be easier if I was married to Klaus. It would be a favor to Klaus, also, his wife being an anemic bore who could not cease suggesting I volunteer at the genbrugsbutik. One of her jobs was to price the furniture and then, after a month's passing, slash the price in half with a red pen. She had told me this several times.

Matias and Klaus crunched down the drive and beeped twice. An hour passed by the big clock and during it, I became immobile.

In my mind, Matias and Klaus turn away from the highway and find a house that looks normal from the outside, but, on the inside, it is dark enough as to be night. The windows are blacked out. A crowded house party gets increasingly explicit the higher they climb. They ascend the stairs, holding hands, looking at one another and licking their lips, so pleased at their luck. Each room holds some new delight. They put their penises through holes in the walls. Strangers tug and pull and suck on them from the other side. They lie on tables with holes in them to the same effect. All the while, they ruffle each other's hair companionably.

There sits the fishing gear, unused in the car, the campsite, unbroken, and Klaus's wife, variously cleaning the genbrugsbutik or masturbating furtively in a bathtub. Meanwhile, her husband—her nice, jolly husband—pulls himself through the eye of one thousand degrading, oily iterations.

* * *

I should have called first, to Hilleborg's aunt's house. I had six hundred kronner folded in my pocket. It was a miracle I got off the couch at all.

Hilleborg answered with wet hair, her face undone. Less

grinning and superior, this time, than the Russian beluga whale. In a room with a raised bed and face cradle, she told me to undress. The room's contents once took up the whole space, but they were now all shoved to one side. The blinds were drawn, a lamp lit.

"Any injuries I should know about?"

"Sciatica. If you could do something for that—"

"Not really," she said.

I expected Holy Rolling. I figured that some hair-clogged drain in me would open. Instead, Hilleborg manipulated my body in a superficial, clumsy way. She swore when she spilled oil on the carpet, dark spots I could see through the porthole of my cradle. She rushed away to get a towel, then blotted the carpet with it. I apologized.

"As if it was your fault," Hilleborg said, a familiar note in her voice.

After the massage, she didn't rise to make coffee. I wondered where her aunt was. Under my clothes, especially at the nape of my neck, I could feel the oil and it made me walk as if all my clothes were too big for me.

I creased the bills, tented them on the table.

"I didn't ask you your rate," I said.

"This is fine."

"I mean, I can go back to the cash machine."

"No, this is fine."

"Well—"

"Thanks for stopping by," Hilleborg said. She folded her hands on some paperwork. If this was spending my time wisely and having a life outside of the marriage, I wasn't interested in it.

I gathered my keys. I wouldn't make one of those apologies that required a lot of work on the part of the other person.

"Hilleborg, I'm sorry for what happened, when we were kids."

She scanned my face. I prepared myself for adolescent wrath.

"I was lucky to leave," she said. "Lars Larsen? Isn't that who you're talking about? He was molesting three other kids."

"Of course, yes, of course," I found myself saying.

"Terrible," she said.

"Terrible," I echoed, and wished her a happy return to the States.

* * *

Lars Larsen, if he still lived in my hometown, would be staying in an outbuilding on the farm, next to the hunting club's headquarters.

I drove north, unheeding of other cars in roundabouts, uncaring of my hunger or my thirst or the fuel gauge dropping ever lower. It rained. Just brief summer bursts of it. I listened to no music and, upon arriving, two hours later, I let the car stall at the base of the driveway.

There was the pond, with its rickety dock, the lawns manicured around it. A small, automated mower ran without a pilot. This was new. The filbert archway remained. Many trees had been cut behind the houses, but the wood remained gloomy, as if by letting more light in, you could better see its degradation. The same black slugs clotted the drive. My shoes became quickly wet at the toe.

The hunting lodge stood empty. My hopes for public shaming and finger-pointing expired on the spot. No dead foxes hung from hooks. No incomprehensible, cigar-smoking men looked upon me with rheumy eyes. No Lars Larsen. No blazing fire in the hearth. No lazy flies, salty salamis, used cheese knives.

I wanted clear evil. I wanted to throw an axe and have it nearly miss a man's head and I wanted to stand, chest heaving, and take well-articulated issue with the men of this world who get to do whatever the hell they want. What I found instead was the groundskeeper's house. Its door hung open. From the inside came a scurry. I walked by, waiting to be summoned. I even sat outside, in the courtyard, sunning my face. Finally, I had to knock.

The little girl who answered didn't know me but bid me enter nonetheless. Her grandmother would return soon, and would I like to come in for cake? This wasn't so spectacular, the town being small and trusting and the customs for hospitality unerring as the country's love of tablecloths. What did seem of importance was the family portrait on the wall, a group of maybe thirty, young and old, and, in the background, the unmistakable flat head and inverted triangle of Lars Larsen.

"Are you in this picture?"

"I wasn't born yet."

"Do you know this man?" I asked.

"That's my uncle. I don't really remember him. He died. Something in the hospital. You know."

So there was that.

The girl led me to the greenhouse addition, sat me behind the sun-bleached placemats, and began to set the table. She sighed and put her hand on her hip, affecting world-weariness, or maybe really feeling it.

"Are you in school?"

"It's summer break."

"Of course it is."

"Would you like some Kringle?"

The Kringle had been put away warm and sat under sagging plastic wrap. I wiped my palms. When the grandmother returned, I wondered how to hide my conviction, so strongly held short moments ago, of throwing an axe at her son, a man now dead and laid to rest in the town's immaculate graveyard.

"Do you like Kringle?" the girl asked me. I hadn't touched mine.

"Of course. Don't you?"

"It's not my favorite, but I like it," she said, and poked her finger on the tines of her fork.

"Anne-Marie," I started, figuring I could lean on the oracle-like quality of children, especially unknown children, "how do you know whether you should or shouldn't do something?"

"Are you allowed to do it?"

"That's unclear."

"Like you're not sure you're going to get in trouble?"

"Kind of."

"Then you should do it if you want to do it."

"And how do you know if you want something?"

The oracle portal closed. A shadow crossed her face before the girl turned away. I couldn't be reasoned with. She opted for hospitality.

"More Kringle?"

I ate most of the cake, the girl filling my plate each time it emptied. I also drank a warm Coke and a microwaved cup of tea.

Time passed, scratching for things to talk about, until the yeast, the sugar, the Coke, the whole room, with its hotboxed air and sunlight, lulled me into a warm, giddy water.

I'd been trying to put myself at the center of something, but here was another avenue. Dissolution. The lack of a center. If there is no me, the whole problem disappears.

"Have some more," she said, indicating the last piece of cake.

* * *

When would I fall back into solid from this liquid undoing? The eastern sands of the country, its wild coast, its duney heather and planted pines, had blown into me. For the space of the car ride, everything had pleasant significance. The plants swayed in the median, the land rose as dough, swallowing the raisins of farmhouses.

It was all dimpled and rumpled and vast. Farewell, worry. Here is the world, giving of itself so freely, making of itself an example. Here are the pointy churches, gleaming in the sun.

Matias stood in the doorway. He was back early from fishing. I said, in a burst, that he could go ahead and patronize the sex dungeon in Aarhus, as he had suggested, conversationally, so many weeks before.

"Poseidon's Place," I said. "Go there. If you want. To sleep with other people."

It was a professional service, after all, superficial to the emotional bathymetry of our marriage. I couldn't do this thing for him. I was a land-based person with legs who lacked the willingness or creativity or fluidity required of me. That's how I thought about it, in these matter-of-fact, near evolutionary terms, before the Kringle and the car ride and the grace-of-God business.

"Great," he said.

I went outside and curled against the house. Inside, the walls could close in on me. The great, deep-blue depth around my navel could open and darken everything, again. Inside, Matias chopped. Soon it smelled of onions. The trees moved at their crowns. The sun went red and the fields turned pink. Birds made their outsized sounds, rustling in the hedges, on to their night places.

I wanted, of all things, new potatoes, from the fenced vegetable garden at the demonstration farm. I wanted them boiled, buttered, with skin so thin as to get swallowed when knifed, as a sheet gets tucked, into its flesh. Rosemary, thyme, and salt and pepper. It was that easy, knowing what I wanted.

"And I don't want that," I said, tapping my head on the house. I drank it, the understanding. "I don't want that at all." ∎

AND SO IT GOES
Richard Huffman

W hen Abe was born the nurses went out to the waiting rooms in search of his daddy, Jake, to give him the good news. They thought he must have gone out for cigarettes or a soda pop, but in truth he was in a green DeSoto sitting beside a man who had picked him up hitchhiking, and they were jawing over who was the best looking—Brigitte Bardot or Katharine Hepburn. Jake just about fell out the door laughing, thinking anyone would pick Hepburn over Bardot. But he settled down and took a swallow of the other fella's homemade, which just about set his throat afire. He got drunk enough that he forgot all about rolling the sap and went into a sulk until he was let out near a bar on the outskirts of some nothing town.

Abe's mother, Adele, was not surprised when the nurses said they could not find her husband. They were sure he would come by soon and tried their best with pasted smiles to assure her everything was all right. Adele held back her tears and asked for her child and one of the nurses gave the other one a "look."

Adele caught the look and asked what was wrong. "Please," she whispered, intending it for God.

It turned out Abe had a foot that seemed more like a little hoof than a foot, the toes being fused together. And with his somewhat pointy ears, it was believed by one of the nurse's assistants that the boy should be drowned. She was released from employment on the spot when she said as much.

There was an operation, and Abe's toes were separated as best they could be and his hitch afterwards became of little concern to Adele or Abe. Still, there were those pointy ears that some could not ignore. It was a sign of something. That was for sure.

* * *

Dillard Dawes laid off frying holes in toads with his magnifying glass when he saw Abe walk by. "What you doin' here?" he demanded.

Abe stopped and looked at the boy who was sitting in the dirt at the corner of the five-and-dime. This other boy was half hidden by a barrel of something giving off a sourish smell. "Doing nuthin'," Abe said and started walking off again.

"Hey, wait a minute," Dillard called out. He pushed his square body with his square head up off the ground and slapped the dust off the back of his pants and grabbed Abe by the shoulder to turn him around. "I said what you doin' here? You one a them retards from the crazy place? Why you limpin' like that?"

"I'm just going home," Abe said, facing the bigger boy.

Dillard looked Abe up and down. He sneered. "You nothin' but skin and bones."

"I'm just going home."

"You already said. I live down the street there a ways." Dillard twisted his head around and motioned over his shoulder. "In a apartment. I got the attic to myself so's I can see everything going on around here, like you trying to sneak around."

"I'm not sneaking anywhere."

"If I say you are."

"I'm going." Abe turned back around and took a couple of steps when he felt a push in his back that knocked him into the dust.

Dillard stood over him, his legs straddling his victim.

Abe turned onto his back and looked up at the boy, whose face was but a dark square mask with the sun behind it. "You shouldn't have done that," Abe said to the boy. "You're going to regret it someday."

Dillard laughed. "Oh yeah … what you gone do about it, sissie? Kiss me? If I give you my bear hug it'll squash you flat. I got arms strong as everything. You wanna get squashed … just git up and you'll see."

"Hey, you boys quit with that and get on home." The store clerk stood off near the store entrance. A cigarette dangled off his lip. He had a broom flung over his shoulder and took it in his hands and swept a spot of something away and then glanced back at the boys and told them again, "Go on home now."

"You pay me a quarter next time," Dillard told Abe when he stepped away and walked down the street toward where he said he lived.

Abe propped himself up with his elbows and watched the boy go and stared hard after him and thought about things he wanted done to the boy. He pointed at the boy's back and made a secret gesture with his fingers just as a woman came around the corner. She gave Abe a hard look and slapped the other boy across the head and pushed him forward and glanced back again, her mouth agape when she saw what Abe was doing with his hand.

A week afterwards, Mr. and Mrs. Dawes, as they presented themselves to Adele and Dane Lemon, stood on Adele's porch glowering, their faces a mix of red ire and gray sorrow.

The Daweses' genetics had been passed on for generations and had not missed a beat between parents and child—their boy, Dillard. They all had the same square heads and square bodies from which well-muscled arms sprouted like smoked hams, with legs in the same meaty configuration. It had taken Mr. Dawes many years searching for a kindred soul to be his wife, and he had chosen a distant cousin whose proportions would not prove a detriment to his own time-tested genes. They looked alike, spoke alike, and dressed alike. Had it not been for the stubble of shorn hair on Mr. Dawes head and the twists of Mrs. Dawes's shoulder-length curls, a body would be hard pressed to tell which was which.

When Adele Lemon came to the door and through the screen asked what they wanted, Mrs. Dawes said, "Our boy, Dillard, is near dyin'. He's over to the county hospital. We know your boy had a hand in this." Both of the Daweses stared hard at Adele and seemed ready to force their way through the screen when Dane Lemon, dressed in his sheriff's uniform, came up behind his wife. "We know you ain't gone do nothin'," Mr. Dawes said, nodding his head toward Adele. "But you, the sheriff," he went on, redirecting his stare at Sheriff Lemon.

"He hurt our boy," Mrs. Dawes cried out from beside her husband. Her face boiled up. She squinted as though in pain. The whites of her eyes were bathed in an angry red. Adele involuntarily drew back.

"Hold on," Dane said. "What are you talking about?" He knew most everyone in town, by sight at least, and had never seen these two. "You sure you have the right place?" he said. He was used to dealing with angry people. It was the biggest portion of his job. Domestic entanglements. Wife and husband. Brother and brother. Uncle and aunt. Cousin and cousin. There was usually alcohol in the mix and usually at someone's house during or after a party, but they seldom came seeking him out.

"Dillard tole us. That boy of yours put a curse on our boy, who done nothing to deserve such a thing."

"A curse?" the sheriff took a deep breath. He realized then he was getting tired of the job. It only made sense anymore when someone did something he was trained to deal with. Robbery, mainly, which did make sense, as far as upholding the law went. But this other was pure craziness. "Well," he said, "I'm sorry about your boy but nobody gets sick from what you claim. Pure and simple as that."

Mr. Dawes puffed up his chest. "I know you think us fools. We don't have the education like t'others but we know what we know and we seen what we seen. My wife seen the hex sign your boy put on Dillard. Not a hoot wrong with our boy till he met up with your'n. Come home right away sayin' what happened and took to bed that night with a poor feelin'. Your boy hexed him."

Dane kept his voice calm. "You call a doctor?"

"Acourse we did. Doctor says its nuthin'. Just a sour stomach. Called him 'gain when things took a turn and he just says nuthin' he can find wrong but says to get him over to the hospital. Who's gone pay for that?"

Mary Beth Dawes leaned her heavy head forward. "He was a healthy boy. Hospital couldn't find a thing off-kilter. Now you tell me what that leaves to figure. You get that boy of yours out here and make him say what he did ... and ta take that hex off."

"I am so sorry about your boy," Adele said. "But my son had nothing to do with this. He doesn't even know your boy."

"Oh, he knows all right." Mr. Dawes sneered. "He sure does."

"Look," Dane said in a quiet, determined way, "you need to go back home now and console each other; pray for your son. Hard to figure why things happen like this in the world. But they do. You blaming someone else—especially another boy—isn't going to help. There's a good man over at the Methodist church. If you want I could ask him to ..."

Mr. Dawes swept his hand outward, like he was clearing the air of spiderwebs. "We don't need no preacher. We God-fearin' for our own selves. And I'm sayin' this ain't the end of things."

Dane felt Adele grip his arm. "You listen," Dane said, his voice strong and determined, "you do anything—I mean anything—to this boy, you will answer to me. Do you understand that? You stay away from him. If I even hear of you coming near him you will not like the consequences." Dane opened the screen door and took a step toward the pair. They backed off the porch and down the three steps and stood at the bottom, glaring up at Sheriff Lemon.

Dane upticked his chin, as a sign for them to go. "Now get on home before I run you both in for making threats, and whatever else I decide to charge you with."

Mrs. Dawes sniffed contemptuously. "We didn't make no threats. Ain't gone hurt your boy. Just so you know what evil you got a holt of there." She pulled her husband by his shirtsleeve and away from the house. He walked backwards a few steps staring at the sheriff, then sneered, spat a gob on the ground, turned with his wife and left.

After they were gone Adele went back into the house and through the kitchen to the backyard, where Abe was sitting on a small hillock of grass and weeds. Beyond the backyard an eight-foot-high wire fence separated their yard and garden from the forest and the deer that would have made quick work of the garden otherwise. Abe was looking through the fence, off into the woods.

Adele tried to calm herself. "What are you doing?" she said.

Abe turned halfway toward her. "There was a fawn there a minute ago. Didn't see a doe. You think it's on its own?"

"The mother's probably close by."

"I s'pose. Maybe we should put some food out in case."

Adel squatted beside her son. She ran a hand through his hair. "You need a haircut. I'll give you one tonight if you want."

"Is it all right to let it grow?"

"A bit more maybe. Don't want it getting too shaggy, do we?"

"No. Guess not. You think we should leave out some food? Carrots or something for that fawn?"

"That fence is there to keep the animals off our garden. Feeding them is probably not a good idea."

Abe shrugged. "I guess so. Just hope its mama is somewhere near."

"I …" Adele began, not knowing what to say to that.

"Dane go to work?" Abe asked

"He's getting ready."

"He's a good man, ain't he, Mama?"

Adele smiled. Her son must have overheard her say the same thing. As far as she was concerned, Dane Lemon was more than good. "I wouldn't have married him if he wasn't," she said. "And 'ain't' isn't the word you want to use, now is it?"

"Sorry. It just slipped out."

She wondered if she should say anything about what had just happened on the front porch, and then it just came out while she was thinking it over. "You know a boy named Dillard?"

Abe shrugged. "I don't know. There's a new boy in class. Maybe him."

Adele shifted her position and smoothed her summer dress

underneath her legs and sat beside Abe. He was still looking off to the woods. "Nice out here," she said. It was quiet but for cicadas while she thought about things. "You know any boys who have been sick?" she asked.

Abe pursed his lips and squinted as if concentrating on the answer. "If they are, they'll be all right," he said, nodding his head.

Adele frowned. He was so young and innocent.

She thought of telling him to be watchful for any strangers approaching him, but reconsidered. No sense alarming him over something that was probably nothing. And Dane would be sure to take care of things anyway. Maybe encourage that crazy pair to leave Galeton for a different town. He had a reputation of not putting up with much from people who didn't listen—as far as the law went— but he treated her about as well as she could hope for from any man, especially considering the one she had married before, Abe's father. She couldn't say she loved Sheriff Lemon in a romantic, heart-palpitating kind of way, but he was decent. Paid half the mortgage on her house and took care of the utilities and chipped in for groceries. The sex was adequate, which for a man his age—fifty-three—was about all a woman could ask for. And she was going to turn forty in another year and a half, so she wasn't exactly a spring chicken herself. She was glad to have Dane, and he got along well enough with Abe.

Still, she thought—it'd be nice to feel that thing that made her want to nearly bust, which was how it was with Abe's father, Jake. But having to put up with his other women and his wildness—it wasn't good for her, and certainly not for Abe. Jake was the right man if you were looking for a good time and feeling like you had a fever all the time. As far as being part of a family, well, as he said just before he left that last time, "Sorry, Adie, honey, this just ain't my cup a tea." It was good he was gone.

"Mama?" she heard from a distance and snapped out of her dreaminess when Abe tugged at her dress sleeve.

"What? Oh, I'm sorry. I was just thinking of some things. Sorry, honey."

"That's all right. I do too sometimes. It's like being in a place different from here, isn't it?"

Adele pulled him to her. "Yes, it is. But we don't want to be like that too often, do we? We're where we are and nothing is going to change that, and where we are is pretty darned good, isn't it?"

"I guess so," Abe said, his voice muffled against her bosom, where she hugged him tightly.

They heard the back screen door open on its rusty hinges and then slap shut.

"Hey, you two," Dane called out, "I'm off to work. Back around six or so. I'll call if it's any different."

She turned and waved and Abe said, "Bye," and Sheriff Lemon waved and went back into the house and through the house and out the front to his cruiser, and gave a brief toot on the siren when he left.

* * *

Three hours later, on his way up the courthouse steps to testify against a man for burglary, Sheriff Dane Lemon was shot through the heart. According to the coroner, he was dead before he hit the ground.

* * *

Eighteen months after Sheriff Lemon's murder, Jackson Dawes, maintaining his innocence to the last, received two thousand volts from the state electric chair, Old Sparky, and a few minutes later, another two thousand volts as assurance that he was dead and done with. Adele's son, Abe, fell into a long depression after Dane Lemon's death, until he founded the self-described Holy Light of Your Religion church at the age of sixteen, going on to become one of the most successful and respected religious leaders of the state.

Adele Lemon, lonely after Abe left home to "lead his flock," remarried a much younger man, Robert Vargas, whom she assisted financially and emotionally through law school and his political career—which culminated in a lieutenant governorship. She was widowed (or abandoned) for a third time when Robert failed to arrive for a news conference and was never found or heard from again. Adele tearfully claimed she had no idea what became of him, or certain "government funds" he had been entrusted with.

As did Robert Vargas, Adele eventually slid off the map of history like dissipating fog. It was later claimed, with pictorial evidence in a national tabloid, that she and her husband were aliens who had gone back to their home planet. Abe, when interviewed, avowed that his mother had been spirited into the Holy Light, dismissing the alien abduction theory as nonsensical folderol.

* * *

Dillard Dawes, abandoned by his mother after his father's death, became a ward of the state. He entered a foster home of a decent family where he hacked a German shepherd and six unweaned pups to death with an ax. He spent the rest of his youth in a residential treatment center for emotionally disturbed children.

When he was released at the age of eighteen and with full intent to shoot and murder Abe at a Holy Light of Your Religion revival, Dillard succumbed to Abe's religious luminosity and became Abe's chauffeur until he died at the age of seventy-six from a failed heart.

Abe lived on, for a full ninety-five years, and died smiling, surrounded by his faithful flock, who had come from all corners of the state. It was said the line of cars wound through downtown Galeton and out onto State Route 10 for nearly a half mile.

Neither Dillard nor Abe fostered any children, leaving themselves as the last in their genetic line. It was rumored that they had a "funny" relationship, as women were never a part of their lives, except as religious acolytes.

When the question of their relationship being "odd" came up, said with a knowing sneer from one Hadley Straw, he was rebuked by a follower of the Holy Light of Your Religion, Danny Hedgerow, who sneered back and said, "Wadda you know, you ignorant hick?" and offered up a meaty closed fist to Mr. Straw's face. "Didn't mean nuthin'," Mr. Straw is reputed to have said. "It's just them ears is all … but I don't know nuthin' about it."

And, in truth, he didn't.

* * *

Primary tenets of the Holy Light of Your Religion.

Forgive yourself.

Loving bear hugs are good.

Help old people cross the street.

Educate yourself. (Bible, Torah, Koran and dictionaries are free at Holy Light of Your Religion churches.)

If you are rich, give to the poor. If you are poor, find a better job. (Career counseling is free at Holy Light of Your Religion churches.)

If you are fat, eat less and exercise.

If you are in pain or sick, see a doctor.

Tithe to the church only if all your utilities and rent are paid.

Come to church and sing.

Be honest.

* * *

What Really Became of Abe's Birth Parents, Adele Lemon-Vargas and Jake Winters

At a gas station/convenience store, lieutenant governor Robert Vargas (Adele's third husband) told Adele he was going inside for smokes and a beef stick. Adele waited and waited, until she knew something was wrong and went into the store to find her husband. She asked the clerk.

"Oh," the clerk said, "I forgot. I was supposed to take this out to you." He handed her an envelope. Adele turned her back to the clerk and pulled off her calfskin glove and slit open the envelope with her fingernail. She imagined Robert standing right where she was, sliding his tongue along the glue edge and pressing the flap tightly and running his thumb across to ensure it was sealed.

My Dearest Darling Adele,

Irrevocable circumstances dictate that I take leave of you and this world. I know not where I go. Please do not try to find me. It would be futile. Use the key in this envelope to access the security box at our bank. Wear your gloves when you do so. Take all the money you will find there. You will need a large hat box or a small valise. Do not take the black ledger, or even touch it.

Do not take money that is in our savings or checking accounts as there is not much in either. They will need to find something.

Knowing you as the intelligent woman you are, I am sure you will understand what has happened. If you do as I suggest you will have a secure, happy, and hopefully, long life.

Your loving, faithful husband,
Robert

* * *

Adele had often dreamed of traveling... perhaps aboard a cruise ship. Being on the vast, endless sea. Visiting exotic locales. A gondola in Venice. The whirl of colors and aromas of India. A Paris café, smoking a cigarette and sipping French wine.

She used the name of her first husband, Jake Winters. She had always liked the sound of it. Adele Winters. It had a certain cache about it. A hint of something.

She took cruise after cruise, always on the *Excelsior II*, a smallish but still large enough liner, on which she made many friends, some of whom she saw semiregularly, always with a smile of recognition. She became much admired by those who met her, including the crew of

Excelsior II, who, when she died in her private berth, two days short of her one hundredth birthday, buried her at sea, as she wished.

Although she never knew, Jake Winters died many years before her. His attempt to go over Niagara Falls on an inner tube, which was at first a joke—until he had so bragged about his derring-do that he could not back out—was, of course, a disaster. His body was never found. The punctured inner tube was hauled out of the Niagara River some days later by a fisherman who thought he had hooked a "big one." The inner tube still bore Jake's name, now faded, and the remainder of the phrase "Mister Adventure." "Mister *Idiot* is more like it," the fisherman said when he brought the artifact to the local newspaper. There was a picture of Jake Winters in the *Buffalo Evening News*. Although no one knew, the resemblance between Jake and Abe was striking—the pointy ears being a dead giveaway. Though Jake never had a problem with fused toes. Just life in general. That, at least, Abe overcame. ∎

SWANETTA'S WAY
Delia Pitts

"**D**etective, I'm sorry to disturb you at this hour. But we need your assistance." Darcy Pierce hated that her lieutenant's voice always sounded like maple syrup. As if his words weren't orders, just suggestions. Like this call contained an option.

Jerked from its cradle on the nightstand, the damn cell was upside down as she held it to her head, the mouthpiece hastily pressed against her ear.

Pierce heard the muffled sounds of John Carbone's voice and wondered how the man could still be cooing at one in the morning. Flipping the phone around, she grumbled a greeting. "Hello to you, too. Don't you ever sleep?"

"New body dropped, Detective Pierce. I can give you the address. Pick up Colfax on your way."

"No, wait a minute. I'm not getting out of bed to chase after your two-legged Rin Tin Tin." Pierce liked her partner, Delphine Colfax. As Black women veterans on NYPD's homicide squad, they'd formed an iron bond of trust. Loyalty and history glued them tight. But Colfax could be a strait-laced bitch with no sense of humor. Especially on murder cases that launched in February snowstorms after midnight. "Call Simpson on this, why dontcha?" Pierce didn't add that she and Colfax had wrapped a deadly armed robbery with two casualties this week. They'd earned the break.

Pierce had raised her voice at the start of this statement, but looking over at the still form beside her in the bed, she lowered it when she got to Colfax's name.

Her connection to Allison Baxter was only a few weeks old. Still in the hot but shaky stage. With their love affair so new, the link felt dicey. Pierce didn't want to risk the good thing they had going by skipping out in the middle of the night if she didn't absolutely have to.

She wanted Allison to have a good impression of her, of her devotion, of her steadiness. Taking off like this could put the kibosh on their affair, relationship, sex thing, whatever it was. She didn't want to do that without good reason.

Lieutenant Carbone's sugary voice swirled through these thoughts. "Detective Pierce. I realize this is an intrusion. Please apologize to Miss Baxter on my behalf for any disruption my call may have caused."

The. Hell. This four-eyed bastard knew about Allison. Pierce clambered from the bed and retreated to the lilac bathroom down the hall, stumbling over Allison's guitar, leather clogs, and flowered robe as she went. When she was perched on the edge of the footed tub with the door secured, Pierce resumed her conversation with Carbone. "What is going on? Why can't Simpson take this one? Call him."

There was a long pause. Pierce couldn't remember a time when she'd heard Carbone express even the slightest hesitation. Only cloying passive aggression. Now Lieutenant Secreto was giving with the silent treatment? Pierce scrubbed fingers through the tangled coils on her close-cropped head. "Hey, you called me. Remember?"

"Well, I don't believe Detective Simpson is able to assist in this matter. He broke his leg yesterday." Carbone sighed. The sound of breezes ruffling honeysuckle vines.

"Okay. Didn't know. Sorry for the big guy." Pierce felt Carbone was dancing around something. "How do I fit in?"

The boss let his answer dribble down the line. "The body in question belongs to George Olivette. I believe you know him."

"Christ." Loud, then muffled. "Jesus Fucking Christ." Pierce knew George Olivette from days gone by. Days that should have stayed gone. Was his wife, Swanetta, safe? Where was their son? Almost two decades had passed since Pierce had last seen Swanetta. If Swanetta was still mixed up with George, this case took on new urgency. But a counterweight—self-protection maybe?—pushed Pierce to resist. She grumbled but held her tongue.

Carbone rushed on now that the essentials were unveiled. "I want you to go to Olivette's bar. Uniforms are already on the scene. I want you and Colfax to take the lead." A drop of frost on the sugar now.

Pierce glanced at the wall clock over the toilet. One fifteen. "And you can't get anybody else? Because what?"

"Because you're my best man. Detective Pierce." Did his voice stumble over a choke? "Please."

Carbone sounded desperate. Perfect. Pierce would tuck this moment away in her memories for use another time. Blackmail was the lubrication that made her job run smoothly. "Well, when you put it that way, Lieutenant, how can I resist?" A sense of duty plus hopes for career advantage shifted her answer. Further animating the decision—curiosity about Swanetta.

"Thank you for your help, Detective."

"Yeah, yeah. Tell Colfax I'll pick her up in twenty minutes. Out in front of her place."

Pierce stood from the tub, staring at the flimsy dress hanging on a hook on the back of the bathroom door. She plucked a long blond strand from the collar and rolled it between her fingers. Allison deserved a scribbled note under the coffee cup in the kitchen. More than that. Pierce wanted to write a sonnet. Maybe carve an essay in hieroglyphics. But the Sharpie scratches on a legal pad would do until she returned home.

* * *

Pierce took twenty minutes to reach her partner's corner. Delphine Colfax was muffled to the cheekbones in an orange mohair scarf when Pierce pulled to the curb in front of the sleek high-rise apartment where she lived with her husband, son, and two cats. Minimal greetings seeped from her full lips. Colfax was gruff in the best of times. This wasn't one of those times. Her eyes were ice-cold. The tips of her nose and ears were so shiny and red Pierce winced looking at them. Pale as a manila envelope, Colfax wore her hair in long dreads. She'd piled the locs in a knot that pushed the top of her black knit cap four inches above her crown. The navy wool reefer coat wrapped closely around her trim figure. Pierce had bought a similar coat at the start of the winter, though the double-breasted buttons strained across her broad torso. Light and dark, slim and thick. They looked like a team, that was the important thing.

After five silent minutes of driving, Pierce offered a warm-up bid. "You know I got history on the vic, right?"

Colfax wasn't buying. "Yeah, LT said."

"You wanna ask me about George Olivette?" Pierce's offer was muttered through a jumble of unruly memories. She was afraid Colfax would ask about his wife, Swanetta. About what Swanetta had meant to her in those long-gone days. About hopes Pierce had buried, chances she'd discarded as impossible. Pierce weighed how much to share with her partner.

"Save the backgrounder for after we survey the scene." Colfax was by the book. Or too frozen to engage yet.

Pierce relaxed. Off the hook for the moment. Since no further talk seemed forthcoming from her shivering passenger, Pierce rolled through the hushed streets toward lower Manhattan in matching silence. She turned up the heater full blast, hoping that the warmth of the vehicle would penetrate, if not thaw, her partner.

After driving fifteen minutes, Colfax had warmed enough to

unleash a doozy of a conversation starter: "Your girl Allison, she okay with you cutting out like this?"

"How do you know her name?" Screeching was unhip, but it burst anyway. "Or the first thing about her? You some kind of witch?" Pierce didn't add that Lieutenant Carbone had pulled a similar surprise earlier.

Sniper Colfax leveled her voice. "Remember last week when you lost your phone?"

"Yeah, what of it?" Forty-eight hours of hell until the dry cleaner had excavated her cell phone from a suit jacket.

"Who do you think fielded that buttload of calls Allison lobbed at you when you were out running the streets?"

"You did. I got the notes you left." Yellow-and-white scraps of paper drifted in mounds on her desk each time Pierce returned to the station house.

"Not quite. I caught four and Carbone answered two his own self. Had quite a chat with your girl Allison while he was at it."

"But the messages were in your handwriting." Whining covered the embarrassment.

"Lieutenant said he'd be damned if he was writing down shit like a freaking secretary. Made me scratch his dictation."

In a traffic light's rusty glare, Pierce glanced at her partner. Had the whole squad analyzed her newest love affair? She tightened her grip on the steering wheel, tapping a thumb to urge the red to change.

Colfax smoothed the planes of her face to skating-rink sleek. Only a twitch at the left corner of her mouth betrayed amusement. "Allison sounded cool." Big praise coming from reticent Colfax. "Like she wants to get you. You ought to give her a chance."

Not like those other times, Pierce heard. She grunted to end the exchange. She didn't want her business in the streets. This Allison thing was still tender. Not prime for dissection yet. The death of George Olivette evoked memories she needed to clear before she could write that sonnet for Allison.

After ten more minutes of silence, Pierce steered her car into a familiar block in the Bowery. She remembered this street. The shadows stretching from the recessed doorways seemed friendly to her, even the potholes dotting the asphalt were in the same old places. Nothing had changed. She liked it that way.

This tired block had escaped the attention of ambitious developers. No aggressive network of scaffolding across its facades supported optimistic plans for renovation and investment. The buildings here were pockmarked by pollution, their stone surfaces rubbed soft and stained by years of human touch.

A few neon signs blinked in welcome at this hour, even though the stores were closed. But, thanks to a man's sudden death, the quiet bar she sought was still open. Red-and-blue light beams from three NYPD patrol cars pierced the shadowed plate glass window of Swann's Way.

Two uniformed officers stamped like show ponies next to the narrow door. Snow mounds slumped on either side of the entrance. As Pierce and Colfax approached, jets of white streamed from the men's red faces. The crystalline air carried their conversation across the sidewalk.

Beefy said, "Who sicced Detectives Shine and Shimmy on us?"

Boney asked, "Which one's Shine?"

Beefy snorted. "You guess, dope."

Pierce was familiar with the snide nicknames. Dark, boxy, and tough, she'd been called worse names coming up through the ranks. The brass blew off her complaints. Locker-room banter. Boys're gonna talk. Roll with it. Chill out. As Black women, she and her partner couldn't luxuriate in those games. But when she crossed the tavern's threshold, she leaned into the gaunt cop's face. "Just so you know, I'm Shine." Maybe a fleck of spittle grazed his chin. He reared back, cheeks pinkening as if she'd slapped him. Maybe she should have.

Swann's Way was small by modern standards. The tavern's vestibule opened to a rectangular space anchored by a bar stretching down the long wall. The room seemed more cramped than Pierce remembered it. The interior seemed dingy and brown, the racks of polished glasses hanging perilously low over the cracked wood of the bar. The ornately framed mirror on the wall seemed to absorb as much light as it reflected, casting a queasy glow over the customers, waiters, and cops posed in front of it.

Pierce smiled to see the golden curlicued letters forming the name "Georges" in a flamboyant arc at the top of the mirror, just where they had always been. The place smelled the same too: a faint whiff of feminine orange blossoms mixed in with the musty male scents of alcohol and sweat.

Pierce expected to find a few men hanging on the bar rail at this hour, stooped by age or worry or alcohol or all of the above. Did some of the older barflies' faces look familiar? No one hiked an eyebrow in recognition, so she walked on.

A cop—freckled, chubby, still a child—escorted them into the place. He announced he'd been first on the scene. Proud, like he'd won a participation trophy in a grade school track meet. A crime scene tech bustled over to hand them plastic booties, which they snapped over their shoes to prevent contamination. Three other uniforms were stationed near the bathrooms, the kitchen door, and the jukebox. A photographer paced, angling her camera for shots of the scarred floor planks and stone fireplace mantle.

No one was behind the bar. Except the dead man. George Olivette lay on his back, right hand flung over his eyes, the left clutched at his waist. Colfax squatted near the right shoulder to get a closer look at the bullet wounds dotting Olivette's white shirt. Two shots to the gut. One to the heart. Pierce didn't need to look closer. This George Olivette was not the same man she'd known in years past. This paunch was looser, unsexy and bloated. His auburn hair had faded to steel wool. His cheeks were pale with death, sure, but the rough skin around his staring eyes lacked the youthful sheen she remembered. George had grown old. Now he was dead too.

Hiding a shiver, Pierce skirted the bar to study the lineup slouched against the round stools. Five white men, three white women, all in variations of dark worsted wool suits. Striped button-down shirts or imitation silk blouses; ties stowed in pockets, gold-plated bracelets clinking on wrists of both sexes. Lug-soled boots that cost a week of her salary. This set was almost posh, not rich, but striving. Not the mud-dappled, grizzled crowd she remembered from her days frequenting Swann's Way.

The missing one, the one she wanted to see, was Swanetta. George's wife. The namesake of the bar. The reason Pierce used to frequent the place. The one who'd brought her back. Was Swanetta dead too? Or fled to another country, as she'd threatened so many times? Or maybe she was at home basking in the final few minutes of peace before some ghoulish cop announced her husband's death. Pierce needed to see Swanetta. But she knew better than to spew that desire.

When Colfax finished her examination of the body, she joined Pierce near the fireplace to hear the report from the freckled first-on-scene. Shots fired shortly after midnight. The vic staggered from the kitchen to where he dropped behind the bar. A waiter called 911 while everybody screamed. A stock broker touched the vic's neck to confirm he was dead. Most of the customers escaped before the police arrived. The kitchen staff fled too. Probably filthy illegals, the cop offered. Vermin, you know. Pierce's glare extinguished the casual racism. Where was Swanetta, the wife? The cop shrugged. A pair of his colleagues had been dispatched to the Olivette apartment to find her. Maybe they'd return soon.

Though her trembling knees urged flight, Pierce said, "We'll wait."

Colfax said, "We'll interview those witnesses." She pointed with her chin at the people along the bar. "Bring them to us, one by one. On my signal." Another gesture, this time with her elbow. "Back there."

Pierce knew the way to the sheltered booth in the rear where she had spent so many nights and weekends. Without hesitation she led Colfax past the gaping fireplace with its embers still glowing and the swinging doors barring entrance to the bathrooms.

They hung up their overcoats on brass hooks flanking the booth and shoved onto the facing benches. The two women, both good sized, could barely squeeze into the compartment. Pierce was surprised it seemed so crabbed now and dark.

"I used to come here all the time twenty years ago. Haven't been back in a while I guess."

Colfax hadn't asked for the explanation, but Pierce wanted to offer it anyway. Being in Swann's Way again after so much time made her feel expansive and warm, even if her partner was not.

"Yeah, I used to bring Rita here a lot when we were first going out. Those were some times. Getting married put a stop to that of course, but Swann's Way still brings back all the good memories." Rita was long gone, a fragment of history she'd shared with Colfax, then discarded as irrelevant. And dismal.

The arrival of a waiter interrupted the reminiscing. Even a murder investigation got service with a smile. Dressed in a tight purple T-shirt and matching jeans, his jet-black hair streaked with a wide band of more purple, this skinny waiter was a boho anomaly in Swann's Way.

But he took Pierce's order like a pro and quickly brought back the two glasses of club soda with tall tumblers of ice water on the side. "Jack Daniels was more my speed, back in the day." Pierce grunted and sipped the bubbles.

Pierce unfolded a small paper napkin and smoothed it on the table between them as Colfax took a first slug of soda. Pierce traced the Swann's Way logo on a coaster, two black swans entwining their necks like lovers. "I wonder what's keeping Swanetta."

"Swanetta?" This was the first private word Colfax had spoken since they entered the tavern.

"Yeah, the girl usually behind the bar. The owner's wife. Swanetta."

"Girl?" Skepticism tightened Colfax's almond-shaped eyes.

"Yeah, Okay. Well, I remember back when she was a kid. The first day she came in here looking for work. Fresh-faced, nice figure, no smile. Honey-blond hair past her waist and brown eyes to die for." The memories were unleashed now. No corralling them any longer.

Both women swirled their glasses until the ice chimed.

"I guess I had a thing for her once upon a time," Pierce continued.

"A thing *for* her? Or *with* her?" Colfax's gaze sharpened, but a smile, the first of the night, played across her lips.

"Smart-ass." Pierce spoke without bite. "All us regulars were crazy for Swanetta back then. Not just me. Women, men, everybody. But George laid down his marker early and it was lights out for the rest of us."

"George, the dead guy?" Colfax scrunched her lips to point toward the bar.

"Yeah. The owner of this place. French, probably. Nice-looking but always had a book in front of his face, always reading. Always quoting from some crusty French writer or other." Pierce chuckled at the memory. "When I first started coming here, the original name of the place was Georges's Bar and Grill. Like the regular George but with an *S*. I guess he dropped that last *S* after a while. He used to talk all the time about making it big in America. Opening a chain of restaurants across the city or maybe even in New Jersey."

Pierce sighed and sipped the ice water to soothe her achy throat. Was this soreness emotion? Or the effects of subfreezing temps? Pierce voted for winter as the culprit.

"But then he married Swanetta. Everything changed. George ditched all his big ideas. Named the bar after her. Said he had all he ever he wanted."

Lines on Colfax's forehead deepened. "Were they happy, do you think?"

"I don't know. What does that even mean? Happy." Pierce shrugged and stuck to the facts. Safer that way. "I do know they had a kid, boy with her blond hair and brown eyes. She came back to work behind the bar when the kid went to school. He must be nineteen, twenty now."

"And George with no *S* ends up dead behind his own bar."

Pierce sucked her teeth. "He didn't even make it to sixty, poor fucker."

"Poor fucker." The echo hung in the air between them as they drew gulps of soda.

Pierce shook her head, adding a grace note to the story. "You smell that orange blossom when we come in the bar? That is Swanetta. She always smelled like that. From the first day. Like you just bit into the juiciest orange slice ever and it was running all down your chin and stinging where you pinched a pimple and making your mouth pucker up. But you didn't mind, you just wanted another slice of that orange. That is Swanetta." Pierce closed her eyes to cloak the feelings from her partner. Was Swanetta's marriage the real reason Pierce never took the chance? Or was cowardice the badge she wore?

They ordered another round of club sodas. At the bar, detained patrons shuffled their feet. One blew his nose, another raised her voice in a whine. The detectives decided to interview the lineup from left to right.

When the fresh drinks arrived, they came with two grilled cheese sandwiches. Pierce's first bite into the gooey cheddar slabs brought a new surge of memories. About Swanetta, about Swann's Way. About choices dodged.

The purple-haired waiter said Swanetta had sent the sandwiches. On the house, for old time's sake.

"She's here?" Pierce asked, eyes popping. "How'd she get into the place without us seeing her?"

"How do I know what you guys see?" The waiter flicked his purple forelock and turned.

Pierce snapped, "Tell her to come here. Now." She cracked knuckles on the table, making the waiter jump. He scurried toward the kitchen. "Let me lead the questioning," Pierce told her partner.

Another bite of the cheese sandwich. Anxiety turned the cheese chalky. Colfax waved off the food, gulping half her drink in the minute they waited for Swanetta.

As the bar owner stepped to their booth, Pierce felt warm currents lap at her shoulders. The scent of orange blossoms wafted across her face, the juicy trace causing her mouth to water. But something tainted the flowers, the metallic tang of blood.

Pierce looked up at the figure hovering beside their table. She swallowed a gasp. Changes—time-wrought and man-made—were harsh. Swanetta was still pale and tiny, maybe even shorter than Pierce remembered. She was dressed in a fuchsia sweater and black pants. That ravishing fall of blond hair that had fascinated Pierce years ago was now chopped into a pixie style. Below a spike of hair, a livid bruise marred the right cheekbone. Fresh pink-and-red stripes draped her left eye like a swollen flag. Tremors shook the inflamed lid, revealing her pupil as a sliver of brass between the purple. Next to the table, Swanetta clenched her hands before her waist. Pierce could see the grated knuckles, where seeping creases scored the flesh. Swanetta's lower lip hung like a crimson bulb, wobbling as she swayed before them.

Colfax rose, pointing at a chair. The battered woman shook off the invitation to sit.

Pierce, rooted to the bench, barked, "Who hit you?" No greeting, no reminiscence. No old times, unforgotten. She knew the answer but needed to hear it for the record. And to erase her own memories.

"You know, Darcy." Swanetta murmured. "I'm sure you've guessed."

The whisper of her first name made Pierce's gut clutch. Regret tinged with desire rose in an acid wave to singe the back of her tongue. "Maybe. But you've got to say it. Out loud."

Swanetta touched an index finger to her damaged eye. "This wasn't the first time. That happened years ago." A tear dribbled down the trench beside her mouth. "George told me to stop. I wouldn't. Couldn't." Shoulders hiked as if the explanation was simple as two plus two.

Heat swarmed up Pierce's neck. She rubbed the indentation behind her left ear to quell the throbbing. The citrus nip of orange blossoms ripened in the air around the table.

Colfax broke the silence. "Stop what, Mrs. Olivette?"

The red bulb stretched with the movement of her mouth. It meant to be a smile. "Let's say, George wasn't the first—or last—man in my life." She nodded once. "Yeah, that covers it." Now the smile sliced straight and true. She looked at Pierce. "Or woman either."

Pierce wanted to slam her forehead on the table, punch her fist into the padded leather cushion behind her shoulder. Deliver loud blow to hammer out the commotion in her head. A violent act to ease the ache in her heart. Instead, she gripped her jaw, sliding it from side to side as if the joints were creaky. She felt old, useless. Dragged by recollection to the edge of futility.

But the routine of her job tugged her clear. "Then we got what we need here. Agree, Colfax?"

"Right. We got it." Her partner, eyes brimming with unshed tears, signaled to the freckled cop.

A brief explanation, an order. A camel hair coat retrieved from the kitchen. As Pierce draped the coat over Swanetta's shoulders, one last whiff of orange petals brushed her face. The boy clapped handcuffs on Swanetta and led her to a patrol car. Self-defense case wrapped with a straight confession. Details to be recorded at the station house in the saner hours of late morning.

Watching the squad car pull from the curb, Pierce's mind cleared. George Olivette hadn't been the jolly ambitious man she'd remembered. Swanetta wasn't the golden icon of her memories. They were a couple shackled first by bonds of dreary convenience, then by hatred. She felt lighter for shedding those fractured memories.

The last Swann's Way clients straggled into the night, steam haloing their bare heads. In the bar doorway, Colfax straightened the lapel on her partner's overcoat. She plucked a long blond hair from the wool and dangled it between them. "Allison will be cool about tonight. She'll understand you doing your job. You know that, right?"

Pierce took the strand, rolling it between her fingers. "I hope she'll go easy on me." She tucked the hair into her pocket and patted her hip. "Until we make new memories."

Colfax nodded, then followed Pierce into the tunnel of frigid air surrounding the empty bar. They flipped the collars of their matching coats and trudged toward their car for the long, silent ride home. ∎

DANIEL TELLS HIS DAD
celeste doaks

This ain't the first time I've tried
announcing it. Crossed wires was all
I got. Figures. That's why I'm feeling
dumber than the idiot box he absorbs,
fumbling for words more elaborate
than "we're leaving."

"Dad, Hec and I are taking a little trip,
but we're not quite sure when we'll return."
No response. My news isn't primetime.
He clicks between *Law & Order* and a local
news anchor saying "And that's how the war's
being fought—with civilians." Surprise!
There's no signal between us. Never has been.
The remote's closer to his heart than me.
Only thing that breaks our silence is
the deadbolt click, as I let myself out.

ALMOST HUMAN
Lis Bensley

Gwyn pulled up to the curb and parked her car as she did every evening after work. Tonight, as she shut off the engine, she looked up and noticed how vivid the sky had suddenly become. Flat earlier, as though beaten lifeless by the afternoon storm, it appeared to be fast gathering its vitality. A young woman's flushed cheeks in some portions, deeply bruised flesh in others with streaks of yellowish addled veins that colored the celestial debris left over from the clouds and the rain. What the sun breaking through had not dissipated. It was a lovely sky, she thought, a confusion of identities, neither stormy nor clear, though fading quickly in the darkening light.

Cracking the window, she closed her eyes for a moment, letting her head drop back onto the headrest as she cleared her mind from the day's work at the office. She and Gordon had acted professionally as always, keeping their romance a secret. About to retire and settle in Colorado, Gordon had proposed to Gywn three days earlier, though she had yet to give him an answer. There was work to be done on a dying client's will, a sudden change of heart over leaving any of his estate to his black sheep of a son, knowing full well the fury Gordon would be met with at the surprise exclusion, Gwyn thought as she typed the documents.

Before she left the office, she placed them neatly on Gordon's desk—the client was bedridden and preferred that Gordon deliver the papers personally—each signature page marked with a yellow Post-it. He had barely nodded to her. There had been no acknowledgment whatsoever of the previous evening, not even a surreptitious grin in the hallway, just the expected formality, Mr. Lutz and she always Gwyneth. She said her usual good evening and closed the door behind her.

When she opened her eyes, the sky was noticeably darker and the streetlights were beginning to come on. Glancing at the solemn, shaded house across the street, she wondered when Marshall would put on a light. Or did he just sit there, night after night, in darkness, living his life by the sun? She knew he was in there—where else would he be? His red pickup truck was parked in the driveway, so faded that it looked like half the metal had sloughed off and he was driving a vehicle no more protective than a tin can. She had offered to buy him a new truck, but she knew it would just sit in front of the curb unused while he continued to drive the old one wherever it was that he went.

Tonight, she had made pork chops with gravy and mashed potatoes, with some greens though she knew he would not eat them. Still she would not be a good mother if she did not at least try. She had heaped his plate full just before she came, then microwaved and wrapped it tightly in heavy-duty aluminum foil. Now, balanced in the middle of the passenger seat, the plate was so well sealed that she could barely smell the rich meat juices she had noticed earlier while assembling his meal. Lifting his dinner gingerly, she so hoped he would open his door to her tonight and eat the plate of good food. There was clean laundry in the trunk of her car that she would take out for him later.

But Marshall did not answer when she knocked. She waited, then knocked again, louder this time. It was getting colder now that the sun had gone down and she pulled her collar up more tightly around her neck. Standing as she was on the front stoop, she marveled at how much paint had begun to peel. It looked awful, really, now that she noticed. How had she managed to miss this detail—this need—when she was diligent about observing all the rest, the torn, dirty clothes, the wild hair, the bare kitchen cabinets, the awkward movements and black hole dark eyes that absorbed all her love and concern and sadness. And never gave anything back.

"Marshall?" she called out again and took a step back. As she did, she saw the front curtain flicker. Then, the click of the front door, which crept open once it was released. Marshall, looking like a sad, numbed animal, a foot from the door, gazing down at her knees. His auburn hair was long and riotous, his dirty clothes hanging like drapery over his thin body, making him look almost a decade younger than his twenty-three years. How Gwyn wished she could get him to gain some weight.

"Hello, Marshall," she whispered, taking a step into the house. As he often did, he touched her shoulder, then turned and walked away. This was as affirmative a greeting as Gwyn would ever get. She followed him as he moved into the kitchen and sat at the table. Every night around seven, she came with a hot meal, whether he let her in or not. Whether he let her help him change into clean clothes or even take a bath. Consistency was very important, Dr. Witkins had told her, confirming her efforts. He was the one psychiatrist out of many who had actually touched Gwyn with even one iota of compassion.

"No matter how he responds," Dr. Witkins had said, "it does bring a measure of stability into his life."

Unwrapping the plate, she laid it in front of him along with the utensils rolled up in a napkin. "It's pork and potatoes." She did not bring his attention to the chard, nor the laundry in the back of her car. He was so easily overwhelmed. She would see first what he did with what was in front of him. Marshall had crossed his arms and was staring at the plate. Gwyn sat across the small table.

"Shall I cut your meat?" she offered.

He began to shake his legs, sending vibrations up through his body. Gwyn reached over carefully and took the fork and knife. "Let me help you."

She cut the meat quickly, then wiped the gravy off the knife with the side of the fork. "Here," she said, holding the fork out for him. But he just stared and shook harder. She knew it was the greenery; she should never have put it on the plate with the meat and the potatoes, contaminating the little that he would let her feed him. But it was too late to remove it now. The green had infiltrated the white potato hill. She braced herself for what was coming any moment as he vibrated harder and harder.

"Radioactivity," he yelled, leaping out of his seat. "Pond scum. Mustn't touch, mustn't touch. The waves are lethal."

Moving quickly, he shot out the back door. Gwyn laid her forehead on the table, an angry voice ranting silently, *Stupid, stupid. You always try for too much.* Then, as she had taught herself to do every time the blame set in, she summoned Dr. Witkin's deep, calming voice, his words of compassion. "You must not take the ranting and screaming personally," he had said, putting his big, warm hand on her shoulder. "The delusions are part of the disease. Nothing, absolutely nothing," he added, making sure they had eye contact, "to do with the quality of your parenting. You must believe that."

She rose from the table and with the napkin wiped away every trace of green and put the plate in the refrigerator. He might forget and eat the food tomorrow. She would scream if she could. Stand at the sink and wail. Instead she should clean up the kitchen, the few dirty plates in the sink. The living room needed vacuuming, his sheets washing. But Gwyn knew he would stay hidden in the bushes out back until she left and she didn't want him to get cold, dressed as he was. She would leave and come back tomorrow.

Getting into the car, she lit a cigarette before turning on the ignition. She had been trying to stop smoking for over a year and had cut down substantially, only two or three a day, whenever stress threatened to uproot her hard-won demeanor of calm. Tomorrow, she thought as she filled what seemed her entire body with smoke, he might be better. He would welcome her presence, the warm sustenance she carried. He might even let her brush his hair, let her touch him, even if it was just a grazing of the back of her hand against his head. Some days he'd come to her, be almost happy to see her, at least receptive. Other days, well, she just never knew what to expect. What enemy, what planet had captured him or whether he was momentarily safe. Almost human.

As she finished her cigarette, she noted the house catty-corner across the street. A new family had moved in recently. A young doctor with his wife and their two small children, she'd heard from the realtor. A slim young thing, too much lipstick, Gwyn had noted as the woman asked questions about Marshall's house, uprooting the For Sale signs just before the family took ownership. Introducing herself to Gwyn, giving her a card, asking so many questions about the house, about Marshall. Did he have any plans to move? If so, they must be sure to let her know. It was an up-and-coming neighborhood. Clearly, Marshall's place was an eyesore. Gwyn hated the pretense of interest the woman showed. Didn't she know how clearly dollar signs gleamed in her eyes? How transparent these people were.

She made a mental note to call Marshall's father and tell him about the paint. It was still his house, after all, and his responsibility, even though he had purchased it for Marshall nearly five years ago, once he turned eighteen. A small bungalow really, enough to give him privacy and a safe haven. He would no longer live at home. Not in her house, half a mile away, from which he had taken to running away. Nor Victor's, even without the new wife and child. But he seemed content to stay here, alone much of the day. Without this place, Marshall would have ended up homeless. Victor seldom came to see Marshall anymore. He had moved to a wealthy suburb of San Francisco and had stopped coming by a few years ago. He and Marshall would only end up fighting in the street, yelling obscenities at one another while Mrs. Myerson next door threatened to call the police. At least Victor kept up with the payments and took care of the taxes, and when Gwyn let him know, arranged the repairs if Marshall would permit them.

Gwyn started the car though she was reluctant to leave. She knew her son had been squatting in the bushes watching her every move, the continuous glow of her cigarette as it periodically lit her face. She could almost feel the weight of his stare taking everything in and though she could never explain it, she felt strangely comforted, even loved. It was selfish, she knew, making him wait this way, letting him get cold. It was time to go.

Gwyn drove slowly past the doctor's house, captivated by the light glowing warmly from inside the windows. Though she could see no one stirring inside, she imagined the mother and girls curled up on the living room couch, the mother animatedly reading a story, the girls giggling at humorous inflections and pulling closer in, nestling tightly into her body.

She tried to remember the feel of her own son against her. Though Marshall had stopped letting Gwyn hold him when he was quite young, even to comfort him when he scraped a knee, he would allow it on his own terms. Their evening ritual. Where after dinner, he liked to nestle into her on the sofa and have her read to him, sometimes the same book over and over ad nauseum. How content she'd felt then, his body relaxing into the lull of her words, the slow turning of pages. And his weight against her was such a comfort. A dim but constant source of hope.

Seeing the glow from the house, Gwyn decided she would introduce herself to the new neighbors soon. She wouldn't want Marshall to frighten the girls. It was important they knew that he was gentle and harmless. Even if he always looked a mess. "Please," she'd probably tell them, "he's really a good boy. You needn't ever feel scared."

* * *

She and Gordon did not see one another outside the office during the week. He often worked late at night and she needed the time to take care of Marshall, do their laundry, do the shopping, the few hours alone late at night when she'd drink too much wine and have her treasured solitude into which she'd only allow Miles Davis or Coltrane and, when she felt any energy at all, Lightnin' Hopkins and John Lee Hooker. Stripped out of her constrained office attire— she did so hate pantyhose though it was a good job for her and paid what she needed—she could easily transgress time and slip into her late teenage years. To that little slip of rebellion when she imagined herself freer than her circumstances allowed. She should have run away when she got pregnant at seventeen, her parents' greatest nightmare, which she'd half-consciously, drunkenly, chosen to bring to life. Instead she'd allowed the abortion and withstood her father's belt afterward, marrying Victor three years later. How pleased they had been.

It was nearly one in the morning. She should remember to drink a lot of water before going to bed. She had smoked too many cigarettes, she told herself as she got up to turn off the stereo. It was only Monday, well, now Tuesday morning. It would be a long week. Maybe she'd take a pill to make sure she'd sleep.

* * *

Gordon would not press her for an answer. He was a remarkably patient man. Kind and gentle too, which Gwyn found ironic considering most other attorneys she knew. His partner, Rick McKierry, for instance. And their colleagues, all easily inflamed and imperious. But not Gordon.

After fixing his coffee and delivering the morning mail, Gwyn sat at her desk to drink her own cup of tea. Before beginning to type the many documents that waited, she gazed at him through the half-open door. Dressed meticulously, he seldom removed his jacket except when he worked late into the night. In his breast pocket was a crisp white handkerchief perfectly folded and peeking just over the brim. He wore bow ties, which looked stuffy on anyone else, Gwyn thought, but on Gordon were perfectly acceptable.

She had always thought she liked how Gordon dressed for work, the care he took with his clothes. Always before getting into bed after he undressed, he paused to hang everything up neatly, put shoe trees in his shoes, his absolute formality, the way he always held the car door open, how he carefully balanced his weight on top of her, how he always addressed her by exhaling her full name slowly, taking time to pronounce the *Gw* in his deep alto voice.

But this morning, for an instant she saw him in a new light. His round, ruddy face looked puffy, his bow tie absurd. She wondered how refreshing it might be to see his shirt open in the front, his hairy chest visible, passion burning in his eyes. She imagined him rumpled and crazy standing beside her son. The picture made her laugh hard out loud, almost hysterically.

Gordon looked up from his work. "Is anything wrong?"

It was all Gwyn could do to stop herself. But she did as though her life depended on it, then smiled and answered, "No."

* * *

While she often ate lunch at her desk while doing the *Times* crossword, today she chose to walk to the park. It was a lovely, warm spring day and she found an empty bench by the playground. Two young mothers were there with five toddlers squealing as they flew down the slide, demanding this or that snack, throwing sand in the air.

The children were in busy dialogue, interactive in words and play. Gwyn remembered Marshall at a similar age, no longer on the charts of normal social development. He had stopped making eye contact, even with her. Soon he eschewed other children and began building forts in the corners of playgrounds and preschools. Elaborate Lego constructions, his foreign countries as he designed his own language that he spoke only with his one friend, Emily from across the street. Or in sharp retort to any other curious child who wanted to venture into his creations.

"Nabu nark," he'd shout and the innocent child would scamper off. Then to Emily, laughing, "Voleott."

A few of the other mothers insisted he was a genius. "Look at what he designs, even his language. It's absolutely brilliant for a four-year-old." Gwyn had only been marginally soothed by such kind words, even as she herself believed it to be true. For a time, she had fantasized that all this ostracizing behavior would one day culminate in a monumental work, something that could only come from the farthest edge of the periphery. An almost otherworldly connection to the mundane.

One of the children suddenly hit another with the plastic shovel. Tears ensued. The two mothers, deep in conversation, did not seem to notice at first. Gwyn was about to leap up and rushed over. But an angry voice stopped her.

"If you do that again, I'll come over and whack you myself." One of the mothers had turned from her conversation and was glaring at the children. "One more complaint and we're leaving, got that?" One or two of them nodded, then they resumed their play.

Gwyn looked at the mothers, back in conversation, seemingly oblivious to anything else. They were young, one—not the disciplinarian—was very cute, in the classic thin, blond way, and both were covered in tattoos. The cute one had several nasal rings glinting in the sun and was dressed in a skimpy tank top that revealed more rings in her navel. The tattoos were intriguing. The mother of the shovel wielder had a huge Lady of Guadalupe up one arm, a Chinese dragon down the other. Her friend had Japanese blossoms and branches curving beautiful around her shoulders. There were words that Gwyn could not make out. She wondered if they were the names of spouses or fathers of the children. Maybe it was names of the children themselves. What would Gwyn write on her body if she dared? Emergency info? Operating instructions? Or maybe something from Marshall's incomprehensible "genius" lexicon?

Gwyn was a half hour late getting back to the office. Guiltily, she trotted back, her shoes too uncomfortable to go much faster, her mind filled with worry about Marshall. Even if Gordon had come up with a perfectly reasonable solution.

"You could come back often. Every week if you'd like," he had offered as they talked it through earlier. "It's not that far, only a few hours' plane ride. I can arrange to have someone bring Marshall meals every day. Check in on him."

Then, his hand holding hers, "You've done more than is humanly possible for the boy. It's okay to let go."

At that moment, she could feel a huge weight lift. Still she could not give him an answer, could not say the word he was in no hurry to hear.

By the time she reached the office, she told herself she would respond to Gordon over the weekend. After the ballet. He was a lovely man. It was time to let go. Of course they'd make it work.

The phone nearly shattered her, bursting through the quiet of the early-morning night.

"Gwyn?" It was Victor, his voice sharp and urgent. She had not yet told him of her upcoming marriage and the changing of the guard. Had he heard? Was he angry? Her first confused thoughts snapping so quickly from a deep sleep.

"Yes," she whispered back hoping the tenor of her voice would give Victor's a more realistic point of reference.

It did not. "I've had a call from the police."

Gwyn gasped.

"There has been an incident, nothing serious," he assured her quickly. "But still it will require some attention."

"Yes." Seated she could better shore herself up.

"It seems Marshall has been looking into windows at night. There's a new family across the street and he has frightened the mother and the two children. I'm afraid the father called the police."

"Damn!"

"They did explain the situation, apparently, but it seems the father was not quite assuaged. I think you should go over."

"I will, first thing in the morning." Gwyn hung up the phone. She was not feeling strong enough for an encounter. Still she knew it couldn't wait.

It was early when she arrived. She found Marshall already busy in the garage, his red truck overflowing with junk, he at work assembling a large construction of rusted metal components.

"Marshall," Gywn said as much to announce herself as to address him. "What happened with the neighbors?"

He was cutting a metal sheet and did not stop to answer. Most likely he would say nothing. At any other time, Gwyn would simply accept his silence, realizing it was futile to press further. He would only just leave. But to her surprise, she was unwilling to give up. She asked again, moving closer. She touched his shoulder.

Marshall immediately jerked himself free, dropped his wire cutters and moved a few steps away. Her voice was firm and angry. "Why were the police called?"

Marshall looked at the floor, then over her shoulder. She could see chaos whirling in his eyes, attempting to fall into a functional pattern.

There had been an incident years ago. Though he had long been relegated to the special class for emotionally disturbed children, Emily had remained his one constant friend. The one child he could relate to. They were separated in school but often played afterward or during the weekends. When he was ten, though, Emily met someone else, a new student, Patty Nye, who suddenly swept her away. Completely. She no longer had time for Marshall. She stopped speaking their language.

At first there were huge outbursts and tantrums. Marshall could barely be contained at home and school was impossible. His doctors tried several new medications and only the tranquillizers seemed to have any effect. He became a ghost being, a soul departed, but at least he could function. Or, as Gwyn realized, everyone else could function around him.

One night soon after, Gwyn was awakened late. It was the police. Marshall was in the back seat of the squad car contained behind wired windows.

"What happened?" Gwyn gasped. She thought he had been asleep.

The officer tipped his hat. "The boy was found inside a home on Palmetto Road. Actually he was found inside a girl's bedroom."

"What home?" Gwyn was dumbfounded.

"Apparently the family knows the boy from school. The parents said he was a friend of a friend of their daughter's. They often found him lurking in the woods near the house when the girls were playing."

Gwyn could barely find her breath. She knew exactly—Patty Nye. After school Marshall had insisted on playing outside until dark, often down by the creek near their home, but he was always back by dinner. She never had any complaints, had no idea he would travel so far, nearly a mile away.

"I'm afraid the family is going to press charges," the officer continued. "The girl was scared out of her wits."

Gwyn felt faint. Though Victor had moved out over a year ago, she wanted him there to take charge, to make decisions.

In the end, Marshall was taken to the psych ward of their local hospital for observation and new medications. After much pleading by both Victor and Gwyn, the Nyes dropped their charges. The new meds seemed to make Marshall more manageable and he fell back into his daily routine without further problems, at least for a while.

Standing in the garage, waiting insistently for an answer—some semblance of justification—Gwyn remembered how he had looked back then inside the squad car. His hair, normally long, was greasy and matted, his face dirty and his eyes erratic, darting frantically about car's interior. At the time, she'd had such an odd reaction, so unlike anything she had ever felt, it seemed almost an out-of-body experience. She could imagine the girl waking to this creature. She could feel her complete terror. She saw, at that moment, Marshall as a stranger—indeed some alien creature to guard against. To push away from. And she remembered how light she had felt at that moment. For one tiny second, free.

"Were you staring in the windows?" she asked.

Marshall nodded, almost imperceptibly.

"Just that? The windows. Nothing more?"

"Watching," he uttered to the floor.

"And you were just watching?"

Again he nodded.

There was a time this revelation would have brought her to tears. She could feel his distance from the world, his need to at least partake of normalcy, if only as an observer. But this time she was angry. She could feel her blood stir. Look at you, she wanted to yell, you are a terrifying sight, all dirty and strange.

Instead she left, walking outside immediately, as though the heat—her own heat—would cause her to faint. She would make something for Marshall to eat from what she could find in the cupboards. But first she'd talk to the family across the street.

It was just eight thirty. A young pretty woman answered Gwyn's knocking. Through the door and the dining room, Gwyn could see the two girls eating at the kitchen table.

"I'm sorry to bother you," Gwyn began. "But I am Marshall's mother, from across the street."

The woman's inquiring face turned suddenly concerned and she opened the door completely and invited Gwyn in.

"Oh, I don't want to interrupt your breakfast."

"No, not at all. We're finished. Really. The girls are just dawdling. Let me make you some tea."

Gwyn was surprised at the hospitality, at the smiling young girls who insisted on showing her their artwork, then offering one of Mommie's brownies.

The young woman—Ellie—told the girls they could watch a movie. She and her guest would have tea in the living room. The conversation was curious though solemn. Before they had moved in, Ellie and her husband had heard stories about Marshall. Michael was a pediatrician, not an expert in the field, but he suspected autism.

"Is that correct?" she asked gently.

Gwyn nodded. "He's really quite harmless, though I know he often looks a sight."

"And he can be very sweet."

"Really?" Gwyn sat up straighter on the edge of the sofa.

"Oh yes, often he's caught little lizards for the girls. Or will bring them some strange toy he's obviously picked up somewhere."

"Yes, he is quite the collector."

"But he's been lurking about at night and staring in the windows."

"More than once?" Gwyn felt her chest tighten.

"I'm afraid so," Ellie seemed reluctant and admitted this sadly. "Sometimes he does scare the girls, his face suddenly appearing. I want to believe that he's just curious, but Michael is not so sanguine. Actually he is quite concerned."

For a moment, Gwyn could find nothing to say. She could not even move her teacup off her lap. More than anything, she wanted to run away. Then Ellie put a hand on hers. "I'm so sorry. This must be so awfully hard for you."

Gwyn felt herself weaken. Any moment she could crumble. Was this the first time anyone had actually said this to her?

One of the girls came bounding into the living room. "Mommie, Mommie, I'm scared."

The girl collapsed into her mother's arms. Gwyn froze, suspecting the worst.

"What happened?" Ellie asked as the other little girl appeared in the doorway.

"Sally put on the other movie. The witch one," the girl explained through sobs.

"Sally," Ellie said sternly to the older child, "you know Morgan is still too young." Then she kissed the child's head and calmed her, "It's okay, Morgan. It's okay."

Watching, not moving a muscle, Gwyn suddenly found herself wanting—no, longing desperately—to crawl into Ellie's lap too, to be held as she sobbed and sobbed and allow herself to be comforted.

Instead she put the tea cup quickly on the coffee table. "I must be going. Thank you for the tea."

* * *

Gwyn did not return to Marshall's. Nor did she call Victor as she had promised she would. Instead she went home and the next morning called in sick, put on Miles Davis and sat in her living room, staring out the window at the clear blue day as she saw the future in a way she had never seen before. Something set in stone, whether she participated or not. The time had come. Marshall would need more supervision than even she could give. Sitting in the dark, smoking her cigarettes, Gwyn realized there was nothing more she could do. Maybe there never had been.

She began to feel rumbling inside. Her containment shaking, a wall of pain about to push through. But not quite yet—there would be time enough for all the sadness, grief, feelings of guilt and blame— indeed half a life ahead. First she needed to stop everything and just close her eyes.

She imagined herself driving. The windows were down and the air outside was cooling her face, blowing her hair erratically. She was driving fast but longed to accelerate. Because the road ahead was straight and wide open, not a speed limit sign nor a policeman in sight. ∎

UNFATHOMABLE
Vikram Ramakrishnan

I

I was barely in school when Oscar died, my first experience of loss that wasn't temporary. There were moments in the first days when he was still there, a black-and-gray-and-white blur in the corner of my eye, or a heavy, furry head on my lap. Once I woke up expecting to find him at the bottom of the bed. Instead, there was a hollow impression where he'd been.

Over the years, my family replaced Oscar—or attempted to at least—with a succession of other dogs, little things with poodles and foxhounds in their pedigree. They didn't have the same qualities of wisdom and gentleness of Oscar. They were never my dogs, not in the way Oscar had been, but rather, the dogs that were around during my childhood.

A dog is a living thing, which means that it must die, and it is a cruel thing to introduce a child to the death of their pet. I was not told about Oscar's death until after his funeral. I remember waiting for him to come home and the slow dawning of the terrible truth.

II

When I understood Oscar was gone, I dragged his bed to the corner of my room and curled up in it, my cheek resting softly on its surface, Oscar's scent embedded in its thick fabric. My mother lingered outside my door, her silhouette like a shadow cut out of a wall. Eventually she came in and tried to comfort me, but I was inconsolable. She told me that death was a natural part of life and that we all had to die someday. "Are you going to die?" I asked her. She hesitated and then said yes. It would be many years from then, she promised. Death is the greatest mystery, the ultimate unknown. The end of life, the end of consciousness. The end of everything. At the time, I didn't care about any of these explanations, and I wanted to know when I'd see Oscar again.

III

We lived in a small Colonial, right on the corner of two quiet streets. Our landlord's name was Mr. Brennan, and he arrived on the first Friday of every month to collect rent. Mr. Brennan was a large man with a red face, and he always smelled of clove cigarettes. Usually my mother and I waited for him at the door, and she would hand him an envelope with the rent money inside. While counting the money, he asked if anything needed work or if there were any problems he should know about. My mother said, "No." He stuffed the envelope into his pocket, said, "See you next month," and meandered off down the cobblestones.

The week after Oscar died, Mr. Brennan came to the door, and my mother invited him in. We sat at the living room table, and she poured him tea, explaining what had happened. He said he'd had a dog when he was young too. There was an awkward pause, and he took the envelope and shoved it into his pocket. He looked at me and said, "I'm sorry to hear about your dog, kid." I remember wondering why he was apologizing. I even thought to ask him this, but I kept quiet, simply nodding.

IV

Outside the classroom the leaves were red and yellow and orange, swaying in the faint wind, drifting to the ground. Inside, fall colors festooned the walls, the kids chittering and laughing, some bouncing in their chairs, others running around the room. My mother had given me a letter for our teacher, Ms. Carey, so I dug it out of my backpack and handed it to her. She clipped it open with ruby fingernails, glancing up at me, offering a quick hug. Sighing, she asked the class to sit down with a commanding voice. "Teaching moment," she said, clapping her hands.

I don't remember what Ms. Carey said exactly, but the other kids formed a single-file line for construction paper, safety scissors, and coloring pencils. Soon, my desk was stacked with little condolence cards. One was black and white and said "Sorry" next to a red heart. None of it made me feel better, though for some reason I kept the black-and-white one, and still have it somewhere to this day.

V

In my early twenties, I had been dating Miranda for a few weeks. Out of nowhere, she told me she was going home to her mother's and that she would be back in a few days. I didn't ask why and just assumed it was to be with her mother. It wasn't until she came back she told me that her father had died. It had been sudden and unexpected. Though they hadn't been close, it had still come as a shock. Miranda said she hadn't told me earlier because she hadn't wanted to burden me. I was struck by her frankness, her selflessness while enveloped in grief. It was then I understood grief as something personal, a threshold where its articulation oversteps an unfathomable mark. That is to say, giving voice to grief is to make it public. In the following weeks and months, she would talk about her father openly, sharing stories and memories. In a way, I got to know him like this.

VI

One day, I was taking the cramped elevator up to my sarcophagus of a studio apartment, and it suddenly stopped, stuck between two floors. I pressed all the buttons, tried calling for help (my phone had no service), even banged on the metal doors, screaming until my throat was sore. Nothing worked. Soon it became hot, and it felt extremely claustrophobic, and I was sweating profusely, my clothes stuck to my skin. I sat down in the corner and fell asleep. I have no memory of dreaming then, but I remember waking up from this nap with a lurch.

The elevator was completely dark, and it felt like all the electrical current in the world had simply stopped. In retrospect, I would clinically call my feeling at the time disorientation, but what I distinctly remember was that I had discovered some secret of mortality, that in that moment, I felt pinned between life and death. I can only describe the feeling as intense, like a thought as heavy as an anvil being gently lowered on your head, the fragility of reality stark and bare. A beat later, the lights flickered on, and the elevator moved again.

VII

On occasion, I still dream of Oscar. In these dreams, he's very much alive, wagging his tail, gesturing to me as if I should follow him. He barks and howls if I don't chase him, so it becomes a race. Sometimes it's through fields of grass, other times it's underwater, and even once we were like spaceships gliding through the stars. His fur is always an arm's length away. ■

TEACH A MAN TO FISH
James K. Zimmerman

Give a man a fish and he will
crave the subtle flavor of sole
scallions and garlic, salmon's
oily meat glazed with soy
and maple syrup, or soft
catfish flesh within the crunch
of deep-fried corn

Teach a man to fish and he will
learn to crave the bobber tucking
under the river's skin like the nod
of a head when a dream tugs
from below the ripples of sleep

and he will wait to savor a rainbow
trout with a barbless hook in its lip,
the roiling flash of a school
of cocktail blues, the breach
of a small-mouth bass, or steady
insistence of flounder deep
in the folds of an ocean floor

Teach a man to fish and he will
learn to brave the flop and gasp,
the flapping of gills, the sharp slice
through vertebrae just behind the head
the gutting from anus to throat, blood
spattering on deck, dock, shoes

and he will learn to read ripples
on water, the inverse of a breeze's
path, the easy flick of a cast
that lands the lure or bait where
it needs to be, at a sunken log,
the seam of a stream, or deep
in the belly of the ocean

Teach a man to fish and if
he is fortunate he will learn
the quietude of early morning mist
in a birch canoe, evening shadows
under sail, the beauty of the placid
lulls and rolling surges of water,

the tranquility of a day
when nothing takes the hook
at all and a meal of beans,
sunset, and roasted corn
satisfies his craving

GRAPES IN THE WATER
Mary Wisniewski

I am a great builder of sandcastles. I have made Stonehenge, the Tower of London, a dragon, and the Roman Coliseum, complete with gladiators. Every summer, on beaches up and down Lake Michigan, I build kingdoms with moats, drawbridges, stables, guard towers, chapels, and long, cavernous passages propped by bits of driftwood.

I am great at sandcastles because I can't swim. I've never been able to manage more than a sixty-second dog paddle. Water is a dangerous element—all right in a teakettle but treacherous at more than five feet. I never saw the fun in a sport that kills you if you stop doing it—you can't decide to take a break halfway across the pond. If I had been given the water test at the witch trials, I would have sunk immediately, drowning as the crowd on the shore applauded my innocence of the demonic arts. Swimming defies my understanding of how the world works. In regular life, you struggle, but in the water, struggling makes you sink. It is a mystery.

My mother, who was dubious about all physical activity besides baking, signed me up for a swimming class when I was nine. "It might save you in case you ever fall off a boat," she said, cheerfully. She told me the story of how she had cracked her head on the bottom of a Chicago Park District pool and never gone into the water again. Then my father told how his transport ship got bombed during the war and they all had to jump into the ocean. He smacked his head on the steel hull of the ship, and salt water poured into the wound. So I had that to think about.

Swimming class started at 8:00 a.m., when it was about twenty degrees. The water was always a harsh blue, no matter how overcast the morning. It was an unfriendly color, the color of antifreeze and hospital gowns. Along the ends of the pool were black marks showing how deep it was at that point. The depths ranged from the reasonable three feet at one end to the absurd and outrageous twelve feet on the other end, where the diving boards were. Our teacher was a high school cheerleader on summer break who ignored us for nine weeks, until it was time to dive off the diving board. My turn came last. I stood shivering on the board and stared for a long time at the poisonous blue water. I wasn't sure whether to hold my breath before

I jumped, or right after, or right before I hit the water. I wondered if after I drowned I would go to heaven right away, and if I didn't, what purgatory would be like, and would it be something like a doctor's waiting room with rust-colored carpeting and old copies of *Highlights* magazine.

Behind me, I heard the Park District teacher. "Come on, like, just do it already." Then I heard her climbing the rails with quick, athletic, confident adolescent feet and stepping on the board behind me. I didn't want her to push me, so I jumped.

I forgot to hold my breath. The heavily chlorinated water rushed into my open mouth and burned my throat. I opened my eyes and saw white bubbles and the flailing of my own white legs but saw no bottom, no top, and no sides to the pool. I reached with my feet for a surface but could feel nothing but water. My mind was bright with panic. I shut my mouth and eyes and kept kicking, hoping to find a solid surface. Suddenly, through my eyelids, I knew it had grown lighter. I was above the surface, sputtering and gasping. I kicked my feet and looked for the sides of the pool. They were miles away. I sank again, then kicked back up. I saw my mother outside of the pool's chain-link security fence. She had her hand to her mouth. One of the male instructors thrust what looked like a flag pole into the water and told me to grab it. Then he pulled me out of the water. My mother took me home, and we baked cookies. We never spoke of swimming again.

I tried again a decade later. At a beach party, I let a friend show me how to move my head to breathe, how to time the stroke. It was a hot, windless August night. Lake Michigan was black and opaque, its low, gentle ripples streaked orange from the sodium-vapor lamps lighting the beach. I liked how the summer water felt on my skin. I swam several strokes, away from the pier, out onto the dark lake. Then an undertow like a sea monster grabbed my legs, and I went under. The pier was far away. I went down a second time, struggled to the surface of the black water, and yelled for help. My friends fished me out.

But I did want to try again, after I had daughters. They looked to me for an example, and I wanted to show them that they could face anything, even the water. Their father was a strong swimmer—a V-shaped champion in his high school yearbook. He would go out long distances on the lake, while the girls and I played in the sand. But I didn't ask him to teach me. I didn't ask him for much.

My husband was not a patient man. There were strange currents in his personality, like in Lake Michigan at night. He could be calm and kind and quiet for long periods, then suddenly, for the smallest of reasons or no reason at all, explode into rage and drag me under, so he wouldn't have to suffer his dark feelings alone. I tried to adapt to this. I tried not to take it personally. I tried to stay in the room and argue. I tried to leave the room and not argue. I tried to ask for things nicely; I tried not to ask for things at all; I tried to relax and I tried to struggle, but I could not adapt myself to his element. It was a mystery. I got sick all the time, with stomach pains and headaches. I apologized for this. But he hated me when I was sick, he hated me when I contradicted him, he hated me when I was late or had asked for something in the wrong tone. If I confronted him with something he had done, he would deny it, or leave out something, and I would become confused and wonder why everything seemed so poorly lit and disorienting, like the bottom of the Park District pool. The feeling flowed into other parts of my life, so I was never really sure if I'd locked the door, or turned off the oven, or paid the grocery clerk. I didn't know where I was, or how to grasp on to the one strong argument that would finally, finally make him understand.

Everyone knew but me, that it was time to go. My dad knew. My friends knew, offering help I failed to grasp. It took a long time to break through the surface of my optimism. Then I fled with my little girls and filed for divorce. It was a strange time, those first couple of years alone. He wouldn't pay support, so money was tight. I couldn't afford to take the girls to even budget movies, so I took them to the lake, which was free. I had them take swimming lessons at the Park District. They had good teachers, so I didn't worry. I vowed not to tell them scary stories about swimming. My older daughter loved the water and never wanted to get out. But my younger one was wary of it.

Once, when they were six and four, we went to the lake the last evening before the start of school. It was breezy and pleasant, and Montrose Beach was crowded with families speaking a mix of languages—Polish, Russian, Spanish, Tagalog. Daddies held their little girls horizontally in the water, letting them splash and kick. Boys pretended to be sharks and swam under the surface. The teenage lifeguard sat in his boat, chatting with his girlfriends, occasionally hollering through a megaphone to stop the horseplay and stay inside the ropes.

I took the hand of each girl and led them into the water. I did not like to let go of their hands. But I let the older girl take off by herself, splashing and playing, jumping into waves, trying the dog paddle she'd been taught in class. When she got too far away, I hollered at her to come back, trying to keep the terror out of my voice. I wished I could be on the shore, building sandcastles, but I had to show them I wasn't afraid.

My little girl would not let go of my hand. When we walked into water deep enough to touch her chin, she scrambled up my body and wrapped her wet, skinny arms around my neck. She was giggling, but frightened, and she squeezed my neck at every wave.

"Don't let the waves get me, Mommy."

"I won't. Don't worry."

She giggled and clung to me, with chattering teeth. The waves beat against us, and I concentrated on keeping my balance. I tried to keep track of her sister. When I didn't see her, my heart beat faster and I held my breath. Then I'd see her curly dark head pop up behind another kid, and my limbs would relax, a little. I tried to convince my little girl that the water was nice.

"Look at the water, honey. It looks like it has gold in it." The sun was setting, and the tops of the waves shone with pink and golden light. The undersides of the waves were deep purple.

"There are grapes in the water," she said, giggling.

"Do you want to ride on the grapes? Do you want Mommy to hold you in the water? You don't have to be afraid."

"No!" She wrapped her legs around my waist. She was wet and slippery, but she clung like a vine. We watched the gulls circling overhead. She tilted her head back and pointed up. Her long, wet hair hung back into the water.

"Look, Mommy. Look at the birds. There's my family flying around up there. There's my mommy and daddy and sister. What's my family doing up there? Hey, come back, family! Come back!"

"I'm sorry, honey." My throat hurt. "I'm sorry for everything." The air grew cool, and I shivered. She shivered too, and squeezed my neck.

"I want to go back to the beach," she said. I yelled at her sister to come back—it was getting late. Then we walked back to build a sandcastle, which is what I wanted to do anyway. Everything was going to be all right. Everything, somehow, was going to be all right. One day, I'd learn to swim for real. For now, I'd build sandcastles, topping the turrets with sticks, and seagull feathers, and shiny bits of shell. The people in the castle had won a victory and were flying their tiny flags. ■

THREE CARTOONS
Charles Johnson

*"By my calculations, their civilization collapsed when they cut
back on the liberal arts and humanities."*

"I think you're making great progress in realizing the Buddhist idea of No-Mind."

"You still waiting for Reparations?"

HOME AND FRONT
Moazzam Sheikh

H e kissed his girls, Judith and Elizabeth, named after his mother and Tracy's respectively, as they dashed out of the house to board the beat-up yellow school bus, their backpacks bouncing. His eyes caught the parking lights blinking before he looked away. He registered how different the two girls were, one eager and curious, the other reluctant, given to introspection. Lisa got his bone structure, but Judy had his temperament, calm and poised even in the midst of a tempest. Boy, had he missed them. What a delicate age to be without a father! *Why did I go? That was so stupid. So I could return with a little money cushion to support my family.* Look what he came back with instead. A duffel full of nightmares, cries, bloody howls, bloody body parts, deafening footfalls of fear, deadened stares from victims of rape and sexual assault, charred bodies, buddies dying in arms. Now he couldn't hold a job. Though he knew it was only a matter of time, he couldn't wait. The girls were growing up fast. Tracy'd been a real weightlifter; *I'm just headed straight to palookaville,* a smirk appearing on his mug.

On duty, off duty, patrolling the streets, swiftly coming into action on a tip, lying back in his barrack, smoking cigarettes, sitting at a table in the giant kitchen's common area working his laptop, reading emails and baseball news, burying the nagging thought of leaving his young wife and two little girls behind. What if they got hurt? What if Tracy was unfaithful! What if some demented person broke in and raped her! Would she call the cops? Would she tell him? *I want to get the hell out of here before my luck runs out. What am I doing here? I got duped, man!* What was he doing there? The question's sharp tip pierced his skin. Already weary of the posttraumatic stress syndrome, everybody was hiding their pain behind their masculine facades. But when he saw his buddies blown up, or even shaken, he shakily believed in the sanctity of his mission, that he was not just a hired foot soldier, a man without conscience—but a thinking person. Or was he? Yes, he was, and he believed in accepting the consequences of his actions. He understood, too, when a person did have power over his actions and when he didn't. He wasn't simply justifying being a part of an invading army; he realized that the larger world was more complicated, and it wasn't good to crank out judgments.

The world wasn't just a matter of saints versus sinners. The bulk of human suffering occurred in the shade. It was healthier to have a deeper look on life. But at the end of the day when the thought circus had run its course, what depressed him was the worry about his little girls and his wife being alone in the shithole called Vallejo, without the man of the house. As he saw again and again the stunned faces of little children and terrified, sleepless eyes of women, and with him not understanding their language, their pleas, he couldn't suppress the thought of his own family getting hurt at the hands of a crazy fuck who might or might not know that he was hurting the family of someone who'd given up everything for his country. As the yellow school bus rolled away from his waving hand, he scanned the neighborhood and though he spotted a neighbor or two, he lacked the desire to engage with them. He turned his back on them and entered his own hell.

He stopped and stared absentmindedly at the family photos on the wall. He missed Tracy and felt terrible that she had to pick up the pieces while he recuperated. He cleaned the kitchen countertop, put the rest of the food back into the fridge and the dirty dishes into the sink. He thought of calling his mother but couldn't make up his mind. He opened the door in the kitchen that led to the space in the back of their tiny house. One day he'd like to move his family away from this pit. He put on a Creedence Clearwater Revival CD, lit a cigarette and sat down on the steps with the soft morning sun glaring into his face. *Long as I remember / The rain's been comin' down.* The smoke stung his wet eyes.

Tracy would be home in a few hours and the time without her became unbearable. He was lucky to have married a tough woman. Someone else would have left him by now. Being held in her embrace made a hell of a difference to his state of mind. Making love to her pushed the demons of the war farther away till they came crawling back when he was not alert. He wished, with immense sadness, his buddy Private James Doniger had had someone like Tracy to pull him out. Perhaps he should have invited him to come and stay with him so both of them could recuperate, heal each other by being around his girls, go to the bay for fishing, do some hiking, go visit Frisco, strum some guitar, listen to some live music. *And now Jimmy Boy is gone, dead, overdosed on aerosol, the fucking computer cleaner! Why could nobody save him, why?* He heard his shout in his head. He saw Jimmy Boy shouting, *Why can't we save him? What's he done to die? I am goin', hey, bud, give me a cover. You fuckin' outta your mind? Just give me a fuckin'* cover! Can you do that? If you've got any fuckin' humanity still left in you? Hey you fuckin' fuck asshole, there's booby traps everywhere, there's snipers waiting for your head, I don't wanna see your crown blown off on my watch. We are not here on a humanitarian mission, soldja! Okay you shithole, I get you. Why don't you just look away and just tell the officer you didn't see me cause I'm goin'. You've been a good pal. Of course I had the bastard covered but I wasn't sure he'd survive. The next I know my Jimmy Boy's a hero, his photo splashed all over the newspapers, rescuing a little Iraqi shit at the risk of his life. The great American putting his life on the line for other people. No mention of his pal givin' cover. While I was coverin' his ass, a stray bullet hit my helmet. Of all the hits and explosions, that's the one that still wakes me up. Well done, Private Doniger, you're goin' to earn a medal if you make it out alive. We'll try our best though, hahaha! Mr. Embedded Photographer, how come your camera can catch my Jimmy Boy's heroics but not mine? Why couldn't you catch the bullet hitting my helmet, missing my face by half an inch? Just as well, no one mentioned what Jimmy and I did to the sand niggers when we broke into the house by the cloth market after a lousy tip! Oh don't get us wrong, we are men with conscience, we suffer from pangs of remorse, we wake up in the middle of the night, even right after we've made love to our wives, shrieking or howling. But Jimmy Boy wasn't married. He spent time alone in his apartment and sometimes at his mother's. But he's gone now, so no more driving his neighbors nuts. I wish I had him come over for a while and spend time with my family. That might have done him some good. That aerosol shit ain't good for anyone. We could've listened to Creedence Clearwater, Grateful Dead and other homies and played our guitars and jammed with folks I know in Oakland. Why did you do that, Private Doniger? Oh God, oh shit, my head's hurtin', explodin' explodin' explo ...

I see now poverty and patriotism don't mix well, kinda like oil and water. Tracy and I are both like water, flowing into each other, cascading through difficult situations, adjusting around each other's rough shorelines. I met Tracy in the lot next to an Ace Hardware store where they sell pumpkins and Christmas trees. It was love at first sight. Couldn't be any other way. We were both broke and wanted a baby Christmas tree and there was only one left, the sad-looking one. We were both hovering around, not letting our empty pockets speak out loud for the other to hear. Her clothes were certainly cleaner than mine, but even if she had been wearing soiled jeans or hand-me-downs, she would've looked stunning with the shine in her eyes and with a dip in her cheeks, her hair curling around her shoulders and dropping over her forehead in carefree bangs, and I thought it would be so good to make love to this woman, spend the rest of my life with this stranger. We were waiting for one of the guys to take notice of us, but they were busy with a family with kids pestering over the kind of tree they wanted. So as I am checking her out as discreetly as possible, she giggles and says, "Are you *after that tree? You can have it," but she just stood there, waiting for my reaction. "Naw, you can have it." I can still hear the squeak in my voice, as if someone had squeezed my balls. She shook her head and the breeze added an extra flick to her hair. I said, "This baby's yours," and I made a mock dash towards the midget tree. "Come on, lemme help you load it into your car." She stopped me with the light stretch of her hand and I obliged and she says, "What's your name?" "Justin. What's yours?" "Tracy. Hi!" And as we shook hands, a current ran through my body and almost knocked me down. "Are you okay?" she asked and I said, "I am not sure. I guess your eyes are making me tipsy," and she goes, "Excuse me?" and begins laughing, freeing her hand. "You're weird. I mean funny."* Every time he looked back at that memory it felt like a scene straight out of a movie like *When Harry Met Sally*. Or maybe *Bonnie and Clyde*. She got the Christmas tree on his insistence but he got her and soon they were married, living in a small one-bedroom apartment in Pinole, another shithole, since she worked there.

He wasn't good at holding jobs but he could always find work and before you know it Tracy was pregnant. Their families helped out, but everybody was poor, struggling to make ends meet. The tests showed she was pregnant with twins. To Justin's surprise he was itching to be a father. He had always been a caring person, to his parents, his younger siblings, to their friends and neighbors. Half of his closest friends were not white. Although Ale—short for Alejandro—had dropped out of high school (unlike Justin, who did make it past high school and even took some classes at various community colleges around the Bay Area), they had stayed friends, and it was Ale who called one early morning to wake Justin up, forcing him to turn on the television. That day Justin sat in front of the tube in a state of shock, watching repeated images of two planes ramming into twin towers for an hour or more. Both Justin and Tracy were scared, angry, confused. Many of their friends showed up that day offering and receiving comfort from each other. But everyone was on edge. Some of his friends were even blaming the country, saying all kinds of shit like what goes around comes around and so on. But many just wanted to nuke a Muslim country.

His girls had turned eight months old that week, crawling all over the place and attempting to stand up by grabbing onto edges and protrusions. Usually he'd be ultra alert, noticing one of the girls was inching closer to a danger zone, but that day Justin couldn't muster any strength, couldn't feel any appetite or any deep love for his wife, his girls or others for that matter. The shock of tragedy had stunned his senses and numbed his body, but periodically there would arise in him a wave of hateful anger, so that when Tracy egged the boys to go out and get some fresh air, he offered no resistance. That evening Justin's buddies tried to run over a Pakistani- or Indian-looking woman with a teenage boy and a younger girl walking back to their car in a Safeway parking lot. His pals wanted to get out of their truck and beat the crap out of those scumbag foreigners, but Justin's common sense prevailed over the itch to assuage national pride. When his friends dropped him off, the twins were asleep, but Tracy sat glued to television. Justin joined her on the worn-out sofa, held her in his embrace, as the two wondered in their grief if they knew anyone among the dead. They didn't. Both Justin and Tracy had not paid much attention to politics up until then and had little to no idea of Afghanistan's relationship to America, but in the next few months he saw an opportunity to lift his family out of poverty by joining the army for a good cause, emboldened by some famous athletes who had given up their sports careers influenced by similar thinking. Justin could feel the country coming together after being bruised by a senseless enemy. Tracy gave in, realizing she wouldn't have to work and could survive on Justin's salary. Justin saw it as a way to get back to college when he returned from his short service. As the moment of departure neared, he wondered why we were invading Iraq and not Afghanistan, but somehow the idea of toppling an oppressor and getting hands on weapons of mass destruction seemed like a noble cause and convinced him he was headed the right way. That's how far his mind could contemplate the complexity of the world beyond his nose and he could live with that. Even before he left for Iraq, enough money to calm their fears about being poor forever began pouring in. The day he kissed Tracy and his girls goodbye he wasn't betting on his survival, his fifty-fifty chance of dying over there; he imagined his girls graduating from high school and getting into good colleges, his wife working some downtown job wearing fancy clothes, and he himself working some city job with full benefits, all due to this sacrifice, this intolerable separation.

When he returned he felt extremely lucky to have come back alive to his wife and children and family and friends in one solid piece. Others he knew weren't so lucky. He and Tracy began taking their girls to church on Sunday as well. He had returned a conflicted man, with an unsettled heart, and found it hard to pin down the source of this deep discomfort. He'd always been a nonreligious person, putting more faith in human beings, which mostly meant his close friends, than in Jesus Christ or God, and though he saw his friends almost daily—they had been extremely helpful in his absence—their company failed to fill the emptiness he'd felt in his heart, in his whole body now. Even making love to Tracy left him dissatisfied. The fact that he'd lost Miguel and Ricardo to roadside bombs and Jimmy to an overdose of aerosol didn't surprise him. He knew they were all taking a chance for their country. Though he was sad and missed them often, the source of his agitation had to be something else. Despite how kind nature had been to him, he found any peace leaking out, leaving deflated organs. It was Tracy who suggested one day that he could try going back to school, take classes at a community college. He needed a change of pace, a change of scenery, a new direction, not just for his own sake but for the future of his family. He saw wisdom in her words and somehow the idea spoke to his heart immediately, and the next thing he knew he'd already enrolled in two classes at Laney College in Oakland.

It worked out well as he made it back from his classes before his girls returned from school. He spent time with them till Tracy showed up. He noticed staying busy was the best medicine and his girls too made him forget the war for a while. He had to be thankful to whatever higher power was there looking out for him, that his posttraumatic stress wasn't too bad. He contacted the authorities about his postwar situation but they could care less. The loose talk about the high number of veterans among the homeless in San Francisco didn't ring true to his ears. His nightmares were manageable. He'd revisit the horrors of the combat sure and his reactions to those gory situations, but most of his shrieks and shouts were within his dreams and the kids never woke up. Tracy could tell when he was wrestling with those demons and she would either embrace him or massage his chest and shoulders and back, even his thighs to divert his attention from violence to love. One of his distant buddies, Val, had become a wife beater after returning and before leaving again, accusing Jenny of cheating on him. He had had similar thoughts, but he'd decided he'd never be a wife beater. He'd sit down and talk, rekindle the love, rebuild the trust. That's what he'd always been, a nonviolent person. But he did believe in self-defense and that's how he'd justified letting Uncle Sam twist his arm into fighting in Iraq. If that guy Saddam hadn't had links to Al-Qaeda and hadn't helped them out, Justin would have had a harder time joining the army as a fighter. He would have joined as noncombat personnel. But now things were messy. He was grateful on the one hand and very disturbed on the other. He was starting to hear a lot of shit about how the Bush clan were oil people and had no reason to attack Iraq, that it was done for the black gold. The real enemy was somewhere else, and in the meantime Americans were being picked off. There was confusion all around. He heard about antiwar marches, but he was glad he didn't have to be near those sickos.

He barely passed his first semester, two classes, basic English and math. Now he had something to look forward to. He thought it would get easier as his brain adjusted to absorbing information. But right now it was a real struggle. It was a miracle in fact that he hadn't flunked the classes. It was probably good karma if you got sympathetic teachers. He'd tried very hard to study, do his homework while leashing his drifting mind, the struggle that left him exhausted at the end. When he sat around his girls, his affection for them would suddenly dip or even go into deep freeze. He'd stare at them, thinking they were adopted. He didn't understand how that could happen, how one heart could just turn itself off, even temporarily, to one's own flesh and blood. He was lucky to have Tracy in his life. She was such a wonderful mother and all her good qualities, patience, perseverance, selflessness, affection, he could see, had already poured into his girls. They were always chirpy, now four, keeping their sibling rivalry to the minimum, their hysterics and tantrums almost nonexistent. How easy to forget the little gifts that made one's life worth living!

One day, Tracy gone to work, the girls played in the small backyard with their toys while he sat on a tall steel stool in the kitchen, his books splayed open on the table, peering at them occasionally, feeling grateful for the bliss, when suddenly something got into Judy's head that prompted her to rush up the steps, stealthily, and scare the hell out of him. In that one instant he saw too many Justins exploding out of his skin. *Fire! Take cover! You are authorized to shoot children!* Justin fell off the stool, rolling under the table, taking an imaginary cover behind a bunker as shells landed left and right. *It's an ambush!* Another Justin leapt out of him to pounce on the ambushing hyena, grabbed and pinned her down to the ground, throttling. One more got to see his own head blown off, splattering dark red color everywhere. Another one stunned, frozen at the sight of a surprise attacker, shocked eyes with a plea to live. The girl simply ran past him to the bathroom *shoot her shoot her blow her head off* and then within seconds ran back out. He exhaled and inhaled and exhaled and inhaled and exhaled. He couldn't concentrate after that moment. He had to keep himself busy or the demons of the war would burst through his head. He got up, put a Tom Russell CD, washed a few dishes, and hollered, "You girls ready to go for ice cream?"

East of Woodstock, West of Vietnam ...

It was clear that the girl's dash had triggered fear in him. At the slightest sudden noise he'd get all tensed up, part of his brain would go numb, and though remaining still, he'd imagine himself reacting as he would in a combat situation. He could hear his and his comrades' and victims' loud, piercing noises. *What's the count, man? How many kills?* Even Tracy noted that his neck and back would suddenly feel like wood. An oil rub seemed to help, and when the girls had dozed off, a couple of beers relaxed his nerves. He did experience an increased sexual intimacy with Tracy, whose body had gone a bit flabby in the last year, but their chemistry still did magic when he didn't come to her with his head full of shrapnel. Even then it was good but not what it should be. It surprised him to see violence and sex mingle so easily. Especially after the war he'd made a point of staying away from booze and smoke, smoke for the sake of his girls. But a couple of beers, he reasoned, were not only harmless, they were like valium and an aphrodisiac rolled into one. The joy of physical and emotional connection with Tracy, however, began to crack when his behavior of getting startled didn't ebb but remained steady throughout the next semester. He began to have, though infrequently, headaches. He had to see a doctor, who recommended that he go to an optometrist. He did and it turned out he'd have to wear glasses now. This helped with the headaches a bit, but they couldn't be fully subdued.

Someone must have drilled that idea into his head, that he try taking at least one class for fun, like acting, or French, American poetry, or a modern literature class; how about modern jazz dance!? Things at home were kind of working out. The girls were in pre-K now and staying longer at school three days a week, allowing Justin to pick up part-time security work at the supermarket Tracy worked at as a cashier. The pay was better as they had relocated to Oakland. That way he was closer to more community colleges. He noticed City College of San Francisco had a wider variety of classes designed partly for intellectual enrichment. There were classes that had to do with the legal world. He would certainly dig that, but perhaps next semester? Anyway, he felt drawn to a class that looked at American culture through its varied ethnic literatures. That sounded exciting. He spoke to Tracy about it and she encouraged him to contact the teacher via email since the semester had already started. The professor wrote back about an available spot, advising him to sign up online. It was being offered twice a week in the morning hours and that suited him well. He would be home before the girls returned from school. He'd have their munchies ready. On other days he did his security guard job. He and Tracy drove together, and then he took the bus back. Two other classes were in the evening at the community college in Oakland, near the apartment they now rented for real cheap. Tracy was home in the evenings.

He'd never been to the City College of San Francisco campus before but he liked its layout, with a decent-sized hilltop in the middle surrounded by buildings on three sides, liked the feel of students milling around different stalls selling food and art and craft. It was groovy. The campus spoke to him in a way no other campus had so far. There was a little uphill walk to the campus and that made him thirsty. Following a steady trail of students into one of the buildings near the administration office, he ended inside a spacious cafe full of students and staff. That day he'd arrived early and had about half an hour to kill. He filled a paper cup with Italian roast and got in line to pay at the cashier. The cashier had to repeat herself to get his attention as he'd become too distracted by the energy buzz, mostly of the female variety, and as he smiled at the cashier, a young woman with an accent, he realized he was for the first time lusting after women other than his wife. Something about it, this realization, made him giddy and irritated at the same time. *I am so much in love with Tracy that I didn't cheat on her even in Iraq,* he reminded himself, *where I could have fucked anyone I wanted, like some of my buddies did. Except once, but did that count?* But this onslaught of sexual energy, which seemed in abundance at this college, had succeeded in enticing his vulnerable heart. It was just an innocent digression, he concluded. *I would not betray Tracy, my soul mate, the mother of my two darling girls.* Commuting to the class here every week would perk up his spirits, he mused. The atmosphere in other community colleges he'd attended so far either bordered on dullness, callosity, or intimidation. The community college in Oakland felt even threatening, with too many brothers and sisters yakking out loud and everybody else imitating the ghetto rough talk and walk. *I am no pussy either, but I know when to leave a battlefield behind.* He had begun to feel ashamed of the symbolism he couldn't shake off and when his mind was out of control, the idea rushed to his mental tongue involuntarily. But here it felt more creative, colorful, the right mix of differences. Intoxicated by the visuals of the campus, he arrived in the class, already enrolled a week late, ten minutes into it. Still, he walked in smiling as if he had just conquered a tiny island of happiness in the middle of Pacific Ocean.

Professor Shams, he learned, was originally from Pakistan. Pleasant, soft-spoken, articulate, humorous; it took Justin a while to get used to his verbal acrobatics. It seemed that he expected the class to have a previous knowledge of things like history and literature. He alluded to events like the Boxer Rebellion and RCD. He wanted the class to know who García Márquez was. He made it clear that he was working with the assumption that majority of the class knew who Gregor Samsa was. What did they think of Huck Finn's leading the big man Jim down the river, the wrong direction for a slave who wanted to run away? What was Holden Caulfield's problem? Who was Uncle Tom? Just as the class became antsy, he'd throw in some humor. He'd flirt too. If it hadn't been Justin's first day in the class, he would have said, Chill out, dude! This is community college, not Cal! But he bit his tongue, not only because he was new. His own ignorance notwithstanding, he enjoyed the challenges Professor Shams threw at them. To his surprise, however, there were students in the class who recognized the allusions and references he came up with. Although that made him a bit insecure, the class excited him. He wanted to catch up what he had missed in the previous two classes. Or most of his life. His American life.

He was already making eye contact with the folks sitting around him. That Black dude sitting on his right had his food splayed out on the pan of his chair. Professor made a joke about it. The guy explained that he needed to eat in order to gain weight so he could pass a fitness test for a job. He didn't explain which job he was chasing after. Justin took his guess. Nightmares will kill you, my friend, he wanted to tell him. The guy took a peek at him as if he'd muttered his thought out loud. Justin smiled, he smiled. They both looked away to Professor Shams's theatrics. The young lady sitting on his left, some sort of East Asian, offered to share her notes with Justin after the professor asked the class to help. As he scanned the class, he was alerted to the layer of sexual temptation bubbling under the surface. *I bet my ass this chick by the window licked her lips as our eyes met.* He closed his eyes, conjured Tracy's face, and made a vow to not take the bait. *Tracy, help me to be faithful to you*, he prayed silently.

The class had already read the story Professor Shams took apart with the help of students. He had never heard of Langston Hughes. He'd heard of Harlem, but not the Harlem Renaissance. He hadn't read the story so hadn't a clue and he stayed quiet, feeling dumb.

He appreciated that the professor said that the purpose of this class or his lecture was not to offend one group or another. He gathered they weren't supposed to turn this class into a white-bashing exercise, especially white male bashing, since they were the source of all the evil in the world. Justin smiled inwardly. "Our collective attempt is to separate the historical and cultural threads," the professor added, "that make up the American quilt." He liked the approach and he later told Tracy that he was not taking a class about American culture but a class about American cultures through literature. Justin felt he needed that exposure and that he was a good person, not after settling scores, that he wasn't some kind of an ex Panther or Viet Cong sympathizer. Justin began to understand the story, putting pieces together, after hearing students chip in voicing their points of view, that it was about a guy named Charlie, an Asian, maybe Chinese, who'd been working on ships, turn of the century, been with whores, mostly white whores, some Russian whores, faced racism at the hands of white men even when he was in China—*I had no fucking idea that the white man had colonized parts of China too before their fucking communist revolution*—he'd faced racism in American cities, in bars where only colored folks were allowed, been roughed up, knocked out by white trash, spat on by a white woman whom he'd bought drinks, jailed for disturbing the peace, missing his ship and so on.

Tracy heard it all in awe. Charlie finally found a benevolent white master in New York, who had a whore for a mistress, addicted to the white powder. When one day Charlie's master had gone to some other big city for an urgent business transaction, the whore took a fancy to the Asian dude, hoping to seduce him. As she pulled him into her bed, the fucker, the psycho killed her by throttling her. *What the fuck! Why not fuck her first, then kill her!! Glad I didn't shout.* Tracy rolled her eyes, guffawing. *I didn't tell her I felt so ashamed the way my mind had responded to the story. I didn't know if anybody had noticed the reddening of my face. I had completely blanked out, disoriented as if air dropped in the middle of a combat zone, ducking the random bullets, praying to stay alive, pleading the hell to be over with.* When he came to his senses, the class was analyzing the opening of the story, where Charlie, aboard a wobbly deck of a ship, is running away, looking at the Manhattan skyline. The professor drew the class's attention to the movies now, to the scenes where the camera was unsteady to give a certain feel, he explained, of uncertainty, of shakiness. Justin remembered how he hated those movies where the camera was mostly like that. He walked out of those films with a headache. The only time he liked that type of camera work was during a war sequence, or like in a horror movie, when a character walks into an abandoned home, wandering through haunted rooms and crooked staircases.

After he walked out of the class and left the Cloud Hall building, the fog rolling all over the place like a big giant tank, his nervousness returned. In the class he hadn't felt twitchy, or scared of being jumped at. He wanted to get away from the crowd as quickly as possible, straight to the train station, and back to Oakland. A queer thought took hold of him, that he was the rich, benevolent white master who'd flown to Chicago on an urgent business-related errand, leaving Tracy behind only to be raped and strangled by one of his friends. As he quickened his pace, he calmed down and he was able to put a lid on his paranoia during the train ride, except for those long minutes underwater in the tunnel. He'd never liked tunnels. It was just that he liked open spaces and wide sky. He didn't mind growing up in tiny apartments as long as there were big sidewalks and plenty of barren land to roam around with his buddies. That was one thing he found hard getting used to in Oakland. There were few places to roam, though the drive to the lake wasn't too bad.

His girls seemed to have appreciated the transition and he'd do anything for his babes, anything! Seeing his girls do their girly things every day made him acknowledge there were things in life one had to be grateful for. He wished and wished and wished there were no wars, there were no murders, no robberies, no rapes, no bruising, no hurting, no meanness in the world. That alone wouldn't take the tragedies out of one's life, though it would certainly minimize the suffering. Human beings had to reckon with natural disasters and illnesses. But we had added to our miseries by the pure evils of our greedy intentions, he reflected. He was glad he was home on time and able to set up lunch for his daughters, who ate ravenously these days, probably about to hit a growth spurt. Looking at them every night snuggled in bed with their pandas and teddy bears, he imagined their legs gaining an inch beneath the fluffy blanket before the sunlight rapped its knuckle at their window.

I had no idea how a war could change a person like me, he thought out loud, *a simpleton, an ordinary fella like me who just wanted some love, bread on the table, a job, a little security in life.* That night as they sat down in front of the TV watching some mindless late-night show, he openly shared some of his apprehensions with Tracy. He was worried if the war demons would get the upper hand. How would that affect the girls? Her massage on his shoulders and neck only did so much to soothe the mind, but he went on and on about how insecure he'd felt lately, that something bad was gonna happen to her or the girls, "I'd come home and witness some tragedy." She tried to laugh it off, then suggested he should see a psychiatrist or a therapist. She said she'd been reading articles about soldiers returning with all sorts of problems, from anxiety attacks to nightmares to sleep deprivation to depression. That's where family and friends come in, she hammered the point. There's professional help out there. Anybody who'd experienced a real combat situation, she had read and come to understand, would walk with a kind of mental disease, fear of being ambushed clinging to his back, and she added, that the families left behind by soldiers suffered equally, though in different ways. The rub of her fingers was starting to have the desired effect. He was calmer now. Holding each other in an embrace, they talked about friends, relatives, childhood. She mentioned a funny little episode from her work, about an older guy in her checkout line, short a couple of dollars, holding up the line, unable to decide what to take off his shopping list. But he was so adorable, so sorry that he was causing an unwanted scene, Tracy explained, she couldn't be rude to him. They had to open another counter to move the waiting line. *That's Tracy*, he thought, *all love and kindness from head to toe. Wouldn't survive combat duty!* He finally picked a small packet of condoms and said he didn't want it.

They decided to make love on the couch. As they undressed, she examined his cock in her gentle firm grip. He could read her wish, if it were half an inch longer, if not more, but its thickness made up for the trivial shortcoming. They were, both his cock and her pussy, a good fit, and they were *hellova* lovers, as they told each other often. Under special circumstances they could fuck like rabbits, go on all night long, with the right kind of music and some weed, so rarely. God knows what got into his head, he asked her if she'd give him a blow job instead tonight. She looked at him, smiling as if trying to read the drift of his mind, and almost asked if he'd like her to belly dance for him too or put on a veil.

"Would you, please?"

"Anything for you, honey bun." And she took the semierect member to her succulent pout. "Lie back and relax, let me give you the best fellatio you've ever had," she said as her other hand smoothed his belly. He said, "What?" She said, "Relax!"

She felt his belly tense up instead, but she persisted and soon it gave way to the stubborn gentleness of her hand. What he didn't tell her was that when she spoke the word *fellatio*, it had sounded like a town in Iraq he had to visit a few times. But love and war didn't mix well, like oil and water. Better not conjure Fallujah at this very moment, and he shook the war out of his mind, he knew, only temporarily. His head rolling back on a pillow, she casually asked about his day, his first day in class. His member grew, eyes closing, his fingers running through her hair, surprised at the parade of female faces from the class donning Tracy's body, speaking briefly about the class and that he was looking forward to it. The moment he described the story's final scene about the mistress being strangled, pure bliss engulfed him inside Tracy's mouth.

His second week in class. He had caught up with the readings, established a cordial rapport with a few students in the class, worked on an assignment which Tracy helped him out with a bit. *See I get a lot of thoughts in my head, complicated but sophisticated ideas—I wish I had opted for education early on and not wasted my time with the kind of friends I had—but it takes a person like you,* he confided in her, *the clear-headed, more rational and less verbose, to sift through the clutter, the crap, the claptrap, to formulate a decent, coherent thought.* She smiled. He loved her smile. The professor was pleased with his take-home assignment about Esther, the Indian chick with a quarter of French blood who got taken away from her reservation to father Paul's missionary outpost, with her father's permission. *This Esther chick grows up at the outpost of Western imperialism, as Professor Shams put it, and falls in love with Paul's nephew while missing her own culture from time to time. She yields to the power of love, as Tracy and I did when we both met over a Christmas tree, but this fucker betrays her, as does father Paul, who convinces his nephew that though Esther might have become Christian she is still inferior to the white race, calling her a snake. Esther overhears the man she has come to consider her father. Heartbroken, mad at the feeble-kneed lover, she kills her amour by poking him with a sharply pointed arrow dipped in poison.* Though he didn't tell Tracy about it, he kept thinking that he understood the metaphors in the story. He had made up his mind to speak up in the class about how he saw a parallel between the story and his own life, especially his decision to join the army and be deployed to Iraq. That he saw Iraq as Esther, that he had fooled himself into thinking that he was headed there to love the people there, to free them of Saddam's tyranny, but what he did there, what they as an army did there even if their intentions were good, was nothing short of raping Esther. And so as a payback she had killed him, almost, by inserting the poison of history into his skin. He was all excited to be making a literary connection. He suddenly saw literature so intricately connected to actual human life. "I had no fucking idea," he hollered once alone in the house.

So here I was in the class, exchanging pleasant stares, revving up my inner engine, collecting my thoughts as the professor began talking. I finally mustered courage and raised my hand; it's like he notices me for the first time, not true, asked me to introduce myself, clarifying that I had missed the early classes and so had missed when others had graciously introduced themselves. I thought it was no big deal laying out bits about my life, nothing to really speak of, in front of others, but then as I mentioned my time in Iraq, the fucker took me for a ride, insinuating I must have seen things I wished I hadn't seen, to which I was stupid enough to nod and even stress on the words too many. *But the asshole wouldn't stop as he had the nerve to further needle me by asking whether I would be going to a march against the war over the weekend. I wish I'd had the guts to blurt out that I had no intention of joining morons and pansies, that the world was a tough place and it was one thing to wax eloquent from the safety of your wife's cunt and another to actually put your own life on the line. Things would've been all right if he'd stopped right there. No, he had to go a step further to show what a low-class monkey he was when he asked if I had any blood on my hands. That was a grenade thrown at me, exploding in my face, and like a stunned idiot I sputtered, "Perhaps!" My mind went blank as night and in that darkness I could see his mouth making weird shapes. Then it seemed he moved on to some other student. I could make out only a word here and there for the rest of the lecture as the spell of darkness evaporated in places. It was like someone had grabbed my hair and dunked me in water repeatedly. I walked out of the class shell-shocked, feeling the pain in my bones, drained of any desire to walk, to make it to the train station, to stick out the entire journey, the time under the tunnel, dreading the ride home, scared shitless to face my girls and Tracy.*

He managed somehow, only God knows how, kept opening and closing his fist, stuffing them inside the pockets, slipping his palms under the thighs, hiding them behind his backpack, obscuring the view of others. Ridiculous, really, since he hadn't strangled anyone, hadn't broken any jaws. His work had been done with bullets; the victims of his weapon were hidden from his eyes. There was no way to tell, looking at a collective mass of dead bodies, whose bullet got who. *There was no blood on my hand,* he sighed. *Then why the fuck did I say, "Perhaps!" What a dumb thing to say, Justin! I'll get over it like I always do. I am no Private Doniger,* he yelled at himself. As he got off the bus, two blocks from his home, he wasn't too sure. He had no strength left, his backpack felt full of rocks, his shoulders and back stiff as wood and his mind suspicious of everybody aiming his way. He became extra cautious, believing everyone on the street was a suicide bomber with a purpose to smack into him, slicing him into a million pieces. If a car sped by, it made a hundred lizards run up and down his spine, and by the time he turned the block and approached the apartment building, his head was ready to burst from the pressure of the battle scenes being enacted inside.

As soon as the elevator door closed, it freaked him out. Despite the weak bulb on in the elevator, he thought this nothingness would swallow him. He couldn't breathe for those long minutes. The door opened and he tumbled out gasping for air. Walking down the corridor, hearing voices coming from his apartment, he stiffened, with crazy thoughts running wild in his head. *Someone's broken into my place?* His fatigue took flight, his body language changed into that of a marine. He was ready to pounce at the door and kill the intruder. Had Tracy forgotten the time he came home? He heard Judy and realized what a moron he could be at times. Tracy had a day off and she was going to pick up the girls from school on the early side. A sigh of relief, but dismay returned. How to tell her about the humiliation that came from saying, "Perhaps!" *No, can't torture her. It's my own private hell.*

He turned the door knob and there was Tracy, the girls and a few of his pals, to his horror, ready to sing. *Fuck, it's my birthday!* They had the cake set on the table with candles. Joel began lighting them. His girls ran up to him. Tracy and he kissed. Life, perhaps, wasn't bad at all despite the nightmares. Joel came to give him a hug. Then Ricky and his girlfriend, Tammy. Ronaldo said, Hey, buddy. Sean came over. Justin blew out the candles. Tammy started distributing the pieces. Somebody was passing beer around. He went to the CD player and played a Creedence Clearwater song... *Long as I remember / The rain's been comin' down.* He nibbled on his cake ever so cautiously and Sean hollered, Hey dude, why the fuck you keep looking at and wiping your hand? Something sticky on your fingers I can't see?... and everybody started to laugh. Including him. With tears in his eyes no one noted. ■

THIS IS YOU
Tommy Moore

Y ou are Casey Malloy.

It's a new day! Get up. Put on the boxer shorts, black cargo pants, black T-shirt, and black baseball cap on the chair by the bed. Put socks on your feet. See the running shoes by your bedroom door.

Be Casey Malloy.

Smoke one tiny bong hit. It helps. Eat a banana. Drink a glass of water.

Parked below your apartment, there is a red 1984 Toyota pickup with construction racks. Find the keys to your red Toyota pickup hanging on a hook by the front door.

Start your car. All the presets are set to the classic rock station. Listen to classic rock.

Drive to the 7-Eleven on the corner of Victory and Vineland. Park. Dump yesterday's coffee from the refillable coffee mug in your cup holder. Go inside. Buy a one-liter bottle of Crystal Geyser. Fill your reusable coffee mug with coffee. Pay the cashier.

Now, take the 170 to the 5 and then the 118 west all the way to Chatsworth, the flower of the valley.

Get off at Topanga Boulevard and park in the shade under the overpass.

Underneath your seat is the first aid kit. Open it. Inside find a small blue container of ten-milligram tablets of diazepam, a pack of Winston Lights, an Altoids tin of pre-rolled joints, one small bottle of peppermint schnapps, eye drops, hand sanitizer, breath mints, chewable Tums. Split one diazepam in half, swallow it with some coffee. Light a smoke.

Drive to Earl M_____'s at 34412 Clover Ct., Chatsworth, CA 91311.

The gate guard will wave you through. He knows you.

Park in Earl's driveway.

Brace yourself.

Go into the side door of the garage. It's unlocked.

Lift with your legs, not your back. Load (3) 30" x 50" black duffel bags, labeled "shoes," into the bed of your red 1984 Toyota pickup truck.

Drink some water. Eat one Tums. By 7:00 a.m., the sun will be shining and the valley will already be hot.

PUT ON YOUR GLOVES.

Load (3) black duffel bags labeled "pillows" into the truck bed.

Load (1) 30" x 50" black duffel bag labeled "scarves" into the truck. The zipper is broken. ARE YOUR GLOVES ON? DO NOT TOUCH any of the silky scarves with a naked hand. They are only washed at the end of the month. Wrap two bungee cords around the bag to keep it closed. There are bungee cords hanging from the wall of the garage.

Load (2) large rectangular, semiopaque plastic containers labeled "kitchen" into the truck.

Open container #1. See list of contents on the inside lid: two gallon jugs of "clear," one twelve-ounce bottle of "strawberry," 5 rolls of paper towels, 2 packs of baby wipes, 1 roll of heavy-duty kitchen trash bags, 1 box of black latex gloves, 2 large packs of hand-sanitizing wipes, 1 sixteen-ounce bottle of baby oil, 1 bottle of spray-on sunblock, 1 half-gallon milk bottle of "Earl's Pearl," 1 box of popsicle sticks, 1 roll of orange biohazard stickers. If anything is missing, restock from the metal cabinet on the far wall of the garage.

Container #2's contents are sex toys, scan over them. They aren't inventoried. There will be various dildos, vibrators, butt plugs, Ben Wa balls, ball gags, leather masks, whips, nylon rope, handcuffs. Just be sure there is a variety and that Earl's favorite floppy red dildo is onboard. ARE YOUR GLOVES ON? Close the lids tight.

Load the semiopaque plastic container labeled "Tunes" into the bed of your truck. Inside there is a binder of CDs and a boom box. Don't forget the tunes.

Wait in the driveway for Chad to show up. Chad shows up.

He checks the bed of your truck and the garage to see if everything is in order. He then gorks a good morning. He has worked with Earl for almost a decade. On your first day, you asked him how to wrap a California Sunbounce and he said, "Step one, kill yourself."

He's wary of you, you know it, but tell yourself that Chad has priorities and the riddle of Casey Malloy isn't one of them. Enthusiastically, load the cases of strobes, light stands, C-stands, Scrim Jims, sandbags, flags; the "clamp" crate, containing A-clamps, super-clamps, Mafers, Cardellinis, C41s, J-hooks; the apple boxes, extensions cords, FX fans, compact electric leaf blower, and adjustable rolling stool into Chad's white van. Chad may come to believe in you but still, he won't like you.

Earl doesn't want you in the house. Chad goes inside and brings out two camera bags. Don't offer to help him. After the camera bags are safely secured inside the van, Earl steps outside.

Earl has retinitis pigmentosa, tunnel vision. He also has a bad back and is lactose intolerant.

Earl rides with Chad in the van. Assume they're talking shit about you.

Hate them. Hate everyone you work with. It will make your day easier.

Don't try to follow Chad on the freeway. Take your time. Smoke a Winston Light. Check the call sheet for the Benedict Canyon address.

Make sure you are wearing the black baseball cap. You always wear that hat. Never take it off. When you arrive at the location, you will see Earl in front of the house. Say, "Hello, Earl!" His vision is getting worse every day and he won't immediately recognize you. He will engage you in small talk, ask you if you've lost weight, gained weight, when did you grow that mustache, why did you shave your off your mustache. Laugh, "Good one, Earl!" and then pick some gear up and move it. He's self-conscious about being almost blind and he doesn't acknowledge that he can't recognize you but yes, he too will come to believe, believe in you, Casey Malloy.

If the makeup artist is Mara Cipriani, thank God. She only works when it's girl-on-girl.

Place the strobe lights, bounce, and negative fill per Chad's instructions. He meters the light while you fire the strobes. Adjust the output from the packs until everything is balanced and the key light is one-tenth of a stop overexposed.

Then, stand on the mark. Chad shoots a test Polaroid of you. Then, lie on the mark. Chad shoots another test of you. He takes the Polaroids to Earl. Notice they chuckle. The light isn't right, you reset the lights and adjust the output on the strobe packs. Chad shoots another Polaroid. You get the thumbs-up. Now, take Earl's rolling stool and put it where Chad was standing when he took the last test. Mark the floor with tape. Four Polaroids are taken of you on this setup. They leave these Polaroids lying about the set. COLLECT THEM. COLLECT THEM. Keep them in one of the large pockets of your cargo pants.

Why? Don't ask why. On average, over 100,000 people move to Los Angeles each year, chasing dreams.

Take a leftover plastic Vons shopping bag from craft service and put an orange biohazard sticker on it. Clamp the biohazard bag to a C-stand.

The talent arrives. There are two girls and a guy. Keep a safe distance, smile.

DO NOT LET THE TALENT TOUCH ANYTHING. Tell them if they want a snack from the craft service table, if they want to listen to a different CD, if they want a tissue, tell them you are here to help, tell them that you will get it for them. The last thing you want to do is to eat chips from a bag after they've had their hands in there, after their hands have been in each other's assholes, pussies, after their hands have been stroking cocks.

The first setup is girl-on-girl. They're friends. They are gentle with each other. They throw in a playful spank. It's a cum-free setup. The girls are in a good mood.

Earl stops shooting and calls for a "deal check." You check "the deal." Get down and take a good look. Is her pussy free of any white flecks, smidges, lint, etcetera? Hand her a baby wipe. DO NOT HAND HER THE WHOLE BOX. REMEMBER, DO NOT LET THEM TOUCH ANYTHING. She's done, hold open the biohazard bag. She tosses the wipe inside. Check "the deal" again. "The deal" is clean.

The morning has become a hot early afternoon and now there are flies. The talent can't shoo them away, that's your job. You stand just out of frame with the small electric leaf blower. Earl shouts, "Blow them out but don't fuck up the girls' hair!" Chad laughs.

Eat lunch.

Now, it's guy-on-girl inside, on the couch. Right before the shoot begins, the guy may go into a corner, just off set, and do something to his dick. Give him some space. Back on set, he will engage the girl (after asking permission) in some personal kink to get himself hard. While the makeup artist is applying the final touches to the girl, he may eat the girl out, or sniff her ass, or suck her toes, her tits. She will ignore his attention, she's somewhere else.

Then it begins. Keep the lube on an apple box, standing by. DO NOT MISPLACE THE LUBE. This is like watching animals fuck. You are aware of the smell and then you are not. They've been fucking for an hour. You've adjusted the lights twice and now they are in the third position. Earl calls for the lube. It's not on the apple box. You can't find the lube. Earl is yelling, "Where is the fucking lube." You go into "kitchen" container #1 and there you can only find strawberry. You show Chad. Chad says, "Earl, he's got the strawberry." Earl isn't happy. "She'll look like she's fucking bleeding. Where's the goddamn clear? Jesus fucking Christ. Find the lube! Find the motherfucking lube! You're killing the mood, asshole!" Look under the couch. There it is. You squeeze the lube into the talent's hands. He says, "Don't sweat it, dude, look, I'm still hard."

The pop shot is the last shot of the day. You stand just off camera with a roll of paper towels. She's disgusted but she doesn't let the camera see it. Earl stops shooting and hands Chad the camera. She leaps up and is lunging for you. Hold out the wad of paper towels. Point to the biohazard bag.

Break down all the gear. Load Chad's van first and then load up your truck. Sitting in your truck, in the Hollywood Hills, take a moment for yourself, smoke a joint, have a pull of peppermint schnapps, smoke a cigarette. Eat the Snickers Mini from craft service.

Drive home.

Walk inside your apartment. Hang your keys on the hook. Lock the door. Sit on your couch. Take the Polaroids out of your cargo pants pocket and put them in the album on the coffee table with the others. This is you, Casey Malloy, on a doggie bed. This is you, floating in a pool, laughing on a swing, standing in front of a fountain surrounded by banana palms and birds-of-paradise, this is you on a bearskin rug in front of raging fire, you on a wooden table in a wine cellar, on a leather couch, on a black silk bedspread. There you are, this is you, this is you, this is you. ∎

OTHELLO ARRIVES IN AMERICA
Faisal Mohyuddin

As Father's warnings about the savagery
of any place where mirrors stand as sites of worship

descend each day more deeply into the murk
of memory, this body will also forget

the swaying of the endless light-starved days
I spent at sea, dreaming no longer

of glory, but of a namelessness, a truce of sorts
with destiny's stubborn indifference

to ambition, or redemption. Until then,
may these lungs still pine for the heartbreaking scent

of sandalwood, for the warm coconut oil
Mother kneaded into my sisters' hair. Departure

depends, like so much of a Muslim's sense of time,
on the fickle logic of the many-faced moon.

To yearn for exile, then, demands a commitment
to madness, to unmooring one's self,

blood and all, from the reach of shame, its power
to unravel resolve. If yesterday,

and the yawning emptiness of its robes,
can transform prayer into confession, then perhaps

rebirth is possible. Or so I tell myself
when we make landfall, the night sky frothy

with stars, its bleakness merely a measure
of flummoxed courage. I emerge

from my coffin of darkness into a darker
darkness, alive but no longer innocent enough

to touch any river without triggering
entrapment, so I make this new life's first ablution

with filched dirt, start with my feet, ears,
and mucky hair, moving backwards—neck, arms—

until I smear my face with it, then belch out
three mouthfuls of mud, and swallow

instead the unuttered Bismillahs I'd ferried here
from home, their protections too risky

to keep, their music too steeped in Father's
voice to allow me to unlace the longing from mine.

HOW TO SAVE THE LIFE OF A WIFE YOU DON'T KNOW
Jessica Breheny

Step 1

Sleep until one thirty. Then spend the afternoon looking out your bay window at the grid of yards and back steps and the neighborhood cats that skulk the fence boards. Think, "I'm in San Francisco, and this is my San Francisco life." This is a thought you have had many times a day in the few months since you moved from Los Angeles with your friend Zoya.

Step 2

Swallow aspirin with coffee. Last night was your shift at Lucky's Dugout, the sports bar where you work. You stayed late, drinking vodka tonics with Theo, the bartender, who you love, who will never love you back, but who tells you how much he loves to talk to you, what a good listener you are, tells you all about the ideas he's learning in his philosophy class, uses words you don't know, like, "perspectivism," and "mutability," while his black hair falls onto his flushed cheeks.

Step 3

Sip your silty coffee as you write in your journal about the wild and ungardened yards. Wonder if Theo will call. Write, "the phone wire, an electric tightrope over the bramble circus." Recognize it is not great writing, but resist the urge to cross it out. You might be able to use it years later when you write about the events of the day.

Step 4

Answer the phone when it rings at four thirty. It is not Theo. It is Edgar, Theo's friend from his San Francisco State philosophy class, a married man, a dad to two kids, a Gulf War veteran, Air Force, you recall him saying. You only know Edgar a little, through late nights in Theo's apartment, playing chess and talking about Nietzsche and Sartre and Kierkegaard, who you are afraid to say you have never read.

Step 5

Say, "Oh, hey, how are you?" In the silence after, take a moment to consider that it is strange Edgar would call you. He must have looked your number up in the phone book. You are not friends. You have nothing in common. You are a twenty-one year old waitress who writes poems in notebooks and plans to enroll – *soon*, you tell yourself – at the community college, who reads H.D. and Virginia Woolf and likes silent movies at the Red Vic theater, who sleeps too late, who is always broke and survives on ramen and toast and the employee meals at Lucky's Dugout.

Step 6

Observe how anger sharpens into the whispery breaths of Edgar's voice when he says your name, *Sarah*, like the S were the "Sc" of scissors as they cut through fabric. Understand that he is serious when he tells you that he will kill his wife, Kerri, when she returns home from picking up their kids at daycare. He will *kill* her. Feel the way the word's double L's are cold and rotted in the back of your throat. Edgar will kill Kerri, a woman who you have never met, who – to you – is just a rayon scarf of an idea floating in the pixeled background of the life Edgar lives when he is not smoking a bong, or moving a rook, or turning over a record in Theo's room. He will do this, he explains, because Kerri is unfaithful.

Step 7

Though Edgar's words are heavy pieces of metal that you – a person who likes to look out of windows – can't pick up, pick them up anyway. You have no time for weakness.

Step 8

Ascertain Kerri's route home. She is supposed to stop at the bank on her way back from the daycare center, so figure you have about an hour at the most. It is now four forty-five. Tell Edgar he needs to leave his apartment before Kerri gets home with the kids.

Step 9

Invite Edgar to your flat with the Victorian ceilings and the algae-green painted floors. Give him directions. You are a block from the Panhandle. It is not far from his place in the Sunset. Say you will fix him a drink. You are not attracted to Edgar, but let the promise of sex seep into the words, "just hang out here for a while and talk."

Step 10
Remind Edgar of his two children. Say "your kids, your kids" like a mantra. Look around your living room with the light deepening to a blue five o'clock. Pull your long hair away from your face. Say, again, "your kids."

Step 11
Forget that you are too young for this conversation. Forget that in your bedroom you still keep the orange-armed teddy bear you once clung to on nights when you thought your father would kill your mother. Don't dwell on the fact that even as an adult you sometimes hold it and think, "I'm floating away, I'm floating away from here," and you don't even know why you are thinking those words, only that, like a lost birthday balloon or a shred of wood from a broken boat, you can't stop how light and tiny you are in this world's bullying currents. This is not a moment to be so young, or so scared, or so insubstantial.

Step 12
Say, "your kids," and "leave," and "drive here now." It is ten after five. You are running out of time.

Step 13
Only when Edgar says he has his car keys in his hand, and only when – at five fifteen – you finally hear them jangle on the other side of the phone, only then may you hang up. This is not a responsibility you can share with a friend, so call Zoya at the café she works at in the financial district and ask her not to come home for a while. Tell her you have a guy coming over. It is the truth.

Step 14
Put on a record. Play something slow and bassy, something with a singer whose voice sounds like it is echoing from a concrete tunnel. Mix a drink with Zoya's gin. She won't mind. Sip your cocktail while you pace the living room. Listen to a siren cyclone through the air.

Step 15
When Edgar arrives, meet his gaze. It will pull you past his blue eyes into a narrow hallway in his head you don't want to enter. Notice how his moustache is a bark-brown minus sign over his lip. Think that the muscles in his thin arms remind you of tangled power cords.

Stay out of the reach of those arms. Pour him a gin and orange juice. Give him a cigarette. Ask him to sit down on the sofa you and Zoya dragged three blocks home on big trash night.

Step 16

Listen to Edgar's story about Kerri's infidelity, about how he found the letter from a man in St. Louis, how, tucked into the letter, was a plane ticket for Kerri to visit the man. Let Edgar explain that all of this is why he must kill her. After he is done talking, remind him of his kids. Remind him that custody doesn't favor the violent parent.

Step 17

Do not show fear when Edgar thanks you and takes your hand. Do not wince when he squeezes the sharp tips of his long fingers into a pressure point on the base of your pinky. Remember that when he was in the military, the man in your living room once loaded bombs onto planes. Stay calm when Edgar lets go of your hand and grips his glass of gin and orange juice so hard that it shatters. Get the torn pink towel from the bathroom. This won't stop the bleeding on his gashed palm, but it may distract him from the dangerous thought that you could – at any moment – decide to call the police and that there is now a deadly three-inch piece of a cocktail glass on the floor.

Step 18

Answer the phone when it rings. It is Kerri. Unknot the spiral cord and hand Edgar the receiver.

Step 19

Go outside so they can talk privately. Walk down the block and sit on the steps of the McKinley statue in the Panhandle and watch the evening turn the cypress branches above you into a cyanotype print. See how the fog rolls in from the ocean in the wind tunnel of the park. A would-be murderer has come to your house, and you are alive. Feel how the word, "alive" is a plucked string in your throat. Think about how the cypress trees hold the years of the neighborhood in their rings, like albums with their oldest songs in their centers. Imagine the music they would play — your own life now in 1991, then into the smaller circle of 1967, when your mother lived on a nearby street a few years before you were born. That was her San Francisco life. If you are very quiet, you can hear the grooves circle even closer inward to when the neighborhood and the park were built, and the grass was first laid down, and the trees were slim-limbed youths, and ladies hovered in melancholic drawing rooms while the folds of their skirts whispered things they could not say. That was their San Francisco life. Promise yourself you will write a poem about this later, but forget to write it. It is not really that important.

Step 20
Return home. Find Kerri sitting in the turquoise velvet chair next to the bay window. Think of a dandelion puff when you look at Kerri's frizzy hair and legs as thin and delicate as stalks in her tight jeans. Think, "this is her San Francisco life." Her life. Kerri is drinking a glass of gin. She does not look scared of the broken glass, or her husband's bleeding fist. She does not seem to be worried that he is standing over her chair. She has given him her blue sweater, and he is holding it against his wound. His spilled blood on the green floor glimmers in the evening light.

Step 21
Retreat to your room with the blankets on the floor, and your stuffed bear, and the moldy closet, and the window that faces the yellow-lit entryway of the building. Let them talk. Listen for violence. Listen to the quiver of footsteps upstairs. Don't make any sounds. Imagine the quiet in the house is water and that you need to hold your breath so you don't drown.

Step 22
Look out into the hallway when you hear the zipper of a coat and the turn of the handle of the front door. See Kerri leading Edgar out the door with her arm vined around his elbow. Make eye contact with her when she turns back to you. Concentrate on the words, "life" and "live" as you look into her pretty brown eyes. Nod your head when she mouths, "thank you." Think, "be careful." Think it like an incantation so that it comes true.

Step 23
Wait tables another five years. Go to college. Get accepted to grad school. Run into Theo occasionally and let your feelings fade like a mournful song on a cassette left too long in a car's tape deck.

Step 24

Remember Edgar and Kerri one chilly June night, thirty years later, while returning home from a walk with an armful of groceries. Look up Edgar on Google. Find his LinkedIn page and see that he works in a marketing department for a hotel chain headquartered in Cincinnati. Try to see if he is still married to Kerri. When you can't find her, check obituaries, and then give up.

Step 25

Take out your old writing notebooks that you store in boxes amongst coats and shoes in the hall closet. Find lines of poems, scraps of stories you'd once started, a Muni ticket, a piece of a map of Noe Valley. Get to the page with faded blue ink where you can still make out the words, "phone," "wire," "tightrope." Sit down at your desk by your window that overlooks the lonely night-cars as they moan past the neon of a liquor store sign. See your reflection in the glass and imagine you can leave your image there for someone to find later, when you no longer live there, when you are no longer alive. Feel how the word, alive, is the cluttered ring of breaking glass in your throat.

Step 26

At your desk, as your reflection watches from the window, write the first poem you've written in nearly twenty years, a poem that tells the story of how you once saved the life of someone you didn't know. At least, that is the story you tell yourself. You have no way of knowing who lived and who died and by what causes. All you can say is that one day, you stopped a man from murdering his wife. And that is enough. ■

THE BIRTHING TENT
Ben Bird

Alison is talking at length about her recent attempts at astral projection, surrounded by my coworkers at the office Christmas party—the same party she insisted would be a good time. *What's the worst that could happen?* And here I am, watching the ice crash into the rim of my plastic cup, listening to my wife talking about a point of contention in our marriage in front of everyone. People I don't particularly like to look at, or hear from, or be near. A circle has formed around her. She's got that magnetic way about her. You know the kind.

In the circle is my boss, Mr. Strangler, a strange-looking Bulgarian man, his eyes far too close together, as though barely resisting the gravity of his nose, obscured slightly by his big, circular glasses, his neck fat like a wattle. He looks like God got bored of making good-looking, serious people. But don't mistake his poultry looks for meekness. The man is a hammer.

I've been having this recurring dream of Mr. Strangler holding a baby in the office supply closet, bouncing it up and down in his arms. The child is very quiet. Once I open the door, I turn to my wife, who is next to me, in the dream. I ask her if the kid is ours. Then, she'll open her mouth to answer. A lifetime passes without her saying a word. I see into the depths of her esophagus, where it seems she is hiding the answer to life's mystery. And then she starts to speak, but I wake up before I can make out what she's trying to say. The strange thing is, I was having that dream before I started working here, before Alison was pregnant. I probably saw his face on a billboard or something. And I knew Alison wanted kids. Those are the only explanations I can think of.

Next to Mr. Strangler is his wife, a kind-eyed, sickly Bulgarian woman who looks twice her age, her head wrapped in a scarf with an intricate pattern of bright blues and yellows. I remember being sick and angry over the party starting so early in the day. Shortly after I threw my little fit about it, Alison reminded me of Mr. Strangler's wife's condition, how she would lose her energy towards the middle of the day, due to the chemo. You know I felt like the world's biggest asshole after that.

Completing the circle around Alison, still detailing her attempts at reaching the astral plane, are the Dougs. The Dougs are six young men, all stocky and average height, each with the same combed-down hair, slick with gel, brows furrowed, eyes eager yet cold. Each of them named Doug or Douglas. Almost like it was a job requirement. I'm the exception, of course. My name is Dan. I must have squeaked past the screening process, just by a hair. Maybe the person screening applications had a date the night before, their first date in ages. It had been so long that anything the person on the other side of the table said struck their heart like a hot iron, and any hope of sleep was stomped out by visions of love and a full life together. I'm only kidding. I know why I got the job. When Alison learned she was pregnant, she asked her father to get me a job working for Mr. Strangler. Her father, not a wealthy man, but a connected one, was happy to help. If you told me every Bulgarian immigrant was connected in some way, I'd believe you.

It was a fair ask, getting a job. Alison would have to take a leave from work, and pretending to be a writer wasn't going to pay the bills. Especially not under my healthy $40,000 of debt from my MFA program, where the only real connection I had made was to my own self-loathing. And then we were forcing a child onto the world.

I'm not sure how it happened. I had gotten a vasectomy the day I was eligible. And I never had a problem, not with getting someone pregnant, not until Alison. And no, I'm not the easiest guy to look at, but I've been lucky enough to have a few women introduce themselves to me for a few minutes at a time. And sure, I've wrestled against a few diseases as a result of said meetings. But nothing serious. Nothing long-term. Nothing like my own eyes looking up at me after freeing themselves from the womb.

We met shortly after I finished my MFA. I was working at a coffee shop in Providence, my hometown, where Alison was also born and raised. Except she never left. That is, until we moved to Los Angeles, for the job, for the baby. Long before we met, she had planned on moving to Bulgaria, to connect with her extended family, her roots. She bought plane tickets and everything. And then her father was diagnosed with Parkinson's. She canceled her flight and spent the years after working for local nonprofits, saving the world in her own little way.

When I first laid eyes on her, I was in serious trouble. She was the most beautiful person I'd ever seen. I know what you're thinking. It's what everyone says. But it's true. Her hair was cut short and rested around the bottom of her lobes. She had a small nose with a crook in the middle and a piercing stare under her big, bushy eyebrows. Deep-brown eyes like the wood of an oak, creased at the sides. Her jawline could cut you open.

When I say I chased after her as she exited the shop, begging to see her again, you'd think I was joking. She sure thought I was. So did my coworkers, laughing at me behind the glass. Until she realized I wasn't kidding. Then, I think she felt bad for me. Boy am I glad she did. We eloped two weeks after our first date. It was one of those things. When a feeling carries you a certain way, and you follow it. She got pregnant a week later.

Alison taps me on the shoulder. I think I've gotten used to her beauty. I'm ashamed to say it. It's the same thing I think of when I see the ocean. *Of course it's beautiful. It's the ocean.*

"Isn't that right, honey?" she asks, dispelling my trance. Everyone in the circle pulls their eyes from her gravity and looks towards me. "I was just telling everyone how small we realized the country really is, when we drove out here from Providence." I remember when Alison and I stopped in the Badlands, in South Dakota. Looking out at the jagged white mountains towering over the sprawling rock desert, Alison said, "What's so bad about this?" That was the funniest thing, to me. No idea why. I still laugh about it sometimes, when I'm on the toilet or thinking about hanging myself on the ceiling fan.

"That's exactly right," I say. "Small country." I don't mention how much my back hurt, cooped up in our shitty little car. How the mosquitos would buzz and buzz in my ear as we crammed into our shitty little tent.

She smiles that smile when I'm full of shit, squinting her eyes into a glare. I take a look around me at the office spread. The Stranglers went all out. They dragged the tables from the board room, slapped some white tablecloths over them, and filled bowls and plates with various Bulgarian delicacies, including lukanka—a big long slab of pork salami. I'm unable to partake, since Alison has me on a plant-based diet. She's been worried about my *longevity* ever since my dad expired due to a triple coronary a few years ago. Alison has been vegan since I've known her, concerned with animal suffering and interested in preserving nature and all that. That's all to say—no lukanka for either of us. All to Mr. Strangler's dismay. You should've seen his face when we turned it down, like we'd walked over to the big map of Bulgaria hanging on the office wall, located the village he grew up in, and spat on the exact coordinates where his mother was buried.

Mrs. Strangler turns her attention back to my wife. "But I'm so curious," she says, "how will you know when you've made it? To the astral plane?"

"I've been listening to some podcasts," Alison responds. "There's this one called *The Birthing Tent*. It talks all about this festival in the sky with these big white tents. It's where all the souls go before they're called to be born. A bunch of people say they've been there, filling in the gaps of each other's stories."

The Dougs all nod their heads with genuine curiosity and intent. I know that they hate me. Hired as their superior with no experience. The truth is, I don't blame them. I have no clue what I'm doing. If you asked me what our company does, I couldn't even tell you.

Over the last month, Alison has been on a tear exploring what she calls *spiritism*. At night, before bed, she will sage away the evil spirits of our small Century City apartment. I understand her need to believe in something bigger than herself, I really do. Even though I think it's a sham. Even though the smell makes me sick.

It all started after that night. It was the last night of November. I'll never forget it. Alison's parents had just left after we hosted them for Thanksgiving. I remember her father's shaking hand caressing her belly. He looked so proud of her. Anyway, it was the middle of the night. I woke up by osmosis. I could feel the primal fear coursing through her body, though I couldn't understand why. She told me she was having contractions, and I thought—*How wonderful. We're having our baby.* I couldn't figure out why she was shaking and crying. Wasn't this what she wanted? What I had grown to want, too? And then I remembered, on the way to the hospital as she urged me to drive faster and faster, that it had only been five months since she'd burst into the room, holding her pregnancy test up like she had just won Wimbledon. And then, at the hospital, we learned that we wouldn't be parents after all. I've never thought of my own death so fondly as in that moment.

Mrs. Strangler braces herself on one of the tables, breaking the circle and dropping the big plate of meat onto the floor. She looks like she herself could expire at any moment. And isn't that the nature of things. Mr. Strangler rushes over to help steady her, the Dougs following closely behind him.

"I'm fine, I'm fine," she says, hacking up the words.

"I think it's time we wrap up. Feel free to stay and eat. Thank you all for coming," Mr. Strangler says, his voice rising and falling like a sine wave, taking Mrs. Strangler into the crook of his arm and walking her to the elevator. She turns to us and blows Alison a kiss.

"Thank you!" Alison calls out to the Stranglers as the elevator doors shut. It all happened so fast, and I had no instinct to help out or speak. Maybe that's all I am—a passive observer of my own life. "Maybe we should go," Alison says, looking up at the analog clock hanging from the wall—3:00 p.m. "You have your appointment soon."

"Good call," I say, grabbing her hand. We walk to the elevator, pressing the pale-orange button, watching it brighten and *ding*.

"Lovely to see you, Alison!" one of the Dougs shouts as the elevator doors creak open.

"Good luck with your astral projection!" another one calls out. The rest nod in agreement, waving goodbye as the doors shut and obscure them from view.

"You sure had a lot to say today," Alison says. "Where'd you go off to this time? I'm sure your drink wasn't that interesting." I do what I do best, which is smile and nod.

"If I could choose where I was going, I probably wouldn't go there." Now my wife is smiling, and as the floor descends beneath us, the weight of everything disappears for a moment. With this new lightness, I am able to float up from my body and look down on us. How special it is, to be next to the person who gives your life meaning, hand in hand, without that invisible wall erected between you.

"All the more to talk about in therapy," she says, and I come hurtling back into my shell.

* * *

After being stuck for an hour in the thick, ever-expanding mud of LA traffic, after dropping Alison back at the apartment, I head out to my appointment. I don't see a therapist. This is a lie I've told my wife, and continue to tell her. The more I tell it to her, the more I have to continue doing so. I've told it too many times now to ever get to telling the truth. You know how it goes. Plus, what I am doing is a sort of therapy, in its own way. This is a lie I tell myself.

The sun has set, which happens early in these winter months, one of the only ways to tell which season is which in Los Angeles. The sky is dark and covered in smog, there are no stars in sight, just the faint red blinking of planes mulling overhead. I pull into the In-N-Out parking lot, exit my car, patting down my coat to locate my wallet. I walk past the drive-through line, the cars teeming like ants.

Inside the restaurant itself is mostly empty. One of the lone patrons sits alone in a booth—a grizzled man with a long gray beard in a frayed leather jacket and a ten-gallon hat. He's got an anger in his eyes as he shoves several fries into the corners of his mouth all at once, like he's packing a tobacco dip. He's the kind of man who could kill me without much effort. Part of me expects him to do so, since he's now caught me staring, to get up in a rage and beat me to a pulp, burying me beneath the dirt under intertwining palm trees by the drive-through window. Instead, he tips his hat to me and continues packing in his fries.

There's no one in line waiting to order, and I can tell by the look on the small, round cashier's face that he remembers me from last week. I fish a one-hundred-dollar bill from my wallet and ask for one order of fries, a grilled cheese, and as many Double-Doubles that the rest will get me, Animal Style. For the uninitiated, Animal Style is In-N-Out's sacred ritual of dousing a burger or fries in liquid cheese and viscous, flavored mayonnaise.

"I can't do that," the cashier says in a voice that registers as a lost career as a Mickey Mouse impressionist.

"Sure you can," I say. "You did it last week. And the week before."

"It makes people uncomfortable, sir," he says. "It makes me uncomfortable. It's not good for you. It's not good for anyone. My manager says I can't." He points to the camera looking down at us from the wall next to the register.

"What happened to the customer being always right and all that," I say, pulling back my hundred and grabbing my credit card. "How about the first few things, and as many burgers as you're allowed to give me. Is that all right?"

"Sure thing, sir," the boy says, relieved, swiping my card. I grab the receipt and walk over to the bench where Kev, Ashley, and their daughter, Crystal, are waiting for me. Kev is a handsome man, approximately six foot four. His frame is broad and large although his clothes are several sizes too big and you can tell he's lost a severe amount of weight. He grew up wanting to be a professional basketball player, but when his talent stopped short of his height after high school, he ended up working construction to pay for his growing child that he shares with his high school sweetheart, Ashley. She is one of the people who you can tell used to break people's hearts just by looking at her, but now her skin is ghastly and sunken in, and she emanates the stench of someone living just because they have no other choice. She wanted to be a movie star herself, that's why she moved them out to LA in the first place. But then she got pregnant, and her father, a renowned pastor back in their hometown, when she came to him for advice, said he'd rather she drown herself than terminate the pregnancy.

When I saw their ad on Craigslist, I thought it was a joke. I was looking through the personals, as I often do to pass the time as I idle at work. I think I spat my drink out onto my desk, I really do. It was an ad for a child actor, seeking stardom. But it was incomprehensible. It said something of the sort:

Child star—our crystal six years old. The Audrey Hepburn. Get in on the ground floor before the time is up. Looking for any and all acting experience. Twenty bucks. Just an hour. Call ME.

There was something about it that stuck to me. What people would be so eager to offer up their child in this way? They kept posting the ad, until finally I replied. My curiosity got the best of me. I told them another lie, which I wished were true, that I was a screenwriter, writing about a child actor, and I thought theirs would be the perfect fit for my next movie. I invited them to In-N-Out, somewhere I knew my wife would never be.

They told me their life story, and it struck something in me. They lived in a tent city under the 405. They were worse off than me. Falling to the trappings of fame. I fell in love with them and envied them. Their desperation was right there for the world to drink in and pity them. And then there was Crystal. She looked exactly as I had imagined my daughter. Small, chubby cheeks. Curly dark hair. A big, beaming smile with several gaps of missing teeth. And that's how it started. Every Thursday at 7:00 p.m., I meet with Crystal, buy her fries and a grilled cheese, and she pretends to be my daughter. It's just acting, I'll tell myself. I'm helping her prepare for the future. And I make her parents promise to spend the money I give them on her. For food, shelter, her schooling—whatever. And they do promise. Whatever that's worth.

I hand Kev the money and he takes my hand, thanking me as he does, with emotion collecting in the bottoms of his eyes. Then, he and Ashley walk out to the parking lot, where they sit on a bench and watch us through the window. This is how the transaction goes. Crystal will sit at the booth. I'll bring us our trays of food, and then ask, "How was school today, Gemma?" *Gemma*, the name Alison had chosen, the one I haphazardly agreed to. And then she'll reply, "Good, Dad. How was your day at work?" To which I'll say, "Good, Gemma. Thanks for asking." And then I'll hand her her fries and grilled cheese and begin working on the mountain of burgers I've ordered for myself in silence. Sometimes, we'll stare at each other and simultaneously burst out laughing, usually to the effect of some food spilling from our mouths. After she's finished with her meal, I'll wave to her, usually my mouth full of meat and sauce and bun. She'll say, "Bye, Dad!" And she'll take off outside, grabbing her parents' hands and walking off into the night.

I'm sitting in the booth now, with my hands covered in slop and my stomach full and pulsating. I look over at the cashier, who is staring at me like he's just seen my face on a poster wanted for murder, and give him a big thumbs-up and smile. I grab as many napkins as I can fit in my slimy hands and begin the process of wiping myself and the table down. Then I walk into the bathroom, bathe myself in the sink, and head out into the parking lot, where I begin the long drive home.

* * *

As I'm unlocking the door, the neighbor lady comes out from her apartment across the hall to greet me. Her face is wrinkled and worn, and I can tell she doesn't have much stomach left for it all.

"I was so sorry to hear what happened," she says.

"So was I. About your husband," I say.

"With everything that happened with Richard I haven't gotten a chance to say it. Haven't left the house at all since the service, really."

"I liked Richard, he was very kind to us when we moved in." I look at her and she looks at me and there really isn't anything left to say. And in that way, we are both taking in the end of everything, before we head into our respective apartments, wishing each other a good night.

The living room, if you can call it that, being three steps from the kitchen and all, is mostly dark. The lights are turned off, save for the little lamp in the corner. Alison must have left it on for me. It's where I like to read at night, when I can't sleep. Alison has been going to bed earlier each passing night, and I don't blame her. But it reeks of incense and my first thought is to get angry, because I hate the smell, and that hatred often turns into a headache. And then I think of the peace of mind it must give her, to have control over something, even if imagined. I calm down a bit.

I take off my coat and pants and unbutton my shirt, shedding the evidence of the long day. In the bedroom, I see Alison passed out above the bedsheets, her back propped up against the headboard, lit up by the glow of the city poking through our window. On her face is a smile, as though she's about to start laughing. I remember telling her I was setting aside some money for facial reconstructive surgery, for the baby, on the off chance it inherited my looks instead of hers. That's the last time I saw that look.

And then there are her arms, one on top of the other, forming a cradle. I'm just brave enough to admit the sight moves me to tears. And then I place myself on the bed, next to my wife, staring at the big white canvas of our ceiling, waiting and hoping to hear what she has to say in my dreams. ■

WHILE WE WAITED FOR THE PHONE TO RING

Maya Miller

My mother, the residue of last night's sleep still
in the corners of her mouth, puts water on

the stove for tea. The AC is broken, or maybe
never worked, my brother and me like two

butterflied fish on the tile floor. Doubled:
the surface area of cool ceramic on too-warm

skin. The wrap-around porch a tired sprawl.
The air so thick I could bite it and chew.

Roots threading through the asphalt.

At some point there is twine and a chicken leg and
then a bucket full of crabs. At some point

three of us share a feast for four. If I told you this
is where I come from it would still be

a partial truth. The water boils over, I wake up
every few hours to keep the dog from gnawing

out her stitches. And there is an empty mug
in every room.

THE GHOSTS IN THE GARDEN
Olga Domchenko

My mother loved her garden, more intensely, more passionately, than anyone I have ever known. To see her in a garden was to witness a woman almost teetering at the edge of hysteria, overwhelmed, overjoyed and intoxicated by the one thing she desperately needed and the one thing she could never own.

The last time I saw my mother before she died was in the month of January, but I only remember her distinctly the summer before, in her garden. She was a widow then, my father having died years ago. I was invited to lunch.

She always left the front door open for me and sat patiently by the window waiting. I remember I was very busy that day and arrived some two hours late. It fills me with so much sadness now to think of how I always kept her waiting at that window.

I remember the dress she wore—brown with tiny orange flowers that exposed her leathery, tanned arms. And her eyes. My mother had very blue eyes, but that day they were bluer—a bright cornflower blue—and looked odd somehow against the brown dress. But what struck me most was her hair, how blond and shiny it was, like finely spun gold above her pink scalp. At first glance she appeared healthy and bronzed, like someone back from a Florida vacation, but when I think back now and remember her, she looked like a dying angel.

As soon as I entered the house, I saw flowers everywhere. A bowl of yellow marigolds, another of pink snapdragons, Queen Ann's lace and blue salvia, a vase of tiny roses. And then, before I had a chance to catch my breath, before she unwrapped the gifts I brought, she ran to me like a gushing six-year-old and literally screamed, "The garden, come … hurry … the garden!"

Stepping into my mother's garden was always breathtaking and I can never explain why, not even to myself, nor can I understand the riot of emotions I felt as soon as I went out there. It was a happy, excited feeling, but also tinged with anxiety, as though any minute something terrible would happen, something ugly and tragic.

The garden was in a working-class Polish neighborhood of squat bungalows, with neat front yards and small sculpted shrubs, white plastic urns and red geraniums on front porches. Her house was the prettiest one on the block—a yellow brick Tudor with stained-glass windows and an old-fashioned lilac in front. There was a magnificent horse chestnut behind it and two huge pines growing next door.

She always gave me a tour of the garden as though I had never seen it before. You didn't just walk into my mother's garden and sit down to eat or drink. You had to meet all her flowers like they were personal friends, specially selected guests at a dinner party. You had to meet them, greet them, smell their exotic perfumes, marvel at their soft and silky skin, their sparkling eyes and beautiful faces.

We started with the pansies, called *bratki* (little brothers) in Ukrainian, one of her favorites. She led me to them solemnly like a priest at the baptismal font, cupping them in her hands and caressing them like the feet of a newborn baby. Sometimes she'd grab her own face out of sheer happiness and squeeze until I thought she would burst. Then came the snapdragons—*katchki piski* (big duck mouth). She took the head of a snapdragon in her fingers, squeezed it back and forth, making it quack like a duck, and nearly collapsed with laughing. She then made a whole row of snapdragons quack.

My mother was born in a small village in the Carpathian Mountains of Ukraine and told stories about it all her life. I sometimes thought it was a made-up tale, because it was too beautiful to be true, but it was real. Her village was surrounded by grassy meadows filled with flowers and wild strawberries, ancient forests teeming with mushrooms. The village priest was a rosy-cheeked cherub who played the accordion, his wife a maiden with long golden braids, and they made cherry wine. In the winter the snow was pure white and in spring the rains came but they were gentle rains falling from a tranquil sky. No one worried about the birds and butterflies because they were numerous and thriving, there were no tornadoes, derechos, hurricanes or wildfires and Antarctica was icy and far away. At night the sky exploded with stars and everyone drifted off to sleep on sweet-smelling sheets dried in the sun. This was my mother's Ukrainian home.

When she turned eighteen the war that had seemed so far away suddenly caught up to her village and she fled Ukraine with her family. In the chaos of the escape she was separated from them and ended up alone in a German DP (displaced persons) camp. She met my father soon after, in a hospital where he was recovering from tuberculosis. He was also alone. My father had suffered through the terror and forced starvation under Stalin, the horrors of war, the loss of his family farm, and later imprisonment in a Russian jail. A stronger, more determined man might have survived but my father succumbed to disappointment, anger and bitterness, eventually losing both his health and mind. My mother didn't know it then, fell for his kindness and charm, got married, and had me, their first child.

My parents started married life in that DP camp, a cluster of ugly low-slung buildings housing numerous families who shared one bathroom. Each family had only one room but everyone had a small plot of land. Our neighbors' yards were just patches of dirt overrun with chickens and garbage cans, but my mother planted a garden with dahlias, roses and lilies and a rainbow of sweet peas on trailing vines. I saw a picture of her in that garden sitting on a bench with my father, both of them so thin and all dressed up, sitting in the sun, but not smiling.

After leaving Germany we ended up just outside Detroit, in a neighborhood of Polish and Ukrainian immigrants, and rented an apartment in an old brick two-flat. The landlord was an old, shriveled-up little man who lived alone on the first floor. He never turned on the lights, sat in his dark house night after night and during the day on the back porch staring into space. He had no visitors and no family; it was like living above death itself.

The backyard of that building was just a scrubby lawn surrounded by a chain-link fence. One day my mother got the nerve to ask the little man if she could plant something in the garden and he broke out into a toothless grin, wheezing out a barely audible yes. She and I bought a small ruby-red rosebush and planted it, rushing downstairs every morning to watch it grow, imagining it would soon be a tower of roses, covering up the ugliness of that yard. It stayed very small, the blossoms grew out like buttons, and I still remember how disappointed we were.

It was shortly afterward that I realized just how unhappy my mother was. I remember walking down the streets with her, seeing the look in her eyes when we passed a real garden and saw a mass of peonies or lilacs, roses tumbling over a fence. I was still a child but quickly learned what heartbreak and loneliness was and remember feeling that I was not my mother's child at all, just a useless purse dangling from her arm.

My parents were well into middle age before they finally had their own house and garden, their American dream, but my father was already on the road to oblivion, too far gone in drink and drugs to feel joy. A garden with flowers meant nothing to him; he preferred things you could eat, like tomatoes or cucumbers. He belittled my mother's love of flowers, screamed at the expense, and made her life miserable. If anyone wanted to give her bouquets or plants for the garden, they had to do it in secret, praying he wouldn't notice.

One day when she was out, my father planted cucumbers in front of the roses. When she saw them she shrieked like a madwoman, turned on the garden hose and chased him around the entire yard with it until he was soaking wet. Then she paced up and down with the gushing hose still dangling from her hands and wept hysterically like a child. It was the cucumbers—they grow into huge fuzzy vines and would eventually strangle her roses. He might as well have strangled her.

"Never be with a man who doesn't give you flowers, who doesn't love flowers. He will never love you, he will never understand you," she said over and over again. It was true. I was given Japanese chocolate pots, vacuum cleaners, ornate chopsticks, odd musical instruments I couldn't play, cheap jewelry bought from starving locals on Mexican beaches. If I wanted flowers, I had to buy them myself.

Soon after they bought their house, my father's drinking got worse, more frequent, and his mind became a cesspool of political conspiracy theories, jealousies and paranoia, but he was still physically strong, with the strength that raging alcoholics often have. Living with him was like living in a nineteenth-century madhouse— there was never a moment of peace, never a moment without fear. My mother and I frequently left the house to save ourselves and spent hours just wandering the streets, staring at other people's houses and gardens, their normal lives, filled with envy for people who lived in peace.

We wandered like lost children, gypsies, prisoners, mental patients, peeping toms, slaves, criminals, like thieves in the night, sailors out on endless seas, peering into forbidden gardens, trying to find some comfort, some beauty. Once we stared so intently at a woman's flowers she came to the window and glared at us. We turned to leave, but when she realized we were admiring her garden, she smiled and waved.

Nothing good happened after we left the garden with the button rose. Years of sour penny-pinching days, stifling summers, shootings, muggings. My mother's weary night shifts at the hospital. I still see her sitting on the couch the few minutes before she had to leave for work, sitting in her white nurse's uniform like a zombie, her expression one of utter defeat.

I remember the day childhood ended. My friends and I were yanked inside forever from our games of hide-and-seek and badminton, happy wanderings in the dark to the hot dog stand for bags of greasy French fries. A demon from hell was loose and killed nine student nurses in their southside townhouse, one by one, in a slaughter that decades later can still make you sick. The images of those nurses and the killer's ugly pockmarked face haunted my days and nights for decades. Even now I can't say his name out loud or write it down.

Home wasn't safe anymore. My mother was in danger like those nurses, would be raped and slaughtered in her tidy white uniform while walking in the dark or waiting at the bus stop.

Late at night I heard doors being broken down by crazed drug addicts, sexual perverts who would tie us to the radiators and torture us, bludgeon us to death in our beds. I saw our pictures in the newspapers like those slaughtered nurses.

The only escape was a garden. No one gets murdered in a garden, underneath the lilacs or roses. No one is beaten to death on a bed of violets. In the garden there is no evil, no unhappiness. The world itself seems to stop, take a breath, sigh at its own beauty with pleasure.

One day in early autumn it was like that. I remember that day distinctly because I think we died that day. I was sitting in my mother's garden, and it was the beginning of dusk, the air was the color of lilacs, smelling faintly of licorice and violets. It was very quiet and suddenly the entire garden was lit by the sinking sun and turned to amber. The snapdragons were mouthing words and trying to say something, changing from flowers to birds to fish like an Escher drawing. The salvias were bluer than any earthly sky and the dahlias looked like exotic beasts, savage dancers, like mermaids, sirens and nymphs diving into the sea. Purple morning glories were trailing through every herb, shrub and flower and ruby roses were climbing on every window, wall and fence. It smelled like Marrakesh, like Egypt, like midnight in Paris, like a freshly dug grave.

My mother had gathered great masses of the flowers and brought them into the kitchen just before dinner. Hardened by night frosts, their colors were electrifying and they released a cold, damp fragrance of lilies and incense, Easter morning in a cathedral, and as we sat waiting for our dinner, the room swirled in scents more intoxicating than the boudoirs of Egyptian queens. Even my father changed and slowly, like a drugged soldier, walked quietly to his room and disappeared.

I sat in the corner, watching the movements of my mother and father, and saw we had already turned to ghosts, the kitchen and garden no longer ours, but still the ghosts persisted, refusing to leave the room, smelling the fragrant meat and desperately trying to chew and swallow through narrow plastic tubes. Then it vanished like a dream, a sudden storm, and I heard the sound of human voices again.

Sometimes my father was away or sleeping or dozing in a chair and we drank in the garden, my mother and sister and I. Those were precious halcyon days. Sipping delicious wines or liquors surrounded by flowers seemed like such an innocent pleasure. Even my mother had a glass or two. I remember cool Alsatian Rieslings, gin and tonics, ice-cold vodka, mingling with the smell of flowers and grass. The more you drank, the more beautiful the garden looked, you could even see it in the dark, every leaf clearly defined, the white flowers floating like swans in black rivers.

The only one who didn't drink in our family was my aunt Sophia. Every night she made a pot of boiled potatoes and well-done steaks for my uncle and his two giant sons and went out chain-smoking in the woods behind their half-finished house in northern Michigan. Six feet tall, her blue-black hair trailing down her back, she wandered for hours like a banished queen. My mother, father, younger sister and I came to visit one summer. No one answered the door and we let ourselves in, standing in the middle of the vast, barely furnished living room, totally ignored by someone sitting in a corner. It was my mother's brother, slumped back in a chair listening to a record of a popular song that year, "If You Go Away." You could tell he had been sitting there for a long time.

At one point he acknowledged our presence, motioning for us to be quiet. "Listen, listen!" he bellowed, like a grizzly Anthony Quinn, his voice thick as the steaks congealing in the kitchen. Like frightened children we obeyed and listened to a gravelly baritone singing in a monotone voice:

> If you go away on this summer day
> Then you might as well take the sun away
> All the birds that flew in a summer sky …
> If you go away
> Ne me quitte pas
> If you go away …

He played it over and over, oblivious to our tired faces and hungry eyes wandering to the plates of crusty steaks and potatoes. Finally, he offered us a drink, as though we were ready, purged of any sense of happiness or homecoming—a final toast before the sacrifice. He filled our water tumblers with a pale yellowish liquid that quivered slightly like lightening, and we drank, while Rod McKuen's voice echoed in that house like the muffled cries of forgotten slaves.

I still remember the taste of that liquor—Chartreuse—sacred water of Carthusian monks. I see them, far from the noise of human lands, mingling berries, herbs, and spices, barks of exotic trees, in the blinding-white kitchens of their monastic mansions, dancing on the cool, wide stones washed clean by tears and silence. I never saw my uncle after that day but still see him slumped in his chair in the house in the woods listening to that old song, and drinking.

I often wander in the evenings in my own garden, always with a glass of wine, a gin and tonic ... and wonder why it doesn't work with tea or lemonade, or why I have to drink at all, and I remember reading that someone asked Richard Burton why he drank so much and he said: "Because life is so beautiful and so sad." He must have been thinking about Elizabeth Taylor. I saw a picture of her once in a magazine wearing tight pink capris and a pink silk shirt, sitting on a terrace in Puerto Vallarta. She looked as lovely as a peony, her eyes purple columbine, and she smelled like honeysuckle, rain-drenched phlox, David Austin roses. She looked like my mother's garden, so beautiful and sad, and like Elizabeth Taylor, the last of the ravishing beauties, it's gone.

If only my mother had met a man like Richard Burton, been a woman in love like Elizabeth Taylor dancing in her pink capris, a woman worth the Krupp Diamond. She could have been Martha Stewart in her Connecticut gardens, the Queen of England in Buckingham, Beatrix Potter in the Cotswolds, Vita Sackville-West in Sissinghurst. But the world of gardens and beauty is not fair.

No one really cares for or understands flowers, the burning, almost savage desire for them, the black void of a world without them. But my mother did. The flowers you dream of, the flowers you long for, the flowers you grow yourself in a silent garden, the flowers you wash with your own blood, the flowers you stare at until you blind yourself with beauty, the flowers of your wasted life, the flowers of your great unbalanced mind, the flowers you will wave at before your own ghastly death, the flowers you will bury yourself in, the flowers you offer to yourself, taking them between your teeth and letting them soak into your brain like poison.

I never saw my mother again after that summer day in her garden. Not my real mother. I have a vague memory of her on New Year's Day a few weeks before she died, making dinner. She wore red and looked massively tired. Old. She was frying something—Ukrainian doughnuts called pampushki. In Ukraine they were a special treat for the New Year and were often filled with a delicate rose-petal jam from roses grown in wild, untainted gardens. I remember her making them over the years and how the delicious aroma filled every room in the house, how hot, plump and sugary they were, piled up in a huge ceramic bowl on the kitchen table.

But that day everything was dull, chipped, ugly. I remember she asked me to get a pitcher that was high up on a shelf. I got on a step stool and grabbed it, feeling sticky old oil and dust and made a nasty remark about her housekeeping. She said it was so high up and out of place, she didn't think to dust it. The dinner was joyless, tasteless, and the memory of everything faded except the touch of that sticky pitcher and my cruel remark.

It's over two decades now after my mother's death, yet I still remember the joy of sitting with her in the garden, and how hard it was to leave. I could barely get up from the chair and would start to gather my things reluctantly while she went and picked a huge bouquet of flowers, thrusting it into my bag. Sometimes she walked with me to the bus stop and I felt like a soldier leaving for war never to return. I was a grown woman but felt like an abandoned child, afraid I might never see her again. She followed me with her eyes as I went the rest of the way and we kept waving to each other, as her little brown figure got smaller and smaller. Sometimes I wanted to run back and sit with her in the garden all night long and stare at the sky, the moon and the stars, until we were both swept away.

Sometimes I sit in my own garden as the skies turn violet in the evening and I see someone bursting through the screen door, running like a breathless child, a regal queen and sometimes just a sad and lonely mother. She bends down to the flowers to say hello, filling her blood with their perfume. She stands quietly inhaling the scent of grass, hay, water, clouds, fermenting grapes on tangled vines, apples withered on autumn trees, the smear of a trampled strawberry on someone's shoe, a licorice stick eaten long ago by some child.

I see the vast and intricate space of ecstatic flowers in that garden, flowers she seemed to create with her own breath. And then as brief as a summer rain, as quick as lightning, the perfume of strange lands calling, the scent of a silent world, as though from a galaxy of shattered stars, fragments of sun and moon flying, someone a million miles away cutting the waving grass. The sky trembles, turning inside out trying to find itself, shifting colors white to yellow, black to blue and gray, finer than mist, falling on the deep dark lilacs in her garden, their perfume knocking you senseless off your feet, but how gladly you fall.

Sometimes I see my uncle sitting in his half-finished house in the woods listening to that Rod McKuen song over and over again. And the little skeleton man on his porch, perhaps he noticed the ruby-red roses a woman and her child planted so long ago. My uncle, my wandering aunt, and my mother, are all there in another garden drinking an elixir pale as tears, sharper than lightning, more brilliant than diamonds, each of them drowning in the bitter yet thrilling taste of their final loneliness. ■

HERMITESS
Greg Tebbano

Approaching the second anniversary of Julian's death, Nadine's dreams grow wild. She is in their old apartment in Hoboken and Julian is not gone, only "out" according to a note left on torn newsprint. He is at this club or that show or just down the block at the bodega buying beer. He is everywhere at once. And in the dream she is bored, opening the freezer, looking for a Klondike bar or something great from 1992 and finding, instead, the freezer frosted over save for a single Popsicle with a pair of lips suspended inside it. Julian's lips. Really, how many pairs of lips could one recognize absent the face? Just these, she thinks, full and lipstick bright, almost a woman's lips. How they parted for her and the words *I do* and *Don't you even* and pulled her into the men's room at Maxwell's with a shameless, *Shall we?*

As she stands in the kitchen of their old apartment trying to exhume her dead husband's lips with her tongue, waiting to feel the excited static brush across her face, Nadine hears a laugh that sounds like her own coming from the next room.

The Popsicle is made of glass.

* * *

Nadine wakes cold and alone, pulling herself to the kitchen in camouflage long johns as the sunrise fires a warning shot through the window over the sink. She remembers once asking Julian if the same tights made her thighs look too thick while he smoked and cooked bacon and eggs in the same pan.

"Don't be stupid," he said. "Can breakfast be too delicious?"

In her memories, Julian is always same age, somewhere around twenty-five, an observation Nadine hopes will one day excite her future therapist. She, on the other hand, is in her fifty-second year on earth and the thinnest she's been since she was a teenager. Though perhaps it is not good thin, if the appraising eyes of her friends are to be believed. After Julian died she gained fifty pounds and just as quickly dropped it. Afterward, she kept going. Now she almost misses the weight, goes looking for it at thrift stores like a dress he gave her that she, in a haze of grief, donated by mistake.

Nadine opens cupboards, shuts them. At some point in the last year her brain permanently replaced the thought *I am hungry* with the thought *I should be hungry*. The last of the pot brownies gifted her by the sisters up the road sits by the coffee maker. She lifts the brownie to her nose, eyes each planar surface, each tanned moonscape. To be safe, she should cut the brownie in half but—too late. It is already a molten pleasure of the mouth. She stands there for minutes tasting it, the butter under the chocolate and under that a warm, green expanse. How it clings, jealously, to the back of her throat.

Hermitess.

Nadine tries the word across her tongue to see if it exists.

In the garage, she dons the old down coat and rubber boots, crampons synched to the soles. According to the Shell Gasoline thermometer, it is nine degrees. The wind drives out of the north, whistling through the soffits. Sometimes two notes catch in the air and she mistakes the harmony for Julian standing with her on the mud floor, a minor third passing through his overglossed lips.

She fills a bucket with grain, another with black oil sunflower seeds. For good measure, she digs out the crowbar. This is how today will pass. One thing, then the next.

The chickens come out long enough to drink. Only the roosters linger in the cold, keeping watch or trying to prove something, each standing on one leg in the snow. They are Dominiques, with cascading white-and-black tails and vocal cords built for six-hour sermons. They watch Nadine pry a ring of ice from the waterer. How she once brought such a ring into the bedroom for Julian, still sleeping, and laid it on his bare neck.

Oh, you fucker.

But look what I got you. It's a necklace.

I bet you went all the way to Macy's.

No. God made it for me. Now I'm giving it to you.

The only thing God was capable of making, Julian claimed, was a mess.

* * *

While Nadine's dreams are unexpected, full of possibility, the nightmares are more like memories. She already knows what's coming.

How many times has sleep taken her back to the exam room, its bone-white walls and noble gases sparring in the overhead lights, floors too tired to shine. The space could have been a classroom or a waiting room, an interrogation cell or an office—the room in which, if you were an American, you might be born, live and also die. It was here a doctor told Julian he had cancer of his pancreas, that it was stage four. As with tornados and hurricanes, the higher the number, the greater the chance your neighborhood would be decimated.

"This is the cancer you don't want to get," the oncologist told them, a woman in her fifties. Like you wanted any of them. Even in that moment, upon receipt of his own ticket to die, Julian's eyes were tied to the woman's shape under her coat, and to her curly red hair.

But in Nadine's dreams of the exam room, Julian is not there, only the bench with its butcher paper upon which no one has yet sat and sweat. Outside the window a team of arborists limb a tree. One dangles from the canopy like a marionette. Chain saws cough against the pull starts and then fire up.

Most of the dream is waiting. There are no magazines or pamphlets about emphysema. There is no one to wait with and bookmake odds about who, of the two of them, will get emphysema first. There is only Nadine. And no one is more tired of Nadine than she is.

When the oncologist returns with news, the biggest branches are just starting to come down. They rattle a set of sterilized instruments laid out upon a tray. Some of the branches break again, a second time, when they impact the concrete.

* * *

After finishing with the chickens, Nadine washes her hands and face in cold water, dries them with a tattered towel that smells of parmesan and moss. She wants to go back to bed and wait for sunset. To carve an X into the back of her hand—like at all those shows they used to go to. To drive into work at the post office. Anything. That there are no drugs in the house harder than the neighbors' edibles is a fact that simultaneously relieves and disappoints.

In a fleeting moment of resolve, Nadine tells herself that today will not be about grief, or, like those stupid hippie funerals, a celebration of life. Julian wouldn't have been caught dead celebrating that.

From somewhere in the kitchen she hears her phone vibrate. The buzzer is a reminder, a message from Nadine of the past to this Nadine, who is surprised by her own foresight.

Take down posted signs, it says. *Deer season is over.*

For all the shit Julian used to do, Nadine must now set reminders.

He hated how the manufactured signs along the road made their five acres seem like a militia proving ground. Property was another convention Julian couldn't abide. The young punk Nadine met in a basement haunt was a professional shoplifter turned anticapitalist, none of it belongs to anyone, etc. Even after they became the very landowners they'd once despised, Julian continued not to care who walked across their fields. He wanted people to. To explore like children, running half-naked down to the lake as the two of them had done years before—same fields, same lake, province then of some other old widow. To leave flags of skin on the barbed wire. To fuck and sink into the silt.

Nadine suits up for an extended expedition—face mask, down layer, a ratty GORE-TEX shell Julian used to fall asleep wearing in the recliner when he could no longer feel his feet. Today she will wander the fields across the street until snow blindness sets in or enlightenment. Perhaps they will coincide, like a fireworks display set to music. On the way home she will take care of the signs.

Nadine is halfway down the driveway when she sees two bright anoraks out on the road. After all these years living on a dirt track once owned by a single, sprawling dairy farm, she is still surprised how often she runs into their neighbors.

Yet here they are, the sisters. Their faces pale and wearing the cold's makeup.

"Nadine!"

For as long as she and Julian had been there, the sisters lived on the opposite side of the lake. In the summer, the four of them would often meet by chance on the floating dock, its decaying decking slick with goose shit and spilled canned cocktails.

Vivian grabs Nadine by the shoulders and squeezes, begins searching her eyes like a mother might for some clue cast away in the irises.

"It's today, isn't it?" she says.

Nadine begins to speak—

"No, no, no. It is. I can feel it. Can't you, Marian?"

From behind, Marian drapes an arm around Nadine's scarved neck.

"He burned brightly," she says. "And went out too quick."

Nadine used to think the sisters might be twins, always finishing each other's thoughts. Julian had a contradictory theory: they were a couple of unrelated widows exploring the unexamined corners of their sexuality—wrenching free the bag from a box of wine, as both were known to do, to wring out the final sweet drops.

"The other day I was looking at your hill and I thought I saw him standing there," says Vivian. "That way he did. With his hands on his hips, you know. Smoking a cigarette till it burned down to his mouth."

"Did you," says Nadine.

"But you know what I think it was? Like when you look at the sun, and then close your eyes and the sun's still there—"

Vivian's unblinking eyes are an open prompt.

"You're not supposed to look at the sun, Vivian," says Nadine.

"Well. You lived with it."

Everyone always liked him more than they liked her. Sure, he was moody, quiet and dark, but that was at home. That was just for her. At a cocktail party he was the one who gathered all the wallflowers into a bouquet, who coaxed the shy and egged on the assholes. And if he didn't make you laugh then you were the dead one, or death adjacent. You saw him gobbling up Jell-O shots in the paper cups and you knew that all this wasn't so important, not in the way you thought it was. Then he proved his point by dying and it hadn't been funny at all.

"I lived with it." Nadine parrots the idea back at them.

"Say," says Vivian, taking Nadine's gloved hands in hers. "How were the brownies?"

"Oh, divine."

"But have you had it yet? The one that *hits*?"

Nadine gives her a puzzled look.

"Before she bakes them, Vivian has to slip an extra pad of butter into one of the corners."

"The seer's portion," Vivian whispers, pumping her eyebrows. Marian asks her to forgive them. They're not bad witches, she explains, just bored ones. She wants to say she's sorry again about Julian but Nadine can barely listen to it. She was never a fan of condolences. How they merely turn her attention to the hurt, spotlight it—the moment she walked in on the end or the postscript or whatever it was, Julian on the bed, not asleep and full of unprescribed pharmaceuticals, his lips half-open as though he'd been telling someone to wait.

Now the sisters are crying beside her. Nadine is nearly jealous, distracted by their authenticity, a trait she thought strip-mined from the earth. Their faces are close, wind-pulled tears on their cheeks. In each frozen arc she can see a tiny sun.

The field across the street is wind-whipped, a snowscape skewered by cornstalks left behind after the combine came through for chop. The land belongs to Nadine's neighbor, who leases its rolling hills to a dairy to grow hay and feed in alternating years. To walk it stoned, however, in the middle of the day, there is no charge.

Soon the feeling Nadine hoped for arrives—to be absorbed by the unbroken horizon. She leans into the wind and marvels at a sky the color of blood still in the body, the clouds ripped from it like torn canvas. It makes sense, she thinks, that we would put god up there.

There is a hill she wants to climb, and she makes her way along a tree line grown in over a stone wall. How often did they hike up here in the summer at sunset, cans of beer sloshing in the plastic rings.

This way to the free concert.

And after, how they'd strip naked in the lit garage, plucking ticks and burs out of the other's hair with the half-hearted attention of two cats cleaning each other. She remembers sitting once, legs spread on the mower, moth wings against her back in imitation of his tongue, flickering.

Coyote prints lead her on to the hill top, doubling back on themselves where the night air must have turned sweet. It is only time that separates the two of them, Nadine thinks, that keeps her and the wild dog from climbing the hill side by side. Time, that heartless motherfucker—the same warden that keeps her from Julian. Without it, she and Julian and the coyote are all climbing the hill together and the snow is grass and the wind is warm and the clouds dream, by afternoon, of becoming thunderheads.

At the top of the hill Nadine can see the southernmost Green Mountains, decked out in white. For once, she can see where she is—how the hills around her make a bowl. At its bottom is the frozen lake and on the near shore up a short rise is their house. She still thinks of it as theirs. Their farmhouse with its sunken porch, its slouch in the frame like that of an old man. And in the front yard, for a moment, she sees someone legs apart and head down, a Julian sort of stance, laughing at some revelation he's had, that he will fold up and pocket to tell her when she gets home from her walk.

Nadine presses her eyes closed and light dances across the lids.

It is a tribute to Vivian's brownies that she does not realize she is screaming. She sees the scream first, in the brush birds that fan out from behind her into the field. Only after covering her mouth does Nadine hear the sound come back at her off the foothills. At first she doesn't recognize it. It's not her voice, but someone else's—someone equally alone, and listening.

* * *

On the way home Nadine has the buzzed idea that she can mitigate her sadness by besmudging Julian's memory. He did cheat on her once. Though even that event, the pain and shock of it, has become something longed for. She misses being mad at him about it, the attendant jealousy, which at first frothed, then faded slowly to a high ceiling.

What happened was Julian had gone and slept with the bartender at McGeary's. What was her name again. Janette? Nadine had a soft spot for her, a woman ten years her junior whose family boarded horses. Maybe it was because the bartender seemed fonder of the mud that tracked into her tavern than the men whose boots had carried it there. Like Julian, she was expert at ribbing you. The first time the two of them walked into McGeary's, she took one look at their peacoats and said they didn't serve anyone with a *New Yorker* subscription. Of course, Julian would always engage. His ego had found a new sparring partner. Maybe that had been the wick.

In all the years they'd been going to McGeary's, Nadine must have jokingly said it once: *Christ, get a room, you two.*

Unfortunately, there was one right over the bar. Julian described it to her the morning after, when he kicked open the farmhouse door still drunk, still dying. It was one of those old hotels—a long room with a tin ceiling just above his head and low windows just off the floor. It made him feel like a giant, he said. Then for some reason he was telling her about the sex and the eagle tattoo they had only ever known as wings, though Nadine could have done without how she felt through the condom, part marine, and how after, he lay awake all night, unsatiated, watching car lights creep up the walls, then across the ceiling. He forgot what it was like, he said, to spend the night above a street where traffic still passed.

Nadine, despite descending into a private well of vertigo, sipped at her coffee as though they were having a normal conversation. "Well, did you enjoy it?"

He shook his head. "I enjoyed the headlights."

Earlier that morning when Nadine had woken alone, she'd had an inkling. Though it seemed just as likely he'd gone out in the middle of the night to find a coyote he could fight barehanded. The diagnosis was fresh. He couldn't just lie with it. She got that. Even so.

She walked around the table to him, cradled his chin in one hand, held it there for a moment as a priest might. This is absolution, Julian, the hand seemed to say. This is forgiveness.

Then with the other hand, a fist now, she mashed in his beautiful lips.

* * *

When Nadine gets back to the house, the posted signs are already gone. She walks the road along their property line, flecks her glove over nails that kept one fastened to a tree. There was a time when she would have needed proof, to get on her hands and knees and punch through the snowpack to find the plastic signs with Julian's illegible handwriting on them. But she is tired and seeing double and Jesus extracted himself from the nails didn't he? Slunk down off the cross, all on his own. No one seemed to need any proof of that.

But Julian would have liked this, she thinks. The stretch of fields with no flags laying claim. No fingers pointing you away.

The Julian Latour Memorial Preserve. Have at it, kids.

Nadine goes inside and the couch finds her, its cushions, which deflate to half their size under her weight. A light switches on over the desk and she watches its glow dance in the dark house like a faulty firework that cannot gain lift.

It's cold. Why is it always so cold now? Maybe she is too thin. She should get up and start a fire. She should eat. She should really— definitely—rinse with mouthwash. She should, for safety, sharpen the one good chef's knife. She should not believe the cold overtaking her is a spirit. She should not expect to see Julian, for Julian is dead, dead of cancer—mankind's penance for a world of industry, cancer, who took her father and their Irish setter, cancer, who even now sticks his forked tongue in her face, tells her sullenly that if her kind are bent on wrapping the earth in spurious signals and caustic dust then he, cancer, will populate it with ghosts.

* * *

When she misses him, there is a day she will revisit. Over the last two years she has meted out her memories of this day, apportioned them like doses of methadone.

It was one of those March days. In the morning it snowed but the sun came out by noon and it was so bright you couldn't look anywhere, so she looked at the road, the water streaming across that turned to glass, then to gold as their tires overtook it. He was taking her out for sushi, in Rutland of all places. Two of his coworkers in production raved about the spot, but according to Julian they were raised on hot dogs and canned-soup casserole, so who knew. He must have seen pictures online because the place fell squarely in the middle of her taste, a long room with tables on both walls, jellyfish lanterns over the bar and beneath their feet a layer of lacquer over wood painted blue and streaked with clouds.

"The sky is our floor," Julian said.

Nadine smiled at that. It sounded prophetic in a way she couldn't articulate.

Julian kept looking over at a man he assumed to be the night cook in the next booth, half-asleep in a big grey coat.

"Why, because he's Asian?"

"Because he keeps looking at his watch."

What Nadine also remembered: the endless list of rolls, the sake not warm but hot, good-hot, and the tokens for the restroom down the hall. She liked the idea of a kind of currency you could only use for one specific, vital thing. How the man in the grey coat began to snore until he was prodded awake by their server, collecting himself and then disappearing into the back. When he came out again he was wearing a white hat and tying on an apron behind the sushi bar.

"I told you."

She turned his chin away from the bar and back to her.

"Nice work, Columbo."

If anyone had asked her in her twenties if she could love one person for thirty years she would have spit beer in their face. Back then she could barely finish an entire drink. But now, all those miles and years from New Jersey, there he was in the same booth as she. What made it possible—the only way she could explain it—was she still had a crush on him. Even now, baggy eyed and higher browed, Julian continued to exude something of the unattainable. Maybe other women would have hated it, having to always work for his attention. But this made it real for her. Made it count. A lifetime of cradling his chin and turning it back to her.

When the rolls came they were the best they'd ever had, even after so much time in proximity to New York.

"Good Christ this is amazing," she said. "I wonder what he dreamt about?"

With each bite Julian laughed a little harder. Both of them smiling like a couple of idiots. It was that good.

Afterward they walked around the cold but sunny streets, ducking into one thrift store after the next. It seemed to be the city's main industry, used clothing. One place claimed the largest selection in the state, which maybe wasn't that big a boast, but Nadine reveled in the smell of the room, thumbing through the racks, like all those places they used to hang around at in the Village. Even the clientele was the same, kids as they'd been, kids with too much makeup, the boys included, in cloaks and spikes and plant-based leather.

Nadine found a sweater exactly the same as one she had in her closet, only this one a more conifer green. She was trying it on in the dressing room when she heard a gasped whisper from beyond the plywood doors.

"Nadine? You in there."

"Nope, this is Claire," she said in what she hoped was an Australian accent.

"You suck at that," Julian said, slipping inside. He was wearing a teenage girl's former pants splattered with paint, one leg intentionally shredded both at the knee and up by the pocket. The upper tear was not exactly alluring. Too much hair maybe.

"How do I look?"

"Like Iggy Pop made out with Bob Ross."

"So, amazing then?"

He was twirling around with agility most had left behind in their thirties.

"Why don't you leave those for some lucky Vermonter to find," said Nadine. "Where would you even wear them? McGeary's?"

"To bed, obviously."

Nadine lifted her arms to take off the sweater but her shoulders froze up. They'd been doing this lately. Some kind of arthritis, she thought. But Julian was there and he was helping, the fitting room barely big enough for the entirety of them. He took an elbow in the jaw pulling her arm out and they laughed; she in her bra, he with a finger pressed up against her bared sternum.

"You know, Claire, I'm starting to like you."

In the mirror she saw herself blush. She thought about it, but there was barely a door—the thrill of whether or not the hook and eye would hold. And she knew he was thinking about it because he always did. But in the end it was he who handed her the shirt she'd worn there, helped her locked-up limbs inside it, then into her puffy coat and at the register took the admonishment of the clerk right alongside her, his turn to blush as a woman their same age told them—for next time—one person only in each of the fitting rooms. She pointed back across the store, though neither Julian nor Nadine turned to look. In case they hadn't noticed, there was a sign.

That was the day. Then he drove her home over the mountain at dusk, Nadine watching collapsed barns pass and houses she would have thought abandoned save for the lights on inside them. When they got home, Julian closed up the chicken coops and they drank too much whiskey and had sex that migrated from the kitchen to the couch.

She was lying on top of him trying to keep the floor fixed in the same place when Julian said suddenly, "His wife."

"What?"

"The sushi chef. He dreamt about his wife," said Julian. "I went up to thank him when you were in the bathroom. Apparently, she died last year."

"Wait, what?"

He pulled her closer, closer, until it felt like a kind of falling. When he fell asleep he was still clutching the back of her leg and when they woke in the next day's light there his hand remained, her flesh bunched under it—how a boy might slumber clenching a beloved bear or his baseball glove, for fear that someone might come in the night to take it.

* * *

Now when Nadine wakes in the world he has left, this is where she feels his touch, on the back of her thigh. How she will scramble then, breathless, for the mirror or the overhead light to see what must be there: a burn or a watermark. Some proof beyond forgery of what had been.

She feels it now as she wakes, still half-high on the coach. Loathe to rise, she puts a hand on the couch, then, up to her knees. A hand on the mantle, then to her feet. One thing, then the next.

In the garage she slips into the chore coat. For no reason she expects it to be warm. In the breast pocket are a couple of Julian's cigarettes, probably with salmonella on them. She lights one regardless, wonders if his lips ever wet the paper while he thought of her, of something he'd promised to do, before returning it, unsmoked, to its hold.

Outside the sunset is tearing the sky apart.

Her eyes follow the unbroken white fields to the wood and from there down to the lake, where a pair of bright jackets stumble from the trees. Vivian and Marian and a box of wine are walking out to the floating dock now buttressed by ice. Nadine whistles and waves her arm at them in a high, wide arc. She knows how this must look: like the word *help*.

The sisters wave back, calling up to her, inviting her to their sunset revelry with enough enthusiasm to land an aircraft.

Nadine walks—no, runs—over the glazed field. Under each step, the world seems to break, to snap and recoil, and its destruction is a mild comfort. But her attention keeps pulling back to the sky where the day's last light has settled on the hillside full of locusts. She and Julian wondered nightly about these trees, all the same age, all in straight rows. Whoever planted them must have lived too quickly to see to their harvest. Otherwise, they'd be fence posts now. And this delights Nadine—the enclosures that will never be built because these trees still stand, their leafless branches coming together, pulling apart, coming together again, at the pleasure of the wind. ■

A NEST IN THE PRISON CLASSROOM
John Brantingham

The classroom's window air conditioner
doesn't work, hasn't for a while. In spring,
sparrows nest inside it. Their tweeting
is music that makes it much harder
for us to concentrate and makes the biggest
guys smile and talk about their kids, stories
of children finding nests or injured chickadees
that the little ones wrapped in towels to nurse.
They tell me not to put in a work order
to fix it until the fledglings have grown
enough to fly on their own. They tell me
whatever heat we have to sit in is better
than silencing the chicks. Once they've flown,
it'll be harder to stay inside these memories.

HIGH NET WORTH INDIVIDUALS
Suzanne Scanlon

I had a plan to meet Carla for a drink after our last engagement that day. I arrived at the Social Club and saw Janet sitting alone at the bar, her back to me. I asked the hostess for a table in the dining room. When I'd met Janet a few days earlier at the happy hour, she told me that she was writing a book about philanthropy. Well, not exactly, she clarified, I met a man last year in New York and he told me that he wants someone to write a book about philanthropy, which is a sham, she explained. What is a sham? I said. Philanthropy, she said. I said, is this what you are writing now, a book for this man? And she said, well I was going to write a book about that but now I think I'm going to write a book about wealth, and grief. Now Carla joined us. She wore a 1980s miniskirt and a low-cut blouse. I felt dumpy next to her. She'd recently transitioned. She'd published her last book as Carl Cook; her latest would be by Carla Cook. What I mean, Janet explained, now including Carla, is that I am writing about High Net Worth individuals. It had become loud in the cafe. On one end of the room an open bar with a limited selection of drinks, on the other, a hallway leading to a room for a poetry reading; crowds were gathering. Carla said, High what? And Janet repeated her description of her clients: High Net Worth individuals. Oh, Carla said, of course! HNWIs. I laughed. Yes! Janet replied, unaware that Carla was mocking her. So, Carla went on, you write about rich people? And what do we need to know about rich people? Tell Mark Zuckerberg he can spend a week in a homeless shelter, and then talk to me. Janet protested: But they aren't all Mark Zuckerberg! Most are normal, interesting people! Yes, Carla rolled her eyes, like all those people who cheated to get their kids into colleges? Janet's eyes widened, Yes! Those were my clients! You don't understand, Janet explained, rich people are the only group you're allowed to discriminate against anymore. If you say something about a Jewish person or a Muslim person or a Black person, you are shunned, but say something derogatory about rich people, and no one objects. Are rich people an ethnicity? Carla asked. No. Okay, next! Carla said, her hand flipping her frosted hair. Janet tried again—it was discrimination, it wasn't fair, not all rich people, etc.

I asked the waitress to seat me at a table where Janet would not see me. That was when I saw Pam at the next table. Pam had been a student in my class the year before. Hi, Scanlon, she said, calling me by my last name. Can I join you? I smiled, said I was meeting someone and she would be here any moment. Pam looked offended, and I remembered what had been so difficult about her: the way she would storm out of the room, or cry, or make inappropriate comments. I suppose what she lacked was a protective layer of self. During one in-class writing exercise, she stood up and walked around, finding a chalkboard on which she wrote her story. It was distracting to other students, but I did not stop her. I knew that if I reprimanded her in any way she might become upset, leave the class, or cause a greater disturbance. But to include her meant putting up with her unpredictable and erratic behavior.

Pam said, Well that's too bad. Anyone I know? You mean the person I'm meeting? She said yes, and I said that well I doubted that, though of course she knew Carla. I looked at Pam, her messy hair, unplucked eyebrows, patchy skin. She had hairs growing out of her chin. The pathos of Pam's life overwhelmed me. When I met her some years ago, I said: How are you? And she said, I'm fifty-three and have my period. How are you? It was so off-putting, though I don't consider myself a prude. Still, it managed to push me away from her, to create distance, physically and emotionally. I too have protective devices; I too have barriers.

Though I see Pam only during the summer, she sends me the occasional email. *Hey Scanlon*, it might begin. Or, apropos of nothing, she'll write, *I had a weird experience.*

Now Pam had moved to the table next to me. She was taking the bread from the basket and putting it on the table, piece by piece. I texted Carla, telling her we might need to find another place and was she close etc. 10 mins! she texted. I drank water and looked to the other side of the restaurant.

Hey, Scanlon! Pam had pulled apart the bread slices, removing the bread from the crust, rolling it into balls. There were crumbs all over the tablecloth. A waitress brought her a Coke.

I wanted Carla there, who would get me out of this. It occurred to me that because Carla had been a man for nearly fifty years, she was far more effective at being a woman than I would ever be. How comfortable I felt with Carla leading the way in her platform sandals. Now where was she? I wanted Carla to experience it, how needy Pam was, how she wanted to be close to the very people she alienated. I would explain it to Carla, what I'd observed: It is hard to bear, to see how, despite having an above-average intelligence, a person might be trapped by her own personality.

But right now I was trapped. Scanlon! Pam was saying. Why don't you like me, Scanlon? I looked over again and saw the breadcrumbs on her shirt, her lap, the tablecloth. Scanlon, what do you have against me? What did I ever do to you? Pam, I said, quietly, I'm sorry, I said. Yeah I bet you are! Others were looking at us, hearing Pam accuse me: It's always this way, people like you and here I am, you know, trapped at my cousin's house. What do you mean trapped? Trapped! You know my cousin's husband? Well this morning he said something about Trump's PENIS and I had to leave the house. I have a lot of problems with husbands.

I put my jacket on. I'm sorry, I said again to Pam, who had stopped talking, was drinking her Coke. I'll have the check, I could hear her loudly call out to the waitress, though I was down the stairs by now and could see Carla on the street, taking her time, laughing and flirting with someone on her phone. ■

TIDE POOL
Aarti Monteiro

You begin to lose weight before the breakup. It's a few pounds at first and then suddenly your pants have a two-inch gap behind the buckle. You lie on your back, Max asleep beside you. You rub your fingertips against the hair on your belly, try to grab at the usual fat underneath your shirt, but there's nothing to grab. Walk to the bathroom, stare at yourself in the full-length mirror, and find that your body has morphed into something you didn't expect. You're embarrassed you like it. Tell yourself you're better than this— you're a feminist, being skinny has never been the goal—and yet there's no doubt in your mind that you look better. Without doing anything, you've lost the weight you've secretly wanted to lose for a long time. Climb back into bed, rest your heel against his calf. It's still too early to think of the obvious metaphor: you're losing yourself.

Two months later, you and Max move out of the apartment you share. You were together for eight years and everyone assumed you'd get married. Tell your friends it's a mutual decision, but you know he'd take you back. The certainty of the relationship is part of the problem. Your falling out of love comes out of nowhere for him; it came out of nowhere for you too, but you couldn't ignore it when it arrived, fully formed. The nagging feeling of wanting to experience life alone, you told him, outside the relationship. The explanation wasn't concrete enough for anybody.

You never had the biggest appetite, but suddenly the knot of anxiety you carry around makes it impossible to eat full meals. Cook food you don't eat, then stop cooking all together. Fall asleep with a sharp pain in your belly. Your jaw locks as you sit down for dinner, unable to open wide enough for food. You're no longer sharing a life with anyone, so the amount of time you spend not eating is yours alone.

You spent most of your twenties with Max, and now, in your thirties, you're doing what most people have stopped doing: dating. "Getting past a breakup takes time, Rani," your friend Molly tells you. "There's no rush." But you've never been a patient person. You wish you could montage your way through the next year and find yourself on the other side.

Your friends give you advice, tell you what images to include in the dating profile, what pithy bio would elicit the right response. You're usually behind the camera and have few photos to choose from. Most of the pictures are on occasions when Max was there; either he took the photograph or he was in the room at the time. See yourself through these potential dates' eyes, aware when you're looking at the lens, when you're not. Whether you're presenting yourself too accurately or not accurately enough. Whether this new body they're seeing is really you.

The dating app becomes a sociological study very quickly. More brown and Black men message you than white men. A lot of South Asian men respond to you, but they're the ones you don't have anything in common with. The South Asians you're interested in don't tend to like you. You're ashamed to admit that you're drawn to those who seem more American. Find yourself wanting to express that you're Indian but not too Indian, you're Western but not too Western, you're a perfect balance of the dichotomies that pull and push you like a fish in a tide pool.

* * *

Your first date is with a Black man. You go out for a drink, which turns into two, and he explains his tech job you couldn't care less about. The lights are too dim to read the menu, so you point to a random beer on the list. People lean over you to order at the bar and you constantly feel in the way.

While the alcohol swirls in your head, he invites himself over. You fear you acted like you had a better time than you did—laughed at too many jokes, didn't move your leg quickly enough when he leaned his against you, asked him too many questions. But then you decide that someone you don't care about is the perfect first experience post-breakup. Low stakes.

His kisses are clumsy, his hands on your neck, your shoulder blades. You think of this stranger in your apartment, how he could hurt you, but you push the thought away because isn't this just what dating is? The risks inherent. Undress yourself and lie on your floral sheets. He pulls you on top of him and your body goes stiff as glass. When he can't hold an erection, worry you're not pretty enough for him. Let him talk about his frustrations of dating. How this happens a lot. He says that sleeping with white women, over Black women, feels like winning. You're surprised he'd tell you this. Maybe since you're not part of the Black and white dichotomy, he thinks it won't offend you.

He spends the night in your bed, but you don't have sex. You tell him you have to wake up early, that he should go home, but he stays, complaining of the winter outside. He holds on to you and tells you how lonely he is. You let him. Or at least you've stopped asking him to leave. Don't want to be rude. Lie awake listening to his breath slow into sleep.

* * *

A week later, you sit on your couch and browse swimsuits online. You can't decide whether to buy one that flatters this new body or whether you're surely going to return to your old self before summer. Is this change one you need to get used to? Stare at your naked self after stepping out of the shower every day, the curves of your breasts accentuated by your small belly. You're attractive in a way you've never felt before. But in another moment, you feel too fragile. Touch the ribs beneath your taut skin. Your skinny wrists could snap easily. You're embarrassed your body is visibly responding to the changes in your life.

You go home to visit family for the first time since the breakup, and because they don't know how to make space for sadness, they complement you. "Have you lost weight?" your aunts ask. In your mind you say, "Yes, twenty pounds." But twenty pounds is too much for someone your size, so you smile and nod. Looking "good" means you've clearly made the right decision—Max was holding you back because look how healthy and independent you are without him. The disconnect between how you look and how you feel is a valley inside you.

Friends you haven't seen in months comment on how you look, as though your body falls into the small talk category. Sometimes you lie and say you've been exercising. Other times you joke it's because Max isn't there to cook for you. Mostly you push away the attention by asking them questions. This is the reason why, Max would say, you don't feel like anyone really knows you.

Every day pushes you further from who you were before. Corny breakup songs hit you in a way you've never experienced. You wander without a net beneath you, the loneliness you've always felt has a different texture now. Carry around your camera but your desire to take photographs has softened. Recording this moment in your life is unappealing. Your friends say breakups are always hard, but your arrogance makes you believe they don't understand. You and Max grew like vines around each other. The worst part is when you realize the relationship wasn't so unique in the end. Everyone thinks they're special.

Guilt of the breakup has seeped through your skin and splatters your insides like paint. Will you ever stop feeling guilty that you made a decision that uprooted both of your lives? It's pathetic, this guilt, because your desire to be forgiven is rooted in your desire to feel better. It's not possible to forgive yourself until he forgives you, and he shouldn't forgive you. Wonder if you're allowed to feel heartbroken too.

* * *

The second date you go on is with an Indian man. He smiles a lot and laughs at your jokes. You see him twice, but neither of you leans in to kiss the other. Brush your hand against his arm, sit near him at the dimly lit bar. You have few common interests, but you talk about your families and Desi comedians. Though your cultures are different, the baseline of understanding between you feels like coming home. For a moment you're relieved you don't have to explain yourself, that he can see what you keep hidden.

He asks the race of your last boyfriend. You tell him Max is white, and he says he thought so. "You're different from all the Desi girls I know," he says. "You're kind of a hipster."

A part of you is pleased—the part you're ashamed of. The part that does everything to fit in with the white people around you. The other part of you is angry, wants to tell him there's no one way to be Indian. But you fear there is and that you're doing it all wrong. You don't know how to say any of this, so keep your mouth shut and laugh because maybe this new person you're being doesn't take everything so seriously.

You would go out with him again but neither of you contacts the other. Maybe you aren't Desi enough for him. Are you Desi enough for anyone? Maybe you've been so embedded in white culture that white people are the ones you feel connected to. That was not the plan. You told your friends that you wanted to date people from other backgrounds—as though you're a company trying to meet a quota, checking boxes so you can't be labeled as a woman of color who only dates white men.

* * *

You attempt to build a new life in the same streets you shared with Max. A memory smudges each corner. You scan every bar and coffee shop and subway car for him. Look closely at each man you pass; any iteration of dark blond and white and medium height causes a stir in your belly. So many men in Brooklyn. You know you shouldn't want to run into him—he doesn't want to see you—but you want it anyway. Want to catch him off guard, make him witness your new life even though it would hurt. How deep can your selfishness go?

You finally find him in your neighborhood. A Tuesday night. You pass a bar and glance inside and there he is, sitting at the counter with a brown-haired white woman. His shoulders and posture are so familiar you can't believe you thought anyone else was him. The woman he's with is exactly what you expected. When you'd first started dating, you imagined everyone assumed his girlfriend looked like her, not like you.

His back is to you and you know she won't notice you. He's wearing a black sweatshirt you've never seen before. She plays with her hair. Maybe she's an artist like Max. Maybe she's calm and relaxed and forgiving. Things you never were.

You remain still. Your breath marks the glass. People pass on the street, but no one glances in your direction. There is no reason for you to be angry, or even jealous. These are the obvious next steps of a breakup. It's not possible to move on at the same pace. But you want to go through all of this together, like you've gone through the last eight years, to see what he thinks about living alone for the first time, or a date's enigmatic texts. He can no longer be a witness to your life.

You watch him touch his face as he listens to her and imagine you know what they're talking about. You have an impulse to rap on the window, barge inside, draw attention to yourself somehow. The breakup was a chance to recreate yourself, to be a new kind of person. It's impossible to start over. Everything you are you take with you; the pull of your personality dictates your every move.

When you get home, you open the app and flip through men's faces without really looking. The idea of Max moving on hits you in the gut. When you've only dated one person, you have little context. Now he will see you more clearly, see that you weren't as giving of a partner as you should have been. Everything comes into perspective in comparison.

* * *

You sleep with the third person you go out with: a white man. You've only been on two dates and you aren't sure you like him. But you need to show yourself you can move on. You invite him back to your place for a "nightcap"—a phrase you've never heard people say in real life. He is paler than Max, and he's gentle as he kisses you. You want it to be more passionate, for him to take you in his arms and carry you to the bed. Want him to show how desperate he is in his desire for you, but instead he's slow and methodical. He undresses you and then himself. You resist the urge to cover up. You're conscious of where you touch him, this man you barely know, so you let him slide himself inside you. Your mind moves out of your body. It's not that the sex is terrible, but rather that you're too consumed by what's happening on a theoretical level. That you are sleeping with someone other than Max, that this man is holding on to you like he loves you, and for a moment you let yourself think he does. Until you remember that he doesn't know you.

He climaxes before you return to your body. He apologizes and you smile shyly saying it's okay. You perform for him because even though you aren't sure if you want to see him again, you know you want him to like you. He pulls away and lays your head on the smooth space between his shoulder and his chest. Only now does he glance around your room, this space that is just yours for the first time, and suddenly you feel exposed. He's talking but you can't focus. You're disappointed that the man you ended up sleeping with is white. That even when you intentionally seek out people of color, you are pulled to whiteness. He leaves soon after and you know you won't see him again.

All these men only know you in this body, the one you haven't had for very long. They see you as a different person. And you suppose you are. Getting used to it means you have to settle into a new life you chose for yourself. Things are different now, though you're surprised you feel the same.

* * *

Slowly, as the winter air lifts, so does your mood. The weight returns. You suddenly feel silly in the small clothes you bought, how tightly they cling to the bulge of your belly. The anxiety has thinned but you don't like your body as much. Wonder whether everyone notices that the changes were only temporary. Your body in the old life has returned like a shadow and you can't tell whether this is a new normal or if you too are supposed to return.

You're ashamed that this is something you would even feel bad about; it is undoubtedly positive you have an appetite again, and yet everywhere you look, being skinny is beautiful. The confidence you gained from a flat stomach has evaporated.

Your friends begin to think you're doing better. They want to hang out with Max, want to move on from talking about your heartbreak. No longer in transition, begin to focus on remaining in this new moment. Moving on feels like a betrayal, like the relationship wasn't as important as you'd both thought. How could yous echo through your mind; your past self tries to yell sense to your current self. Hold on to the familiarity of your body; it is with you regardless of anything else.

You meet Max for coffee on a Sunday. He looks healthier than he did when you were together. Wonder whether it was actually you holding him back during the relationship. It has been over a year, and you fall easily into laughter and chatter. The space between you shrinks and expands like a jellyfish. In moments you feel the comfort of how he knows you, and in others, the distance presses against your chest, making it hard to breathe.

The coffee shop is impersonal, a neutral space that doesn't belong to either of you. The sweat of iced tea falls onto your shirt as you bring the glass to your lips. You avoid the topic of dating; he tells you about his art projects, how much he's been able to focus and accomplish. Where was this discipline before? Does being alone always teach you more?

You let yourself imagine starting over, taking what you've learned from the time apart and rising from it. You touch his hand and he clasps yours. Everything you've kept to yourself rushes out like water from a pipe and he nods at all the right times. Tell him you miss him. Tell him that it's been the hardest year of your life. Tell him you feel like you should be different but you're not. Let him hold you for a moment, on a street corner. He's taller than you remember; lift your heels to rest your head on his shoulder. Cling to a past that's steadily drifting. He's the first to pull away. Your arms fall to your sides like banyan tree branches; your feet hit the pavement.

You walk the three long blocks home, in the opposite direction of Max. The sky dims and you remember the downpour the day you moved into the old apartment together. Boxes surrounded the bed, one small succulent on the windowsill, a pile of novels on the wooden floor. You thought little of the future then, wide-eyed about living with him, creating space for another person. You want to turn and run back to him, explain that it's been a mistake and let's go back to where we were. But you know he's gone. This isn't a movie. Walk into your empty apartment, the mess of your life everywhere. Books, clothes, water glasses. Now everything there is yours alone. Spread yourself out, your body that is no longer shrinking. ■

APPLE PIE
Eleanor Spiess-Ferris

W orld War II had been over for two years, but the war between my sisters continued. This sibling war would last through their adulthood and end only when one of them was pronounced dead.

I wonder when I first noticed their dislike for one another, being that I am ten years younger than the eldest sister and eight years younger than the other. Perhaps my enlightenment happened when I moved from high chair to a "big person's chair" at the dinner table, where our family dramatics were copiously exposed.

While I may never, until this writing, have truly realized the family pecking order, I must have always been subconsciously aware of it.

My brother, Randall, at thirteen, seemed totally unaware of his sisters—myself included. He had discovered girls.

Mother ruled all members of our northern New Mexico family and most of the fifty acres of our small farm. She was keeper of the chicken coops, churner of butter, director of mores and middle-class values; administrator of chores, homework, and cleanliness. She held court at the end of our rectangular table closest to the root of her kingdom—the kitchen.

My gentle father sat facing her at the nominal head of the table. The only dinnertime deference Mother gave him was that we didn't say grace, being as he was an agnostic, leaning toward atheism.

My sister Jeannette, green eyed and dark like my mother, sat at mother's right. Randall, fair haired and handsome, sat to our mother's left. Next to my brother and at our father's right sat my blonde, chubby sister Ann. For some reason, I sat between my sister Jeannette and my father. Ann and Jeannette sat at a diagonal to each other and while I did not have full view of my eldest sister, I could hear her. I did see Ann clearly.

I seemed to be the only one that was fully aware of the disgruntled sounds and looks they shared. Hairy eyeballs, rolled eyes, side-glances, and muffled coughs and groans were tossed from one to the other and returned—a volley of covert messages from one citadel to the other.

Mother had, perhaps unconsciously, defined each of us. Jeannette, the eldest, was the intelligent one. Ann was the difficult one. Randall was the golden one, and I, the youngest, was simply "the accident." My conception, Mother would often reveal, had happened after a party when she was drunk.

* * *

When I got older I bravely asked my mother why my sisters disliked each other. She paused, looked out of the window, and said, "When Jeannette was five I gave her a red dress. Ann was jealous because I had not given her a red dress." That was all she said and, judging by her demeanor, that was the end of that particular conversation.

When my sisters weren't ignoring me, each one would draw me separately into her confidence and start a narrative of blame and mistrust about the other. This made me uneasy. I liked being accepted, albeit one sister at a time. I was the jury in two separate trials and learned quickly that I shouldn't choose sides.

The rest of the time, I was their toy. When I was four, they dressed me up as Carmen Miranda. I was made to parade around the living room with a towel around my head balancing the oranges and apples tucked into the folds. I was prodded to repeat "I, Yi, Yi, Yi, Yi, I Like You Very Much," Miranda's signature song, while wiggling my hips. I enjoyed making them laugh!

When I started school, I worried that there would not be enough oxygen in the classroom. Witty sister Ann presented me with empty Mason jars and suggested I take them to school with me.

"Don't worry," she said, "there's a lot of stored oxygen in these jars."

If I asked Jeannette a question, she would look at me from over her book, shake her head, and continue to read.

At one moment, I was to be played with and at another I was to be ignored or teased. But all the while, they, it seems, were busy carrying on their personal vendettas.

I was the "baby."

They were teenagers in their bobby socks and saddle shoes moving quickly into adulthood.

I was cremating stink bugs with stolen matches and roaming among the struggling fruit trees, hunting for butterflies and worms. I was wading in the muddy irrigation waters with my dog.

They were dating young men from their high school and dancing the jitterbug in the high school auditorium.

They were wearing red lipstick and blotting their lips on tissue paper.

I was wounding myself on hidden barbwire fences and, in my seven-year-old way, contemplating nature in all its tribulations of birth and death.

My sisters and the rest of the world were celebrating a time of peace.

When the school year was finally over, it was my habit to spend mornings patrolling the expanse of land along the irrigation ditch with Tootsie, my mixed spaniel.

We always had several dogs. They would greet my mother with wagging tails and happy faces. My mother, in turn, would respond joyfully.

Mother had gifted Tootsie to me when I was three. The dog, who slept with me every night at the bottom of my bed, still seemed to know that my mother was the ultimate boss and dutifully met Mother with love and respect each morning.

Leaving by the kitchen door, Tootsie and I would weave among the cottonwood trees on the water's edge, dash across a wooden bridge, and run past the dried-up cornfield that my brother had attempted to cultivate the year before. Together, we would circle the grove of blossoming plum trees and then, doubling back, I would give a military salute to the tall, spindly cherry tree. At excursion's end, we would cross another bridge near an abandoned pig shed. All the while, a flock of magpies that called those trees home would caw loudly. The greatest wonder was seeing the black-and-white birds hopping from one branch to another, keeping their eyes on the intruders. It was nesting time.

One morning I had escaped home for an early, before-breakfast, walk along the water's edge. The ditch water was high and the trees had fully leafed out. Spring was beginning to leave. Summer would be arriving soon. I could smell the change in the air as the spring scents of lilac and tulip and new growth were becoming faint.

The magpies were calling to each other in great distress. They flew down into the brambles and up again to their high nests.

Tootsie and I were busy turning leaves over.

Leaves of faded red and washed-out brown.

Leaves soggy from the winter snows.

Leaves that certainly now should harbor all sorts of small, squirmy creatures.

We, me with my scuffed school shoes and she with her wet dog nose, were on the hunt for anything that crawled.

Then suddenly, hidden among the dried fall leaves, we saw the baby magpie. It lay on its side, its beak moving silently and its wing extended out from its small body.

I scooped the small bird up in my sweater, leaves and all, and held the bundle close to my chest. I ran home, hoping and praying that there was some way I could save this tiny creature.

I burst through the kitchen door and into the dining room, where my family was finishing their Sunday breakfast. I presented the fallen bird to my family.

At first glance, my sister Ann fell back in terror. She was afraid of birds.

My mother pointed to the door and suggested I take it back to its "found" place.

But my sister Jeannette suggested the old rabbit hutch as a safe harbor for the bird.

My brother, with a mouth full of scrambled eggs and bacon said, "No use. It gonna die."

My sister Ann, gaining composure, suggested a diet of hard-boiled eggs and plenty of water.

All agreed that the old wooden rabbit hutch would be a good place for the injured bird.

As I turned from the family gathering toward the kitchen door, bird bundle cradled in my folded arms, my sister Ann asked, "What are you going to name it?"

Farm folk don't often name animals, especially ones that will appear on the dinner table. However, I had named a rooster King Lear once because of his temperament. But this naming was different. This was like the naming of a dog or a cat or a milk cow or the bull with curly fur or the brown colt that lived with the old palomino by the second chicken coop.

I paused.

"Apple Pie," I answered.

It took three days for Apple Pie to die.

No matter the water, or the hard-boiled eggs, or the songs I sang to it, the beautiful bird passed away. I cried and cried.

I made the announcement at another family breakfast.

"Told you so," said my brother with a slight touch of sympathy in his voice.

But my sister Jeannette left the table and came back with a shoebox that I knew had housed her favorite high heels.

Ann declared, "It is time for a funeral. Randall, you make the cross. Jeannette has the box. We all shall go to the rabbit hutch and start the proceedings."

"May, I suggest hats?" added Jeannette.

"Yes, absolutely," agreed Ann.

"Gloves?" said Jeannette.

"I will dig the grave," interjected Randall.

Ann gave a nod to the gloves and to Randall's suggestion as well.

Within the hour Apple Pie had been gently placed in Jeannette's shoebox and both sisters had donned their Sunday hats. Ribbons were tied around my braid ends.

A white kitchen towel became the casket's lining.

The dead creature seemed even smaller nestled in the white cloth. Its black-and-white plumage was just beginning to be prominent. Its tail was still short and immature. Apple Pie's eyes were closed. The eyelids were a deep purple. It had been barely a fledgling. And I, in tears, carefully closed the lid.

Randall presented me with a cross, made from two twigs from the lilac bush that grew near the dining room window. The cross was carefully tied together with white string.

Both Ann and Jeannette had gathered all the sad flower remains from my mother's spring garden. They held the bouquets tightly in their gloved hands.

"Music?" questioned Jeannette.

"I fully agree," said Ann.

"Something we all know," replied Jeannette.

"Ah, yes. 'Onward Christian *Shoulders*'!" responded Ann.

"Great idea," replied Jeannette, sharing a wink with her sister while they both sweetly smiled at me.

I was at the head of the line carrying the shoebox and the cross.

My sisters followed according to age.

My brother was at the rear with a collapsible World War II army shovel.

We marched in single file toward the wild orchard singing at the top of our voices, "Onward, Christian *shoulders*."

There, between the old green apple tree and the grove of plum trees, we buried Apple Pie. I placed the twig cross at the head of the grave. My sisters adorned the small pile of turned dirt with wilting spring flowers. We bowed our heads and I said a prayer.

I, during quiet times, return to that day and fondly recall how my warring sisters put aside their feud to help their baby sister. I march and sing down to that little burial site with my siblings following me. We are all singing the only hymn we knew together—

with a slight word change.

I again feel the New Mexico breeze as it stirs the aging trees, as stink bugs hide under dead leaves and as magpies build their nests high in cottonwood trees. I feel the mud that forms under my feet as my ghost dog and I wade in the irrigation ditch.

While I wish I could have saved that lovely bird, I wish more that my sisters could have found pleasure in each other.

Their hostilities continued.

Our mother, after her stroke, decided to stay in her own separate home. Ann moved in to help her as they, over the years, had become close. Jeannette was very disappointed with her decision, as she had wanted Mother to move to her home many miles away.

When Mother died, my sisters argued over the silver, the Victorian furniture, the Indian pottery and especially over whom mother loved best.

I became weary of their continuing feud and sent a letter to each of them.

"Mother, in my opinion," I wrote, "didn't love any of us best. Time to get over it and realize that she loved her dogs best!"

They never acknowledged my letter. ∎

MID-MORNING OFF THE ROACH
Sarah Anne Stinnett

I wear your waders this spring
nymphing in the easy riffles,
those wavelets crisp and swashing over
out-jutting rock heads.

Why are waders so ugly? Their khaki
is a spoiled hunter-green gone pale,
an overripe avocado.

I cinch the waist, yours twice mine,
belt the net, tin box of pupas, a spare line.

Waders underwater fill, you said,
carry you with the current.

A lean trout, rusty olive, young
and keen, idles in an eddy
around the brushy bank. I wade

deeper into the cold, thigh high,
but the trees are still too close behind
so I roll-cast—
                    and the rod,
buoyant in my hand, cheerful even,
sings the line downstream,
reel humming, a murmur, voice, your
cork grip grooves so familiar.

The wet nymph drifts, rivered
toward the whirling countercurrent
and the parr, too fresh to be cautious, bites—
I strike, I miss;

then reeling back in slowly,
I see the branches have broken
lines tangled up and knotted, stringy webs,
one streamer of chestnut with fluttering white feathers.

I circle to pitch the cast overhead again
and let it unspool and fly and settle,
traveling with the water
as it dead drifts.

VISITATION
L. Annette Binder

The dog pulled hard at the leash, up the last hill before home, past the Fournalts' winding driveway and the Malones', where kids were shouting, and then the three hundred acres that belonged to a Benedictine monastery somewhere in New Jersey for reasons nobody knew. Forest on either side, ferns unfurling and birch and maple just coming into bud and everywhere the sounds of spring, the peepers in the neighbors' ponds, the phoebes with their *ee ee* calls, back and forth, back and forth, and it was the most relaxing part of the day, her morning walk with Brutus. She liked to watch the neighborhood kids when she walked. Sometimes they zoomed past her on bikes, the littlest ones on wooden balance bikes that had no pedals, and they raced along the hard pack road in their swimsuits and their Crocs, but not today. All night it had rained, and the road was empty.

"Go easy, boy," she told him, jerking back at the leash when he pulled her, but not hard enough to hurt him or even to deter him from his bad habits. "You've got no manners, no manners at all." She stopped to tighten her shoelaces and he watched her impatiently. She felt her left hip as she bent down, her left hip and her right knee. Left, right, left, right, a terrible symmetry that stole what little grace she had. She walked like an old woman in a street of young families. Every step cost her, but she walked anyway because walking was better than sitting still.

She straightened up and stretched her hip before easing on the leash. "Now we can go," she told him. A beef bone was waiting for him back at home, he knew this without her saying so. The wind blew through the branches, showering her with raindrops. A stone wall led into the Benedictines' forest; everywhere there were stone walls built by farmers two centuries earlier. They'd cleared the land and planted it, but the cities had more sway over them than the rocky fields. The farmers left to work in the factories and the mills in Boston and Springfield and Manchester, and the forest came back. It grew around the walls they'd raised and covered the fields where grain once grew. A hundred years later new people came and renovated the old farmsteads or cleared just enough land to build new houses and they raised their families in these houses and commuted ten miles south to Hanover and Lebanon, where they worked at the hospital or the university or the tech companies clustered on the narrow roads behind the fitness club. She'd lived for thirty years on this dirt road, twenty-six of them with Philip, who'd built the house himself and terraced the garden and built her a little greenhouse. He cleared the snow and resurfaced the driveway every spring, and all these years later, everything still reminded her of him, how he held his coffee mug and how he tilted his head when he looked at the land.

An owl swooped overhead and settled on a branch just a few yards in. It was a lucky sign, her mother always said. Owls bring luck and crows bring rain. She looked up at the maple tree and the owl turned its neck and watched her, too, and there was a flash of color just behind the tree where it sat. A motion and a flash of red, the sound of laughter in the distance. It was a child, she was certain, a child hiding between the trees. The littlest Malone girl maybe, who always ran ahead. "Don't go in there by yourself," she called out. "Come on out before your momma starts to worry." But there wasn't any answer.

She left the road though she was wearing rain shoes and not her leather hiking boots. Brutus strained against his leash, not wanting to follow her. It wasn't smart to go through the tall grass and into the forest this time of year. She'd be covered with ticks, and Brutus, too. They'd be impossible to see in his black fur, but no matter. She climbed down into the gully where the snowmelt flowed every March, and then back up and deeper into the forest, and there was a light just ahead. A soft light suffused with green and amber and it flickered like a flame. How many times had she passed this spot? Every day she walked this way with Brutus, and she'd never noticed how the light shone here behind the rotten log where children left colored stones. How the forest was lit like a chapel by the sun shining through the branches.

She walked the ten yards to where the light was strongest, stepping over rotten logs and puddled water. There was a humming under the branches, the sound of swarming bees, and Brutus pulled harder at his leash, straining to get back to the road. He started to whimper, but she pulled him toward the spot where the light was strongest. "That's enough," she told him. "We'll only be a minute and then you'll get your bone." She looked up between the branches at the streaked April sky. She forgot about the flash of red and the child she thought she'd seen. She breathed in deep and the humming sound grew stronger.

Peace, ease, peace, ease. All generations will call me blessed, the words came all at once, and somewhere an owl called and then another and Brutus had started growling. He scratched at her legs, but she stood fast. It wasn't time to leave yet. The air was gentle and it felt like June and not April. She stood there until the humming stopped. Until the light flickered and went dark. And when she finally turned to go, her hip didn't hurt and her knee wasn't stiff and she felt freshly awoken to the world.

* * *

Philip lived on the first floor. Every afternoon at four thirty she went to see him. Past the front desk where she signed in and through two sets of locked doors, past the nurses' station and all the open rooms where residents sat dozing in recliners, and it smelled like bleach in the hallway. It smelled like Lysol and chicken fingers, and the nurse aides were rousting the residents from the art room and the library with all its picture books. "It's time," they were saying. "Let's head on over to the dining hall." Some of the residents were fast and moved in packs along the hall, and others resisted or ignored the staffers and stayed in their chairs, their faces mildly stunned.

Philip was already in his usual spot, at the round table next to the window. His chin was tipped against his chest. He'd started dozing in the afternoon no matter where he was. He dozed in the library during movie hours and in his wheelchair when she pushed him down the halls. "Philip," she said, touching him lightly on his shoulder. "It's Helen, sweetie. Time to wake up." She pulled her mask down so he could see her face.

He opened one pale eye, reluctantly, like a cat. "You're not Helen," he said. "My Helen's got black hair."

"That's right," she told him, pulling her mask back up. Every day they had the same conversation. "My hair used to be black. Just the same as yours. We're two gray foxes now."

He laughed at that. His lips pulled back from his teeth. "You're a funny one," he said. "My Helen was funny, too."

She cut his food when it came, and he worked his fork, his brow furrowed in concentration. She talked about the garden, how the beets had come up already but not the carrots, no, they were the slowest and it'd been a chilly spring so far. The cold snap from last month had killed most all the fruit tree blossoms. There'd be no apples this year, no pears and no plums either, but the sour cherries had somehow survived and she'd cover them with netting when the time came. She'd keep the birds away and make him his favorite jam. "You'll eat like a king this summer," she told him. "I'll bring you something different every day." But he wasn't listening. His eyes were closed again, and she couldn't wake him, not even for his frozen yogurt bar. She wrote his name on the wrapper with a Sharpie and set it inside the freezer. The hardest part of the day was when she left him in his chair, his head tipped low against his chest. He was alone as a man could be, lonely as a sailor adrift at sea, and every day she walked away from him and went back out into the world.

* * *

She left Brutus at home though he gave her a mournful look when she closed the door. She used her umbrella as a walking stick and she stopped every few minutes to stretch her hip. *Breathe,* she told herself, four counts in, hold for seven and eight counts out, four, seven, eight, four, seven, eight, and sometimes she felt her heart beating inside her ears. It hammered inside her oceanically until she was certain it would burst.

She came to the spot just before sunset. It was twenty yards from the road. She heard the familiar humming under the branches when she got close and she felt it underfoot, too, the gentle vibration that came through the rubber soles of her shoes. Nothing hurt when she stood there. For a little while her knee and her hip were healed. She braced herself against a fat maple trunk, and it was thrumming, too. *Be careful,* a voice said, and it was her mother standing by the window of the old house. *Those Lucash boys are bad news,* she was saying. *The way they rev their engines. Stay away from boys like that. They're always looking for trouble.* Her mother was in the kitchen and her father in the garage, hammering while country music played on the little transistor radio he kept on his workbench, and her father sang along. She hadn't heard him speak in fifty years but she knew his voice and her mother's, too. She recognized all the familiar places. The little brick ranch house and the yard and the narrow steps to the basement. She recognized herself, too, sitting at the chipped Formica table.

"You better come out." Two of the Malone boys stood on the road with their scooters, wearing helmets like little policemen. Hands on their hips, heads tilted at the strangeness of their old neighbor standing alone under the trees.

"I'm just listening," she told the boys. "I'm listening to my mother."

They looked doubtful. "There's nothing but bugs out there and maybe some bears," the older one said. "They're waking up now from their long sleep. They don't pee all winter."

"I don't see any bears just now. I think I'll be okay."

He shook his head. "They're sneaky, especially the mamas. They're always watching for their babies."

"That's what mamas do."

They waited for a minute, unsure of what to do. "It's gonna be dark soon," the younger boy told her. "That's when the snakes wake up. Nighttime's their favorite because the eagles can't see 'em." They waited a moment longer and then stepped back on their scooters and pushed off together in perfect unison.

She felt relief when they left. This spot belonged to her. Warmth rose from the forest floor, from the moss and damp needles, and she needed no jacket though the sky was growing dark and the air would soon get crisp. An owl called and then another. The crickets chirped in the meadow across the road, the crickets and the peepers in the pond, and there was no better place anywhere than this little patch of earth. She tried to conjure the voices back. She tried to find her parents, but they were someplace else. She stood there waiting until the sky was black and the stars showed between the branches.

* * *

The air grew heavy in late June. Sometimes it rained even when the sun was shining, and everything was green, lime green and emerald and darkest forest green, and the mist rose from the valleys and floated like a phantom across the tops of the hills. The choppers fluttered down from the maple trees later than they usually did, and the beets were growing and the tender corn shoots, the potatoes in their rows. Her climbing roses and the hydrangeas fat like snowballs along the driveway. She worked the garden every morning with Brutus by her side. He carried a tennis ball in his mouth and fixed her with hopeful eyes as she knelt on her gardening pad.

She lacked faith, she understood this only now. Her parents were dead and she had no siblings and no children. She should believe in Jesus or the vengeful God of the Old Testament. If only she believed the world would open up. There would be potlucks and picnics, there would be people who came to visit if she was ever in the hospital, but she couldn't find it in her. All the faith she had lived in the dirt. It lived in the red beet seedlings and the blooming summer squash, in the irises that came back year after year after year. The bulbs that waited out the cold and the stubbornness of the trees that budded every April, these were no less miraculous than walking on water or spreading the sea. The flowers and the trees were her company. They were her children and her parents. They were her closest friends, and at night with Brutus at her feet she dreamt of the spot beneath the trees. It was waiting for her, always waiting and always warm. The air smelled of sap, and she wasn't in her bed, no, she was sleeping on the pine needles and damp leaves.

* * *

Mondays and Thursdays she volunteered at the local library, helping kids with their summer reading lists. Brutus came with her, and the kids all gathered around him and stroked the ridges on his forehead. Neighbors filed in, making themselves coffee at the Keurig machine and reading the Manchester and Boston papers. They talked of the weather and the garden, of the town budget shortfall and the beavers that were damming up the stream at Post Pond. They were messing with the water levels and something needed to be done. Josephine, who lived in a big house on River Road, leaned over the circulation desk. "I've got those damned jumping worms," she told Helen. "Watch your dirt, watch your dirt. Nothing works when you get them, not coffee grounds or dish soap. The birds won't eat them either. Wait till they get to the forest. Then we're all done for," and she wandered off again, holding her coffee mug.

One of the neighbor boys came to the counter. His red hair stood up in spikes. "Are you Oren?" Helen asked him, "Oren Malone?"

He shook his head. "That's my brother. I'm Tyler." And he set his books on the counter, dissatisfied. "I'm looking for something scary."

"There's lots of scary books. How about *Harry Potter*?"

"I read those already," he said. "I'm looking for something new."

She walked with him to the young adult fiction shelf and pulled *Coraline* for him and Poe and the collected works of the Brothers Grimm.

He wrinkled his nose at the last one. "Fairy tales? Those are for little kids," he said, but she took the book anyway and led him back to the circulation desk.

"Give them a try. The old stuff can be scary, too." She scanned his books and set them in a pile. "You won't know it's spooky until after you've finished."

He looked doubtful. "Are you the lady who stands in the woods?"

"Sometimes." She smiled at him. "Sometimes I'm that lady."

"Is there ever anything out there?"

"Sometimes," she said again, handing him his books.

* * *

The light flickered between the birch trees. It moved and danced and threw strange shadows and Brutus cried when he saw it. He sat beside the road and wouldn't budge. She dropped the leash. "Wait here," she told him. "I'll only be a minute." She went to the light, and it was farther from the road this time. Every time she went the light was farther back in the forest, this is how it seemed. It receded like an ocean wave. She leaned against a maple tree, her maple tree and no one else's, and waited for her parents. *He doesn't know you*, the voice said, and it sounded like her mother. *He doesn't know your face.* The forest went quiet then. Even the birds stopped their singing.

* * *

The trees changed their colors in early October, and it was the best fall the valley had seen in years. Orange, yellow, purple and scarlet red, with no rain to knock the leaves down, no clouds at all to dampen their brightness. Every day she went to her spot. She hobbled into the forest with her walking stick and when she emerged she had no need for the stick. All the things her mother told her while they were standing under the branches, about the neighbors and the brown-eyed Susans and how tight money was now that Poppa was gone, it all came out in a torrent. *You need to eat more*, her mother was saying, *you're skinny as a noodle*, and, *You need to tie your hair back so people can see your pretty face.* She'd been saying these things since Helen was a girl. *You're getting taller than your poppa, You're smarter than you think*, and *You'll die alone in that house of yours. It'll be weeks before they find you. You're lonely as a spinster*, the voice said. *Why didn't you have children.* And the words struck hard as any blow.

* * *

She made soup for families in need. The whole house smelled like chicken broth from the copper stockpot simmering in the oven. She wrote greeting cards for children at the hospital and knitted scarves for seniors. Every month she brought platters of cookies to the veterans at the hospital across the river. Every day was busy and every day was full, and she thought only of the snake under the swing set, coiled like a spring in the cedar mulch until a child comes toddling through. It was the only poisonous snake in the Upper Valley but rarity provided no protection. The distraught lover who crossed the median. The woman who left her twin newborns alone in their crib so she could fly to Bermuda. The stories weighed on her. Sometimes it was hard to catch her breath. Life's tragedies are just one exception after another to the rules we assume to be true.

* * *

Philip knew her before she'd even pulled her mask down. He reached for her hand and squeezed it. "It's about time," he said. "I've been waiting here for hours. What a place, what a place. I've never seen so many sick people." He looked at her and not the window. He waited for an answer.

"Getting old isn't easy," she told him.

"How are the apple trees? Did Chipman come and deal with the fire blight?"

"We've got full barrels." She cut his pork chop and set a piece on the fork. "I'll bring you some tomorrow," and it wasn't true. She'd bring him some grocery store apples.

He took the fork from her and fed himself, and there was nothing better in the world than to see him smiling. The good days, people called them. The days when he was restored to himself, and they were rarer now than they used to be. They were few and far between, but they were a reminder when they came. He was still among the living, and he saw the world with those eyes she'd known since she was twenty. She didn't want to leave on days like this. She wanted to sit forever in the dining hall at their little round table. She'd eat the underseasoned food with him and let all the clocks stop and let the sun never set because he was back beside her. All the noise in the room, all the music and the chatter and the instructions from the nurse aides, these all fell away, and it was only the two of them. The two of them in an indifferent world—the way it had always been and the way it would always be—and her heart was a balloon full to bursting in her chest and it carried her upwards.

* * *

Once there was a poor boy in Germany who had to walk into the forest every day and pick up sticks for kindling. He was afraid of the forest, the story goes. He tried to find reasons not to go. *I'm tired*, he'd say. *Everyone has picked up the loose branches and there aren't any left*, but his mother only smiled. *The forest makes new branches every day*, she told him, and she kissed him on his head. Out the door he went with only a piece of bread and a bruised apple for his lunch. One morning he went farther than he'd ever gone before. He'd eaten all his food and the sky was growing dark between the branches when a boy came to him, a beautiful boy with skin so pale it looked almost blue. *I'll help you*, he said. *I'll show you the best branches*, and he was wonderfully strong. He carried more than two grown men. Together they gathered the wood and brought it to the house but the beautiful boy was gone before the mother opened the door. *Mutti*, the little boy said, *oh Mutti, I met a new friend today, he lives deep in the forest where there aren't any houses*, and the mother scolded him because it wasn't right to make up stories.

Every morning the boy went into the forest and visited his friend. They ate like kings under the branches. Rouladen with red cabbage cooked in wine. Liver-dumpling soup. The beautiful boy opened up his basket and every time he brought out something different. They sat together when they were done and intertwined their fingers. They ran the path and fought like pirates with their sticks but the evenings were growing chill. The air was damp from the river, and late one afternoon when the forest was gray with fog the beautiful boy stood up. *I have to go*, he said. *Don't be sad, we'll play again—sooner than you think*, and he reached inside his vest and pulled out a single rosebud. *When it opens I'll come back*, he said and he kissed the little boy full on his lips.

The boy brought the rose home to his mother and she set it in cold water and sleep was so sweet that night when it came. He dreamt of his friend, who took him by the hand. *I told you it wouldn't be long*, that's what he said, and the sun was warm on their heads in this dream and the light shone through the branches. The next morning the rose was blooming on the sill. In all her life his mother had never seen a fatter blossom. *Time to get up*, she called from her spot by the stove. *Time to drink your morning milk*, and her boy didn't answer and he didn't move. He lay dead under his feather blanket.

* * *

Every good day is followed by a bad day, a terrible day—ten, twenty, a hundred terrible days. Sometimes she forgot this, but Philip always reminded her. He was bent over in his chair when she came to see him. She touched his shoulder but he didn't notice and he didn't move his eyes from the darkening window. "He's been that way today," the nurse's aide told her. She softened when she saw Helen's face. "Maybe tomorrow will be better." Helen sat with him at dinner and told him stories about Brutus and the jumping worms and the

Sadlers, who'd finally gotten tired of winter. They'd loaded up their car and they'd bought a little place in one of the Carolinas. "Fools," she said. "Winter is the best part of living here. You always told me that. Woodsmoke and snowdrifts and no ticks in sight." She spooned some mashed potato into his mouth and he chewed it mechanically, unwillingly, before swallowing it down. "How about a little meatloaf?" she asked him. "You could use a little protein, too, and not just those carbs you love." But he closed his eyes and turned away, a double rejection, and when dinner was done she left him there with the pinpoint light haloing his gray head.

* * *

Maybe she should be bringing wood to the pile under her eaves. Or doing laundry and making fresh chicken stock, but here she was instead walking the road without Brutus, crossing over the rocks and into the woods. She knew just where to go, always farther back, always farther into the forest. And waiting, waiting but for what? *What do you want?* This was her only thought. *What do you want from me?* Silence everywhere but for the sound of her steady breathing. She waited for a voice, any voice. She waited for her mother, and it was a tunnel there between the trees, she could see it extending deep into the Benedictines' acreage. A tunnel and a balustrade and it was expecting her. It would wait for her forever, this lonely pathway. She needed only to begin walking.

* * *

The snowplow trucks scuttled like beetles along the roads. A polar vortex was coming down from Canada. The forecast was saying eight to twelve inches starting around six in the evening. She'd go see Philip before it started and then she'd ride out the storm at home. She'd set a log in the wood-burning stove and cozy up with Brutus. There'd be time to write her Christmas cards and to make soup for a family that had lost their pet schnauzer. The charitable committee that helped people with their heating bills had scheduled a virtual meeting at seven to talk about a flurry of last-minute applications. She sat by her window with her empty coffee mug. It was time to go if she wanted to beat the weather. The granite sky and the bare black trees and snow clouds over the hills. Christmas lights along the street and every house was a jewel box lit from within, waiting for the storm. She had so many things to do, she remembered them all. She wasn't forgetting a single thing, but she didn't go to her car. She didn't drive the twelve miles to where Philip was waiting.

* * *

She slipped a little on the ice, even with her spikes, but each time she caught herself, and her knee hurt in the cold and her hip, too, but she moved quickly. She felt the pull of the trees and their strange light that nobody else could see. She climbed over the rocks piled beside the road and into the forest where everything was quiet.

Time holds no sway under the trees. Look how beautiful it is in the gray twilight. How sweet this place and its silence that pressed down on her like water. She looked for the light and it was always just a little farther ahead. She walked until she was winded. She walked until she found a rock and she sat down and rested her sore leg. She'd climbed Cardigan Mountain with Philip back in '86. Halfway up they stopped on a boulder and ate their salami sandwiches. He wasn't even forty yet and he still had a young man's appetite and a young man's grace. He stretched out on the rock while she finished eating, and when he looked to the clouds she saw them reflected in his strange gray eyes. He was her world and she was his, this is what she thought, and it was still true now. Her future lay with him. She should bring apples and sit with him in the dining room. The sky was growing dark. The first flakes were starting to fall, and he'd be lonely there by the window. She needed to go see him but she didn't move from her spot. ■

THE WHITE NEGRO
LeVan D. Hawkins

"I just stabbed somebody!" My nephew Raynell blurted out at my mother's front door.

I froze at my thirty-two-year-old nephew's news while his breath and body jerked in spasms. Though friends and relatives enjoyed pointing out Raynell's resemblance to his father, my brother Ernest—the same long blockish face, dark coloring, and wide forehead—that afternoon, Raynell's face was distorted by panic and fear, a complete turnaround from the smirk he'd worn the first time we'd met five years before. On that day, he seemed to brag about "the thuggin" he had done when he was young after telling me it was no longer part of his life.

"You don't want to hear about the things I did," he'd said, amused.

"No. Don't tell me," I said.

He leaned towards me from the recliner and chuckled, sending me back to my high school cafeteria. I was a fourteen-year-old freshman honor student who didn't fight back sitting across the table from fifteen-year-old Kevin Riley, a proud member of the Elbachos Street Gang. Kevin clinched my food tray; his eyes staying on me as he did it. He nibbled a piece of meat, then spat it out on my plate. "I want you to bring me your mother's gun," he said quietly.

Shocked, I searched my brain for a reply. "I don't know where it is," I told him. I didn't think my mother had a gun but felt telling Kevin *We don't have a way to protect ourselves from you* wasn't information I wanted to share with someone who had done time at the Audy Home. I may have been reluctant to fight, but there was no way in hell I was going to take a gun registered in my mother's name and give it to someone who could possibly commit a crime with it or at the very least, sell it to someone who would.

Suddenly, Kevin punched me in the face, my head jerking from the full force of bone against bone. I grabbed the edges of the table, riding the shock of the pain unsure of where it was going to take me. I blindly reached for the napkin on the food tray that I had forgotten was no longer in front of me; I needed something to wipe away the taste and tickle of blood. Just as sudden as the first punch, Kevin followed with a second to my chest that was so strong it felt like it had powered its way through my ribcage. As I fought the pain, I wondered how all this looked to the others in the cafeteria. I hoped no one had seen Kevin hit me and prayed that was the last time he would.

"Man, oh man," Raynell had chuckled. "Hey, it's all in the past but I walk through my old life every day. It's like walking through landmines," he said.

"That's no way to live."

"How can I avoid it? Shit's everywhere."

"It's *not* everywhere. There are other worlds here—you just can't see them. You tell me thuggin' is in your past but you talk about those days like you're talking about all the candy you used to get at the Robbins Day Parade."

He pondered over what I had said, then surprisingly, he nodded.

* * *

There was a time when Raynell's judgement held great sway over me. Even though I knew better, when I first met him, I cared so much about being accepted by him I altered the way I spoke—I dropped consonants, mumbled, and used slang I had never uttered before—I felt like I was a foreigner struggling to communicate in a foreign land—all to keep the Kevin Rileys of the world at bay.

Seventeen miles south of the Chicago Loop, incorporated in 1917, the Village of Robbins is one of the oldest African American municipalities in the United States. It has also made lists anointing it as one of the poorest suburbs in the country. As you drive through Robbins today, you can see remnants of those times but the dilapidated houses with red notices of condemnation are disappearing—these houses are being replaced by new homes and apartment buildings that are sprouting up throughout the village. In 2007, the year Raynell stabbed somebody, the village's population was 6,188. In 2022, the population of Robbins was 4,521.

* * *

I quickly glanced down 142nd Street where I lived—it was empty and quiet. If I had the ability to stand outside my mother's front door and magically transport myself to 1931, I would see airplanes. Much of the land near our home was once occupied by Robbins Airport, described by the Robbins Historical Museum as the United States' first Black-built, Black-owned and Black-operated airport and hangar.

In my mother's hallway, Raynell was terrified. As he began to speak, I quickly raised my hand to silence him; my eighty-two-year-old mother was watching. How much had she heard? Did she understand what he had done?

"It's just Raynell," I casually told my mother. "He dropped by to talk to me for a while."

I calmly moved out of the doorway so she could see her grandson enter. I touched Raynell's thin shoulders underneath the oversized white and black New York Yankees jacket he wore, then instinctively drew away when I smelled the stench.

"Say hi," I gently guided him.

"Hi Grandma," he said, still catching his breath.

My mother waved. I kept an eye on her as she left the kitchen and returned to the home-improvement show she was watching. I turned to Raynell.

"Breathe," I told him. "I'll get you some water."

"I ran all the way here," he told me.

"From where?"

"Mom and Pop's."

"Mom and Pop's?" I asked, surprised.

A little over a mile from my mother's home, Mom and Pop's was a liquor store that I occasionally drove Raynell to so he could purchase two-for-a-dollar Kool Menthols. Though the store has been open for decades, I've never been inside. I still haven't. The forlorn faces of the men who stand guard at the door, some my former elementary and high school classmates, keep me away. Driving down 130th Street at twenty-five miles an hour, I still have enough time to read the cautionary tales on their faces. Whenever I drove Raynell to Mom and Pop's, I locked my car doors and kept my head down until he returned. The first time he saw me fiddling with the front passenger door, he sadly shook his head at this confirmation that I was bougie, soft, and white. Despite my precautions, I never pictured anything as wild as Raynell stabbing two men in Mom and Pa's parking lot then running hysterically into a busy street wielding a bloody knife.

* * *

"I'm thinkin' about going back to school," Raynell had told me.

Instantly, to my shame, I doubted him. I couldn't imagine an almost thirty-year-old man who used the words bougie, soft, and white returning to school. One who was admittedly an indifferent student intent on thuggin.

There was also the possibility that all the unspoken judgments, all the pressure from his bourgeois family played a role in him telling me about his college ambitions. So perhaps he mentioned college as a way of defending himself. "I could help you with that," I told him. "If you would like some help." I had spent months helping a fatherless inner city high school student prepare his college applications, listening to him describe the business he wanted to start, pushing him when I thought he was slacking, praising him when he stretched beyond his comfort zones and worked hard, my energy lifting every time we interacted. I had mentored strangers; that week, I would help my own blood.

"What do you plan on majoring in?" I asked Raynell.

There was a long pause before he answered, "I'm not sure."

"This isn't bullshit, is it?" My voice was flat and direct. It was not the voice I expected to come out of me after I stopped the slang and got real. "You're not telling me you want to go back to school because you think that's what I want to hear?"

"No." He sounded offended.

"I am interested in you. In *you*. Not made-up shit."

"No, I'm thinkin' about going back to school."

I was delighted, ready to turn to the computer and begin, but he had something to do that night and assured me he'd return before I left for my apartment in California in two days.

"If I don't see you, I'll know what this was." My directness surprised me.

"You'll see me," he said, full of charm and flashing the whites.

When Ernest arrived home from work that night, I excitedly told him Raynell was returning so I could help him with his college applications. Ernest shrugged. "He's not going to do it," he said firmly.

I was taken aback and frowned in disapproval.

"He seemed interested. I think he will."

"It would be nice if he did but he's not going to." I shot Ernest a look. "I told you what he was like. I'm not making the shit up."

I didn't see Raynell again until three years later.

* * *

The day Raynell showed up at my mother's door and told me he'd stabbed someone, I was free from being concerned about what he thought of me. In his presence, I said what I thought. Even if he thought it bougie, soft, and white. I wanted a better life for myself and for him and made no apologies. I lectured; I fussed; I gave advice; I listened.

He'd visit me multiple times a week, sometimes daily. Occasionally, he'd get in a huff and leave; I'd assume it would be weeks before his return. If ever. Often, he'd return the next day—as if nothing had occurred.

It is a tricky thing: to help someone who insists they have no hope.

"There's so many things to do and see in this world," I told Raynell months before the stabbing.

"Why are you so worked up?" He asked me. "Why do you care?"

"Because I see you. I see who you are. I see all you can be. No one knows how many bad decisions you can make before you run out of opportunities to get your life right. I worry before you step into the world, you're going to get hurt or you're going to hurt somebody. Or end up in jail."

When we reached the top of the stairs, I firmly instructed Raynell to go to the upstairs den while I stopped in the bathroom to grab some much-needed water and towels. I looked at myself in the mirror. I had expected to see my mother's worried face: my nostrils flaring like an Igbo mask— my lower lip pulsating uncontrollably to its own beat—the way hers does when she's struggling to tame her emotions. Instead, my face was relaxed. Authoritative. As if stabbings were something I experienced daily. As if I were the worldly and streetwise uncle and my helpless innocent nephew had rushed to me desperately seeking guidance.

Still, I felt myself tighten when I asked, "Is... he alive... she?"

"He. Two of them."

"Two!" I exclaimed, way too loud for someone who thought of himself as a calming influence.

"They were alive when I left." He chugged his water then took a towel out of my hand to dry off.

* * *

Before Raynell arrived that day, I had been reading writer Norman Mailer's noted essay, "The White Negro." Literary great Mailer, one of the titans of the New Journalism movement, had died that morning. It was November 10th, 2007. Most of Mailer's obituaries mentioned "The White Negro." I was intrigued by the title. I assumed Mailer's essay was about Black assimilation which would have been the context in which Raynell called me "white." Instead,

"The White Negro" depicted whites in the 1950s who patterned themselves after the behavior of Blacks of the urban streets. During my reading, Mailer continually called Black people, "the Negro" as if we were a scientific project, as if we were all the same. According to Mailer, the Negro lived in the present like a child, with no past or present memory or planned intention. He also wrote: *The psychopath is incapable of restraining his violence.* I dismissed Mailer's essay as condescending bullshit but as I continued to read it, I thought of Raynell, my history with him and the things he had done and said during the few years I had known him. It was then, as I debated with Mailer in my head, that Raynell had rung our doorbell.

"What happened?" I asked Raynell as I handed him another glass of water.

"I got in an argument with the first one over some he said-she said bullshit. Then the other one jumped in, and I had to stab them to get them off me."

"Why were you carrying a knife?"

"For protection."

"Where is it?"

He tapped his front right pocket then reached inside. All I could think of was dried blood.

"I don't need to see it. You need to find places to hang out where you don't need to carry a knife for protection."

"Where would that be?" he asked sarcastically.

I had him recount what led up to the stabbing. My intention was to show him there were other ways to react to conflict. Remarkably, he cooperated with me though he stubbornly held on to the belief that the stabbings were unavoidable. "I want to know what he said that led you to fighting in public. What was so bad?"

"It was self-defense!" he yelled.

"Now that it's over," I said calmly, standing up to his anger. "Think. Focus on what happened. You had to fight? You had to stab him? Was there a time you could have ended it?"

"You let people get over on you and don't react to it, everybody will think you're weak and dog you. You know that! You act like you don't come from here!"

His voice was full of anguish. He seemed a frustrated teen who after his best efforts, couldn't make his uncle understand the perils he faced. The vulnerability in his voice shocked me, as did my reaction: I took a deep breath to stop the tears that were on their way. I wanted to throw up my hands, sit down, and turn on the television.

I wanted to pretend Raynell had entered the front door the way he had hundreds of times before. Somewhere along the walk from his apartment to my mother's home, he made a decision that didn't lead to blood.

I knew firsthand that perceived weaknesses make you prey. Teenage bullies had chased me in my adult nightmares for over twenty-five years. When I first met Raynell, he reminded me of my predators. When he returned to visit me the next day, he seemed to delight in making me feel ill-at-ease. "You don't want to know all the things I did," he smirked.

"No, I don't."

Raynell grinned at me, sizing me up, directly stripping me of all pretense, "You probly wouldna wanted to know me."

"No. Probably not."

I felt his fear. He was me. I felt the impulse to stop interrogating him, but he could have killed someone or gotten himself killed. What is the right action in this situation? I pressed on, though I no longer did so with the naive zeal of an uncle teaching his ex-felon nephew how to go straight.

Any Negro who aches to live must live with danger from his first day, and no experience can ever be casual to him, no Negro can saunter down a street with any real certainty that violence will not visit on his walk.

I had dismissed Mailer's statement as "condescending hyperbole" because he didn't leave room in his grandiose observations for any other type of Black person but the ones hanging out at Mom and Pop's front door. What about the whites who were the systemic perpetrators of this state of existence? How can you analyze the Negro and ignore the lenses of racism and poverty? And not only are descendants of the enslaved totally responsible for our condition; we are also responsible for the misbehaving of misguided whites who have decided to mimic us?

The Mailers of the world don't have the inclination to see me or my father who was born in 1921, eight years before Mailer. Mailer didn't know that nearly twenty miles from the Chicago Loop, in a poor small Black town, there was a group of Black men and women building an airport. There was a man who was denied Aviation classes because of his color. He decided to become a janitor at the Aviation school. Daily, he went through the garbage and studied it until he taught himself how to fly.

Mailer couldn't see Raynell though Mailer thought he understood him. Yes, Raynell stabbed the two men, which I didn't condone in any way, but he viewed it as self-defense. This same Raynell was the person who sat with my mother and spoke to her in the gentlest of ways. Once, he reprimanded me for snapping at her. He refused to drink alcohol in her presence at a family barbecue. He worried that his paternal grandfather was getting older and couldn't take care of himself. He wanted to do better but didn't know how.

"If I had been around here, I would be more than what I am," he once told me. His limited view of his life made my heart ache.

If he wanted someone to tell him the stabbings were righteous, he would have run to someone else's home. In my mind, running directly to me when he was in trouble meant that he wanted to do the right thing but was stuck between his desire for a new way of living and his comfort with the old.

Three years later, after Mailer wrote "The White Negro," Mailer stabbed his wife Adele Morales and almost killed her. Perhaps he was influenced by "The Negro."

* * *

Before the doorbell rang, I had decided Mailer was writing from the perspective of a pontificating liberal white man living in 1957. I couldn't, however, ignore his 2007 Negro prototype standing before me.

Raynell never told me specifically what set the fight off and chuckled when he realized there was a moment when he could have walked away from the fight with his dignity and reputation intact. Instead, he had angrily returned and jacked-up the confrontation.

"That's all I'm trying to make you see. We have choices in how we react. Choice is power," I told Raynell.

"I was too pissed to think straight."

"Bullshit. If one of them had had a gun—which they certainly could have—you would have kept stepping."

Raynell told me he needed to call a few of his homies to see how badly he had hurt the two men he stabbed. No one answered the first number he dialed so he left a voicemail message that he was at his grandmother's house and left our contact information. Silently, I objected—he should have asked me before he left his contact information and location—but only someone "bougie," "soft," and "white" would be upset with his nephew for giving out his telephone number for an emergency. Raynell's second friend answered his phone. Raynell was casual and loose as he spoke, laughing easily. The laughing bothered me. Couldn't he see how this situation could have escalated into something uglier? And unlike Mailer's stabbing of his wife, Raynell wouldn't have high-priced lawyers to negotiate his way out of trouble.

Raynell was a man, a declaration he made repeatedly. "I don't take shit offa people, I'm a man!" Adult men and women are supposed to consider the consequences of their actions. The men he stabbed could have died. The store owner at Mom and Pop's could have called the police. Raynell could have given in to his emotions and attacked the police or resisted them when they tried to arrest him. He could be in jail. Or it could have been worse.

Once, Raynell and I had a big argument over a hypothetical situation: What would I do if someone hurt his father, my brother? I told him first, I'd probably call the police. "You'd snitch?" he bellowed. "What kind of Black man are you?" In his mind, he didn't cooperate with the police, you took matters into your own hands. "You hurt me or mine, you will pay," he told me when he shared how he would have reacted to someone hurting his loved-ones. If those are the rules in his world and the men he stabbed lived in that world, wouldn't they seek revenge for the stabbings? Would word get back to the two men who were stabbed that Raynell was hiding out at my mother's home? They could wait for him outside—my mother and I caught in the middle of violence and gunfire.

"Everything's cool," he told me after he hung up the phone, smiling at me as if it were just any other day. "Time to jet." When I rose to walk him downstairs, my legs buckled. All the tension had gone straight to my legs. I grabbed ahold of the computer station to steady myself, our family pictures crashing to the floor. ■

NEW YEAR'S IN CHIANG MAI
Cooper Young

Two women sing karaoke
in front of their barber shop,
while a man plays an electric guitar
on a wooden stool. They invite
my brother and me to dance,
and we don't hesitate to join.
The owner opens beer bottles
with a wrench and never lets
our glasses get empty. We haven't
even exchanged names, but we feast
on grilled pork on the sidewalk.
A Frenchman and a Japanese man join us,
and add to the choir of languages
I can't understand. It is 2019
in the Gregorian calendar, and 2562
in the Buddhist calendar. Everyone
has a reason to celebrate.
We light fireworks that explode
into blossoms of light, level with the roofs.
We've missed the countdown,
but no one minds. Lanterns
released hours ago still linger in the sky.

ESTHER AND MAX
Jeffrey Wolf

1.

They sit in the sun-stained room near the slow river. The Venetian blinds have left stripes on the carpet, the furniture, an old bookcase without books. This apartment on Whipple Street, their penultimate resting place. Max sits with his eyes closed, his face wrinkled like a canyon. He looked like this in 1943. That year, his arthritis got so bad he had to give up his corner grocery, boarded it up and let the rent expire. Two decades later, barely anything's changed. Every year a little slower, a little less able.

Esther had prepared herself, for so long, to wake up beside his cold body. And he kept living. So long that she's becoming unprepared again, even musing that he might outlive her. So long that she's started getting annoyed.

He sits. He sleeps. He sleeps while sitting. Sometimes he rises, quivering, and shuffles to the john. She follows him in so she can hold him steady while he wipes and clean the seat once he's finished.

Once a month, their son Fred stops by to examine the bills and give Max a shave. Sometimes—God forgive her—she imagines Fred's hand slipping with the blade. Morbid, horrific. But then, at least, it would be over. She could mourn.

2.

On Sunday morning, they cab uptown to their daughter Ruthie's. One of their grandkids is having a birthday, and all the others will be there, too. Esther helps Max fold into the back seat. She grips his forearm and ribs, bearing his weight. Some days he's heavier than others. Today he drapes himself like a stuffy meat coat. She glances over to make sure the meter hasn't started.

His expression stoic, but she knows he's in pain. A subtle twitch. Crow's-feet crinkling. She ought to know his looks after forty years. He used to be so prideful, rebuffing all gestures of aid. Now he gets impatient when his human crutch isn't there waiting. He grunts and grabs at her shirt hem. She thinks fondly of abrasive self-reliance.

At Ruthie's house, the grandkids greet their arrival with indifference. They keep zooming across the yard in various toy hats, ignoring orders from their parents—who stand in a cluster holding cocktail flutes—to stop and say hello. Esther holds Max by the arm and together they creep toward the house. The grandkids pass in another wave, rushing around and between their legs like floodwater. Ruthie erupts. *Go to the backyard right now or the party's canceled*, she screams. She'll take back all the presents and eat the cake herself. The children stare at Max and Esther, not sure what to make of these odd, wrinkled people who are already half ghost.

Later, after food has been served and "Happy Birthday" sung, they sit around the patio in collapsible chairs. Max's high-waisted pants and curved spine accentuate his potbelly. The mothers dote in waves. Plates of cake. Kids' messy cheeks pulled close. Napkins dab, wipe, crease. Max too wears a stain, a reddish sauce from the meal dribbled down his breast. Someone hands him a baby. A little boy, just shy of a year, who fits snug between his thigh and belly. Though his joints ache, he bounces the boy lightly until the squirming subsides. Esther watches her husband's puckered face erupt with joy. Suddenly forty years melt away, and he seems like he could click his heels and dance the Charleston. In the distance, the light-rail rushes on electric wires.

3.

Max rarely speaks. Even when they're alone, which is most of the time. Sometimes Esther goes next door to Mrs. Goldberg's just to hear her own voice.

Trina Goldberg keeps her door locked, but Esther has a key. Often she'll let herself in and stand there, waiting for words to spring up from her gravelly pit of silence. Seeing this, Mrs. Goldberg rises from her needlepoint and fetches another teacup. There's always hot water on the stove.

"He wet the bed again," Esther says.

The first few syllables are always unsettling. How they rattle in the space behind her jaw. The sound uncanny, something like an invasion. That she feels this is itself strange. She's long been a talker, struck by opinions too strong to contain. It was the one thing Max ever chastised her for. *Would you please not complain so much, dear?* he'd say from the living room of their old house in Lawndale. *Please, for just a moment, so I can think?* Even this he said calmly, politely. Max never raised his voice. And he never complained, though he had every reason to. Three years into their marriage, he lost his business and went bankrupt. Nobody, not even once, offered a lifeline. He soldiered on as a laborer, through constant pain. They lived each day on rotted planks over an abyss, but he never stopped marching. He was perseverance defined.

And there she goes again, thinking of him in the past tense. Like he's already gone. That's what there is to complain about: how he's morphed from presence to object. A machine that turns chicken stew into shit.

"Have you tried incontinence garments?" Mrs. Goldberg muses.

She is small, shrunken, wrapped around her teacup like a fruit holding its seed. Older by a decade, but startling green life darts from her eyes. Esther has only ever known her as a widow.

"I ought to get plastic covers for the mattress," Esther says.

"Do they make those?"

"They make everything. I told Ruthie she should take me to Sears."

Mrs. Goldberg pauses, then gives one of her looks. "Does he know it happened?"

"I'm not sure," Esther says, pausing. Then she stammers, "Changing baby diapers is one thing. But him? No, some things you can't go back from."

As she slumps in the chair, her shoulders crackle. "Haven't I earned a rest, Trina?" she says. "Haven't I done enough?"

Mrs. Goldberg adjusts in her seat. "Maybe it's time to think about it. Putting him somewhere."

Esther sits up straight. "What kind of heartless do you think I am?" She sets her teacup on the table and doesn't touch it again.

Mrs. Goldberg understands much, but this, she senses, eludes her. Her husband died before this phase. It was painful, but swift. Years later, she still finds his unfinished crosswords mixed with old papers and albums. Other times, she'll wake in the morning having forgotten he's gone—having pulled the bedding into a fat pile that she'll think, for a fleeting moment, is him.

4.

Esther always felt she would die young. Ever since she was thirteen and fleeing Russia with her sister. They got caught by a deputy constable in Lublin, held overnight in a cell. They laugh about it now, she and Lena, but the experience opened something. She'd never come so close to the steel nose of a rifle. To the reality that she could be snuffed out like a candle with barely a pinch. Afterward, she stared uneasily at the train tracks crossing Germany, and on the ocean liner to America she felt the water's dark pull.

Yet it's true too that the idea was with her earlier. A mousy, nervous child, she often sat in the overfull schoolroom, or at home among all her brothers and sisters, convinced that she wasn't really there. Just watching. That one day soon she might dissolve into air and be gone. It felt inevitable.

Perhaps she's disappearing now, she thinks. Her hair thinned to wisps. She hides her womanly shame under scarves, hats, wigs. Meanwhile Max's hair keeps growing. His shock of white, like a weed that sold its green for extra vigor.

Disappearing? she thinks with an inward laugh. Even when silence reigns in the flat, she's distinctly aware of herself. Her body stooping, scrubbing, stirring. Resetting the tables and lamps he upsets on his rickety voyages. He wouldn't last long without her—in this she could find twisted solace. Yet without him there to need her, might she feel free to disappear once more?

5.

It's Tuesday morning, and the weather is nice, so they go outside to sit. Behind their apartment, a strip of park follows the river, lined with trees and wound through by a paved path. Esther has two folding chairs and a basket of sliced oranges, but she leaves these outside their door so she can guide Max out first.

She walks him down the stairs, one step at a time. Then they cut across the grass, damp and fragrant from new spring, the ground squishy beneath. The going is slow. Max keeps getting his cane stuck. Soon Esther's shoes are drenched, and probably caked under with mud. She leads him to a park bench and eases him there to wait.

Before going back inside, she drags her foot bottoms across the concrete stoop. Knowing there'll be no way to get Max's shoes off before he's tracked mud halfway across their carpet—fating her to a miserable hour on her knees scrubbing it out, rushing to finish before it's too dark to tell mud from shadow. She grumbles up the stairs. These stairs that seem to multiply like rabbits, more every day. She pants and sweats. Then back down with the chairs, which are too wide and smack on every step no matter how she holds them. So flustered and breathless by the time she's outside again that she has to stop and rest.

In the distance, Max is sitting where she left him, but he's not alone. Three other figures surround him, grabbing him from all sides. Her panic—and anger at Max, that she can't leave him for a minute, that her husband's the only soul on earth more helpless than her—

fades instantly. They're all old women.

Permed widows caked in blush, they eye him like hungry flies. Their grabby hands snatch at whichever arm is closest as they jockey for his attention. Pulling him apart like a challah loaf. Max sits up straight in the crisp air, calm and unbothered—as if they really are flies, and he feels none of it. Still, Esther burns. As she arrives, she clears her throat loudly and watches the women react. Max looks up at her and smiles. Dutifully, he takes her arm and lets himself be raised.

6.

It's dinnertime, and Esther serves Max at the kitchen table. She slops cholent into a bowl, then plates helpings of tzimmes and applesauce. It isn't Shabbos, but she makes these dishes two, three times a week because they're easy for him to chew. He was always more observant. When they married, she accepted having to cook kosher-style for him, and he accepted that she wouldn't keep a kosher kitchen. He built her a sunroom, replaced the floor, changed the wallpaper and upholstery. She did laundry five times a week, gave him a child at thirty-eight. Compromise and sacrifice wound like threads of the same rope.

She helps herself, then returns the serving platters to the stove, but Max is still fussing. He grunts. Points his bony finger.

"Do you need something, dear?" she asks.

His eyes move from her to the table and back.

"Need me to cool it? Cut smaller pieces?"

Max pauses. He draws a breath and opens his mouth to speak— then winces sharply, and deflates. His brow furrows. Then he sweeps his arm across the table, upending his glass and throwing milk everywhere. He lets out a roaring, gum-heavy moan, so primal and terrible that Esther jumps from the table in fright.

Before she can realize it, she's fled the kitchen, around the corner and into the living room lit softly by lamps. Telling herself to call someone, as options flash in succession. Her children. Sanitarium. Police.

She closes her eyes and tries to breathe. Images of a younger Max surface, but she pushes them down. When the ice in her veins finally recedes, she returns to the kitchen. An ivory pool thins and spreads across the table. Multiple drips slap the floor. In her bowl of cholent, spots of milk expand like cataracts. Max sits there staring at her, red-faced and sobbing.

7.

The first week of May, all the gnats burst from hiding. Even with the flywire and the windows shut tight, they slip through into the kitchen. They colonize the windowpanes. They buzz in little circles and throw themselves against the glass. It seems, to Esther, like the gnats are throwing a party and it's she who's the uninvited guest. Soon, their dead form a dark layer on the window ledge. Their bodies fall and become husks.

Esther can feel her own body brittling. It's becoming strange inside. New pains simmer. New pressures bloat. Yesterday, she dropped a dish. Something is surfacing, but as long as there's no name for it, it can't kill her.

8.

After dinner, they sit in the sun-stained room as the light changes from wheat gold to tangerine red. He occupies his usual place in the faded chair, she kitty-corner on the sofa. Across from them, the television stands dark and dull beneath the cabinets. It's used only when grandchildren visit.

Max sits with his forearms atop the arms of the chair, like he's occupying a throne. Esther reaches over the side table and places her hand lightly atop his. Always lightly. Today, he turns his wrist and squeezes. She imagines the pain, his dry finger bones grinding and chafing. Still he grips her, tight as an infant. ■

FOSTER, OREGON, SUMMER OF '73
Karen Fort

Tim winked at me and offered me a turn with his fly-fishing pole. He watched how I could land a fly without thrashing the water and I winked back. When I picked up random litter from the shore of the McKenzie River, he didn't join the others in teasing me for being an "eco-teen." Tim played banjo and guitar, knew botanical names for plants, described Frisbee arcs as fluent calculus formulas, and showed me how to make apple cider from scratch. His love was as enthusiastic as a big puppy's, which helped to mend my recently broken heart. When he got a job on the Forest Service fire crew in Sweet Home, I decided that I wanted to traipse along after my new boyfriend, a privilege I could afford, I admit, only because of my Great-Aunt Mable, who'd left me just enough to avoid employment if I lived like a Walden Pond gypsy. The job started in ten days, but Tim didn't have a paycheck yet to rent a place, so we drove my pickup truck past Sweet Home, past the logging mill, and turned onto Wiley Creek Road from Foster. We chose a spot to park the truck and waded across the creek into a half-wooded cow pasture. In a secluded place we pitched my pup tent, laid out our sleeping bags, and prepped a safe fire pit, with a bucket of water, the axe and shovel handy. Our camp was bordered on one side by an old mossy log, sheltered by brush and connected by grassy deer paths. I decorated the mossy log with the eight tiny porcelain horses that I had brought back from my hitchhiking trip to San Francisco. Deer, rabbits, possums, owls, hawks, ducks and, of course, the cows visited.

Every morning we would wade the stream. I would drive Tim to the station and drop him off holding his cork boots, sack lunch and Stanley thermos of coffee. While Tim was at work, I got our day's groceries. Back at our spot, I waded home towards the pup tent, tucking the quart of milk in the cold river's edge. I soaked the beans and burned the paper garbage, washed last night's dishes in the rubber tub and dried them in the sun. Sometimes I heated a second pot of water on my Optimus stove, washed my hair, and took a sponge bath. I sprouted tiny batches of alfalfa sprouts in a lunch box cooler. Later I might fish off the riverbank or drive back up till the road turned to dirt and pick wild blueberries. I chopped the veggies for the salad. I could gather kindling from the meadow with the small hand saw and split the pieces further into kindling. Keeping the fire minute was strategic; the pasture didn't belong to us.

One day Ben Hodges, the farmer who owned it, was driving down the road and parked by my pickup. He waded across the stream. He made noise as he came down the path and I froze in the pup tent, scared as could be. I peeked out from between the folds of the tent door. Ben Hodges picked up my little white china horses from the mossy log and then set them back. He looked at the ground cleared around the tiny fire pit, at the bucket of water and the axe. He saw the camp stove, the closed food tins and clean dishes. Then he went away without looking in the tent. I found out later from him that he figured that if this homeless couple with a little child needed a campground, he would allow it. But the toy horses were mine, although I was all of twenty-one. That got a chuckle out of him.

There was a good swimming hole upstream, past Ben Hodges's farm, where I could go cool off if it was hot. One time when I was swimming, I heard a pickup full of rowdy young men park. I hid back on an overgrown deer trail until they passed me and dove into the swimming hole. Then I raced back to the truck with my heart pounding and took off. I knew I wouldn't be safe if those guys ever found me alone at the swimming hole, but I still went swimming; I just parked my truck a bit off.

I got to be friends with Cynthia and Mary, whose boyfriends worked on the crew also. They had a big garden by their geodesic dome. I learned how to can tomato sauce and belly dance. They both worked at a church preschool part-time. They packed their boyfriend's lunches and urged me take responsibility so my boyfriend would eat healthier, but Tim and I had a different deal; he packed his own lunch. On days off Tim and I would drive into Eugene to see a dozen friends at the big old Patterson house where we all used to live. We'd shower there and sleep in whatever spare space there was.

One evening in the camp, as we were cooking some chicken, a starving redbone hound dog crept into our circle, begging for food. She was skin and bones, so we took pity on her and shared our supper three ways. We nicknamed her Bones and made a few lost dog flyers by hand, hoping to help Bones find her hunter-owner and her pack. After picking Tim up from work, we went into the Timbers Tavern in Sweet Home and asked if we could tape up our flyer. A logger with one eye sat at a back table muttering belligerence. Tim explained later that they said "Ol' One Eye" was a choker setter. His job was to run the thick wire cable around the fallen tree trunk and hook it. At the winch end of the steel rope, they would cinch it snug and haul it up the hill. One day, hauling a tree trunk toward the yarding equipment, the hook slid off the cable, flung out and took out the choker setter's eye. I put up the next flyer at the Baptist church with the sign that read "Adam's Rib plus Satan's Fib Equals Women's Lib." Sure enough, Ben Hodges claimed Bones, coming to the Forest Service station at quitting time to inquire. Bones was eager to greet him, so even though we had a moment's sadness, we knew she was going back home. Ben Hodges must have recognized my short-box Chevy, just as I recognized his pickup, but he didn't let on until later.

It rained hard for days sometimes. That made me want to find a place with a roof. By July 1 we rented a one-bedroom cottage in Foster, Oregon, 720 people, just outside Sweet Home. Foster had a post office, a sporting goods and gun store, a gas station, a church, and two bars. We lived across from the train tracks. Neighbors on one side were a couple with a six-year-old boy named Chris from the mom's first marriage and a new baby. An old woman who called herself Bitty lived alone on the other side. Bitty taught me how to plant a garden and I taught myself how to make yogurt and, once the garden came in, how to bake zucchini bread and chocolate zucchini cake and make a stir-fry with cheese that we named zucchini delight.

After dropping Tim off at work, I would scramble some eggs and split them onto two plates to share with Bitty, who woke with a hacking, juicy cough every morning. We sat outside at the picnic table in what she called her beer garden. She always drank a full pot of coffee to help her get rid of her hangover, walked to the store to buy two quarts of the cheapest beer, then started in on one of those right away. I drank tea and orange juice. Bitty was a talker, and she asked personal questions, which I answered. We'd laugh at ourselves. She collected metal junk sculptures for her garden, carrying round stones up from the stream bed under the railroad bridge to make borders around her found-art statues. She'd had a wild youth compared to me. She winked a ribald wink with every other sentence and smoked cigarettes delicately, to make them last, holding her little finger out. She tried to convince me that the evergreen branches that she stuck deep in the ground would root and grow into trees. When she told me her tale of being divorced from her husband because she was barren, I hadn't the heart to correct her; the evergreens gradually faded to dead over the months. Bitty would stand back proudly and eye her sculpture garden's beauty with a wild grin. She would rub her swollen knuckles with lanolin and rub Nivea lotion on her tan, wrinkled face;

her "beauty routine," she called it. She was the one who told me that she worried about the little boy who lived on the other side of me. Chris had flunked out of first grade last year because he wet his pants, so he was ashamed to be back in kindergarten. His father had disappeared after his parents' divorce and mother's remarriage. His mother's pregnancy delighted Chris's stepfather so; but Chris was a reminder of bad times and got reprimanded often.

I got to know Chris's mom a little. I asked her if she would mind if I brought Chris some library books to read to him. She was all for that; she was worried about Chris heading into a second try at first grade in the coming fall.

The Sweet Home library had very few fiction or kids' picture books. Just lots of cookbooks, how-to, self-help, outdoorsman, mechanical, crime detective and dime-store romance. It had a meager few I-Can-Read books, which I checked out. I brought some from my folks' home too. Five days a week Chris sounded out letters and then words, rewarded by bites of peanut butter and jelly and powdered lemonade. By the end of summer he understood phonics and could read a hundred words. He confided in me that he was not going to get scared again this time, because he knew now that he was smart. I worked, too.

My other friend, from the house behind ours, was Myrtle. Myrtle was a plain, meek soul, who used to want to be a nun but was now wife of an unemployed welder. They had twin three-year-old girls. When I drove to the laundromat, I helped Myrtle to load up all her laundry bags in the back of my pickup. She hogged almost every washer and dryer, and we folded laundry together until the cows came home. When the food ran out, Myrtle would make white-rice pudding with lots of white sugar, and those blond waifs would scoop up each milky spoonful until they scraped their bowls. I could feed them protein and vitamins when I invited them over, but Myrtle wouldn't accept my help with her groceries; she told me her husband would beat her if he caught her doing that. They were saving up to pay his union entrance fee so he could work a job: at least that was what he said. But he drank Mad Dog 20/20; that's where the money went.

One day Myrtle showed up at my door with a twin in each arm. She was in a state and asked me to watch the girls but not to open the door if her husband knocked on the door. I asked her to stay also, but she said she had to be home to try to soothe him and get him sobered up afterwards. She would be back before midnight. My mouth hung open. She disappeared, going home to take a beating, in order to spare the girls. I packed a picnic in my day pack and walked along holding the little girls' hands, down the path under the railroad bridge. After tuna sandwiches, the little girls slept on the picnic blanket in the shade. After their nap we picked up Tim from work and played with ice cubes on the linoleum floor. We waltzed around on old towels until the floor was clean. We sang along to Tim's guitar, some Grateful Dead, some Waylon Jennings, some Merle Haggard. I put them to sleep on our bed. Tim and I talked over a toke or two, and a couple of beers, until Myrtle showed up with a blackening eye. She carried one and I carried the other. Tim came along to protect us, just in case her passed-out husband woke up. But he was out cold. We tucked in the sleeping girls and promised Myrtle never to tell, never to speak of it again. I realized how different I was from all my neighbors. Her husband would drink up his union fee over and over. Maybe her plan to become a nun had been safer. It rained a lot in the fall there, giving time for thought; I loved wilderness, but I couldn't hack hard-core country full-time. My artistic values, education and cultural upbringing meant that I remained alienated somehow no matter how much I empathized with country folk.

It was becoming hard to keep me down on the farm, as the saying goes. I could try out being a country girl for a few seasons, but without the current of fine arts and performances flowing around me, the artist in me would wither.

Eventually, Tim and I split apart. Looking back on it, I made that romance move clumsily, with some sloppy overlap. But what did I know? So little about how to teach a lover how to slow down, what worked for me, and what didn't. Besides, it was becoming hard to keep me down on the farm, as the saying goes. The theater stage howled a siren's call to me.

By late fall we had moved to Marcola, halfway to Eugene. Tim was planting trees and burning slash piles in the wet Oregon fall. I started taking a writing and an acting class at Lane Community College two days a week. I got cast as Ruth in *The Effect of Gamma Rays on Man-in-the-Moon Marigolds*.

Then I played Honey in *Who's Afraid of Virginia Woolf?* at the University of Oregon. Tim bought a cheap car. We could each drive less than an hour to our destinations: he to work, me to rehearsals in Eugene.

We rented what used to be a goat shed from Ma and Pa Ferguson for a pittance. They had a farm up the side road. Occasionally together we would drive to freshly clear-cut patches of forest and use Tim's chain saw to cut firewood stumps in extra-small lengths. Once we were done with the sharp tools, we drank sips of Jack Daniel's as we loaded the box of the truck.

He'd bought a wedge and a splitting maul to crack the stumps into firewood but went to work before teaching me how. I tried but, beginner that I was, I caught Ma Ferguson's eye trying to split a stump and she offered free advice. She was old but she showed me how. She tapped the splitting maul, flat side up, into the stump so one edge pointed straight to the center, and the other straight out to the bark. She choked up on the handle, so it was easier as she lifted it above her head. She led with the flat side of the axe, pulling down on the swing to fall smack bullseye on the flat top of the wedge. The wood popped apart like corn. I got so I could split wood for a good while before I got too tired. I learned to shift my weight back as I let it go from above my head, so my wrist power turned to centrifugal force.

Heating with wood meant waking up to our cold room that winter, and we got better at banking the fire in the stove so the ashes would keep the coals hot enough to last. There was an outhouse in the field. In winter I put a cover over the toilet seat and cut the center out with scissors, so my butt wouldn't freeze. There was a bathtub inside the goat shed with running hot water, set at sink height in the pine counter, for both bathing and dishes. Those hot baths were luxurious. Sometimes the roof would leak, and we would set pans, bowls and jars about to catch the drips. Then Pa Ferguson would bring his ladder and climb up to tar the roof again, the next clear day we got. He was so old and frail, but he didn't see himself that way. One day he fell off, onto the hood of our pickup. He acted like it was nothing, but Ma told me later that he'd sprained his ankle. I learned that Ma's real name was Mary, but her nickname came from the first lady governor of Texas.

Once in a while Tim and I would cross the road with our fishing gear to catch trout in the wooded stream that fed into the Calapooia River. We'd clean the fish, bury the guts, walk home and put flour, salt and pepper in a paper bag, and then shake the fish in it one at a time. I got as good as my grandma had been at stoking the wood fire just the right amount of cooking hot. But if we came home hungry and the fire had gone out, we used the Coleman stove, because it was quicker. A slice of lemon made it gourmet.

Tim loved the country and was meant to settle down on a

farm, but I needed to do theater in a city. All this earth-mother, going-back-to-the-country stuff was a lot of drudgery. There was something wrong with how the hip country mamas, dragging their long skirts over hiking boots, walked behind their men and held their tongues when the men were around. I had an image of myself as an old farmer woman, lying on my deathbed, wondering, and having regrets.

A gay couple, Richard, my director, and Joe, the actor who played my husband, Nick, in *Who's Afraid of Virginia Woolf?* would breakfast at the pancake house in Eugene. I'd get wired on coffee. The next play moved to the hotel ballroom downtown. It was a musical and I was in the chorus. A chorus girl named Linda and I decided to fly to San Francisco to see *A Chorus Line*. She set up an audition for ACT, an acting school in Frisco, and she got in.

Tim never knew that Joe, who was bisexual, was coming on to me, and that I had given in to the temptation of coming right back on to him. Joe drove Richard's black Cadillac out to Marcola to do some mechanical work on my broken engine, and then we flirted like crazy and used the Cadillac's back seat. It wasn't long before Joe put a halt to it because he realized that Richard would be really hurt. After that we settled for being just friends. Richard had lots of professional acting and directing experience in New York and teased me for hemming my jeans with embroidery, which he considered a waste of my talent. Sometimes I spent the night at their rented home. I learned a bit more about responsible gay couples from seeing the saline solution by the Fleet enema, the tube of KY lubricant and the wet wipes and the condoms by the bedside. Joe cooked gourmet for Richard. They invited me along to Joe's mom's for Christmas. Joe gave Richard a cactus garden, because it didn't need to be watered. They lived for theater and coaxed me to audition for the Goodman School of Drama in Chicago for the next fall. Tim visited me in Chicago and hated the city. I dropped out of theater for winter term and fled back to the Oregon woods, but it was like Heidi in reverse; I kept getting sick because I was unhappy. That was when Tim carved me a wooden tray with rounded edges inside, for cleaning seeds and stems out of marijuana. It had a handle at each end, one longer than the other on purpose, because humans are never perfect, but still pretty good. That lesson has helped my marriage of forty years, and the tray is still used on a daily basis. ∎

STRAWBERRY FIELD
Jey Ley

~~^~~   ~~^~~   ~~^~~   ~~^~~   ~~^~~
{:·······:} {:·······:} {:·······:} {:·······:} {:·······:}
{:····:}   {:····:}   {:····:}   {:····:}   {:····:}
{:·:}   {:·:}   {:·:}   {:·:}   {:·:}

~~^~~   ~~^~~   ~~^~~   ~~^~~   ~~^~~
{:·······:} {:·······:} {:·······:} {:·······:} {:·······:}
{:····:}   {:····:}   {:····:}   {:····:}   {:····:}
{:·:}   {:·:}   {:·:}   {:·:}   {:·:}

~~^~~   ~~^~~   ~~^~~   ~~^~~   ~~^~~
{:·······:} {:·······:} {:·······:} {:·······:} {:·······:}
{:····:}   {:····:}   {:····:}   {:····:}   {:····:}
{:·:}   {:·:}   {:·:}   {:·:}   {:·:}

~~^~~   ~~^~~   ~~^~~   ~~^~~   ~~^~~
{:·······:} {:·······:} {:·······:} {:·······:} {:·······:}
{:····:}   {:····:}   {:····:}   {:····:}   {:····:}
{:·:}   {:·:}   {:·:}   {:·:}   {:·:}

~~^~~   ~~^~~   ~~^~~   ~~^~~   ~~^~~
{:·······:} {:·······:} {:·······:} {:·······:} {:·······:}
{:····:}   {:····:}   {:····:}   {:····:}   {:····:}
{:·:}   {:·:}   {:·:}   {:·:}   {:·:}

SO MANY PROMISES AND SO MANY LIES
S. Afzal Haider

My last salutations are to them
Who knew me imperfect and loved me.

—Rabindranath Tagore

After four days and three nights in Paris, Joyce and Ved headed toward the sun-drenched south of France for four nights and three days. From the Gare de Lyon they boarded an afternoon train for Avignon.

As the afternoon drew to a close, they arrived at Avignon and rented a sky-blue Peugeot at the station. With the evening sun behind them, Joyce drove towards the village of Gordes, less than forty kilometers southeast of Avignon.

"I used to vacation in this area with my grandparents," said Joyce. "They were always reminiscing about days gone by. Immigrants always look back. My grandfather used to say, 'You have to know and understand where you come from or you're lost in the present.'"

But it doesn't hurt to know where you are going, either," Ved said. "I'm an immigrant, and all they call me is *déporté*."

The pristine beauty of the red rock filled Durance Valley, the spectacular views; variegated shades of the area's red stone houses blended in with the surrounding rock quarries and the magnificent terrain of the Alps, which Provence shared with Italy in the distance. Field after field of vegetables and fruit, especially the tiny sugar-sweet melons for which the region was well known, stretched out in the horizon. The heat-baked hills, the picturesque villages, medieval castles, old churches, citadels; nothing much ever changed around there.

They stopped for coffee at a café on the banks of the Durance in Cavaillon. A large Jewish community had once flourished in this region, Avignon, L'Isle-sur-la-Sorgue and Carpentras, with papal patronage. Sitting in the café with Ved, Joyce thought and talked about the days of going to the eighteenth-century synagogue in nearby Carpentras with her grandparents. Ved imagined Joyce wandering through the markets dressed in a pink-and-periwinkle-blue floral printed frock alongside her French-speaking Jewish grandparents. After visiting the markets and then during picnic lunches with them, devouring wonderful crusty bread, cheeses and the sweetest of melons. Ved pictured little Joyce picking up a twig and tossing it into the river and watching it drift, gather speed and disappear out of sight.

Joyce looked up from her coffee at Ved lovingly and smiled.

"I still dream of my childhood days running in these foothills, trudging around the riverbanks, salty beads of perspiration burning my eyes before I would plunge into the coolness of the river. In the evenings I would sit gazing at Grandpa's face shining in the campfire. He would tell tall tales until I fell asleep."

How impermanent, how transitory is life, Ved reflected.

In her apartment in Manhattan, Joyce had an old, battered tin box that once had held LU Champagne Biscuits and was now filled with black-and-white photographs of fading vestiges from an equally fading past. There was a photograph of her grandfather when he was about twenty years old, gentle eyes, warm face, winsome smile.

"My grandpa was a classmate of my grandmother's brother. As a young woman, she had a wild crush on my grandpa. She told her brother that one day she'd marry him. And so it was—they were married when she was eighteen. Within months she was pregnant with my mother. She remained in love with Grandpa all her life and they were blissfully happy." She paused for a moment and continued softly, as if talking to herself, "Unlike my parents, who got divorced when I was a year old.

"In America my grandparents were always reminiscing about the days back home," said Joyce, nodding her head, as if she were acknowledging a mental image of them. "Here you can sit for hours listening to silence, you can walk down to the local bakery to buy a baguette and the bread is still warm by the time you get home."

They finished their coffee and moved on. They drove past a Romanesque church standing in ancient solitude, alongside a village cemetery; it glowed rosy peach from the sun setting behind the heat-baked hills.

"Cemeteries in the villages of France always enjoy the best views," Joyce pointed out.

"They should. The occupants will dwell there until eternity," Ved responded.

He turned his eyes away from the graveyard and looked towards Joyce. She looked ahead. On the surface, he wondered, they both seemed to be living in the moment. These precious days of love and mercy, the joy he felt now, well aware of the pending loss, lucky for the day, gloomy for the emptiness in waiting that would engulf him.

They drove by the city of Apt, with Luberon National Park looming on the horizon, sheep grazing on pine-covered hillsides.

"The Greeks were the first foreigners to occupy these parts, but it was the Romans who built the great towns with churches and bridges and left their mark." Joyce talked as they drove on. Ved didn't mind the lecture. "Apt was originally called Hath but was renamed Apt Julia, after Julius Caesar, during the Roman occupation. Over the years, the name collapsed to be just Apt. Throughout Provence, you can see the Italian influence on French cooking, there are pasta dishes as well as a French version of pizza!

"One of the region's specialties is fleurs de courgette, squash flowers deep-fried in a light batter," Joyce said, "and you can choose if you want male or female flowers."

"How can they tell?" Ved asked.

"It's pretty obvious if you look carefully," she said, raising her eyebrows.

Beehive-shaped stone huts with no windows appeared on the horizon.

"What are those buildings?" asked Ved.

"They're *bories*. Some people believe the *bories* predate Christ, but most believe that residents fleeing from the plague built them in the sixteenth century for protection. The Village of Bories is about four kilometers from Gordes. We can visit them if you'd like."

Joyce looked away from the road and asked, "Are you hungry for dinner yet, my love?"

Before eight in the evening they arrived at the elegant seventeenth-century château with twenty-two guest rooms, nestled in the foothills of the Plateau de Vaucluse, in Gordes, their home for the next few nights, surrounded by a park and an imposing garden with centuries-old trees, fountains and ponds, impressive yet tranquil. Built around the hilltop château were five detached suites intended for guests who desired more privacy.

The restaurant at the château served the best food in the region. Travelers came from far and wide to patronize the kitchen. They had a corner room with a balcony, filled with potted plants with blooming flowers and an exceptional view of the Luberon mountain range and a nearby nature park. The side windows overlooked an open-air swimming pool and tennis courts. The windows in the back looked out onto a garden, like a painting, with potted orange and fig trees that defined the boundaries of blooming beds of lush color. Their room was furnished with antiques and had a stone fireplace. The bathroom was outfitted with a deep double whirlpool tub and a multi-jet shower.

Since dinner wasn't served until after sunset, there was ample time to freshen up. Joyce, tall, tan and voluptuous with a fetching smile on her face said, "Let's try out that shower together, shall we?"

Freshly showered and body heat exchanged, they forayed into the gardens. Joyce wore a deep-blue silk dress and a pearl necklace. A thing of beauty and joy forever. Ved sported his blue blazer with a blue Oxford shirt, a red-and-blue striped tie and grey linen pants. He felt a character in some French mystery movie. Wandering back through the maze of color, they found their way to the maître d'; after waiting to be seated in the dining room, they were seated in the garden at a table for two and ordered their aperitif. There was still sunlight left but a cool breeze blew gently. Happy together.

"Don't turn around," said Joyce, in a low voice, "but George Harrison of the Beatles is sitting over there in the gazebo. Yep, it's George all right, all dressed in black polo shirt, black jeans and pointed black shoes with three other men, chatting and drinking their pastis. But the three others aren't John, Paul and Ringo."

"Are you sure?" said Ved, twisting his torso to get a good look.

"I said don't look!" whispered Joyce.

So he didn't.

Their waiter returned and noticed them noticing Mr. Harrison. He informed, "That is Monsieur Joseph Haydn from Liverpool," as he served their drinks.

"Obviously Mr. Harrison is traveling incognito—George doesn't want to draw any attention," said Joyce with a little grin.

At ten, Joyce and Ved were ushered into the dining room and seated at a table for two by a window looking out onto the courtyard garden.

"Joseph Haydn" and his friends were seated six feet away at a table for four.

"Did you know that George Harrison and I have the same birthday?" Joyce asked.

"February 25," Ved said—he knew her birthday. "I guess that is between you and George," said Ved, closing his menu.

They ordered from the prix fixe menu *gastronomique*. "It's what George and his friends are having. Don't look." The chef fed them crusty oysters and warm pâté of duckling as appetizers. For the main course they had fricassée of sole with lobster and an upside-down tart of snails with buttery parsley juice, followed by a salad of freshly picked greens and lightly sautéed courgette flowers, both male and female.

"I'm so glad we let the chef decide for us," said Joyce, who rarely let anyone decide anything for her. "Everything was delicious."

In her book *Sexual Attitudes and Reassessment*, published in 1977, Joyce wrote:

Sex is not only a beautiful thing. It is also a thing of beauty as well as a beauty treatment. A person's skin can show whether that person is sexually active or not. The sweat that is produced during long, slow, relaxed conjugation serves to clean the pores and make the skin glow. It actually reduces the risk of skin rashes and blemishes.

The sexually active body produces pheromones in large quantities that release a subtle sexual aroma that drives the opposite sex wild. In other words, the more love you make, the more love you will be offered. Sex is ten times more effective in calming one down than Valium or alcohol. It is the safest tranquilizer. A warm, caring congress can release the tension that restricts blood flow to the brain and relieve headaches. Copulation also produces antihistamines that can help fight asthma and hay fever. A healthy, hardworking aphrodisiac can unblock a stuffy nose.

Intercourse is one of the safest sports. It stretches and tones almost every muscle in the body. It is most certainly more fun than swimming, jogging or lifting weights. Lovemaking releases endorphins into the bloodstream, producing a sense of euphoria that leaves a feeling that life is worth living.

"Is George still eating?"

"Yes. Don't look."

He looked. "Coffee?" he asked.

"No. Let us go to our room."

"Tired?" asked Ved.

"Not at all," she said. "I'm all charged up for you."

George was still enjoying his dinner. He looked up and smiled, mostly at Joyce.

* * *

Sitting outdoors among the potted blossoming red and white geraniums, hibiscus and roses at Café Lou Pastre, Joyce and Ved ate a late breakfast of croissants and café au lait in bowls. Ved took a deep breath of fresh air, listening to the cicadas sing their eternal song of time passing by. The people around noticed them, à deux, the Indian man and American woman. Joyce was at home, perfectly natural. She walked with her head up, chatting in her best colloquial French with the locals and enjoying the pleasures of French country life. It was warm and tourists filled the spacious square and the cafés, surrounded by old cut-stone houses, art galleries and small shops selling Provençal oils, essences, herbs and spices. The church at the heart of the village was a reminder of the time when houses of worship were the center of village life. An imposing castle with lofty walls converted into a church, studded with towers, turrets and carefully spaced crenellations. Steep cobblestone alleyways led from the square to the old village. Two-story cut-stone houses clinging to the rocks, turned to the sun, standing against the deep-blue sky and the red mountains, reddish-brown facades, tiled roofs and stone portals, stout wooden doors; streets paved with river stones—old flattish dry stone, *lauzes*, red. The air was strikingly fragrant and the setting was beyond colorful. Unforgettable purple fields forever.

After breakfast they walked the twisting narrow streets holding hands. Ved stopped at an ancient fountain and washed his hands, before cupping them, filling them with cold water and then drinking. After he finished he flicked his fingers and playfully splattered a constellation of water droplets at Joyce.

She growled at him.

"Amazing," she said, "how everything looks the same, after all these years. But I wish it were summer. That's when the lavender fields smell their best."

For the next three days they did things that the young in love did. They visited Saint-Rémy, Bonnieux, Carpentras and Aix-en-Provence. They hiked up a hill through a forest interrupted by striking cliffs, breathtaking canyons at Les Baux-de-Provence. They went to the Musée de la Lavande and watched a film, sitting thigh to thigh holding hands, that showed the love and labor involved in harvesting and making lavender oil. For centuries, lavender oil had been used not only as a fragrance, but also for medicinal purposes, supposedly curing many ills, including arthritis and migraine headaches.

"Interesting," said Ved.

"I wonder if it's an aphrodisiac."

"I don't need one. I'm with Aphrodite."

"And I desire you beyond words."

They climbed up the splendid Renaissance spiral staircase of Musée Pol Mara, to the top floor, and walked down to the first to follow the artist's work in chronological order. There was much to observe, sketches of voluptuous bodies that evoked sensuality, desire and pleasure. A testimony of colors, rhythm of life, as well as Pol Mara's writing on love. Joyce and Ved walked out holding hands.

They drove to Apt to see the Cathedral of Saint Anne, built over two crypts, one on top of the other, the upper one carved out of rock in the eleventh century, the lower crypt said to contain relics of Saint Anne, mother of Mary.

"The discovery of the relics of Saint Anne brought pilgrims from all over to worship," informed Joyce. "Anne of Austria came in 1623 to pray for a child."

"Was her prayer answered?" asked Ved.

"What do you think?" replied Joyce.

Joyce had to buy boxes of candied pears, peaches, apricots and figs. Apt was known for these delicacies, favorite of the popes, who lived in exile in Avignon during the thirteenth century.

A baguette is always worth rioting for. The Musée de la Boulangerie, the Bakery Museum, was yet another highlight of their trip. The social and agricultural history of bread was told through engravings and the tools that harvested the wheat and the process it took to make the flour and, ultimately, bread. Antique scythes, thrashers, scales and kneading machines were also on display. "A baguette is worth rioting for," repeated Ved. Again they held hands.

They ate lunches at local restaurants, regional specialty dishes— tender white anchovies with cold beet salad. Sea bream or saddled bream or eel, or fresh sardines, sea bass or mussels or snails cooked in garlic and tomato or daubes, à la provençale. Joyce's favorite was porchetta, or suckling pig stuffed and spit-roasted. But for all four evenings they came home for the ten o'clock seating and dined in the panoramic peach-colored dining room along with George Harrison and friends. By now they nodded and smiled at each other before and after dinner.

> *Open thy door to that which must go.*
> *For the loss becomes unseemly when obstructed.*
> —Rabindranath Tagore

Emerging rays of sunlight filtered through the hand-tatted lace curtains to awaken Ved at daybreak. He lay beside Joyce, his mind filling with Keats's "A thing of beauty is a joy for ever." He was the one leaving.

"No one to blame," Joyce had said.

In the luminous light of dawn, Joyce's eyes moved behind her eyelids, her blond hair glowed silver. She puckered her lips. He wanted to touch her but didn't want to awaken her. He took pleasure in watching her rambunctious sleep.

He slept straight through night until morning like a plank, on his back without moving. She, on the other side, kicked and jerked and rolled all over the bed. As much as sleeping with her was a pleasure, he cherished waking up with her, as well as waking up before her. He loved watching her rumple the linens in her sleep.

Little over a year they lived together, they would never go to sleep angry. He treasured their morning caresses. Every morning before getting out of bed and starting their day, they lay tangled together for a long time, embraced in blissful ecstasy, a cradle of love. Even on rushed mornings they took a moment to hold each other, snuggled, enfolded, breathing in sync together.

The morning sun shone brightly when she awoke after eight. She opened her eyes, smiled at him and asked, "How long have you been watching me?"

It was Sunday morning, their last day in Gordes. They lay in bed cuddled and connected, each one fulfilling, satisfying and pleasing all the curves, angles and corners of the other. Being together like this was the most peaceful of moments. Everything moving smoothly, in sync and harmonious, erection of lingam swallowed in the depth of yoni, yang with yin, He happy, She happy, Life good. The birds chirped in the morning fog, and flowers blossomed on their balcony and in the lush green garden outside.

* * *

They sat down in the peach dining room for breakfast. "We all live ordinary and extraordinary lives," said Joyce. She talked of Laing's philosophy and George Harrison's music and how greatly it affected her. She loved and admired John Lennon a lot.

"Do we all need to have heroes?" Ved asked.

"Yes, of course we do."

"All right, then. I admire John Fowles, R. K. Narayan, Bernard Malamud, Albert Camus, and my father."

"What I like about George is his childlike simplicity. He seems so full of love and fun."

"There you go again," said Ved, "always concerned with George."

"Passion, my dear boy, passion," Joyce said with a smile. "He is here. We are here, and we see each other every day."

"Yeah, you are right. By now we are like best friends."

"Rain I don't mind, shine, the weather is fine," Joyce sang as she got up from the breakfast table.

She suggested they go to L'Isle-sur-la-Sorgue, the "Venice" of the area, built on pillars over swampland. She said, "I used to go rummaging there with my grandparents. There are hundreds of antique shops in the village, and on Sundays hundreds of vendors come to L'Isle-sur-la-Sorgue for the flea market."

With a gentle wind blowing and the sun occasionally peeking through clouds, it was the perfect day to walk around for hours. They circled the lower River Sorgue, which flowed around the island town. The locals shopped for everything there: fresh-caught seafood, freshly baked bakery goods, cheeses, fresh paella on the burners and live poultry. Fresh-picked fruits and vegetables, preserved jams and jellies; and there were knickknacks, household goods, new and old clothes, belts, shoes, tapestries, tapenades and paintings. A shop called Aphrodite sold only old bathroom accessories. Copper, ceramic and even marble bathtubs.

There was an abundance of noise, mingling of smells, and lots of smiling faces. Vendors offered samples of bread, honey, jam, sausages and cheese. There were elaborately framed paintings, art deco and art nouveau objects. There were classic linens and laces, old and new brass objects and sepia photographs and postcards. The antique stores in town sold furniture fit for a king or a peasant, also vintage dolls, antique jewelry and much more.

L'Isle-sur-la-Sorgue was a fishing village. Until 1884, the townsfolk, in small flat-bottom wooden boats, used to catch as many as fifteen thousand crayfish per day from the river, then an epidemic killed off all the crayfish. Now a festival took place, on the first Sunday in August each year, to recall the old tradition. The small flat-bottom boats returned to the River Sorgue and created a floating market, selling fish and produce to the eager customers along the banks.

On a music stall, in front of an ancient stone wall, was scribbled in red an old anti-war slogan, *"Faites l'amour, pas la guerre."* The stall also sold new and used books, tapes and videos. Joyce picked up the Beatles' *White Album*, brand-new, still cellophane wrapped. Without bargaining, she paid twenty francs, the asking price.

"This is the sign I was waiting for," she said. "It's no coincidence that George Harrison is staying in our hotel and that out of the blue I find the one and only copy here of the *White Album*, which contains a set of mug shots of the Beatles."

"I see," said Ved, smiling. "And tomorrow morning George is going to walk over to our table before we are done with our breakfast and autograph his photo for you: 'With love, for Joyce.'"

"We shall see, we shall see ..." she said with confidence.

* * *

Back at the hotel she removed the cellophane from the record jacket, and from inside the jacket she removed the enclosed sheet of paper folded in quarters, the eight-by-ten color photographs of the four Beatles, John and George side by side on the top and Ringo and Paul below. Joyce carefully separated the photograph of George from the sheet, folding and breaking it away at the perforated lines. She took her journal out of her purse, slipped the photograph into the middle and returned the journal back to its destination.

* * *

During dinner in the dining room, Joyce and Ved sat immersed in the present, not thinking about the future. As they contemplated dessert, their waiter brought two snifters of brandy over to their table on a shiny round silver tray.

"Compliments of an esteemed admirer," he said. Joyce looked up. From his table, George nodded and smiled at her. She saluted him with her drink. George got up and walked over to their table.

"I felt the spirit of my friend sitting six feet away. I couldn't leave this place without saying hello to splendid you," George said. "Where is that photograph you'd like me to autograph?"

As Joyce pulled out the photograph from her purse, George pulled from his inside breast pocket a black Montblanc fountain pen.

Dear Joyce,
We'll meet again.
Yours,
George

And Joseph Haydn walked away.

"Did he see me buying the *White Album*?" asked an astonished Joyce.

Ved smiled with joy for his beloved Joyce, much grateful to Mr. Haydn, a known stranger, for providing a pause, making an all-things-must-pass moment most memorable, like a framed a photograph sitting on a mantel of everything that was there and all that will be gone tomorrow.

"So many promises and so many lies."

He watched Joyce, the woman he was about to leave behind. The Indian man and American woman were coming to an end of their journey together. In two days from Paris he was going back to Shanti, India to marry Sanela, the woman he had pledged his faith to, and Joyce was letting him go. "I know that love is just a word, it means one thing to me and describes another sensation to you, but I am not the type who would devote my life to looking for love. I believe one needs to find her purpose in life, and that love will follow." ∎

CHARLENE IN XANADU
John Blades

O nly two ports into the cruise, Charlene was sick—dizzy, nauseated, and unable to take further advantage of the many all-you-can-eat international buffets, from Mandarin to German to Moroccan—and so angry she was ready to jump ship. This was guaranteed to be a seasickness-proof, virus-free voyage, and Charlene expected a full refund if she was forced to abandon ship this early, pleading illness and claiming she had been deceived— misinformed she thought, with bitter irony. The next port was Casablanca, where Humphrey Bogart was scheduled to personally welcome her and her fawning shipmates.

As extra insurance against such infirmities, she had splurged on an upper-deck stateroom, with a panoramic view rather than a porthole. It was a perfect way to watch the passing oceans in all their calming splendor and torrential fury. Last night, after leaving Clark Gable and his crew of *Bounty* mutineers in Pitcairn, the ship had passed through a typhoon. But Charlene was able to navigate its thunderous waves and violent winds from the stabilized comfort of her cabin, finding it no more threatening than the special-effects storms of the *Poseidon* or *Titanic* movies.

For temporary relief from her ailments, Charlene took to her cabin, venturing out only when she felt an absolute need to connect with the humanity packed and piled onto the decks and passageways around her. She mostly remained in bed, switching her focus from the passing spectacle on the gigantic immersive VR screen outside her window to the classic movies that played continuously on the conventional TV on the opposite wall of her cabin.

* * *

The stateroom was a substantial upgrade that put a dent in the dwindling nest egg Howard had left her upon his premature death from acute gastritis five years earlier. He'd hardly left her a rich widow, not after she was legally obliged to honor his bequests to his two adult sons from a previous marriage. But she was comfortably well-off, after selling their house and moving into a retirement home, which was as well-appointed as a luxury hotel, with the added benefit of having a medical annex and doctors (and morticians) handy as the declining residents lumbered and crept from there to eternity.

In her late fifties, Charlene barely qualified for the retirement home, and she remained aloof from the rest of the female occupants, most of them much older in body and spirit. She still considered herself middle-aged and refused to take part in any of the group activities offered by the home, whether the minibus outings to the opera and other musical and theatrical performances or the twilight happy hours that involved sing-alongs to Broadway musicals, bingo, charades, and limerick contests.

In comparison to the other widows, Charlene was in superior health, as fit and shapely as a prize fiddle, she thought, discounting the knee and elbow issues from years of playing tennis and golf, which set her apart in good and bad ways. The older women were obviously jealous of her youthful face and her curvaceous figure, gossiping about Botox and tucks and suspicious of the exaggerated courtesies paid to Charlene by their husbands or boyfriends. The women nearer her age were unhappy that she was able to monopolize the attentions of the limited supply of widowers and bachelors, privately tagging her with such snarky labels as Jezebel and Delilah and Lucretia.

Charlene reveled in the flirtatious attentions of the men. At the same time she rejected all but a select few, physically and emotionally. She did casually participate in several one-night stands, mostly out of amusement, boredom, or pity for the inadequacy of her fumbling lovers—especially the one whose infantile and embarrassed efforts caused her to dismiss him as Mister Softee.

For Charlene, the cruise aboard the *Emerald Palace* was a cautious plunge. Even though it came with money-back guarantees and insurance covering shipborne disorders and calamities, it was not an offer she would have ordinarily accepted. But it caught her in a moment of boredom and sleep deprivation, when she was longing for a change of scenery, an escape from her monotonous social life, and she impulsively signed on.

Except for a day trip to Catalina, she and Howard had never taken a floating vacation. They'd seriously considered Atlantic crossings and passages to the Caribbean and Mediterranean, but the negotiations inevitably floundered, not just on the cost but on the specter of collisions, infections, quarantines, seajackings, the multitude of catastrophic possibilities, real and imaginary.

If the sight and sound of synthetic rough seas weren't responsible for Charlene's present discomfort, what else could it be? Not the coronavirus, she'd assured herself. That lethal scourge now seemed a blurry memory, vanquished by masks, authoritarian restrictions, and vaccines, and the big cruise lines were once more swamped with delirious passengers, even though by all accounts they were still plagued by the usual mishaps and lesser contagions.

Charlene thought it could be a mild case of food poisoning or a bug passed along by her shipmates, who were more aggressively afflicted with similar symptoms. She rejected the notion it might have been the complimentary bon voyage champagne. Or the carbonara she'd eaten at the Italian buffet on the second night of the voyage, or the two helpings of tiramisu she'd had for dessert, a harmless reward for the shipboard yoga sculpture class she'd taken that morning.

Whatever the cause, Charlene was baffled because the *Emerald Palace* never put out to sea. It was permanently docked in six feet of water inside a former film studio, which had been abandoned and repurposed as the centerpiece of an amusement colossus. Spread over several acres, including the backlot, the indoor park was designed to compete with the studio tours, berry farms, magic mountains, monkey jungles, and outer space odysseys from Disney, Universal, Warner, and other merchants of fantasy and wish fulfillment.

Like a gigantic ship in a bottle, the *Emerald Palace* had been meticulously constructed inside the studio—a palatial liner with amenities to equal or surpass those of Carnival, Norwegian, Viking, and other deluxe cruise lines: first-class cabins, restaurants, cafes, pools, ballrooms, casinos, theaters, shuffleboard courts, workout centers. Except the *Emerald Palace* was never intended to be launched into deep water, where it would have instantly sunk. It was a facsimile cruise ship for tourists who foreswore cruises, whether for reasons of cost, snobbery, or paranoia—"Aqua-nots," as they were called in the promotional brochures.

For Charlene a major selling point of the cruise was that it was sponsored and widely promoted by the Vintage Movie Channel (or VMC), the cable network that broadcast old films around the clock. These ranged from certified classics to dismal sub-B duds, stretching from the silent era to the end of the previous century.

Besides the grab bag of televised movies, VMC offered exclusive bonuses for film-struck members of its fan club, such as T-shirts, fruit baskets, discount DVD collections of golden oldies, and private screenings. But the one bonus—the particular one—that appealed to Charlene was the whirlwind virtual cruise around the world of landmark movie locations over six days and nights, New Orleans to the South Seas, Casablanca to Xanadu, in the intimate company of film and musical celebrities recruited to spice up the journey.

While the ship never left its permanent berth inside the park, the simulated voyage managed to deliver passengers to a half dozen or more ports via rotating movie sets. These backlot reconstructions were wheeled into place by robot stagehands at each stopover, allowing the passengers to cavort amid the classic locations, whether Rick's Café from *Casablanca* or the palmy huts and shoals from *Mutiny on the Bounty*.

Charlene had never been a fan of these ancient movies until she married Howard, who was. She watched VMC along with him, obediently if not always happily, concluding that the majority of them—even many of the certified classics—were puerile, poorly made, and badly dated. But before long she'd become a reluctant devotee, perversely appreciating the antics of Cary Grant, the glowering mug of John Garfield, the sexpot flouncing of Marilyn Monroe, finally becoming an encyclopedic collector of vintage trivia, able to name many of the stars and their definitive roles.

And after Howard died, VMC became an essential diversion to ease Charlene through her insomniac hours. She found the simplistic plots and stagey performances a merciful relief from the repetitive, depressing twenty-four-hour news channels, the infomercials, the makeovers and bakeovers, and other recycled postmidnight programming.

So the prospect of a golden oldie adventure appealed to Charlene, a welcome escape from the humdrum but seductive routine of the retirement home. A simulated voyage—powered by an avant-garde virtual reality process—would provide the illusion of sea travel without its discomforts and hazards. She saw herself luxuriating beneath a three-dimensional canopy—a bubble formed by a 180-degree Ultra Hi-Max projection screen—with views of the sky above, the oceans below, surrounded by seascapes that ranged from the serene to the terrifying.

After only the first full day on board the ship, however, Charlene began to have the queasy sensations in her stomach, mild enough but troubling, partly due, she decided, to the mechanical waves and swells, the jolts, rolls, tremors, and other realistic devices necessarily programmed into the landlocked ship's special effects. Her condition worsened with an embarrassing incident that occurred after the buffet, later that first night, which she thought might be as much to blame for her digestive problems as the suspect meal and the mechanized motions of the liner.

The *Emerald Palace* had embarked from New Orleans with a carnival salute to *A Streetcar Named Desire*—a marching brass band that went from the Bourbon Street set to the top deck of the ship, followed by a luncheon banquet of crawdad gumbo and alligator fritters, a communal screening of the movie, ending with a chorus line of Marlon Brando impersonators doing a Dixieland burlesque.

Charlene slipped away from the festivities well before the finale, wanting to keep a low profile and distance herself from the frantically partying passengers. She sank into her king-sized bed—a special request in case she got lucky and needed extra room to entertain a visitor—took a deep breath, closed her eyes, hoping that a brief nap would ease her nausea in time for a late dinner.

She was roused by a hard knocking on the cabin door. She opened it expecting to find a maid or attendant with extra bedding. But she was greeted by a rotund, elderly, elf-like man wearing a ship's officer uniform and bearing a bouquet of flowers.

"Hi," he said, "I'm your captain, Andy, and I wanted to personally welcome you to the *Emerald Palace*. I didn't see you among the passengers partying on deck and I thought I'd better encourage you to take part in some of our activities. We've got a lot of fun things to do on this ship."

Charlene accepted the flowers reluctantly, afraid she might be the target of a swindle. Captain Andy did have a familiar look, with an artificial twinkle in his eye, cotton-white hair, and a bushy mustache that drooped over a folksy smile. He looked suspiciously like the grandfather character who appeared regularly on TV commercials, promoting retirement housing, car insurance, and virility drugs for seniors.

"I've been busy unpacking and getting oriented," Charlene said, accepting the flowers as she nudged the door closed. "It's so thoughtful of you to reach out like this. You must be terribly busy just steering the ship. I do want to get out and around and enjoy so many of the things your boat has to offer but I'm still a little exhausted from all the excitement of boarding and everything. But thanks so much ..."

"You especially don't want to miss our Halloween ball tonight," Captain Andy said, drawing away so the closing door wouldn't snag his walrus mustache.

"I wouldn't dream of missing that," Charlene said, "and thanks again so much for reaching out."

I wouldn't dream of going to the ball, she thought, leaning against the closed door. But as she thought about it, it didn't seem like such a bad idea—she might just meet a dreamboat and justify the extra expense for that king-size bed.

Because the cruise coincided with Halloween, passengers were encouraged to dress in costumes from beloved movies. Charlene hadn't been able to leave her cabin without encountering faux James Bonds and Dirty Harrys, Mata Haris and Lorelei Lees, along with dozens of Marvel superheroes, cross-dressers, and ghostly impostors from dozens of other vintage flicks.

The main event was a fright-night stopover in Transylvania, where a party in a mockup of a peasant village drew hordes of monsters from cobwebby horror movies—Draculas, Frankensteins, Wolf Men, Mummies, along with some secondary ghouls, like the passenger dressed as Peter Lorre being choked by a severed hand, from a forgotten forties chiller.

It was a "spooktacle" that Charlene couldn't resist, and while she hadn't packed a costume, she decided her chiffon nightgown might pass for one worn by Barbara Stanwyck or Joan Crawford at their most glamorous, while allowing her to mingle anonymously with the freaks and geeks in more outrageous regalia. That turned out to be a terrible mistake, she learned during a shout-out contest to identify characters in off-beat costumes. Standing in a crowd, she suddenly found herself singled out in a spotlight and heard drunken cries of "Blanche DuBois!" and "Norma Desmond!" and "Baby Jane!"

The shock and embarrassment, followed by ridicule and laughter, sent her fleeing to her cabin, where she fell into bed, too aghast and wired to sleep. After an hour, she turned on the television, hoping to ease into a narcotic slumber. But the only available channel was VMC, and she numbly watched a garish fifties dynasty opera, with a slutty Dorothy Malone in a peekaboo nightie, doing a Salome dance around her bedroom—a debased reflection of Charlene's own humiliation hours earlier at the Halloween party.

She was nearly asleep when she heard a cautious rapping at her cabin door. "Who's there?" she asked, in a trembling voice.

"Elliott," came the reply, matter-of-factly, as if she should recognize the name.

"Elliott who? I don't know any Elliott."

"You don't know me, but I'm the talent director for the cruise. I noticed you at the contest and I was struck by how gracefully you moved, how elegantly you whirled, like a ballerina, when you made your exit from the room. I think I have a part for you in one of our little set pieces from the movies."

Charlene hadn't realized the party doubled as a talent contest. Disarmed, she opened the door a few inches to see a face she vaguely recognized—dark and devilish, fashionably whiskered and topped by a slickly receding brow. He had been on stage, at one point, explaining how he was recruiting volunteers for roles in key scenes from *Mutiny on the Bounty*, *Casablanca*, and *Citizen Kane*.

Still dubious, but reassured he wasn't a deranged stalker or gigolo, Charlene moved aside, letting him take a few tentative steps into the cabin.

"Thank you," Elliott said, with a theatrical bow. "I realize my conduct may seem questionable and I hesitated to reach out to you at this awkward hour but I'm under some pressure to cast the Ingrid Bergman part in a scene from *Casablanca*. I wanted to approach you at the party but you left so precipitously and I felt it necessary to contact you as soon as I could."

Charlene knew about the reenactments at the various ports, inspired by the movies, but she hadn't considered auditioning for one of the leading roles, certainly not Ingrid Bergman.

As if sensing her hesitation, Elliott looked her down, then up, stopping with a stricken gaze directly into her eyes. "Yes," he said, "you do bear a resemblance to Ingrid Bergman at her most enchanting ... but you'll need a little touching up here and there ..."

Charlene stood aside as he took another step into the cabin. "Your lips could be a little fuller," he said, putting a finger to her upper lip. Then he cupped her cheeks with both hands. "Your cheeks could be a little more sculpted ..."

He lowered his voice seductively, sliding his hands onto her shoulders and drawing her near to him. "I realize you're not an experienced actress and you may feel intimidated, but I think I can help you find the confidence and reassurance you need. You can start by relaxing."

Charlene could see where this was leading, and after a moment's hesitation she was willing to be led. Rather than take offense at his proposition, she was flattered that he had chosen her from among all the available younger women on the cruise, who might have more willingly surrendered to his advances.

Looking him over slowly, almost coquettishly, Charlene saw a man several years younger, sturdy, not especially attractive, but compared to the losers and bumblers she so casually frolicked with at the retirement home, he was Valentino, Gable, Clooney. Opportunity had knocked, why not answer?

He was gone when she awoke the next morning, and she remained in bed, drained from the physical exertions and still feeling sick from the rich food and the unsteady sway of the ship. Midmorning, she heard a rustle outside her room, and getting out of bed, she found an envelope had been slipped under her door.

"Darling," it began in florid cursive. "I apologize for leaving without saying good-bye. But you looked so blissful and beautiful I hesitated to wake you. I had to prepare for rehearsal and I'll plan to see you there at two. I'll have a part for you."

When Charlene arrived on the set, Elliott was busy rehearsing the actors for a scene from *Mutiny on the Bounty*, being staged on a dockside replica of a Tahiti beach. He barely acknowledged her, a quick glance then back to business. He was coaching the Gable stand-in, one of the professional actors hired for the cruise to play key roles with passengers in the mini-drama excerpts from movie landmarks at each of the stopovers.

Charlene took a seat, waiting nervously as Elliott fixed his attention on the passenger he'd chosen to play a native girl. He adjusted the girl's sarong, then demonstrated to the fake Gable how to pin an orchid into her lush hair, wriggling seductively against her. The actress was considerably younger than she, Charlene noticed, with a shudder of doubt and envy.

When he called a break, Elliott hurried over and took Charlene's hand in both of his, apologetically. "I'm so glad you came, but sorry to have to say that I don't have a part for you. Oh, maybe a bit part, if you don't mind playing an extra, one of the background native girls. But tomorrow you're going to play Ingrid Bergman in a scene from *Casablanca*."

Charlene was encouraged, assuring herself that she was more than just a passing one-nighter for Elliott. But she was disappointed when he didn't return to her cabin that night. She waited up until well after midnight, dozing restlessly and watching out her window as the ship fast-forwarded from the South Seas to North Africa. Just as well that he didn't show, she decided, another amorous adventure would only add to her stomach upset and her anxiety about playing Bergman.

The *Emerald Palace* had docked hours earlier and lowered the gangplank onto a mockup of *Casablanca* set when Charlene arrived.

She was expecting to be ushered to a replica one of the more famous scenes, in which the memorable dialogue was spoken—the piano bar in Rick's Café or the airport where Bogart delivers his noble farewell to Bergman.

Instead Elliott posed Charlene near a window in a flimsy copy of a Paris bistro, the location for the flashback liaison, when Bogart and Bergman listen to the rumble of invading Nazis and she utters a much-remembered (and ridiculed) line: "Kiss me ... Kiss me ... as if it were the last time."

Charlene was sorry she hadn't been given more dialogue, in a more familiar *Casablanca* setting, but she had a problem with her single line, largely because she found the professional actor playing Bogart playing Rick so offensive.

"Call me Bogie," he said slyly. But he was squat and swarthy, certainly not a romantic type, Charlene thought. She immediately recognized him from the shipboard Halloween festivities, guessing that he was an Edward G. Robinson impersonator.

After flubbing her one line a half dozen times, Charlene saw how frustrated Elliott was becoming. Afraid he might replace her, she asked to see him during a break. She started by apologizing for her blunders, then shifted the blame to her costar. "He smells bad," she said. "How can I act like I'm in love him?"

"You pretend you love him," Elliott insisted. "That's what actors do."

"He's fat and sweaty and I can't concentrate on my line because he has terrible BO and it's making me sick," she said, avoiding any mention of the lingering nausea and fever she'd felt for days from the ship's automated swells.

Elliott looked at her with obvious annoyance. "You'll just have to fake it, like a real actress would. Bogart himself stank to high heaven. Bette Davis ... Joan Crawford. . . a lot of other actresses wouldn't work with him because of his alcoholic breath and his skunky smell. So let's just get on with it."

The pep talk convinced Charlene that she had to behave like a trouper, even if she had no theatrical ambitions. She returned to the set, took her spot next to Bogart/Rick, and braced herself for their obligatory embrace. But when he smiled, she saw the grimy teeth and the blubbery lips, and she was barely able to utter, "Kiss me ..." before she retched and recoiled, spilling her glass of champagne down Bogie's pants.

There was a hushed moment of shock and disbelief on the

set, then Charlene's victim exploded in a torrent of rage and recrimination, far more threatening than any of the immortal screen eruptions of Bogart or Robinson.

"You klutzy fuck!" he screamed, pointing to his soaked crotch. "Look what you did to me. It looks like I wet my pants. They're ruined. Who's gonna pay for this? I'm a professional actor. I've worked with all the big stars. They don't pay me enough to work with amateurs like you ..."

Charlene didn't stay around to hear the rest of his tantrum or attempt to apologize. She dashed back to her cabin and tossed her belongings into her suitcase, so frantic to leave the ship she didn't bother to change out of her nightgown.

Wheeling her suitcase behind her, she stumbled through a hatchway and headed along the narrow tunnel formed between the ship's hull and the jumbo VR screen that curved around it. She sought an inconspicuous way off the boat, other than the gangplank leading to the dockside gaggle of actors and spectators at the *Casablanca* set.

Many yards ahead, she came upon a service gangplank, where nobody would witness her premature departure. At the bottom, she crossed a fake moat and followed a pathway through the entrance of a medieval castle. Walking cautiously down a dark hallway, she heard ghostly echoes of ancient horror movies with every footstep, while half expecting a swarm of bats to descend from the cobwebs on the ceiling.

She found herself in the great hall of an ancient fortress. This she knew was Xanadu, the pleasure dome of Charles Foster Kane. *Citizen Kane* was the next port of call on the simulated voyage of the *Emerald Palace*, and she recognized this as another faux movie set waiting to be rotated and positioned onto the main dock for the VCM passengers.

She approached a palatial fireplace, more threatening than welcoming, as enormous as the mouth of a whale. It was flanked by tapestries and statues of goddesses and gargoyles, with a thousand pieces of a jigsaw puzzle spread on the floor around the hearth. She conjured the haunting scene from *Kane* where Kane's mistress, Susan, complains pathetically how she is being kept prisoner.

Charlene dropped onto a throne chair to recover before moving on. Looking around, she saw that the palace was made not of marble and granite but of plywood and plaster, with walls that soared to a ceiling of painted canvas. The abrupt transition from the heat and dust of Casablanca to the vaulted chill and gloom of Xanadu left her disoriented and agitated. She shivered and hugged herself for warmth, wishing she'd changed clothes before leaving the ship in such a panic.

Whatever lingering regrets Charlene had about abandoning ship vanished when she glanced up at the *Emerald Palace* through a castle window. In the shadowy light she saw a menacing behemoth, a beached sea monster—certainly not a luxury liner but a prison ship, from which she'd managed a tricky escape.

It occurred to Charlene that she was still imprisoned within the walls of the vast amusement complex that housed the ship, along with rocket boosters, roller coasters, water slides, and other thrill rides. She forced herself off the bench when she heard distant echoes of "As Time Goes By." Its final crescendo signaled the end of the *Casablanca* performance and the imminent rotation of the Xanadu replica into position for the ship's arrival.

Charlene felt like a displaced person as she rolled her suitcase through a dizzying labyrinth of packing cases and towering boxes, past Greek and Roman and Oriental statues—the loot of the world as it was called in the movie, plundered by Kane and stored in a catacomb of his pleasure dome. She saw a balsa replica of the Rosebud sled, propped against a cold furnace, awaiting incineration, a nearby snow globe, and dozens of other oddities and artifacts from Kane's pillaged stockpile.

She left the castle, headed down a dusty street lined with Western saloons and horse troughs that merged onto a cobblestone path to a Moscow street, both of which she recognized as staple locales from VMC movies. She continued past plywood storefronts, row houses, and assorted urban facades, until she came to a yellow brick road, winding through a candy-colored landscape.

Not far ahead, the yellow road turned into an ordinary paved walkway, which led to the entrance of a pedestrian tunnel. Charlene entered apprehensively, spooked by the spectral light at the end of the tunnel. But halfway along she lost her fear of the unknown, telling herself that the tunnel would deliver her from the fantasy universe, the bubble in which she'd been a virtual hostage.

Charlene was greatly relieved to emerge onto a loading dock, though momentarily blinded by daylight and caught up in a state of organized chaos. She was forced to dodge the dozens of wheeled robots unloading trucks and stacking boxes of food, drink, drugs, electronics, replacement parts, and other necessities, many of them presumably intended for the *Emerald Palace* and other amusement park operations.

Charlene was about to descend a short stairway down from the dock when she suddenly felt feverish and dizzy. She waited until the spell passed, then regained her balance and struggled down the stairs, with her suitcase tumbling behind her. At the bottom, she was confronted by one of the dockworkers, evidently a foreman, who said, "You're not supposed to be here. Only authorized persons."

Noticing her weak and confused state, the dockworker assumed a worried look and reached out to take her elbow. Charlene drew away and snapped. "I'll be all right. Just leave me alone."

But when she saw how genuinely startled and concerned he was, Charlene said: "I'm grateful for your offer. But I don't now and won't ever depend on the kindness of strangers." Then she rummaged through her bag until she found her cell phone and called Uber to take her home. ■

2013 (LYDIA FANNY LUPITA)
Christina Drill

I hate it here so I will go to
secret gardens in my mind ... —Taylor Swift

That was the year we moved in across from the Lydia Fanny Lupita hair salon, in a neighborhood of Chicago far from the lake. I was working as a nanny for a family in the Northwest suburbs teaching their child to swim, while my husband worked from home on a screenplay set in the street outside our apartment. He met Sara at the Starbucks near the Jewel Osco, which was a mile away and our closest coffeeshop. The affair lasted two months or around there.

Tom asked if I'd noticed the tiny sheet of confetti Sara from Starbucks had in her left eye. He described it as a delicate UFO. That Sunday, I watched her knock the cardboard cup against the counter violently to set the bottom layer of caramel for my macchiato before brewing two espresso shots at once and pouring them in tandem into the cup. She avoided eye contact.

At no point did I think to confront Tom and instead let overthinking eat me like a disease. One evening, Tom arrived late from his evening run. He'd stopped at Jewel to pick up groceries for a recipe that reminded him of his childhood: pastina meatball something soup. The Starbucks had been closed for hours, but I had a nervous breakdown anyway—it was clear to me he'd gone to see Sara. By the time I felt appropriately consoled it was too late to cook, so we ate leftover wantons in bed instead and watched detective Gillian Anderson play cat and mouse with serial killer Jamie Dornan. I got so high that the television show seemed even more like a television show, a comforting feeling.

Tom said he wouldn't move until the screenplay was finished. He thought he was Weegee the Famous, he refused to miss a thing. I thought about leaving but I, too, was inspired. On my days off I went on long walks towards the lake. I'd listen to Conor Oberst and cry, my eye rims and nose tip red, and at every red light there was a trucker, a father, or a carpool of law students who rolled down their windows and asked me if I needed help. Each of them seemed alive with a feeling they seemed eager to transmit to me. In each instance I'd imagine myself saying *yes*, getting into their Challengers or Explorers just to say *yes* a second time, to whatever their next question might be.

On a Sunday in early March when the weather was absolutely gray, forty degrees, and windy on top of that, I went on my walk without my fleece hat. Once I reached Western, with its deco revival Chinese cocktail bar and the French Café serving egg patty sandwiches on potato bread, it started to hail. This intersection normally made me feel hope for my life, because the area was more monied than ours, but not too monied that it made me feel inferior. I was being pummeled by the hail. My coat had a high collar that I tried in vain to pull up past my head, as if the soaked corduroy fabric would grow to protect me instead of curling into my neck. I mowed ahead and decided I'd cut my walk short if I passed a dive bar, where I could order a small light beer and see what befell me. I hoped the drink would trigger an endorphin release to lift my spirits temporarily.

I ordered a light beer at the last remaining dive n this block of Western. Its bartender was aging, wrinkles softly setting over his brow, and everyone was chain smoking so I bummed a cigarette from a drunk woman with two inches of grey crown and allowed time to pass. Every so often I would smooth my hair down with my fingers to chip off some ice and watch it melt against the dark wooden floor. The more I did it, the less hair I had. The veins on the backs of my hands became fatter, and my knuckles widened. When I was done with my beer I finally felt ready to speak to a therapist, or at least, a sympathizer. I needed someone to tell the story of Sara and my husband to. I waited for a face open enough to absolve me of a pain that felt relentless.

Ten years went by until I learned that Sara, in 2013, ran the popular Tumblr DreamPoets that reblogged photos of women in which only one of their eyes was visible; the other eye was always hiding behind a hand, bangs, leaves, a camera. That Sara went on to become a manager at another Starbucks location, then a Communications Officer at their corporate office, and that she was now raising a set of twins in the Pacific Northwest, her babies' names anagrams of one another, in a rehabbed house trimmed in scallop molding she'd painted the perfect eggshell color, finally, on the third try. Ten years in that dive until Sara swivels toward me to update me on her life. I forget I'm supposed to be looking for a tiny UFO and am relieved to hear where she's been— faraway. She says she's been reevaluating a difficult time in her life, then asks me what I'm doing here.

I live here, I explain. Well that way, I say, and point west of Western.

By Lydia Fanny Lupita, right?

I nod and smile. I still love the name of my hair salon. The name *Sara* sounds beautiful to me now, too.

Well that's what's been going on, Sara says, on my side of the world. She hands me a five and I'm alone again. I could wait another ten years, or order another beer, but it's finally time to walk myself home.

My fleece hat was in my jacket pocket. My corduroy collar has dried stiff. The weather is fair. I am pushing something out. A moment of clarity wants to be born. I ask myself, *What was so wrong? Why were you so unhappy?* I hear myself reply: *I was young and coming to terms with everything that happened to me, and I am not done doing that.*

I don't respond. I mean, what do I say to that? The further I get from the lake, the longer my hair gets. It grows back in downy layers, and my hands shrink small like a child's. Tom is not home when I unlock the back door and enter through the kitchen because he is at the library, printing his final draft. I sit at his desk and open a notebook where I begin to process the pain that his affair, which I invented, brought me and continues to. ∎

VIGNETTES
Gary Houston

Pincer

And then one time we went to what I took for a nightclub in a woodsy region somewhere outside St. Louis, where we joined my dad's colleague Mr. Burch and his wife. I ordered my favorite dish, a hot roast beef sandwich with mashed potatoes and gravy, but when it came I was perplexed at the *oval* plate, the field of buttered corn, the gravy—not the flour-based goop I knew but a spattering someone called au jus. I felt cheated of what I desired, except it was delicious. Leaving our table to escape the cigarette smoke, I found myself standing outside on a stoop wondering, *Is this what a real nightclub is like? Oval plates? Au jus?* The light above burned brightly in the cool night and from a distant forest came an insect symphony playing counterpoint to the jazz piped inside, clearer now, really, because when I was inside it competed with loud voices, laughter, coughs, belches and wheezes. On the stoop sat a metal bucket full of sand littered with discarded butts. Feeling suddenly very alone, I looked down startled to see a pincered creature twice the size of the basement dwellers we called water bugs. Petrified yet curious as children can be, I raised a foot to squish it but could not lower it with confidence or conviction. The sole of my shoe had barely touched it when, in the blink of a child's frightened eye, it scampered to the top of my shoe, then slid up the laces and shot beneath my pants. I stamped to shake it off. I jumped to the path leading to the stoop and dragged my foot through the gravel, praying the agitated little rocks would oust the monster. I stamped again for good measure. I ran back inside not sure at all I was rid of it. I never really knew, but I saw my mother at the table laughing at something Mr. Burch had said. She saw me and smiled, and this reassured me of love and safety. Yet much older I still often think something is climbing through the hairs on my shin.

Shop-Around Protestants

New to northern New Jersey, vaguely Presbyterian, Dad wasn't particularly religious and when provoked rather irreligiously combative, yet "for the kid's sake" hell-bent to settle on *some* church somewhere. Every Sunday morning took us to pews beside staring strangers in search of a denomination that "fit"—Lutheran, Methodist, what have you. It so happened my schoolmate Mike

Allingham came from the Deep South, so when his parents were away he asked, "Why don't you try our church?" We hadn't tried *those* people, Baptists, yet, which the very next and cold Sunday morning put Mike in the back seat with me. Dad drove, Mom sat to his right, and Mike navigated up to the point he dozed off. We knew we'd be late. But then Mom saw a sign, Valley Baptist. "Turn left, Ken!" He did not see the oncoming car until almost too late. It was a near miss. The other car slowed next to ours. We could see the other driver's face contorted in anger as he yelled at Dad. "Ken, don't," said Mom, but in an instant Dad braked and was out of the car. The other man, seeing this, did the same. Our window muffled his voice, but Dad's was crystal clear and starkly familiar: "Yeah, well, you want to make something out of it?" The man said something else. Then Dad shouted: "You don't tell me what to do!" How it escalated to the physical I couldn't tell. I just see Dad has the man in a bear hug and the man has Dad in a headlock. We are blocking the road and other drivers have stepped out of their cars. Mom rounds the front of the car screaming: "Ken! Stop! Stop! We're going to church!" The fight ends as suddenly as it started. Dad is at the wheel, his hair at the back of his head mussed. Over decades that memory of the mussed hair and the exertion it represented has stood as a message to me never to take any guff that heads your way on the road of life. He often tried to teach by example, you see. He knew I was the kind of kid prone to walking away from a fight. He had me pegged. He still does even though long gone. We drive on. "You haven't done that since you were a little"—Mom searches for a word—"tyke." A few moments pass. "He was very weak," says Dad. Eventually Mike speaks up: "My dad used to do that until he was saved."

Bob's Dad

Edward Andrews played snide, oily, often southern characters to great effect and whenever he's on the tube I think of Bob McKnight's dad. Bob was our team's star pitcher, whose dad scarcely attended a game because, well, he just didn't care. A big reader, he frequented the library as addictively as Bob watched Cardinal games and gobbled up books with a smug cheeriness. He loved throwing new words at others his age, like "dysteleological," and exulted in their bafflement. He relished making his wife, Edith, feel inferior for reading the *Reader's Digest*. And you'd be right to suppose he had little faith, intellectually or otherwise, in Bob's prospects. "I suppose he could drive a truck," I overheard him say with a dry chuckle. One day he actually came to a game. We were a last-place team aptly handed the name of the majors' much-joked-about Senators. Which says right away that as pitchers go Bob was the best, yes, but the best of the worst. Since the league-leading Hawks were leading us 5–0, Bob was a sweaty nervous wreck the moment Mr. McKnight showed up at the bottom of the third, the Senators at bat and retired one-two-three. Coach Saluga was of no help when he sent the team to the field with the order, "Just try, boys, to make it respectable." Before his second pitch, Bob heard the voice, not so much the words as the wearied, plaintiff tone, "Come on, Bob." Not a loud voice, just one that carried. A nasal voice. As the innings rolled by and the score worsened, the voice coiled over Bob and he started walking batters in. "What's wrong *now*, Bob?" The voice seeped into his pores and coursed in his blood. "Surely you can do better than that." His head pounded. Mr. Saluga approached the mound. He said nothing but gave Bob a questioning look as he removed the ball from Bob's glove. "I want him to die" is all Bob had to say.

Still Life

Months later, after a miserably failed self-aware groping stopped short by fears of failure brought to comic ripeness, she said she'd *respected* my restraint that other night we lay still in that clean, unfurnished apartment, key lent by a friend's brother's wife, together on that mere mattress on that leafy hill among a ring of them high above that famously cultured town in that faraway country. *Respected* my restraint, my sensitivity against playing out the cinematic obvious, my gentlemanly understanding (would she have said breeding?) in matters of intimacy—the *truly* intimate, she surely would say, that surpasses carnal tedium, the lying-stillness and lying-togetherness of it, the supine side-by-side apposition of it, the timeless picturesqueness of it, no, the Picture of it, that which says what's possible is surely more than enough: that a bare foot may or may not in innocence brush that belonging to another, that one breathes the self-same air as does the other, that noises from one's organs may be taken for the other's, that dreams, or if not dreams the slipping mind's thoughts, or if not those then those of that that's fevered and wide-awake, that these, furrowing one's brow, bringing teeth to grind teeth, may by one so enjoin two, and so goes the erotic vision of one whose *respect* was earned months before an errant undoing.

The Havisham Ball

Mantua glide to round the still
and quiet eyes, indeed fulfill
what presence on the Saturn floor
comes round avoid conjoin and more:
to speak, with solemn breath eschew
the tempo swirl from me to you.

Vertigo moan to brush the flakes,
white flung the fragments, yellow cakes.
To talk of times as times transpire
to you, transfixed, with lung suspire.
Release the fire to festooned face,
to rotted soul, to mantua lace.

A Dog Found

A dog found, a mutt mottled brown and black, big, muscular, short
haired, broad skulled, like a fighting dog,
    eyes so dark they pierced themselves,
    young with easy movement,
    a panting beast seeking home,
    no collar, but teeth white, nails trimmed, for you didn't hear
them ticking stone, testifying once someone loved him,
    may miss him yet, or another may yet,
    following me homeward at discreet distance, but following still,
lolling about trees on city parkways,
    lampposts, fence corners, pissing with dignity beyond our ken,
and still a stalking flirtation that flatters,
    picks at, peels the human self-containment, a kind of courting,
    just as we might if homeless and scared, we might, we might,
pressed enough.
    Then to home, a bowl of milk set down,
    he eagerly laps in its goodness,
    his panting, rearoused, resubsides, his handsome animal bulk
now drifts
    into you where you sit, black eyes into yours burning with a love
beyond our ken, and this is it is what they say, and
    this will do is what they say, and
    this at last is what they say, this
    moment held for a dog's eternity.
    Does one often see the like?

He does not know about the phone call
to someone who just came to mind,
that soon he will be led away,
that he was wrong in a sureness
that we cannot know, own or have.

Natural Leader

Benny's curiosity about the class reunion got the better of him, so he clicked on the YouTube link. He made out a ghostly group of elderlies—his very classmates, none whom he recognized—bending over carefully to remove shoes and socks while tittering over their own infirmities.

The image of the leader, Bill Waterman, was equally blurry; still it jarred Benny to see the shaved head.

Another barefoot man stood close by, his hair gray but thick, his expression not a happy one.

Bill asked the man, "Mel, what seems to be your problem?"

"Well," said Mel, "people keep telling me I am round-shouldered. And I have heard others say my head juts forward or they say I don't stand up straight. I heard someone say the word 'kyphotic,' but I don't know if that's true. Actually, I guess I don't even know what it means." The audience chuckled, and Bill softly said, "Uh-huh, kyphotic." Both men were quiet for many moments as Bill scanned Mel's contours. The whole room too had grown hushed.

Bill's fingers began to fall lightly upon strategic places along Mel's spinal column as he addressed the audience: "I am merely *inducing* something here, ladies and gentlemen, *inducing*. You see, Mel's body is making the decisions." As minutes passed Benny saw Mel's body by steps and degrees straighten up, his shoulders and his head come into alignment with his upper back. And Mel looked taller and seemed to know it as the crowd gasped in what sounded like astonishment. But it was Bill's transformation over the decades from opportunistic climber to holistic priest that gripped Benny's attention. What on earth had induced the change in that man who had confided to Benny that grand design for his future over so many pitchers of beer? What became of those careers Bill saw for himself in international statecraft, in commerce, in politics, in academia, one leading to the next so deftly, divinely, it was as if it all had been set in stone before he was born?

Abruptly the video ended.

All Shook Up

It was a bright day. Sunlight dappled the rolling park lawn and the crowd dressed as folks did back then, fit for Easter. The class of '57 valedictorian spoke from the dais like a young god. Some girls still preferred their dreamboats to look like Tab Hunter and not, they'd say, "hoody" like Elvis, so the speaker's blond flattop fulfilled their hearts. He was also "cute," they'd say, not except when he was serious but especially when he was.

This was demonstrated as he turned to world affairs. It made the assembled parents chuckle discreetly that such a young person might think himself one day to be another John Foster Dulles. Oh, but what matter? Maybe he would. And it was such a beautiful day.

Of course he had to cite the struggle against Russian Communism—the struggle his generation was expected to face. And valedictorians wherever they spoke felt required, on the eve of joining adult humanity, to speak for their generation. It was a sort of group destiny thing.

Yet just when "Communism" left his mouth, there arose from the throng a clarion boo—loud, male, angry. It made the boy stammer and scared even those girls vigilant enough to shush the offender whose whereabouts no one could tell.

Perspiring, the boy pressed on. His text forewarned that the word was coming again. It called upon him, like destiny—or history, for maybe it was—to say it again.

"Boo!" Now it filled the park like the blast of a bullhorn. Whoever was doing it, the now-murmuring audience couldn't figure out if the jerk disagreed with the lad's politics or loathed Communism so much he wouldn't abide its very mention.

Our hero, stricken, could not go on.

A lasting confusion thus dogged him the rest of his life. The occasion meant to herald his manhood had become a joke remembered at reunions he declined to attend. He married but unhappily. His kids despised him. In old age, meaning only to recover the vibrancy of his youth, he voted for Trump.

Neighbors

I spent a few nights putting her to bed. If you saw our apartments exposed from above, you would see hers wrapped around mine like someone's leg hooked around someone else's. But don't infer we slept together. What we did together was drink, she more so.

I can't recall a single conversation. Yet this membrane that separated our living quarters portended what movies once implied but wouldn't show. You feel the prickle of it in *The 39 Steps*, where handcuffs oblige a man and a woman, otherwise strangers, to share a dingy room. Or change the scenery with a bottle of rye, the Lost Generation's aphrodisiac of choice. Only a prude or naïf would think it all concerns cigarettes and cool patter about a string of murders.

But I digress. Inside her entrance was a narrow passage impeded by a daybed you had to scoot by to reach the open area where you'd find a sofa. Sometimes I led her, inebriated, to the daybed, other nights to the sofa. I never removed any article of her attire, not even a shoe. I suppose I wanted to merit her trust when she awakened. One evening she passed out in the bathtub. My exertions to heave her out got no further than sitting her up. I left content that she wouldn't by accident activate the faucet and drown.

Finally comes the night I pretend I'm the first to pass out. You know, to see what she'll do. I hear her steps approach the sofa and close my eyes. The steps withdraw but then they return. A weighty blanket drops upon me. I lay stupefied for an hour before I arise and creep past her on the daybed, the rasps of her troubled breathing almost forming words. Soft now, I tell myself like Hamlet as I ease out her door and in a flash slink through another one, mine.

Decades later she sends a letter. It apologizes for the pains I took on those occasions. "They coincide precisely," she writes, "with a strange spell in my life when I absolutely believed I was controlled by someone else."

The Invited

Our company had been invited to a daylong party by people we didn't know but who apparently held us in high regard. Some of our employees had already returned from the gala enraptured by its fairy-tale delights and charms. As if to confirm their reports, I found myself listening on the phone to the hostess, her voice rich and seductive, insisting I join them and whispering, "We should meet."

Two white short-haired terriers were my companions when I parked where a mown glade cut into the woods like a boulevard. Beyond a curve in it we beheld the event in the distance. Guests sat convivially at tables but some happily on the grass. The terrace that overlooked them was retained by a stone wall.

I looked about for the woman on the phone, unconcerned that the dogs had vanished. All the women were indistinguishable except one descending from the terrace, elegant in what in afterthought I conceive as an evening gown that shimmered. Her hair was bunched, pale green and pitted with dots of shadow like a floret of broccoli. I saw only a bit of profile but was certain that she was Mediterranean and knew her to be ravishing.

I entered the party from the right and walked counterclockwise within it to look and, by her, be looked at. I felt her eyes as she rotated with me, always to my left, from a remove of several yards. Not wishing to give myself away, I would not allow myself to turn and face her but instead held her in peripheral view. I would certainly not abandon my pattern in order to cross to her and ask, "Are you ... ?" What I wanted was for her to tap my shoulder unexpectedly so she might pose that very question. In truth I awaited it.

But I had come full circle and found myself returning to the glade whence I came. No further development concerning the woman with green hair was possible, for nature, a jealous mistress, had called with the imperative that I quit my bed and attend to her.

Memorial

There were one or two who took us through the grand pageant of her life, the passions and themes of it. A sister came to tears upon realizing that the words she spoke about the secrets of her sister's heart were also her own. Others noted her talents in many activities, her tireless energy, her many acts of charity and empathy for all. Inevitably, over and over, the tragedy of losing one so young with so much to live for was stated. Why then was I asked to speak? I was not good at summarizing a life, much less my feelings about it. I could not muster a theme. My memory gathered details about any encounter—a gesture, an inflection, a smirk someone had made— never what had brought it about or was really being said or going on. You don't have to tell me: a terrible failing. That's my ugly little secret if you must know. Now in a sweat as I climbed to the podium, a silly, absolutely insignificant scene bounced within my brain, but I held on to it. One Christmas we were talking about the songs of the season, and she said "O Holy Night" was her favorite "because of that part, you know, that says 'fall on your knees.'" I can't remember if I said anything, but I did have a reservation. The demand that we fall on our knees took me away not from the Jesus who, I'm told, said it but to that angry, unforgiving God of the Old Testament. Yet I could still understand the power, the majesty, the audacious beauty within the music. Well, that was it, the sorry fragment bereft of meaning I delivered to those closer to her than I was. But then, a funny thing.

I started extemporizing way beyond my usual capabilities. Going on and on about what? Just a moment of union knowing, feeling, what she'd meant. Suddenly I shuddered remembering how our eyes had locked. Now glistening eyes were looking up at me, possibly supposing I was her lover, which made me late to comprehend as I descended the steps that I wished I had been.

Ralph and Me

We'd moved east when we heard Ralph died in seventh grade overdoing laps in the gym. His coach, someone claimed, had it in for him. The shock still reverberates down through many years about losing a childhood friend a thousand miles away where we played football in a vacant lot and hurled aloft grapefruits punctured and stuffed with lighted firecrackers just to see, Ralph explained, how a citrus explosion looked.

He was a curious kid.

So was I.

One day we joined his older brother, Ted, and Ted's sweetheart, Carleton, for Pepsis in Ted's room. Ted was a clean-cut paragon of fifties youth—"college material," meaning sports, enthused my own dad. And Carleton? A raven-haired beauty who evoked, and still does, the unattainable Veronica of *Archie* comics.

They'd just played hours of tennis. Hot and browned, clad in tennis whites, Carleton shed her sneakers and stretched out on Ted's bed. Her athletic socks contrasted so strikingly with her calves I flashed on sundaes with chocolate ice cream and marshmallow sauce.

The couple laughed gossiping about classmates I didn't know as Ralph and I listened in quiet. They spoke of Ted's approaching college life, leaving unsaid what prolonged futures in separation might bring. But it was in the air.

Funny how the very youth of a storybook couple of so long ago still, despite their anxieties, makes us wish we'd been more like them.

But Ralph upended everything. He beelined for Carleton's left foot, announcing, "I want to know how they smell," and sunk his nose deep into that recess, sock notwithstanding, at the sensitive ventral underside of her second, third and, debatably, fourth toes. Her leap into the air was instant, her scream imperious. I doubt he had time to inhale.

The couple lost no time: "What's the matter with you?" "Are you nuts?" "You're really a jerk!" "That was stupid!" "You are stupid!" "Stupid!!" See, while "pervert" was just around the corner, "shit for brains" came much later.

Well, that was something.

Ralph couldn't explain it.

Neither could I.

Unless it was those sundaes.

Chocolate Eyes

Upstate New York, while parents, mine, and adoptive parents, hers, play poker wafting cigar-cigarette smoke and bursts of laughing banter over cocktails through a closed door into the room where we are on the floor before a fireplace and in the heat of embers she is excited to discover we both dig horror movies—those at long last televised, the old Universal Studio cut-ups once manufactured for the consumption, ironically, of the very elders a room away who now announce spit in the ocean as the next deal. We tout favorite monsters the way I once did baseball players over cards wrapped with bubble gum waiting for the grade school bell to ring—a mimicry of bargaining adults on an exchange.

Now eleven, or twelve, I'm on the verge of what? I don't know. I see her chocolate pupils, blazing softly like the embers, the shiny, irresistibly easy smile, a forwardness that scares me that I'm too timorous to take advantage of—a paralysis of ignorance even if with a blink I could whisk the chaperoning grown-ups to Bayonne or South Bend. So we talk about Karloff, Lugosi's Dracula versus John Carradine's and Lon Chaney Jr., the Wolf Man, and those "atmospherics" like the chilling ominous score first exhibited in *Son of Frankenstein* as Karloff's monster rises from the steaming sulfur pit and looms unseen by the son of his creator. But she really fell for Karloff the Mummy, she says, after he's regained the appearance of his first existence in defiance of the deity. "A man like that in my country," she says, chocolate eyes searching, taunting mine, "would be seen as very attractive."

What *was* her country? I ask that now as I did then though not to her, only to myself. Mexico, I guessed, not Egypt. What more did I want to ask, should have asked? What more did I need to know? For my waste of time on distractions, my life ahead finds me trying to reconstruct but never believably our moments over embers and monsters. ■

WEST IN THE MOUNTAINS
Chuck Kramer

I was in Starbucks on a dismal winter day and ran into Jill Shelton. "Danny," she said. "You haven't aged a bit."

We'd grown up on Chicago's South Side and gone to school together. We hadn't seen each other in years. I barely recognized her in a stylish tight green wool coat and a sleek blond haircut but I was glad to see her because she'd always been friendly and down-to-earth. We hugged, took a table together, and caught up while our lattes cooled.

"I've been working in New York since college," she told me. "I'm a vice president with Citibank in the foreign investments section."

"I'm not surprised. You were the smartest person in our class. A hard worker too! I remember people teasing you about being 'the extra credit queen.'" We both chuckled, Jill pleased I remembered her. "You back in town on vacation?"

"No," she replied, running a hand through her hair. "I'm here to help my mom pack up and move. My dad passed on last summer and Mom's moving East with me. What about you?"

"I never went anywhere," I said. "Got a job with the city and bought a house here in Mount Greenwood when I married Gwen. I like the area. My family's nearby. It suits me."

Jill nodded. "You keep up with the old gang?"

"Yeah, I do," I replied, sipping my coffee. She asked me about some of the kids we'd grown up with—Tom Jordan shot dead in Nam, Eleanor Feldstone operating her own restaurant, and Myron Goldbloom, the chubby boy with bad teeth who'd had them capped and became a TV star.

"What about Eric Schultz?" she asked, wiping some foam from her lips. "You two were tight as I remember it. You ever hear from him?"

"Yeah, Eric and I were real close until he retired and moved away." I sat for a moment, thinking about my old friend and his daughter, Sara.

"Where did he go?"

"Out to Colorado. He built himself a place in the mountains, his own little Eden. I see him every so often. Drive out and spend some time with him. He still looks pretty much the same as he did in high school—a buzz haircut and fleshy cheeks pockmarked from acne. Not a handsome guy, but he has a fiery intensity that makes him look younger than his age, despite the gray hair and wrinkles around his eyes."

"So, how's he doing? I always thought he was someone special."

"He's all right but he's sure had a strange life."

"Strange? What do you mean?" She looked across the table and leaned forward to hear better over baristas steaming milk and calling out the names of completed orders.

"That's a long story and it didn't start well."

"Why not?" Jill asked, unbuttoning her coat and settling back in her chair.

"Because he looked like his dad. That was a real problem, since his mom hated his father after she found him with a seventeen-year-old girlfriend. She divorced him, just like that. She felt betrayed and took it out on Eric because he reminded her of the man who'd humiliated her. Beat him with a belt the old man left behind. She was a little crazy."

"It must have been horrible for Eric."

"It was, believe me. He had this dog, Buddy. It was his best friend. One night he forgot to take out the garbage and his mom went ballistic. She threw Buddy down the basement stairs and broke three of the dog's ribs. She wanted to teach Eric a lesson and make sure he'd do his chores the next time, so his dog wasn't hurt."

"God, that's awful."

"Yeah, it was but it worked. Eric made sure nothing happened to Buddy from then on and protecting that dog shaped him, made him someone who thought it was his job to take care of others and help them out if they were in trouble.

"I think that's why he took the job as a probation officer with the juvenile courts. He thought the boys who got in trouble were good kids with bad parents and hated how the judges sent them to jail at St. Charles like they were criminals. After they served their time and were put under his supervision, he tried to teach them how to stay out of trouble and live a good life. He made friends with them, played pickup basketball on weekends, and treated them to hot dog lunches. He figured that way they might listen to what he had to say instead of looking at him like some kind of cop.

"And it often worked. He had a lot of kids return to school, stay out of jail, and get a good job once they graduated. Then he brought these older guys back to play ball with his new kids and that worked too. They were examples of success and Eric called the older guys 'my dream team.' They also played together as a basketball team in park district tournaments. One year they won the Englewood championship—Eric and four Black guys. That was something else."

"He wasn't afraid?" Jill asked.

"No, he's not that kind of guy. One of the things I always liked about him. He just went ahead and did what he thought was right, what needed to be done. And he was really good at it. That's kind of how he got involved with Carmen Sanchez."

"Who's that?"

"She's the woman he married but when he first met her, she was divorced with five kids. She'd married young and was just a little older than Eric. A real beauty, a young woman in her thirties, slim with a big, happy smile. She was a knockout.

"But she needed help. She didn't have a car, so Eric drove her grocery shopping on Saturdays. He got along well with her kids and took them to the museums on Sunday afternoons or to a ball game at Sox Park. It wasn't anything serious at first, just Eric doing what Eric does—helping someone out.

"But Carmen was crazy for him, couldn't believe he was so caring and thoughtful. She cooked him huge meals with the mole sauce he loved. She was also a woman who loved sex. Her idea of dessert was to tell her daughters to wash the dishes, take Eric to her bedroom, close the door, and give him a blow job."

Jill giggled and got another latte. When she came back to the table, I continued my story.

"Well, it wasn't long before they were going together. Eric had finally fallen in love. He told me she was the perfect woman—a hot lover, a devoted mother, and a hardworking teacher in the public schools, doing what she could for the Latino children in her barrio classroom. He glowed when he told me that. I'd never seen him happier.

"Carmen was happy too. Her kids liked him and so did her dad, who owned a couple of apartment buildings in the old neighborhood. Eric's good with his hands and helped the old man with the upkeep on the buildings. He's a natural craftsman who can do anything—carpentry, plumbing, electricity—and Carmen's father really appreciated his assistance.

"So, after a couple of years of this, Carmen says to him, 'You love me, right, Eric?'

"'Yeah, Carmen, I love you.'

"'Then we should get married.'

"'Sure, Carmen, I thought you'd never ask,' he said with a teasing smile. They went down to city hall the next day and he took to marriage like a duck to water. He was also a great stepdad for Carmen's kids. He helped them with their homework, cheered at their Little League games, and sat with them on the sofa watching Saturday night HBO movies with homemade popcorn and Cokes.

"Two years after the wedding, he and Carmen had a little girl they named Sara and Eric was crazy about her. I mean he was devoted to that child and Sara worshipped the ground he walked on. She was daddy's girl—not momma's—and she let everyone know it. Carmen initially bragged about that, seeing Sara's affection for Eric as proof her husband was a good father, but deep down I think it rankled her she wasn't her child's favorite.

"He also got around to building his dream house in the Colorado mountains. He'd bought a couple of acres on an overgrown gravel road south of Colorado Springs when he went West on vacation after his first year as a parole officer. Came back to Chicago telling me it was peaceful up there in the Rockies, where he could breathe fresh, clean air and see the stars at night. Said he was going to build himself a house on that land one day for his retirement.

"And after they were married, that's what he did. He spent his summer vacations with Carmen and the kids building it. He'd sawed every board, hammered every nail, and wrenched each pipe into place. It was his pride and joy and from that point on, he thought of himself as a mountain man, somehow exiled to the city until his time was up and he could enjoy the splendid isolation of the mountains, close to nature and far from the city problems that filled his nights with disturbing dreams."

"Sounds wonderful. I'd like a place like that."

"It's really beautiful. Great views, fresh, clean air but I don't know, Jill. I mean it's really out in the backcountry. For a guy like me, it's just too rural but for Eric, it was heaven on earth, something to look forward to and he needed that when his marriage began to sour."

"What happened?" She leaned forward and waited for me to continue as I took another sip of coffee.

"The usual. Carmen put on some weight, the normal middle-aged spread, and wasn't pleased to be growing older. Her kids brought home boyfriends and girlfriends and were getting married, leaving the house, and she didn't handle the empty nest syndrome too well. Especially since she and Sara fought like cats and dogs. Sara felt Carmen didn't love her as much as her older kids and Carmen was jealous of Eric's doting indulgence of their daughter and I think she was also becoming jealous of Sara's dazzling good looks just as hers were fading."

"I'm not surprised," Jill said. "Sometimes there's a lot of jealousy between mothers and daughters, a lot of bad feeling."

"That was the case with those two and Eric always took Sara's part in their fights. That led to constant tension between him and Carmen. She was also working long, long hours and wasn't home much. She was an ambitious woman who had her sights set on being the school superintendent one day, anxious to prove she was more than a señora, a stereotypical housewife and mother. She'd passed the principal's exam and was heading a school in the neighborhood.

"That left all the domestic responsibilities on Eric's shoulders, including the maintenance of her dad's buildings, which she'd inherited on his death. Eric didn't complain and took care of everything.

"But he told me he felt like 'a single parent' and understood Sara's resentment of her mother. He really loved that girl. Seemed like he gave her all the love that Carmen was too busy to enjoy. He cooked her favorite meals, encouraged her to read widely, and made sure she understood she was living in a new age of women's liberation and urged her to take advantage of her 'girl power.' He drove her everywhere—to dance lessons, basketball practice, and concerts at the symphony. They went grocery shopping together, the movies, and every Thursday night they bowled at Cermak Lanes in a father-daughter league. They were more like a couple than parent and child. It wasn't your typical father-daughter relationship.

"The last straw was the year Carmen was too busy for the annual vacation to Colorado. She didn't want Eric and Sara to go without her, arguing it was time for a change and they could enjoy all Chicago had to offer during the summer without abandoning her.

"Sara wouldn't hear of it, having her heart set on the two weeks in the mountains, and she prevailed. She and Eric drove to Colorado and when they returned, Carmen was furious and blamed Sara for being left behind. She stormed into the girl's bedroom the night of their return, accusing her of being selfish and inconsiderate. They screamed at each other until Sara burst into tears and threw herself on the bed.

"That was it for Eric. After years of witnessing Carmen's angry attacks on his darling child, he couldn't stand any more. He filed for divorce and wanted sole custody of Sara, who was entering high school."

"Wow! I bet Carmen fought him tooth and nail. No mother wants to lose her daughter."

"You're right. She was outraged and argued as a professional educator she should have custody of Sara, not Eric. He responded she was an absentee parent, always busy with work and too tired to pay much attention to Sara when she was at home. He said she'd be a lousy parent for Sara because her job meant more to her than her daughter. The judge wasn't sure who to believe and finally asked Sara, 'Is your mom a good mother?'

"'No,' Sara answered.

"'I am too a good mother,' Carmen snapped, standing next to Sara at the bench and glaring at her.

"Sara gave her a dismissive wave. 'My dad's always around but my mom's never home.'

"'Where is she?' the judge asked, peering through the thick lenses of her glasses.

"Sara looked at Eric, who was worried he'd lose his cherished child, and said, 'At work. That's all she does—work.'

"The judge leaned back and tapped her lips with her pen. She nodded and ten minutes later, Eric had full custody of Sara.

"He heaved a huge sigh of relief because he had big plans for his daughter. He thought she was someone special and wanted her to be a generous, conscientious person helping others. When she went off to high school, he told her to work hard so she could get in a good college, get a degree, maybe go on to law school and be a lawyer helping the people in the community."

"So, what happened?"

"Sara grew up like most kids. She did it her way. She met Fred Chance, a tall, thin kid in her biology class, and fell in love. After that she no longer had any interest in going to college. All she wanted was to get married. Eric tried to talk her out of it, but she was wild about Fred and turned a deaf ear to Eric's pleas to reconsider. 'I want to be a mother, a good mother, and raise my kids so they have a happy childhood. What's wrong with that?'

"Eric didn't have an answer and the fall after she graduated from high school, she married Fred and that's when things got really bad."

"Bad? Why? What happened?" Jill's eyes were bright with curiosity.

"Sara refused to make peace with her mother. The rancor from the divorce lingered and the girl wouldn't speak with Carmen, never answered her phone calls and didn't invite her to the wedding, even though she invited her stepbrothers and sisters.

"I was surprised Eric didn't advise Sara to be reasonable and forgiving. I guess he never got over Carmen's hostility either and was willing to see her suffer. But Sara was the one who really suffered because breaking things off with her mom left her unmoored, like a rudderless ship, just drifting in the wind.

"That wasn't clear right away and things went well at first. She and Fred had Albert a year after the wedding and Rosa was born three years later. Fred sold homes, Sara worked as a cashier in a Walgreens, and Eric worked toward retirement with the courts, looking forward to spending months at a time in his mountain retreat.

"That didn't mean he'd decided to move to Colorado by himself, because he couldn't think of life without Sara and his grandchildren. He needed to keep them close so he could go on being the kind and loving parent, sharing their lives and protecting them from any danger that might arise.

"So, he sat down with Sara and Fred, and they devised a plan for a simultaneous move to Colorado Springs. As his retirement date neared, they flew West on weekends and scouted neighborhoods until they found one they liked. They bought two homes not far apart and once Eric finished working, they sold their Chicago buildings and went West.

"The transition was smooth. Fred had no trouble hiring on with a local real estate agency and was soon a member of the Colorado Springs Million Dollar Sales Club. The kids liked their new school and quickly made friends. Sara found a job working in the school lunchroom and made friends with other moms who had kids in attendance. These women often got together after school to chat at each other's homes and enjoy a glass or two of wine. They also went shopping together once a week and had a girls' night out every Wednesday. Sara went along, Eric glad to watch the kids with Ada if Fred was working late."

"Who's Ada?" Jill asked, wiping her lips with a napkin.

"Ada Lawson—Eric's girlfriend. She's a real sweetheart, a petite little thing with unruly black hair, a chipped front tooth, and patient eyes. She's a widow and a real good match for Eric. They spend a lot of time at his mountain home, where they hike, barbecue steaks on the deck, and take advantage of the privacy for long afternoons of lovemaking. He told me they're both early risers and too tired after dinner to fool around.

"He thought things were fine until his grandkids got to high school. That's when everything blew up like a Fourth of July firecracker."

"What happened?"

"One morning he got a phone call from Sara. 'I need to talk to you, Dad,' she said, 'like right away.'

"'Okay. Come on over,' he said. He told me he heard something like panic in her voice. We were up at his cabin, walking the deck and admiring the stark, cold peaks. Eric pointed out the fresh rabbit tracks that crossed the snowy slope just below the deck. His dogs picked up the scent and nosed the drifts, disappearing into the underbrush.

"We went inside and warmed ourselves in front of the fireplace. Eric explained Sara and Fred had learned they were about to lose their house. Hadn't made a mortgage payment in months.

"Eric was stunned. They'd always been careless spenders and he knew Fred had been having a hard time after the housing bubble burst and the real estate market dried up. But he had no idea they were broke. Sara wanted to borrow twenty thousand dollars.

"He told her he didn't have any extra cash after loaning them the down payment for their house. He needed the rest of his money to keep himself going. She wanted him to sell his mountain home to raise some cash.

"He said he couldn't believe she was asking him to do that. It would be like cutting off his arm and he said, 'No way, Sara. I can't do that.'

"Said he had plenty of room in his house and they were welcome to live with him until they got back on their feet. They didn't want to do it but didn't have any other option, so the bank took their house, and they moved in with Eric—Sara and Fred in the guest bedroom, Rosa in what used to be Eric's office, and Albert in the basement in an unfinished storeroom next to the furnace.

"It wasn't pleasant with five people and three dogs crammed into the house. But living cheek by jowl like that, Eric discovered Sara had a drinking problem. A few glasses of wine with her girlfriends was one thing, he told me. but almost every morning he'd find an empty wine box in the garbage. Most days she made it in to work but on others she was too hungover and slept in.

"There were also numerous times she forgot to pick the kids up from school or band practice or a dance class, and Eric was called to come get them. And there were the unexplained dings and dents in her car, her wearing the same unwashed clothes all weekend, and her losing three phones in a year. Finally, there was the DUI arrest and the expensive legal defense, which got her a suspended sentence but stained her record with a conviction.

"He was heartbroken. His precious daughter who was going to change the world was just another drunk. He tried to talk to her, but she was in denial. Said she didn't have a problem and had things under control.

"Then they all went to Albert's end-of-the-year orchestra concert at the high school. He plays the cello and the lights had gone down when in came Sara and Fred, late from dinner. 'Wait, wait for us to sit down,' Sara yelled at the conductor, who turned with an annoyed grimace as she and Fred hurried to their seats. But when she went to sit down, she missed the chair in the dark. She crashed to the floor with a loud "Oomph!" which resounded across the quiet auditorium. 'Are you all right, Mrs. Chance?' the conductor asked, drawing even more attention to Sara sprawled on the floor.

"'Yes, I'm fine,' she said, as Fred helped her up. She plopped into her chair and looked at the stage.

Eric was mortified and Albert was beet red. Billy Floyd said something under his breath and the string section broke up in snide laughter as Albert twisted uncomfortably in his chair.

"After the concert Eric talked to Fred and they did a family intervention with Albert and Rosa a few days later. Sara was stunned when confronted but agreed to go into rehab. Eric said it was the saddest day of his life.

"He had tears in his eyes as we sat in front of the fire in his mountain cabin. 'I thought I was helping her out, shielding her from Carmen because she hated that woman. But now I see that was a mistake. Every girl needs a mother. I should have pushed her to work out some kind of reconciliation. Then maybe she wouldn't have had that hole in her heart that mothers fill and wouldn't have turned to the booze instead.'

"'You did the best you could,' I said.

"He frowned and shook his head. 'Pretty lame excuse for a guy who saw himself as a protector of children and a great parent. Quite a comedown to realize you screwed up.'

"'So, how's Sara doing?' I asked. Eric dried his eyes. 'She's still sober. Goes to AA and it seems to be working for her. But I have a hard time looking her in the eye. Just seeing her reminds me of all the mistakes I made. So, I spend most of my time up here and let Sara and Fred have the house. Ada comes up most weekends and that's a comfort.'

"I nodded as I watched him stare into the fire. 'This mountain home has always been your refuge,' I said.

"'Or my home in exile,' he whispered, and then looked at me with resignation, shrugged, and got up to refill our coffee cups."

"That's a sad, sad story," Jill said, reaching across the table and patting my hand. "But you've been a good friend, Danny, keeping in touch and letting him know you still care. That helps a person with problems, knowing he has friends who care."

"I hope so," I said as she got up and buttoned her coat. "Good to see you, Jill. Give me your phone number before you leave, and we'll keep in touch."

We exchanged numbers, even though we both knew we'd probably never use them, and kissed each other on the cheek. She smiled and then was off into the gray winter afternoon, leaning into the wind as it whipped the ends of her scarf over her shoulders. She got to her car and drove off without looking back.

I finished my coffee, pulled on my jacket, and went outside. I thought about Jill moving away to New York but still feeling obligated to return and help her widowed mother while Eric lived in the splendid isolation of his mountain home. Lives full of turmoil and upheaval. I wondered if they were happy but couldn't answer that question. It was all too complicated.

I was glad I'd kept my life simple by staying put in Chicago and marrying Gwen, who had promised beef stew for dinner, my favorite meal. I smiled at the thought, took a deep breath of the brisk, cold air, and walked home in the early-evening dusk, humming to myself and wondering if we'd have blueberry pie for dessert. ■

HENRIETTE'S TRICK
Signe Ratcliff

Awoman appeared in the doorway. Glint of sunlight, hesitant smile bouncing off drab walls. Nathan eyed her cautiously as she stepped into the room and wound fast around the obstacles of the floor: diaper boxes, sweatpants, laundry basket, socks. She landed at the foot of Nathan's mud-colored La-Z-Boy and tilted her head.

"Hi," Nathan said and waited. His voice oozed out of him like runny egg in need of being slurped back up. Had he said something bad? He was never sure.

"Hi, Dad." Her narrow face moved in, a pink lipstick kiss on his cheek. The lipstick was damp, greasy on his cheek. His hand began a slow ascent, aiming for a little touch of the lipstick, not sure if he would wipe it off or keep it there. She wore a black sweater strewn with red tulips, the smell of her like well water, like his house long ago. You could never get the smell off your clothes; it had you marked as someone from the sticks—a town outside of town outside of town. The well-water woman reached down and pulled a lever on the side of his chair. His feet thumped the floor. Some trick. Nathan thought of the robots that came into the plant late in the game. They twirled, bent, the school bus yellow of their arms strong like the big lady who gave him a shower, who folded the droopy curtains of his body onto the white shower seat and transported him to the mud-colored chair. Not unlike boxes on a pallet being shoved and rearranged and put someplace new. His fingers found the lipstick on his cheek. He wiped it off.

Now fully upright, Nathan moved at turtle speed, reaching across the expanse of armrest to claim a minibag of Fritos from the chairside table. The well-water woman zigzagged around, folding socks and towels, smoothing the blue blanket over the bed. Such alacrity and speed, her movements like that of a species different from Nathan's; she snapped an empty diaper box off the floor like a cheetah attacking a gazelle. As she collected a row of empty water bottles from the chairside table and delivered them into a garbage bag, the sound of crinkling plastic filled the room.

"Stop that!" Nathan roared.

"Sorry, I know you hate that sound." She threw her hands up, as if shielding herself from further roars, her eyes wide. He had a daughter who did that. Yesterday she had a soccer game. Got in a fight. Scrappy and angry and mouthy. Just like her dad.

"Aggie?"

"No." She flattened a palm against her chest and hunched forward, her voice loud. "I'm Jean, Dad."

"Jean. Right. You played soccer yesterday."

She shook her head. "That was Aggie. And that was forty years ago." She lightly gathered the rest of the water bottles and crossed the room to the trash can. Nathan looked at the television. Packers were on, zipping across the screen in their succotash colors.

"I haven't seen Aggie."

Jean froze in place, her back to him.

"I don't even remember what she looks like."

He searched the violent mess of tulips on her sweater, trying to find her eyes. "Don't want to talk to me. Aggie. See me. How I treated her mother. That's why."

She bowed her head, spoke over her shoulder. "I'm going out for a smoke. When I come back, we'll walk." She dangled a purple rubber belt from one hand. Nathan knew the thing. It embarrassed him, that belt, but he couldn't remember why.

"Not today."

"Yes. Today."

Alone again. His eyes wandered the room, recalling each item, finding the word for each: bed, sink, walker, cabinets. Blue blanket. Windows covered by a series of rectangles, hospital beige. Nathan looked over at the well-water woman—Jean—who'd returned with a box of bottled water and was loading the minifridge.

He pointed to the window. "What are those rectangle things that cover the window called?"

Jean looked over her shoulder. "Blinds." She returned to the minifridge.

"Blinds," Nathan repeated. "Right." He mulled the word over. Familiar, but with a tinge of discomfort. It was a mean word, he decided: *blinds*. "Why are they there?"

Her shoulders fell in exasperation, two water bottles tight in her hands. He should be careful or she might start crinkling them again. "Why are *what* ... where?"

"The blinds."

"Oh. Because of the light."

"What's wrong with light?"

"It hurts your eyes, Dad." Her voice, loud. Everyone spoke loudly on matters in which his memory failed, to drive the memory in. He thought of golf tees, the way they sank so viciously into the ground.

"Open them!"

Jean nestled the final load of water bottles into the fridge and turned, hands on her hips. "Dad, if I open those blinds you'll start screaming and you'll accuse me of trying to kill you. Everyone will run in here thinking I whacked you or something."

"Who? Barely anyone here these days."

She shook her head. "Well. That's true ... But I don't want to be hollered at." She picked up the television stick and turned up the sound. Television stick. That wasn't right. But he'd better not ask another question. Nathan followed the little green-and-yellow men running across the screen. Football players. They'd be huge bulking men if they were standing here considering the spectacle of Nathan, heavy and toad-like in his chair. But on the TV they were quick, tiny, thoughtless things, like trapped bugs trying to escape the screen. It was confounding.

"Turn that off!"

She turned from the laundry she was folding. "You don't want the Packers? You want *Law & Order*?"

"I want to see out the window!"

"Dad, I told you. The *light* hurts your *eyes*—" Suddenly, she turned. "Oh! Hi, Henriette."

Goddammit. Henriette had crept into his room again in her rickety wheelchair. She never spoke but was always socializing, using her decrepit stocking feet to slowly maneuver down the halls and sidle wordlessly into rooms. Her body was like a coat thrown over a very tiny chair, her head at an unnatural tilt, a constant amused play at her lips. She hovered in the doorway like the world's most boring Mormon.

"Get out of here!" Nathan roared.

"Dad!" Jean followed the shaky point of Henriette's finger. From the minifridge, she retrieved a bottle of water, twisted it open and placed it in Henriette's waiting hand. As Henriette sloppily drank, she stared at Nathan, her gaze beaming from the cave-like hoods of her eyelids so intensely, Nathan had to close his eyes and wait for her to leave.

* * *

Mason wriggled in his coat, searching for the mittens Mom had secured in his sleeves by tethering them together with a long string of yarn. Loser's yarn, Upstairs Jack said. Upstairs Jack called him a stupid baby shit with his mitten string, pushed him down, rubbed his face in the yellow patch of snow where the upstairs dog peed. Mason had begged Mom to remove the yarn, to give him another chance. "I can't keep buying you new mittens, Mason," she said. "You've lost them too many times now." Mom moved fast through rooms like bees that go from flower to flower so that Mason had to follow her around and wait until she hovered in one place, gathering her purse, applying her brownish lipstick, checking the thermostat. "Go in the yard and play with Jack. Samantha will be here in a half hour to watch you. I have to go."

There were shifts Mom had to go to. Food on the table, she said. Sometimes, if the snow was the packing type, the shift would go fast. He'd roll fist-sized snowman heads, build tiny snowman replicas, small enough so Upstairs Jack couldn't see. But the snow today was the powdery type, the kind that burned your hand as it melted. Mason spent a minute kicking great clouds of it around so that it caught the bright sun and sparkled blue and green like Grandmom's rings. Upstairs Jack would be down soon. He considered ways to get rid of the loser's yarn. The sharp hair scissors were Off Limits and his school scissors were at school. There were knives in the kitchen, but if he cut himself he'd be in trouble.

He faced the Hardee's side of the yard, where the road that Mom drove on rose to a hill and then disappeared, the Hardee's sign poking up in the distance. Mason sometimes pretended that Mom drove to the Hardee's and spent the day eating hamburgers, instead of driving into Germantown, where she cut hair at the Klassy Kut, so that if he needed her, all he had to do was climb over the fence and walk up the hill and down again to the Hardee's. If it was a Sunday, she would come home for Break and Mason would watch the cars come over the hill, betting to himself the next one would be hers... no, the *next* one, the *next* one. And when he saw her car at the top of the hill (ham colored, long, and sputtery) it was like it wasn't a car at all, but a familiar face rolling down the hill and into the lot.

He turned and faced the other side of the yard, past the bird feeder and the wood fence, where the red-brick Home sprawled across three lots. He'd never been in the Home but Upstairs Jack said people went there to die of oldness. Mason tried not to look at the Home, but he couldn't help it, the long rectangular windows like eyes staring back at him, most of the time closed with their lid-like blinds or half open so Mason could just see a tiny slice of room, bluish with TV light, illuminating a roll of toilet paper on a ledge, a dried-out poinsettia, the glacial movement of a robed backside. It was like watching a broken TV, where you could only see a sliver of life moving around and you had to guess what the story was. Mason kept his eyes on the building, hoping no one would drop dead of oldness as he watched. He wondered if dying of oldness involved blood. Maybe they melted onto the floor or turned to ice and shattered. Or did the building somehow cause the death-from-oldness? Was there a little elevator-like room where one stepped in and didn't step out again?

In the apartment building, Mason heard the angry slam of the door as Upstairs Jack's father thundered down the stairs to warm up his car, the sound of his feet like the many slams and thuds upstairs that Mason heard as he huddled in bed at night. The dog followed him, a big-headed beige one that drooled and didn't like to be pet. It scampered down the stairs and trotted to its pee area, watching Mason as it lifted a leg against a birch tree. Mason avoided the dog's gaze, the smell of its pee still fresh in his nose.

He would have to act fast. Jack would be out soon. Mason shook the mittens from his hands and pulled the loser's yarn free from his sleeve in one swoop. He stepped on the yarn and yanked the mittens upward until his hands turned raw and red. The cold had gotten in, the achy, stingy cold. He needed to warm his hands in the mittens for just a minute. But he didn't have that kind of time, so he tossed the yarn over the branch of the dog's pee tree and in turns, began to saw it against the wood and swing back and forth. If he did this long enough, Mason thought as he listened for the slam of Upstairs Jack's door, the yarn would break and he would be saved.

* * *

Nathan startled awake in his chair. Before him, the room pulsated with television light. *Law & Order* o'clock. He slowly took note of the minifridge, the chairside table, the view of his feet propped in the mud-colored chair, the television stick, the plastic bottles of water. A well-water smell permeated the room, but she was gone. He must have fallen asleep after the walking, the ugly procession down the hall. He'd shuffled on the walker, the well-water woman behind him, grasping the purple rubber belt that bisected his waist and pulling the wheelchair behind just in case his knees gave out. They made it as far as the director's office, Nathan secured by the purple belt like product, like the hundred-pound cartons he'd once tossed onto pallets like they were nothing.

He was thirsty. Time to sit up and drink water from the bottle on the chairside table and wait for someone to come in again. But he couldn't sit up because his feet were up on the footrest. There were buttons for these things. Mechanics. It wasn't long before they had a mere button to press in the plant, the cartons lifted and placed with robots. Hateful monsters. Rob a man of his dignity. Nathan watched his hand swat the air in a dismissive gesture. He had things to say to the goddamn plant manager but he couldn't get his bearings due to the setup here. He grabbed the stick and aimed it at the chair, pressed its buttons, but that only made the television louder and flutter through channels. It landed on the weather, the newscasters speaking Spanish.

"Goddammit!"

There was another button, the red one. That made the smock ladies come. Or had, in the past, if it wasn't a weekend or a holiday when they all called off. He pressed. Waited. Pressed and waited again. The corridor outside his room was silent. No rattle of the meds tray, no cheery greetings. Not today.

He watched the Spanish weather for a moment, a man pointing at whorls of snowstorm on a map, headed straight for Milwaukee. He was late. The snow would be piling up and icing over if he didn't get up soon and shovel the driveway. The plant manager would shake his head, signaling the numbering of Nathan's days.

He pressed the red button again, pounded the arm of his chair. "Help!" Nathan wailed until he heard a series of echoing squeaks in the corridor. A smock lady, at last. But as he peered at the doorway, he saw it was only that woman again. Henriette. She crept her way forward into his room, her head stuck in that eternal tilt and her goofy smile set on him. She was coming to steal his water again.

"Get out of here!"

Nathan frantically aimed the plastic stick at his chair, trying to get the goddamn thing to work.

Henriette inched forward in her Christmas socks, her eerie gaze locked on Nathan. She jerked a hand toward the side of the chair. Nathan followed the shaky point of her finger. The lever! Of course! He reached down and pulled. The footrest thudded down. For a moment, Nathan marveled at the ease of the contraption— how could he have forgotten?—not noticing that Henriette had crept closer. What did she want? His water? She jerked a hand forward, tossing something onto his chairside table. A pair of sunglasses. Pink. With a trio of yellow stars at their edges. She jerked her hand again, gesturing across the room, to the window. The window. His eyes. The light. He remembered. *She* remembered. She turned her chair around in slow increments, jerking her hand toward the handles of her wheelchair. *Hop on.* Slowly, Nathan began to understand the plan— but what if he fell? There was no one here to save him. The journey across the room was marked with peril; boxes he could trip over, the objects of the cramped room to be navigated: bed, sink, a forgotten pair of sweatpants lingering there like a dead eel. But Henriette's frantic arm was insistent, the window just a few steps away.

Nathan fumbled with the sunglasses until he had them secured on his head. He grasped the handles of Henriette's wheelchair and stood, his heart thumping. Henriette steered with her feet, navigating the narrow channel between the bed and the wall as Nathan pushed behind, shuffling one foot forward, then another. After several minutes, Nathan let out a long sigh, hunched over Henriette's chair, the window before them. They made it! But now there was the matter of the beige scales. The blinds. Henriette had that figured out too. She pointed to a string, jerked her arm up and down, like someone imitating the whistle of a train. Simple matter. Choo choo. Nathan reached, his knees trembling. He pulled hard on the string. The scales flew up and light flooded the room. Nathan reached behind and lowered himself onto the side of the bed, the light drenching and warm.

As his eyes adjusted, he saw a small hill of clean snow, glittering blue and green in the late afternoon light. A little fence and a bird feeder. Two cardinals swooped from a tree. And then, in the distance a figure. A little one. Nathan felt his face stretch, the air on his teeth. There was a word for that. He was smiling. "There's a little girl," he told Henriette. "And a bird. Cardinal. The red kind of bird." Why was he describing all this? Henriette wasn't blind. But she nodded appreciatively, and he went on. "She's swinging from the tree. A branch. It's a tree I know. A maple—no, a birch. It's a girl I know. Aggie ... My baby girl. I don't get to see her play. Always at work, you know?"

Henriette nodded again. Nathan was quiet a moment, caught flashes of Aggie's face as she swung from the tree—a morose face, dark-eyed and creased. Not Aggie's round sunflower face. He narrowed his eyes, tried to find Aggie again in the shifting glimmers of light as she twirled on the rope. But she wasn't there.

"No. It's a boy. A boy I don't know."

The boy Nathan didn't know suddenly dropped to the ground,

sending up a poof of snow. The rope had broken. Henriette made a mouselike squeak and Nathan jolted to the edge of the bed. But the boy stood, unharmed. He put on his mittens, shielded his eyes with one mittened hand as he looked west. Nathan squinted. A road disappeared over a hill. A Hardee's sign sprung neatly into the sky. Three cars—one red, two white, made their descent down the hill. The boy's shoulders fell.

Henriette sighed.

Suddenly, the boy turned and looked straight at them, at this place. This lockup. This institution. Whatever it was, Nathan knew he deserved it. The boy knew Nathan deserved it too, his face frightened. But then the boy's face changed as he stared at Nathan. He smiled and raised a mittened hand. Nathan felt his face stretch again, wide this time, wider than he could remember. He raised his hand. Henriette, in very slow increments, raised hers too. The boy waddled to the fence in his snowsuit and threw his weight against the fence. Henriette made small burbling noises like a bird at a feeder as Nathan clapped his hands and whistled like he did when there was a touchdown. The snowy path between the window and the fence seemed narrower, the glass of the window thinner, their collective joints and ligaments looser, younger, stronger. No trouble at all, Nathan believed, as the boy continued waving, to unlock the window and roll his body onto the snow, to stand and dust himself off, to greet the pink-tinted sky. But then, another boy, an older boy, came up behind him, and the younger boy—*their* boy—turned and gripped the fence behind him. Nervously. As if expecting a blow.

* * *

Mason gripped the fence, knowing his legs were stronger than his arms. He could kick hard if he had something to hold on to. But Upstairs Jack stopped a few feet from Mason and started to kick clouds of powder snow just as Mason had earlier, his gaze stuck on the ground. In the pink sunset light, Mason saw the purple under his eye, a large bruise, similar to ones Mason got on his knees, but never on his face. Upstairs Jack only had a Dad. There was no Mom he was waiting for to roll down the hill, to come home for Break and patch up his face. To stop bad things from happening.

Mason loosened his grip on the fence. "Hi," he said.

"Hey," Upstairs Jack said, speaking to the ground.

"They're not dying from oldness," Mason said, pointing.

Upstairs Jack followed the point of Mason's finger, his eyes hound-like and sad. "Not yet." But he leaned over the fence and set his gaze on Mason's discovery: two smiling, nice old people like their Grandmoms—if Upstairs Jack even had a Grandmom. It looked warm inside the window. Quiet. Safe. Upstairs Jack flicked his wrist, returning the wave quickly, as if he didn't want Mason to see. They leaned over the fence and watched the window grow brighter as the light around them dimmed. They stayed there a long time as the cars rolled over the hill and starling birds warbled in the bush, until Samantha whooshed open the sliding glass door and called Mason in.

* * *

Nathan startled awake in his bed. He took note: television stick, water bottles, the purple belt, the blue blanket under his chin. The well-water woman was back, taking away his empties from the little table and unloading more from the fridge.

"Hi, Dad, ready for breakfast?"

She smiled hesitantly. No, he thought. Prison pancakes and eggs made from dust.

"Where's Henriette?"

Her smile disappeared. "Henriette... Were you looking for Henriette, Dad?"

"We want to see our boy." He pointed at the window. But it was gone. Covered in scales. "Where's the window?"

"Dad, I told you. The light hurts your eyes... And what boy?"

Nathan frowned. Henriette had a trick. She knew how to do it. He cast his eyes around the room and—there! The pink sunglasses. Nathan rushed to point at them as if they'd disappear at any moment.

"Look. Those things. The glasses. That's Henriette's trick. Get her over here."

"Dad..."

"Aggie, stop arguing with me, go get Henriette for me... please!" He needed the handles of her chair, the navigation of her feet. She needed his strong hands to pull the string and let in the light. They had figured it all out, together.

The well-water woman looked at him with pitying eyes. She held the empty water bottle lightly, was careful not to crinkle it. "I'm sorry, Dad, Henriette didn't make it."

A pause.

"When? Last night?"

"Yeah."

Nathan eased back onto his pillow. All the urgency and fight suddenly escaped him and his body was a rock in the bed. "Well. That happens."

The well-water woman set the bottle down on the chairside table and put her hand on his arm. "But I'll help you ... Henriette had a good idea. The sunglasses."

Nathan looked up. The wary smile. Everyone was afraid of him. Everyone had always been afraid of him. "Not the belt."

"You don't need the belt. Look. Just sit up. Yes, like that ... Now I'll put on your glasses, okay?" Nathan felt the plastic slide against his head. He sat up straight as she yanked on the string and the room filled with light. There it was: the fence, the snowy hill, the feeder. And the boy. Two boys. The youngest was his.

"That's the boy you're talking about?"

"The little fella. You see him?"

"I see them both ... Just like me and Aggie. Do you remember? How we used to build forts like that?"

The two boys were packing snow against a tree, constructing their fort. Strange how children used these military terms. As if a war were on. Prepare for the attack. Hide. Or maybe that's just the term Aggie used—Aggie and the other one. Taller and wiser like the older fella here who was surveying the construction and deciding it needed buttressing with a row of tight snowballs around the perimeter. As he rolled the snow, packing it tight, Nathan saw glimpses of her in flashes of bright morning sun. The narrow moon face. The serious, watching eyes. Jean. The one who was so up close all the time, it was easy to miss her.

"Jean?" Nathan said and reached across for her hand.

The older one, his daughter, turned on her seat, faced him and offered that slow smile she'd always had, the one that spread minutely, as if pressing against doubt. "Dad?"

"Let's go get breakfast." ■

CHICKEN MAN
Elizabeth McKenzie

The chicken man cleans like no one else. Got his beak in everything, a tornado of order, a machine with feathers, but mostly a friend. The chicken man moved in before I could stop him, but the chicken man knew what was right. I have a new day ahead of me now, every day, there's no looking back. No more sleep till noon, dragging myself from bed full of dread and headaches. Now I'm up at sunrise. The chicken man insists. He shows me the light coming up over the hill. He gets busy, so I get busy. We cluck in time. I feel content. I'm part of a chain of activity now and the chicken man helps me see it. By midmorning the chicken man's got the house clean and he's on to the next thing. Maybe we'll sit outside and see ants in line and hummingbirds hover and dragonflies settle and crows glide. We'll feel the sun move on our skin. The chicken man puffs up and dozes, but only for a minute. He recharges in the sun, airing out his down. He leaves nothing to chance. He's the original double-tasker. He only stretches out his wings when there's something to give shade to. He only scratches his back when he needs to look behind. He only tells me something when there's a reason to be heard. He's gotta keep up the good work. Gotta maintain a high standard. Gotta work hard to send help back home. He's discreet. He keeps me free from worry. He makes me flatten my hands in the sun. When I clench my hands, he presses down on my fingers. The chicken man knows these tricks. He knows how good it feels to have your hair brushed, so he brushes my hair. He knows how good it feels to have a cup of hot coffee brought to you, even though you could do it yourself. He knows how good a flower smells. He'll bring me a sprig of honeysuckle. I see him sniffing it on his way to my chair. He likes it, I can tell. I can see the small smile on his lips. Yes the chicken man has lips. They're real lips, just like my lips. No, not like my lips, but lips just the same. Sometimes they pucker. Sometimes I joke around with the chicken man and give him something sour.

The chicken man sings and the chicken man swings. He's got air under his feet, and his toes are long. He's got it all going on. The chicken man has strategy. The chicken man knows there's a chain of command. The chicken man knows how to dodge it, so we can do our thing yet another day. He reads the classics. He speaks foreign tongues. He's got about eight ways to be that make sense and I've seen him in action. I've seen him pull people from a burning house, seen him lecture on the beauty of mathematics, seen him clean out a pile of trash in the alley. I've seen him catch a fly ball and absorb a stack of books about despots. I've seen him go undercover and lay a trap for a mastermind. But when it's time to come home, the chicken man comes. The chicken man has a warm feeling for me, and when the chicken man's down, I'm there for him. The chicken man doesn't like chicken soup, but the chicken man loves to roost by the hearth and hear a good story. When I read to the chicken man, his eyes go half-mast. His neck collapses, his head falls onto his breast. He's an incubator of words. When I finish he comes alive full of ideas. He's a master, a planner, and he makes the scene. He eats his words. Never misses the beat. He's got a canny way of making time. He's got feathers under his belt. He's got wings and tries to fly. When he flies, he fills the sky. He's got wide perceptions. He's not one to compete. He's not one to give false answers. The chicken man does what a chicken man does. He turns his back on the clock. He's got his eye on the prize. Got his fingers in the cash box but never turns his back on a needy hand. Gives the shirt off his back. Gives the right answer and gives the time of day. Loves color. Loves muffins. Won't buy unless he has to. Makes do. Builds a ladder. Climbs to the top. Crows from the rooftops. Keeps me safe. Makes me warm. Fills my pillows. Cradles my head. Says it again: Don't look back!

Maybe the best thing about the chicken man is the way he can seize the moment, seize the instant, seize the smallest particle of time and make it count. The chicken man's life is too short to waste. The chicken man's here and then the chicken man's gone. He won't be here every tomorrow. He knows but he's not afraid. That's the chicken man's bargain. The chicken man's life is an exquisite string of moments, threaded on a silver spool. The chicken man's moments could blind you. The chicken man's life could shoot a clean hole through your head. ■

WALKING ALONG THE POINT
Jake Young

The lake is choppy today,
and clear, blue-green waves
crash against the concrete sea wall
like bottles thrown against the ground.
I once dropped a wineglass
and watched as it touched tile,
bursting into crystal dust
like the first soft snow of winter,
except for a small, flat piece of the foot
and the base of the bowl
left shining like fragments of bone
after cremation, a sliver of ankle
or vertebrae in a pile of ash.
After Bonny Doon stopped burning
and the ash in the air settled, I drove
the desolate moonscape,
whole swaths of forest
scorched, a white scar, chimneys
all that remained of the skeletons
of homes, cars melted away,
reduced to a greasy outline
on the ground like shadows
burned into walls at Hiroshima.
The scent of smoke, even toast
burning, still makes me anxious
two years later. The water here
is clearer than I remember
and lacks any scent. Where's the brine
of salted kelp? It's there, far to the west.

NOTES ON CONTRIBUTORS

LIS BENSLEY is the author of the award-winning novel *The Glimpse,* as well as *The Adventures of Milo and Flea* and *The Women's Health Cookbook.* She has written articles for *The New York Times, The International Herald Tribune, ArtNews, Elle Décor, Fine Cooking,* and the *Santa Fean.* She lives in Santa Cruz, California.

L. ANNETTE BINDER's short fiction has appeared in the Pushcart and O. Henry Prize anthologies and has been performed at WordTheatre and on Public Radio's Selected Shorts. Her story collection *Rise* (Sarabande) received the Mary McCarthy Prize and her novel *The Vanishing Sky* (Bloomsbury) was published in 2020. Her nonfiction book *Child of Earth and Starry Heaven* is coming out in April 2025 from Wandering Aengus Press. She lives in New Hampshire with her family.

BEN BIRD is a fiction writer based in California, where he lives with his two dogs, Ari and Olive, and his wife, Lora, whose support means everything. He can be reached at birdwritings.com to chat about writing or life or anything that separates the two. He is working on a short story collection.

JOHN BLADES is the author of the novel *Small Game* (Holt) and of numerous short stories in literary magazines, among them *TriQuarterly, Catamaran Literary Reader,* and *Chicago Quarterly Review,* where he is presently fiction editor. He is the retired book editor and cultural correspondent for the *Chicago Tribune.*

JOHN BRANTINGHAM was Sequoia and Kings Canyon National Parks' first poet laureate. His work has been featured in hundreds of magazines. He has twenty-one books of poetry, memoir, and fiction including *Life: Orange to Pear* (Bamboo Dart Press) and *Kitkitdizzi* (Bamboo Dart Press). He lives in Jamestown, New York.

JESSICA BREHENY's work has been published in *Chicago Quarterly Review, Catamaran Literary Reader, Eleven Eleven, Fugue, LIT, Otoliths, Other Voices, Santa Monica Review, Santa Cruz Noir Anthology* (Akashic Noir Series), and *Wild Roof,* among other publications. Her stories have also been produced as audio books by Audible. She is the author of the chapbooks *Some Mythology* (Naissance Press), and *Ephemerides* (Dusie Kollektiv). Her collection, *Broken City*, was selected as a finalist for the Flannery O'Connor Award for Short Fiction. She lives in Santa Cruz, teaches writing and literature at San Jose City College, and serves as the Vice President of her faculty union.

CHRISTOPHER BUCKLEY's recent books are *Naming the Lost: The Fresno Poets—Interviews & Essays*, Stephen F. Austin State University Press, 2021(editor) and *One Sky to the Next*, winner of the Longleaf Press Poetry Book Prize, 2023. *SPREZZATURA* will be out in early 2025 from Lynx House Press.

EMILY COLETTA is a writer based in Santa Cruz, California. Her previous publications appear in *Catamaran Literary Reader, Adventure Cyclist, Good Times Santa Cruz,* and *Metro Silicon Valley*. She is the recipient of the Graduate Steinbeck Fellowship at San José State University, where she earned an MFA in 2023. She is currently at work on a novel which follows three characters as they navigate a human-manufactured bird flu. Picture a literary, ornithological *The Da Vinci Code*, minus Tom Hanks and the sex rituals, but somehow just as exciting.

ALICIA DEROLLO is a lover of words and moments that will never be repeated. She is proud to be part of the writing group, "Mediocre Poets Unite," where weekly sessions keep the laughter and pen flowing. A native of the Santa Cruz, California mountains, Alicia enjoys the sea's temper and the mountains' secrets. A mother of six and stepmother of two, Alicia values the excitement of life's discovery through her children's eyes. As an educator, Alicia has encouraged a love of literature and writing in every student she has had the pleasure of teaching for the past twenty-four years. During times of procrastination and power outages, Alicia enjoys reading realistic fiction, drinking wine, and puzzling.

OLGA DOMCHENKO was born in Germany and is of Ukrainian descent. She writes short stories and poetry and blogs on whennothingworks.com. She is an avid environmentalist, organic gardener and public transit advocate, and co-author of *A Simple, Inspirational Guide to Greener Living*. When she is not writing she works in her garden on the North Shore of Chicago. This is her third piece published in *CQR*.

celeste doaks is the author of *Cornrows and Cornfields*, and editor of the poetry anthology *Not Without Our Laughter*. Her chapbook, *American Herstory*, was Backbone Press's first-place winner in 2018. *Herstory* contains poems—which have been featured at the Whitney Museum of American art, Brooklyn Museum, and most recently the Smithsonian American Art Museum—about the artwork former First Lady Michelle Obama chose for the White House. doaks is a Carolina African American Writers' Collective (CAAWC) member and has received fellowships and residencies from Yaddo, Atlantic Center of the Arts, Community of Writers Squaw Valley, and the Fine Arts Work Center. doaks has been nominated for a Pushcart award three times and has been a creative writing professor for over a decade. Her poems, reviews, and cultural essays have appeared in multiple US and UK on-line and print publications including *Ms. Magazine, The Rumpus, The Millions, Huffington Post, Chicago Quarterly Review, Obsidian: Literature and Arts in the African Diaspora, The Hopkins Review, Bmore Art Magazine, Asheville Poetry Review* and many others.

CHRISTINA DRILL is a writer from New Jersey currently based in Chicago. Her fiction has been published in *Washington Square Review, Boston Review, Triangle House Review, Hobart*, and other places, and has been nominated for *Best of the Net* and The Pushcart Prize, and her nonfiction has been published in places like *New York Magazine, VICE*, and *The Adroit Journal*. She is the social media editor for *Chicago Review of Books* and runs the pop culture substack *Annoying Blondes*. She is at work on a novel.

PATRICIA ENGEL is the author of five works of fiction including *Infinite Country*, a *New York Times* bestseller and winner of the New American Voices Award; *The Veins of the Ocean*, winner of the Dayton Literary Peace Prize; *It's Not Love, It's Just Paris*, winner of the International Latino Book Award; *Vida*, winner of

Colombia's Premio Biblioteca de Narrativa Colombiana and a finalist for the Pen/Hemingway and Young Lions Fiction Awards; and most recently a short story collection titled *The Faraway World*, a finalist for the Joyce Carol Oates Award and longlisted for the Story Prize. A recipient of the John Dos Passos Prize for Literature, an O. Henry Award, and fellowships from the Guggenheim Foundation and the National Endowment for the Arts, Patricia's short fiction has been anthologized in *The Best American Short Stories, The Best American Mystery Stories*, and elsewhere. She is a Professor of English in the Creative Writing Program at the University of Miami.

PETER FERRY's stories have appeared in *McSweeney's, OR, Fiction, Chicago Quarterly Review, StoryQuarterly, HyperText* and *Catamaran* amongst other publications. He is a winner of an Illinois Arts Council Award for Short Fiction and has written two novels, *Travel Writing* and *Old Heart,* which won the Chicago Writers Association Novel of the Year award in 2015. *Old Heart* has been turned into a stage play by the theatrical and movie producer Roger Rapoport, and it opened at the Redmond Theater in Detroit in May of 2022. Rapoport has also purchased the movie rights to *Old Heart.* Ferry's short story "Ike, Sharon and Me" appeared in *The Best American Mystery Stories 2017.* His short story "The Hitchcocks" was named a Distinguished Story of 2023 by *The Best American Short Stories.* He lives in Indianapolis and Van Buren County, Michigan with his wife Carolyn O'Connor Ferry.

KAREN ORENDURFF FORT currently writes memoirs and co-hosts Writers Aloud. She has been published in *The Reader, Sociology 101* and in *Miracles.* She has acted professionally at Victory Gardens, Organic Theater, Pheasant Run, St. Nicholas and Open Eye. She has written and produced the plays *Groundswell* and *Accidents* and been in Brecht plays at Prop Thtr. She's directed fifteen Shakespeare plays, *Slaughter City, To Kill a Mockingbird, Life Is a Dream, Summer Brave, Pastoral* and *Sally and Marsha.* She was community theater director for the Chicago Park District for twelve years. She has petitioned and marched over nuclear waste, for peace, climate justice and the ERA. She's a grandmother, married to Keith for forty-two years so far, and a member of the Second Unitarian Church. Her porch continues to be a weekly drop site for boxes of vegetables from community-supported agriculture, so maybe she's a bit of an old hippie.

KATHLEEN FOUNDS is the author of the novel-in-stories *When Mystical Creatures Attack!* and the graphic novel *Bipolar Bear & the Terrible, Horrible, No Good, Very Bad Health Insurance.* Her work has been published in *The Sun, Good Housekeeping, McSweeney's, The Rumpus,* and *The New Yorker* Online. She teaches fiction writing at Cabrillo College and Philosophy of Nonviolence at Cal State Monterey Bay.

KAREN JOY FOWLER is an author of science fiction, historical fiction, and literary fiction. She has written seven novels and has seven grandchildren. Her novels include *Sarah Canary, Sister Noon,* and a *New York Times* bestseller, *The Jane Austen Book Club.* She has also published three short story collections including *What I Didn't See. We Are All Completely Beside Ourselves* won the 2013 PEN/FAULKNER, the California Commonwealth Prize, and was shortlisted for the Man/Booker. Her most recent novel, *Booth,* a story about the fascinating family of the infamous John Wilkes Booth, was published by Putnam and longlisted for the Booker. She lives in Santa Cruz, California, with a dog and a husband.

SYED AFZAL HAIDER is the author of two novels, *To Be With Her* and *Life of Ganesh,* and the newly-released collection *The Dying Sun and Other Stories.* He is the founder and senior editor of *Chicago Quarterly Review.* His stories have appeared in many literary magazines. Oxford University Press, Milkweed Editions, Penguin Books and Longman Literature have anthologized his work.

MILES HARVEY is the author of *The Registry of Forgotten Objects* (Mad Creek Books, 2024), a collection of short stories that includes "Song of Remembrance," first published in *CQR* #38. Among his works of nonfiction are *The King of Confidence* (Little, Brown & Co., 2020), which was a *New York Times Book Review* Editors' Choice selection, and *The Island of Lost Maps* (Random House, 2000), which became a national bestseller. He chairs the Department of English at DePaul University in Chicago, where he serves as director of the DePaul Publishing Institute and is a founding editor of Big Shoulders Books, a non-profit, social-justice publisher.

LEVAN D. HAWKINS of Chicago, performer, poet and writer, received a Pushcart Prize for his essay, "Both Sissies," which was published in the *Chicago Quarterly Review*'s *Anthology of Black*

American Literature in 2021. "Both Sissies" was reprinted in 2023's *Pushcart Prize XLV11: Best of the Small Presses*. Hawkins is also the winner of the *2019 Great River Writers Retreat (Writing) Contest*. He has appeared in such publications as *Chicago Quarterly Review, Mountain Bluebird Magazine, Lunch Ticket Literary Journal, EDNA, Bleed Literary Blog, LA Times,* and *LA Weekly*. He has read and performed his prose at This Much is True Chicago, John and Nancy Hughes Theater, Filet of Solo Festival, Don't Be Ridiculous Series at Steppenwolf Theatre, Outspoken series at Sidetracks, Links Hall, Rhino Theatre, and The Center on Halsted. An award-winning public speaker, Hawkins was Diversity Day Speaker at North Shore Country Day School in Winnetka, Illinois. He has received fellowships from MacDowell, Lambda Literary, Millay, Marble House Project, Mailer Writing Colony, and Renaissance House. Hawkins received his BFA from the Art Institute of Chicago and his MFA from Antioch University-LA.

CHARLES HOLDEFER is a writer based in Brussels. His stories "The Raptor" and "Paracletus" appeared in *CQR* issues 21 and 34; "The Raptor" won a Pushcart Prize and was included in the 2016 anthology. Other short fiction has appeared in the *New England Review, North American Review, Litro* and elsewhere. His recent books include *Don't Look at Me* (novel) and the forthcoming *Ivan the Terrible Goes on a Family Picnic* (stories). Visit Charles at www.charlesholdefer.com.

GARY HOUSTON is managing editor of *Chicago Quarterly Review*. Formerly a writer and editor for the University of Chicago-based *Chicago Literary Review* and then the *Chicago Sun-Times*, his stories, articles, interviews and reviews have appeared in that newspaper as well as the *Chicago Tribune, Chicago Reader, Catamaran, Harper's, Aware, Libido, Kinesis, Michigan Quarterly Review, New England Review, Chicago Quarterly Review, Detroit Free Press, Christian Science Monitor* and *Los Angeles Free Press*. Among his interviewees: Studs Terkel, Joseph Heller, Saul Bellow, Tom Miller, Ginger Rogers, Walter Matthau, John Carradine, Robert Altman, George Cukor, Arthur Penn, Peter Bogdanovich, William H. Macy, Hume Cronyn and Jessica Tandy and Mr. Frick of Frick and Frack. Many of his "Vignettes" were delivered (half not by him) on two oral reading platforms, Writers Aloud and Ubiquitous Players. As an actor he has portrayed onstage such literary or otherwise worthy figures as William

Blake, Ring Lardner, Nelson Algren, Saul Alinsky and George M. Pullman and appeared in the feature films *Fargo, Hoffa, Proof, Watchmen* and the adaptation of Judy Blume's *Are You There, God? It's Me, Margaret*. Please note that he can be heard in the audiobook of Mary Wisniewski's biography of Algren, *Algren: A Life*, as the man himself.

RICHARD HUFFMAN has had a lifelong passion for creative writing. First short story ever published was in a grade school newsletter. Publications include *The Reed, Chicago Quarterly Review, Catamaran, phren-z*, and the *Good Times Weekly*. His writing, especially of novels-in-the-works, highlights strong female characters, who 'go against the grain.' Tough determined women who aren't always nice. Stories that take place in the frontier west, the Vietnam war era, and traditional noir with tough guy, tough gals and murders around every corner.

DR. CHARLES JOHNSON is a University of Washington (Seattle) professor emeritus and the author of twenty-seven books. He is a novelist, philosopher, essayist, literary scholar, short-story writer, cartoonist and illustrator, an author of children's literature, and a screen-and-teleplay writer. A MacArthur fellow, Johnson has received a 2002 American Academy of Arts and Letters Award for Literature, a 1990 National Book Award for his novel *Middle Passage*, a 1985 Writers Guild award for his PBS teleplay "Booker," the 2016 W.E.B. Du Bois Award at the National Black Writers Conference, and many other awards. The Charles Johnson Society at the American Literature Association was founded in 2003. In February 2020, Lifeline Theater in Chicago debuted its play adaptation of *Middle Passage*. Dr. Johnson's most recent publications are *The Way of the Writer: Reflections on the Art and Craft of Storytelling*, his fourth short story collection, *Night Hawks*, and *GRAND: A Grandparent's Wisdom for a Happy Life*. With Steven Barnes, he is co-author of the graphic novel, *The Eightfold Path*, and his most recent book is *All Your Racial Problems Will Soon End: The Cartoons of Charles Johnson*. Johnson is one of five people on posters created in 2019 by the American Philosophical Association (APA) to encourage diversity in the field of philosophy.

CHARLES KENNEY is a writer from Omaha, Nebraska, who currently resides in Chicago, Illinois. His work is featured in *Notre Dame Magazine* and *The Underground*. He holds degrees in history and political science from the University of Notre Dame.

CHUCK KRAMER's poetry and fiction have appeared online and in print, most recently in *Lothlorien, The Raven's Perch* and *The Good Men Project*. He has also been a finalist in the Gwendolyn Brooks Open Mic Poetry Awards in 2017 and 2023. Memoir in *Chicago Quarterly Review* (a Notable Essay in *Best American Essays 2023*), *Sobotka, Evening Street Review*. Journalism in *Chicago Tribune, Sun-Times, Reader, Windy City Times* and *Gay Chicago Magazine*.

DAVID LADWIG is an artist and graphic designer who lives in Evanston, Illinois. He studied at The American University in Washington, D.C. and earned his BA at Columbia College Chicago. When not creating designs or working as a butcher, David enjoys time with his wife Kate, son Charlie, and Pooka, the Siberian forest cat. david.ladwigdesign@gmail.com

RICHARD M. LANGE's short fiction has appeared in *North American Review, Sixfold, Cimarron Review, Eclipse,* the *William and Mary Review, Georgetown Review,* a previous issue of *Chicago Quarterly Review,* and elsewhere. He has twice been a finalist in *Mississippi Review*'s annual fiction contest and two of his stories have been nominated for the Pushcart Prize. His essay "Of Human Carnage" was included in *Best American Essays 2016* and cited in *Best American Science and Nature Writing 2017*. He lives in Santa Cruz, California.

JOY LANZENDORFER is the author of the novel *Right Back Where We Started From*. Other work has been in *The New Yorker, The New York Times, Raritan, Ploughshares, The Atlantic,* and *Poetry Foundation*. Her nonfiction was notable in *The Best American Essays* 2019, 2020, and 2022 and her essay on the poisoned marshmallows of Carmel won the 2023 Excellence in Journalism Award from the Society of Professional Journalists. She has earned honors from the de Groot Foundation, The Discovered Award for Emerging Literary Artists, Cuttyhunk Island Writers' Residency, Hypatia-in-the-Woods, and Hedgebrook Programs. She lives near San Francisco with her husband, son, and three cats.

DORIANNE LAUX's sixth collection, *Only As the Day is Long: New and Selected Poems*, was named a finalist for the 2020 Pulitzer Prize for Poetry. Her fifth collection, *The Book of Men*, was awarded The Paterson Prize. Her fourth book of poems, *Facts About the Moon*, won The Oregon Book Award and was short-listed for the Lenore Marshall Poetry Prize. Laux is also the author of *Awake*; *What We Carry*, a finalist for the National Book Critic's Circle Award; *Smoke*; as well as a fine small press edition, *The Book of Women*. She is the co-author of the celebrated text *The Poet's Companion: A Guide to the Pleasures of Writing Poetry*. Her latest collection is *Life On Earth*.

JEY LEY's poetry appears (or will) in *Chicago Quarterly Review*, *Magma Poetry*, *The Rialto*, *Tokyo Poetry Journal*, *Door is a Jar*, *VOLT*, *South Dakota Review*, *The Hollins Critic*, and elsewhere. Jey is a visual artist and new writer in Gem City, Ohio. IG: @jeyleyjey

LOU MATHEWS lives in Los Angeles just below the Hollywood sign and is a fourth generation Angeleno. Married at nineteen, he worked his way through UC Santa Cruz as a gas station attendant and mechanic and continued to work as a mechanic until he was thirty-nine. His first novel, *L.A. Breakdown*, about illegal street racing, was picked by the *Los Angeles Times* as a Best Book of 1999. He has received a National Endowment for the Arts Fellowship in Fiction, a California Arts Council Fiction Fellowship, a Pushcart Prize and a Katherine Anne Porter Prize. His short stories have been published in more than forty literary magazines including *Short Story*, *ZYZZYVA*, *New England Review*, *Witness*, *Catamaran*, and *Black Clock*, twelve fiction anthologies and two textbook series. He has taught in UCLA Extension's renowned Writer's Program since 1989 and is a recipient of Teacher of the Year and Outstanding Instructor Awards. His last novel, *Shaky Town*, was published in September 2021 and was long-listed for the 2022 *Tournament of Books*. "Bat Fat" is from Mathews' new novel, *Hollywoodski*, to be published in January 2025. More details on Mathews, *Shaky Town* and *Hollywoodski* can be found at https://www.tigervanbooks.com/shaky-town

ELIZABETH MCKENZIE's novel *The Dog of the North* was a *New York Times* Editors' Choice and a finalist for the Los Angeles Times Book Prize in fiction. Her novel *The Portable Veblen* was longlisted for the National Book Award, shortlisted for the Women's Prize, and received the California Book Award. It was named a Best Book of the Year by NPR, *The Guardian, The San Francisco Chronicle,* and *Kirkus,* among others. She is the author of the novel *MacGregor Tells The World,* a *San Francisco Chronicle* and *Chicago Tribune* Best Book of the Year, and *Stop That Girl,* shortlisted for The Story Prize. Her work has appeared in *The New Yorker, The Atlantic, Tin House,* and others. McKenzie is the senior editor of the *Chicago Quarterly Review* and managing editor of *Catamaran.* She recently completed a translation of Giacomo Sartori's *Anatomy of the Battle* through an NEA Translation Fellowship with partner Michela Martini.

KAT MEADS is the author of the essay collection *2:12 a.m.,* essays inspired by insomnia, which received an Independent Publishers (IPPY) Gold Medal and was a *Foreword Reviews* Book of the Year finalist. Her earlier essay collection, *Born Southern and Restless,* was published by Duquesne University Press as the recipient of the press's Emerging Writers in Creative Nonfiction Award. Her newest, *These Particular Women* (2023), features essays on convicted murderess Jean Harris, author Lady Caroline Blackwood, the mothers of Sylvia Plath and Flannery O'Connor, and other famous/infamous women. Her nonfiction has received five *Best American Essays'* Notable citations, has been anthologized in *Golden State 2017: The Best New Writing from California,* and published by numerous literary journals, including *Chicago Quarterly Review, New England Review, Southern Review, AGNI online, Southern Humanities Review, American Letters & Commentary, Chautauqua, Zone 3,* and *World Literature Today.* A native of North Carolina, she lives in California.

DAN MILLAR lives in Richmond, California with his cat Mouse. He has work forthcoming in *Cathexis Northwest Press.*

JOSEPH MILLAR's latest collection *Shine,* where this poem will appear, is due out this fall from Carnegie Mellon. His poems have won fellowships from the Guggenheim Foundation and the NEA, as well as the Pushcart Prize. He teaches in Pacific University's MFA program and lives in Richmond, California.

MAYA MILLER's writing has been published in *Hanging Loose, Cleaver, Polyphony, Up North Lit, Bluefire, Skipping Stones, jGirls Magazine, Cargoes, Hadassah, One Magazine,* and *Sierra Nevada Review.* Miller's prose, poetry and nonfiction has been recognized by Princeton, Columbia, Hollins, Rider, Library of Congress, Skipping Stones, and The Leyla Beban Foundation. Miller co-wrote and co-edited the book *Salt and Honey: Jewish Teens on Feminism, Creativity, and Tradition* published by Behrman House (2022).

FAISAL MOHYUDDIN is the author of *Elsewhere: An Elegy* (Next Page, 2024), *The Displaced Children of Displaced Children* (Eyewear, 2018), and *The Riddle of Longing* (Backbone, 2017). He teaches English at Highland Park High School in suburban Chicago and creative writing at Northwestern University's School of Professional Studies. He also serves as a Master Practitioner with the global not-for-profit Narrative 4 and is a visual artist. www.faisalmohyuddin.com

AARTI MONTEIRO is a fiction writer who holds an MFA from Rutgers University-Newark and has received support from the Virginia Center for the Creative Arts, the Tin House Writers' Workshop, and the Sewanee Writers' Conference. A Kundiman Fellow, her work has appeared in *Epiphany Magazine, wildness, Kweli Journal*, and *Joyland*. She lives in Chicago.

TOMMY MOORE was born in Santa Monica, California. In 1998, he graduated from UC Santa Cruz with a degree in film and video production. He works as a producer and director creating branded entertainment, documentary and commercial content. In 2013, Tommy was one of six writers selected for the PEN Emerging Voices Fellowship. Currently, he and his wife Amie along with their three children live in Los Angeles County. "This is You" is his second published story.

Ricardo Eliécer Neftalí Reyes Basoalto (1904 – 1973), better known by his nom de plume and later legal name **PABLO NERUDA**, was a Chilean poet-diplomat and politician who won the 1971 Nobel Prize in Literature. Neruda became known as a poet when he was just thirteen years old, and wrote in a variety of styles, including surrealist poems, historical epics, overtly political manifestos, a prose autobiography, and passionate love poems such as the ones in his collection *Twenty Love Poems and a Song of Despair* (1924). Inimitably, from Neruda and the egalitarian stride of his poems, an international Whitman emerges, the poet for everyman. In Neruda's odes, especially, the legacy he has bequeathed to us is in the astonishment of the awareness of living simply but deeply. The three books of odes he composed, for regular newspaper publication in *El Nacional*, in Caracas, in the 1950s, were possibly some of the happiest periods of Neruda's creative life.

LISA ALLEN ORTIZ received her MFA from Pacific University in 2014. Her second collection of poems, *Stem*, won the 2022 Idaho Prize judged by Ilya Kaminsky, and her first collection, *Guide to the Exhibit*, won the 2016 Perugia Press Prize. *The Blinding Star, Selected Poems of Blanca Varela*, collaboratively translated with Sara Danielle Rivera, won the 2022 Northern California Book Awards Prize for Poetry in Translation. Born in the wilds of Northern California, Lisa has spent a lot of time on earth wandering around in the forest, smelling trees, ferns, rain-wet earth, etc.

CLAIRE OSHETSKY's novel *Chouette* (Ecco 2021) was longlisted for the 2022 Pen/Faulkner Award for Fiction and won the 2022 William Saroyan International Prize for Writing. Their latest novel is *Poor Deer*, published in January 2024 by Ecco. Oshetsky lives in Santa Cruz, California.

ROY PARVIN is the author of two collections of short fiction, *In the Snow Forest* (Norton, 2000) and *The Loneliest Road in America* (Chronicle Books, 1997), as well a humorous yoga book, *Yoga for the Inflexible Male* (Penguin/Random House 2019), written under the nom de namaste Yoga Matt. His work has been included in the *Best American Short Stories* and awarded the Katherine Anne Porter Prize in fiction. One of his novellas was turned into a motion picture, *Voyez comme ils dansent*, which won the Grand Jury Prize at the 2012 Rome International Film Festival. "Blood" is from a short story collection he's writing entitled *Bicycle Shorts*. It was inspired by a vague footnote in a biography of the great Italian cycling champion, Marco Pantani.

Born and raised in Chicago, **DELIA PITTS** graduated from Oberlin College with a Bachelor's degree in history. After working as a journalist, she earned a Ph.D. in African history from the University of Chicago. She is a former U.S. diplomat and university administrator. After assignments that took her from West Africa to Mexico and from Texas to New Jersey, Delia left academia to begin writing the Ross Agency mysteries about a neighborhood detective firm in contemporary Harlem. Between writing her full-length novels, Delia has also found success with briefer crime fiction. Her short story, "The Killer," first published in the *Chicago Quarterly Review*, was selected for inclusion in *Best American Mystery and Suspense 2021*. Another story, "Talladega 1925," was published in the CQR's *Anthology of Black American Literature* edited by Charles Johnson. In 2022, Delia signed a book deal with St. Martin's Minotaur Books to write her new Queenstown mystery series featuring Black private investigator Vandy Myrick. The first book, *Trouble in Queenstown,* was published in July 2024. Delia is an active member of Sisters in Crime, Mystery Writers of America, and Crime Writers of Color. Delia and her husband live in central New Jersey and have twin sons living in Texas. To learn more about Delia and her books visit her website, deliapitts.com.

VIKRAM RAMAKRISHNAN is an alumnus of the University of Pennsylvania and enthusiastic member of Odyssey Writing Workshop's class of 2020, where he received the Walter & Kattie Metcalf Scholarship. He's the winner of the 17th Annual Gival Short Story Award, and his stories have been published in *The Minnesota Review, Meridian,* and *Asimov's Science Fiction.*

SIGNE RATCLIFF is a Chicago-based writer and painter with Wisconsin roots. Her short fiction has appeared in *Chicago Quarterly Review, storySouth, Conclave: A Journal of Character,* and has been listed in *Best American Short Stories 2020.* She currently serves as Contributing Editor of *Chicago Quarterly Review.*

SUZANNE SCANLON is the author of the memoir *Committed: On Meaning and Madwomen* and of the novels *Promising Young Women* and *Her 37th Year, An Index.* Her writing has appeared in *Granta, BOMB Magazine, Fence, The Iowa Review, The Los Angeles Review of Books,* and many other places.

Born in Pakistan, **MOAZZAM SHEIKH** is the author of two short story collections and two novellas, *Footbridge to Hell Called Love* and *Unsolaced Faces We Meet In Our Dreams,* as part of his San Francisco Quartet. He guest-edited the special *Chicago Quarterly Review* (2017) issue on South Asian American writing. He has translated fiction across English, Urdu, Hindi and Punjabi. He is a librarian at San Francisco Public Library and is married to artist Amna Ali and has two sons. He lives in San Francisco.

PAUL SKENAZY has published two novels, *Temper CA* (2019), which won the 2018 Miami University Press Novella Contest, and *Still Life* (Paper Angel Press, 2021). His autobiographical essay on Chicago and Saul Bellow was selected as a "Notable" essay in *The Best American Essays 2015*, and stories and essays have recently appeared in *Catamaran Literary Reader, Chicago Quarterly Review* and elsewhere. He revised and edited a posthumous novel by a friend, Arturo Islas (*La Mollie and the King of Tears*, U. of New Mexico Press). His nonfiction work includes a book on James M. Cain, a collection of essays on place in San Francisco literature, and a selection of interviews with Maxine Hong Kingston, as well as more than three hundred reviews of fiction and nonfiction for newspapers and magazines nationwide. For a dozen years he served as a mystery review columnist for the *Washington Post* and has twice been nominated for the National Book Critics Circle award for reviewing. Skenazy taught literature and writing at the University of California, Santa Cruz for thirty years before retiring to devote full time to his writing.

Inspired by Hispanic religious icons, folk art and the wild orchard behind her Northern New Mexico childhood home, **ELEANOR SPIESS-FERRIS** has become a widely exhibited visual artist nationally as well as internationally. She has received numerous fellowships and grants, including an Arts Midwest Fellowship grant and several grants from the state of Illinois and the city of Chicago where she now resides. Her art work is in the permanent collections of several museums: these include the Art Institute of Chicago, the Montana Museum of Arts and Culture in Missoula, the Racine Art Museum in Racine, Wisconsin, the Illinois State Museum in Springfield, Illinois, and the Minneapolis Institute of Art in Minnesota. Her previous publications in the *CQR* include "The Rodeo" and "The Dangerous Eater." Both, along with "Apple Pie," are part of a memoirist work-in-progress about the artist growing up on a small farm in Northern New Mexico.

SARAH ANNE STINNETT teaches at Berklee Online and holds an MFA in Creative Writing from Lesley University and an ALM in Dramatic Arts from Harvard University. Her work appears or is forthcoming in *Plume, Booth, Palette Poetry, On the Seawall, Tar River Poetry, The Shore, Barely South Review, Summerset Review, Cider Press Review,* and elsewhere.

WALLY SWIST's *Huang Po and the Dimensions of Love* (Southern Illinois University Press, 2012) was selected by Yusef Komunyakaa as co-winner in the 2011 Crab Orchard Series Open Poetry Contest. He was the 2018 winner of the Ex Ophidia Press Poetry Prize, by unanimous judging, for his collection *A Bird Who Seems to Know Me: Poetry Regarding Birds and Nature* (2019). Recent books include *Awakening and Visitation* (2020), *Evanescence: Selected Poems* (2020), and *Taking Residence* (2021), all with Shanti Arts. His books of nonfiction include *Singing for Nothing: Selected Nonfiction as Literary Memoir* (Brooklyn, NY: The Operating System, 2018), *On Beauty: Essays, Reviews, Fiction, and Plays* (New York & Lisbon: Adelaide Books, 2018), and *A Writer's Statements on Beauty: New and Selected Essays and Reviews* (Brunswick, ME: Shanti Arts, 2022). His translation of *L'Allegria* by Giuseppe Ungaretti was published by Shanti Arts in 2023. Swist is a recipient of Artist's Fellowships in poetry from the Connecticut Commission on the Arts (1977 and 2003). His essays, poetry, and translations have appeared in *Asymptote, Chicago Quarterly Review, Commonweal, Hunger Mountain, The Montreal Review, Poetry London, Today's American Catholic, Transference: A Literary Journal Featuring the Art & Process of Translation,* (Western Michigan Department of Languages), *Vox Populi,* and *Your Impossible Voice.*

GREG TEBBANO lives in rural upstate New York. His fiction has appeared in *Noon, Epiphany, Witness, Southern Humanities Review, Post Road, Zone 3* and *Meridian.* In 2022, he was awarded second place in the First Pages Prize competition judged by Justin Torres. He has been a resident at Vermont Studio Center and a finalist for the Robert C. Jones Prize for Short Prose.

PRISCILLA TURNER's work includes creative nonfiction, short fiction, and journalism. She has won awards for creative nonfiction from *The Missouri Review* and *New Letters,* and published a short story in *The Massachusetts Review.* In decades past, she earned a living as a freelance writer, contributing to newspapers and magazines ranging from *The Village Voice, Ms., Travel + Leisure,* and *The Christian Science Monitor* to *People* and *Life.* She also edited an alternative weekly newspaper, worked at *Alaska Airlines Magazine,* and taught creative nonfiction to adults. She took her first cross-country road trip with her parents and three siblings the summer she turned six, in a pink Rambler station wagon where she was often allowed to sit in the "way back." She lives in Bellingham, Washington.

MATTHEW WIMBERLEY grew up in the Blue Ridge Mountains. He is the author of two collections of poetry, *Daniel Boone's Window* (LSU, 2020) selected by Dave Smith for the Southern Messenger Poetry series, and *All the Great Territories* (SIU, 2020), winner of the 2018 Crab Orchard Poetry Series First Book award, winner of the Weatherford Award. Winner of the 2015 William Matthews Prize from the Asheville Poetry Review, his work was selected by Mary Szybist for the 2016 *Best New Poets* anthology and his writing has appeared most recently or is forthcoming in: *32 Poems, Image, Poem-a-Day* from the Academy of American Poets, and *The Threepenny Review.* Wimberley received his MFA from NYU where he worked with children at St. Mary's Hospital as a Starworks Fellow. He teaches in western North Carolina.

MARY WISNIEWSKI is a Chicago writer, reporter and teacher. Her biography of Nelson Algren, *Algren: A Life,* won the Society of Midland Authors prize for best biography. A former columnist for the *Chicago Sun-Times* and the *Chicago Tribune,* Wisniewski has won numerous journalism awards, including recognition for community reporting and theater criticism.

Originally from Des Plaines, Illinois, **JEFFREY WOLF** has been a finalist for the *Third Coast* Fiction Prize and the *Arkansas International* Emerging Writer's Prize. His writing has appeared in *Conjunctions, Prairie Schooner, Tupelo Quarterly, Bat City Review,* and elsewhere, and he has received fellowship grants from the Chicago Department of Cultural Affairs and the Memorial Foundation for Jewish Culture. He holds an MFA from Southern Illinois University Carbondale, teaches English and Creative Writing at Columbia College Chicago, and is currently writing his debut story collection.

COOPER YOUNG is a cyber security consultant, poet, and mathematician who hails from Santa Cruz, California. His most recent work has appeared in *California Quarterly, Urthona, Shō Poetry Journal,* and Orison Books's anthology of *Best Spiritual Literature.* His chapbook, *Sacred Grounds,* was published by Finishing Line Press in May 2020. More information can be found at coopergyoung.com.

GARY YOUNG's most recent books are *That's What I Thought* and *American Analects,* both from Persea Books; and *Precious Mirror,* translations from the Japanese, and *Taken to Heart: 70 Poems from the*

Chinese from White Pine Press. His many honors include the Shelley Memorial Award, and the William Carlos Williams Award from the Poetry Society of America. He teaches creative writing and directs the Cowell Press at UC Santa Cruz.

JAKE YOUNG is the author of the poetry collections *American Oak* (Main Street Rag, 2018), *What They Will Say* (Finishing Line Press, 2021), and *All I Wanted* (Redhawk Publications, 2021), the co-translator with Rebecca Pelky of the poetry collection *Desnuda/ Naked* by Matilde Ladrón de Guevara (Redhawk Publications, 2022), and the essay collection *True Terroir* (Brandenburg Press, 2019). He received his MFA from North Carolina State University and his PhD from the University of Missouri.

JAMES K. ZIMMERMAN is an award-winning, neurodivergent writer, frequently a Pushcart Prize nominee. His work appears in *American Life in Poetry, Chautauqua, december, Folio, Lumina, Nimrod, Pleiades, Rattle, Salamander,* and elsewhere. He is the author of *Little Miracles* (Passager Books), *Family Cookout* (Comstock), winner of the Jessie Bryce Niles Prize, and *The Further Adventures of Zen Patriarch Dōgen* (Poetry Box).

"Patricia Engel
is a wonder."
—LAUREN GROFF

THE FARAWAY WORLD

STORIES

PATRICIA ENGEL

NEW YORK TIMES BESTSELLING AUTHOR OF
INFINITE COUNTRY

ELSEWHERE
AN ELEGY

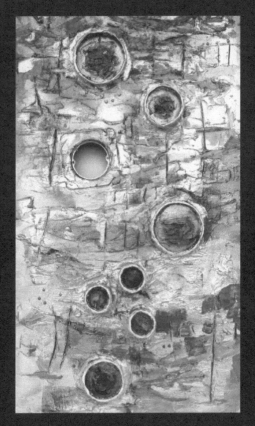

Faisal Mohyuddin

Poetry/Next Page Press

THE WORLD WE WANT

The New York Herald Tribune World Youth Forum and the Cold War Teenager

CATHERINE BISHOP

Soon available from Australian Scholarly Publishing

WEAVERS PRESS
Presents

"*Syed Afzal Haider displays a range and sophistication that is all too rare in American fiction. From the trauma of the partition of India to the meaning of baseball, from parenting to explorations of eros, The Dying Sun and Other Stories is thoughtful and provocative, tackling difficult subjects with sensitivity and wit.*"

*--**Charles Holdefer**, author of Don't Look at Me*

The Dying Sun and Other Stories by **Syed Afzal Haider**

Publication Date: October, 2024

ISBN: 9798987215234

Weavers Press, San Francisco

http://weaverspress.com

Available from Weavers Press as well as Asterism Books

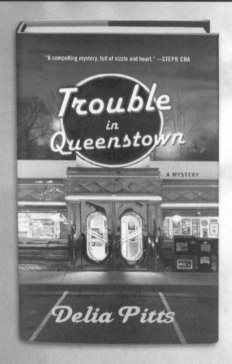

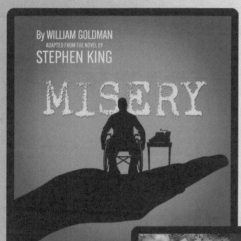

2
Classics

1
Season

American Blues Theater

5627 N. Lincoln Ave.

Chicago, IL 60659

(773) 654-3103

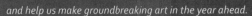

The Stuart Brent Children's Book Club

TODAY A READER,

www.stuartbrent.com

Share your passion.

CavanKerryPress

Celebrates this year's new releases:

Glitter Road / January Gill O'Neil
History Is Embarrassing / Karen Chase
Seraphim / Angelique Zobitz
The Curve of Things / Kathy Kremins
All at Once / Jack Ridl
In Inheritance of Drowning / Dorsía Smith Silva

cavankerrypress.org/product-tag/2024

The
Nelson Algren
Committee

On the Make
Since 1989

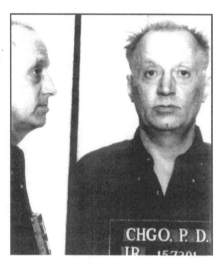

Party Like it's 1893–or 1931

Northwestern University Press

Journey back to the past of night life in *Chicago by Day and Night,* a quite unofficial guide to Chicago's more salacious attractions around the World's Columbian Exposition of 1893. This pocket book for the man-about-town is annotated and explicated by Paul Durica and Bill Savage.

Then skip ahead to 1931, where Chicago journalist George Ade attempted to explain American urban and rural drinking culture (to a generation who had never raised a glass legally due to Prohibition) in *The Old-Time Saloon,* annotated and introduced by Bill Savage.

The University of Chicago Press

Season 44 Subscriptions Now on Sale!
www.citylit.org
or call 773-293-3682

THE HOUSE OF IDEAS
by Mark Pracht
August 23, 2024 - October 6, 2024

In the 1960s Marvel Comics began creating dozens of memorable characters, one after another over a period of years, and built a single cohesive world for them to inhabit. But the two men at the center of this renaissance struggle with the idea of credit now that they've made it something worth struggling over. *The House of Ideas* examines the rise of Marvel and the fraught relationship between the Lennon and McCartney of comic books, Stan Lee and Jack Kirby. Part Three of The Four-Color Trilogy, about the men and women who created a body of literature Americans both embraced and loathed.

SEVEN GUITARS
by August Wilson
October 18, 2024 - December 1, 2024

The Chicago storefront premiere of this searing August Wilson drama about six friends in the Hill District of Pittsburgh in 1948 mourning the death of their friend Floyd "Schoolboy" Barton, a rising blues star cut down in his prime. One of Wilson's "Pittsburgh Cycle" of ten plays depicting the African American experience in each of the 20th Century's decades.

GLASSHEART
by Reina Hardy
January 10. 2025 - February 23, 2025

Chicago premiere of a new play by Chicago playwright Reina Hardy. A modern-day reimagining of the Beauty and the Beast fairy tale. The Beast has moved into a low-rent district in Chicago with his last loyal friend, a lamp named Only. They meet a neighborly witch and a young woman who might, somehow, still break the curse.

R.U.R. (ROSSUM'S UNIVERSAL ROBOTS)
by Karel Capek
freely adapted by Bo List
May 2, 2025 - June 15, 2025

Karel Čapek's early science fiction classic *R.U.R.* coined the term "robot" and looked ahead to the wonders and dangers of artificial intelligence. "Rossum's Universal Robots" is a mysterious island factory that manufactures artificial human beings, run by the eccentric scientist Harry Rossum. When Helena Glory arrives to advocate for the rights of these machines, a series of events is set into motion that sees Harry and Helena married against the backdrop of a global robot uprising.

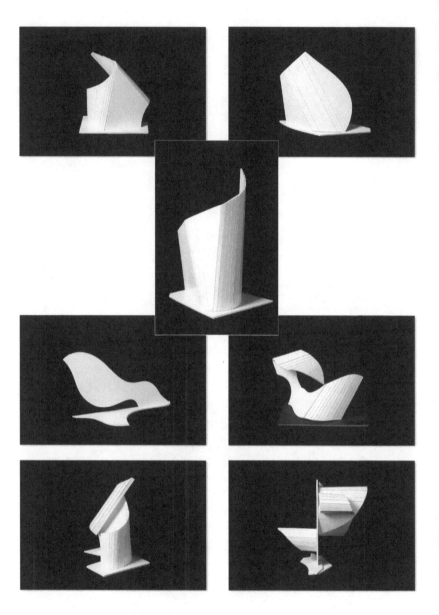

"Art Post Cards from Italy" for mailing or framing. $10.00 Per Package.

Concept Sculptural Prototypes made of Foamboard
(Architects, Landscape Architects and Developers)

Contact: Alicia Loy Griffin   323. 293.1858 (studio)   alicialoy@icloud.com   alicialoy.griffin.com

THE GEORGIA REVIEW

NEW TITLES FROM GEORGIA REVIEW BOOKS

TRIPAS

BY BRANDON SOM

**WINNER OF THE PULITZER
PRIZE FOR POETRY**

CUE
BY SIWAR MASANNAT

PRESENCE
BY BRENDA IIJIMA

FREE SHIIPPING ON ALL DOMESTIC ORDERS

SUNDAY SALON CHICAGO
IS AN IN-PERSON CURATED LITERARY READING SERIES
THAT TAKES PLACE EVERY OTHER MONTH
with Zoom reading events held during
the in-between months to include non-local authors.

NAMED ONE OF CHICAGO'S BEST LITERARY ORGANIZATIONS
BY NEWCITY

THE SALON SERIES HAS BROUGHT WORD POWER TO
NEW YORK CITY, NAIROBI, MIAMI & CHICAGO
MAKING OUR BEST LOCAL AND NATIONAL WRITERS AVAILABLE
TO A LARGER COMMUNITY FOR 17+ YEARS

WE MEET AT **ROSCOE BOOKS**
2142 W Roscoe St. Chicago, IL 60618 in Roscoe Village
(between Leavitt and Hamilton)
FROM 7 PM TO 9 PM ON THE LAST SUNDAY OF EVERY OTHER MONTH
(w/ Roscoe Books selling authors' titles at ea. event)

MAKE NEW FRIENDS, BUY BOOKS
AND ENJOY EXCELLENT READINGS WITH US!
OUR EVENTS ARE ALWAYS FREE

SUBSCRIBE TO OUR MAILCHIMP E-BLAST LIST TO RECEIVE
OUR EVENT ANNOUNCEMENTS
Info at https://sundaysalon-chicago.com

https://www.facebook.com/Sunday.Salon.Chicago/
www.roscoebooks.com

THANK YOU, CQR, FOR SUPPORTING US!

The KENYON REVIEW

**PATRICIA GRODD POETRY PRIZE
FOR YOUNG WRITERS**
SUBMISSIONS OPEN NOVEMBER 1–30, 2023

POETRY CONTEST
SUBMISSIONS OPEN NOVEMBER 1–30, 2023

SHORT NONFICTION CONTEST
SUBMISSIONS OPEN DECEMBER 1–31, 2023

SHORT FICTION CONTEST
SUBMISSIONS OPEN JANUARY 1–31, 2024

All adult contest winners receive publication in the print edition of *The Kenyon Review* and full scholarships to attend the 2024 Kenyon Review Writers Workshops, and all runners-up receive publication on our website.

The winner of the Patricia Grodd Poetry Prize for Young Writers receives a full scholarship to the 2024 Kenyon Review Young Writers Workshop. The winner and two runners-up will have their selected poems published in the print edition of *The Kenyon Review*.

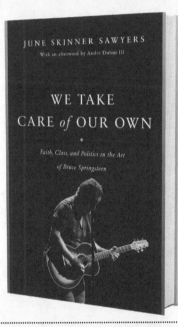
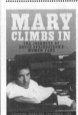

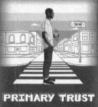

New from Swan Isle Press

The Azure Cloister

Thirty-Five Poems

Carlos Germán Belli

Translated by Karl Maurer
Edited by Christopher Maurer

"Belli's work seeks the limits of human experience in forms that summon 'the bodies in which we dwell,' sometimes with what Maurer calls the 'tortuous Gongoresque syntax' of the Spanish Baroque, and in evocations of the timeless, abject, and ineffable."—*Harriet,* Poetry Foundation

Alias Caracalla

Daniel Cordier

Translated by Rupert Swyer

An English translation of Daniel Cordier's epic portrait and memoir of the French Resistance during WWII. *Alias Caracalla* is a brave and passionate story of action and self-discovery in times of war, with a sensitive and nuanced translation by Rupert Swyer.

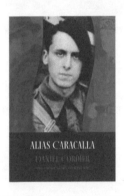

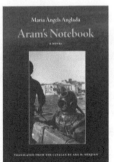

Aram's Notebook

A Novel

Maria Àngels Anglada

Translated by Ara H. Merjian

Aram's Notebook examines the Armenian Genocide through a narrative in which poets and poetry loom large. Aram's tale evokes a struggle not simply for physical survival, but also for saving memory from the clutches of destruction.

S W A N
I S L E
P R E S S

Distributed by the University of Chicago Press www.press.uchicago.edu

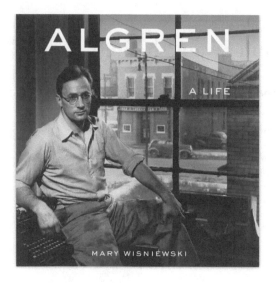

M
THE MENTORIS PROJECT
A NOVEL INSPIRED BY THE LIFE OF
GUIDO D'AREZZO
MUSIC'S GUIDING HAND
Kingsley Day
"The reader can almost hear the notes rising off the page."
—Kirkus Reviews

Writers Aloud

A monthly first read, by and for writers who
don't necessarily think of themselves as writers.
Take it out of the drawer and let's hear it!

First Sunday of the month, via Zoom.
Want the Zoom link? Want to read your writing?
Contact Karen.O.Fort@gmail.com,
DKDunlap@aol.com, or CordisHeard@gmail.com.

Made in United States
Troutdale, OR
08/21/2024

22154897R10271